T0354593

THEO'S GOLD

A novel by
Gordon Knight

Gold, Characters, and a Lost Treasure Mystery.
Have Fun

Order this book online at www.trafford.com
or email orders@trafford.com

Most Trafford titles are also available at major online book retailers.

This is a work of fiction.
Names, characters, places and incidents either are the product of the author's
imagination or are used fictitiously, and any resemblance to actual persons living or
dead, events or locales is entirely coincidental

Printed in the United States of America.

ISBN: 978-1-4269-7441-0 (sc)
ISBN: 978-1-4269-7442-7 (e)

Trafford rev. 02/10/2012

 www.trafford.com

North America & international
toll-free: 1 888 232 4444 (USA & Canada)
phone: 250 383 6864 ♦ fax: 812 355 4082

Dedicated to those who are
overcome with the fever
Gold fever that is.

CHAPTER ONE

Georgia, circa 1852, near the small mining and farming community of Dahlonega, we meet up with Theolonius Raphial Calhoun. The almost 17 year old son of Amos and Beatrice Calhoun.

Theo, as his family and friends call him, is a strapping 5 ft 10 inch 180 lb all muscle, still growing farm boy. The family live on a hardscrabble tenant farm eking out a living as best they can raising corn, tobacco, and truck vegetables to sell in town.

Theo's mother, who once aspired to be a teacher, gave Theo and his 15 year old sister Amelia a good education, reading, numbers and as much bible teaching as the youngsters would absorb without being too pushy.

Their father Amos, was illiterate, but wise in the ways of the world as he knew it, and would listen with great attention as Beatrice would read stories out of the books she collected and guarded with great care. The family was poor, but happy.

One Saturday a couple of months before Theo's 17th birthday, the family packed up their wagon with vegetables and proceeded to go to Dahlonega to sell their goods and get some supplies. While in town Amos met up with an old friend of his, Chastain Castle, otherwise known as Cuss, because of his habit of spitting tobacco juice and cussing to make a pertinent point across when he was talking.

Now Cuss was an independent sort who owned a small placer gold claim near town. In visiting with Amos he mentioned that he needed a helper at the mine. Theo standing next to his father, asked, "what kind of help did he need?". Cuss then went on to explain some of the methods of mining a placer claim and that it was hard physical work, mostly pick and shovel, loading wheel barrows and moving the gravel to the sluice boxes where the gold is washed out of the dirt and concentrated in the sluice boxes,

Theo was so curious as to how a person could find gold in dirt that he asked his dad if he could go to work for Cuss. Amos was always ready to give his son and daughter a little push to see what was on the other side of the hill so to speak. So acting reluctant he asked Cuss what the job would pay and what would Theo learn from the hard work and experience.

Cuss told him he would pay a dollar a day plus found, for a ten hour day, and that he would teach Theo how to prospect for gold and other minerals, and the methods by which to recover them.

Now Theo is getting excited, a dollar a day plus found is a mans wages, plus the aspect of learning how to prospect and therefore some day be his own man, it was all he could do to keep from getting down on his knees to beg his dad to let him go to work for Cuss.

You see Theo has heard of the gold strikes in California and has been dreaming of going there to get rich, but he is also smart enough to know that you do not rush off and get involved in something you have no knowledge of. So this was his chance to learn about gold mining from someone who is modestly successful at it.

"Please dad, may I go to work for your friend, I promise I will work hard and learn everything I can and make you proud of me". Amos looks at his son and asks him,

"what about the farm?, you know I depend on you for a lot of the work that has to be done".

Cuss interrupts and tells Amos, "I only need him 4 or 5 days a week, I'm sure Theo could spend the off time helping you on the farm, Amos", Amos then agrees and said "that would work out".

Theo goes to work. After spending Saturday evening and all day Sunday catching up on all his chores, he is up before dawn Monday, to start to get ready to go to work in the gold mine, He has his rucksack packed with a couple of extra sets of work clothes and his toilet necessarys. His rifle that his dad gave to him on his 12th birthday is cleaned and ready to go, along with extra powder and shot, his mother makes him take his small bible so he can keep up with the lord and his reading skills. And a blank journal, that he can use to write down his experiences in. He and Amos then have breakfast and put bridles on the two mules they have and head to Dahlonega where they are to meet Cuss

Upon arrival in town they see Cuss standing out in front of the General store and hardware, "Good morning to you both". "Theo, come on into the store so we can fit you up with some gum boots and a heavy wool shirt for those cold nights that you are about to experience". Theo climbs down off the mule and goes with Cuss into the store, whereupon they find Theo a pair of gum boots, two pairs of heavy work gloves, a heavy wool shirt jacket and some extra wool socks. After that Cuss picks up some supplies, flour, sugar, coffee, beans,. bacon, salt pork, salt, and a small keg of black powder and fuse.

To pay the store owner Cuss pulls out a leather poke and dumps some fine gold on the gold scales that the store owner uses for buying and selling gold. The store owner weighs the gold and tells Cuss he has more then the bill comes to. Cuss tells him to write up a credit for the extra and when Theo comes to town he can get supplies for the mine and pay for the goods with the credit Cuss has on the books. The store owner is agreeable to that arrangement as there are few customers who would pay for goods in advance, most of them run up a credit bill and try to pay once a month if they can.

While this transaction is going on, there is a character over in the corner eavesdropping, with his eyes popping out at the sight of the poke that Cuss has. Arnold the town roustabout is beside himself at the size of the gold poke, and is filling his mind with ways to steal it.

He leaves the store and runs down to the livery stable that he mucks out every day and borrows a horse so that he can follow Cuss, Amos, and Theo to the mine and figure out a way to get that poke away from Cuss. Now everybody in town knows that Cuss has a mine that pays well, but nobody knows where the mine is, as Cuss keeps the location a secret.

So with everything packed on the mules, the trio head out of town toward the mine, with Arnold following. Going west for a couple of miles following the main road, they come to a little used track that takes them north in a winding path till they come to a small canyon that goes to the west again. When turning into the canyon Cuss spots movement on their back trail. Being cautious he tells Amos and Theo to keep going up the canyon till they come to a grove of cottonwoods that has a small stream running through them, and wait there for him while he sees who is following them,

Theo and his dad continue up the canyon while Cuss hides in the trees and undergrowth, shortly here comes Arnold, looking for Cuss and the others. Cuss comes out of hiding cocking his pistol and confronts Arnold, "Arnold why are you following us?" "Could it be you're trying to steal my gold from me?" Arnold throwing up his hands sputters out "no! no! I'm just out hunting for my dinner," "Is that so, then where is your rifle or shotgun that people usually go hunting with?" "Arnold you are up to no good." "I know it and you know it, so I'm going to teach you a lesson. Take out your bandana and make it into a blindfold and wrap it around your eyes... now!" "That's a good boy, now bend forward over your horses neck, I'm going to tie your hands together, if you make a sudden move I will shoot you, understood." "Yes! yes! don't hurt me" pleads Arnold.

So with Arnold tied to his horse's neck and blindfolded Cuss starts up the canyon to meet up with Amos and Theo. Arnold cries, " I can't see, how am I supposed to ride this horse without bumping into something?" Cuss tells him to trust the horse, he can see and "I don't think he's dumb enough to run into a tree or bush that could hurt you."

Within a few minutes Cuss and Arnold meet up with Amos and Theo, who ask, "who or what do we have here?" Cuss explains how Arnold was out hunting without a rifle or shotgun and Cuss accused him of being up to no good as usual. "So we are going to take him with us and teach him that it's not a good thing to be following people who don't want to be followed."

Arnold hears this and whines, "What are you going to do to me?" "Cuss exclaims, you'll find out, I've got a few old Indian tricks that will fix you up real good". Arnold cries out, "please Cuss don't hurt me, please I didn't do nothing wrong, please Amos, Theo don't let him hurt me," With that Cuss reaches over and backhands Arnold in the face and tells him to stop sniveling, that it's an embarrassment to his folks what raised him up. "Now be quiet and stay on your horse or we will let you walk to where we are going". Arnold gulps, and says "yes sir, anything you say."

"Amos, I'll lead the way dragging the whiner behind me, if he tries to get away just shoot him and we'll leave him to the buzzards or bears to pick his bones clean". Arnold whimpers again, and Cuss says, "I told you to be quiet."

So up this little ravine they go, the mules and horse walking in the small stream single file through the grove of cottonwoods, soon they are coming out into a small meadow, and looking ahead Theo sees a small cabin and some lean-to's. "There she is boys, home sweet home". "Amos when we get to the cabin I would like you and Theo to get the sniveler off his horse and tied up in one of the lean-to's, while I get a fire going, it'll be dark soon, and I'm hungry after all the excitement we've had today".

Amos and Theo get Arnold off his horse and tie him to a post of one of the lean-to's, then take the mules and the horse and let them roll, then hobble them out in the meadow so they can feed on the grasses there, by this time the sun is down and darkness is descending fast.

Cuss hollers, come and get it, so they each get a tin plate and cup and load up on beans and salt pork and hot black coffee to wash it down with. Arnold whining, hollers out "I'm hungry too, ain't you going to feed me?" Cuss hollers back, "Naw, you can just lick the sweat off your upper lip while we figure out what to do with you, my Indian friends taught me all kinds of torture tricks to use on cowards like you, right now we are eating; so shut up".

When the men and boy are through eating, Cuss fixes up a plate of beans for Arnold and puts it on a small stool in front of him and told him he would have to slop like a hog if he wanted any dinner. Arnold being blindfolded bent forward too fast and put his whole face in the plate, getting beans all over himself "Look at that uncivilized human over there, a hog has better table manners then that". At which the trio have a good laugh at Arnolds expense.

Theo asks Cuss what he's going to do to Arnold? "I don't know yet, the Injuns learned me so many tricks that I can't make up my mind, I think I'll sleep on it and see what I can come up with in the morning, course I've always been partial to the stake em out over a ant hill trick and pour honey on them, but it's a waste of good honey, especially in Arnolds case, he's not worth a nickels worth of honey." Arnold groans.

Amos, getting to his feet, says "gents I think it's time to bed down for the night, we all have a busy day tomorrow." "You're right, Theo why don't you take you and your dads bedrolls into that lean-to over there and make yourselves comfortable". "Amos can you help me with Arnold?". "It's time to untie him so he can take care of his toilet, we don't want him to smell up the place because he can't control himself'. So while Cuss unties Arnold, Amos stands guard with his rifle and a mean look on his face, after Arnold relieves himself, Cuss takes him back to the pole in the lean-to, an ties him up, arms behind his back and ankles tied together, then Cuss gets a blanket and puts it over Arnold. "Sleep tight Arnold, don't let the bugs, or snakes, or whatever bite, then walks away laughing". Amos whispers to Cuss," you sure got him scared". "Yeah maybe it will teach him not to try to do bad things to other people".

Just before sunup, everybody starts to rouse themselves up to get the day going, Cuss puts on a pot of coffee and fries up some bacon, and warms up some beans in case someone wants some. After breakfast Amos starts to get the mules ready for the trip back to the farm. He asks Cuss what he's decided to do with Arnold? Cuss tells him, "Why don't you take him back to town trussed up the way we brought him here, only when you get close to town, approach it from a different direction and about a mile out of town let Arnold off the horse, untie him and take his boots off and tie them to the horse and ride away". "By the time he gets over the fright of what's going to happen to him and takes the blindfold off, you should be out of site". "He can then walk to town in his stocking feet." "When you get to town, drop by the sheriff's office and let him know what happened, and gives the sheriff the horse so he can check to see if it was stolen". "By the time Arnold gets to town he's going to have a lot of explaining to do". So with that, Amos takes off for town leading the other mule and the horse with Arnold on it.

Cuss tells Theo it's time to take a tour of our camp and the diggings. "By the time we get that done, we should have time to hunt us up some fresh meat, preferably deer, as beans and salt pork gets mighty tiresome after awhile".

The Camp and Mine. With Cuss leading, Theo is given the grand tour of Cuss's little world. They start with the cabin, a typical miners log cabin, about 12 feet x 12 feet, with a wooden door as opposed to just a skin of some animal hanging over the opening, a couple of windows, with mica isinglass to let in the light. A fireplace, stove with cooking utensils, a bed larger then most, shelves, table, four chairs, a rack to hold a rifle, shotgun, and a couple of cap and ball pistols. Hooks on the walls for clothes, caps, jackets, etc,

Next up, a couple of lean-to's, one for the mule, and pack donkey that Cuss keeps, the other one for all purpose use such as a place for people to sleep in while visiting. Cuss tells Theo that is where he can make himself at home while he is working with him.

The next structure is something that Theo had never seen or heard of before. Behind the cabin there is a platform with three tubs, one is larger then the other two and looks like it could hold about four people at the same time, plus it is sunken into the platforms floor so that to get in you have to climb down into it, the other two tubs are big enough for one person at a time.

Theo asks "what in the world is that?" Cuss tells him it is a Hot tub. Theo asks "what do you use it for?" Cuss tells him, "that after a hard days work, you get in and soak all your aches and pains away, and it also lets your mind relax so you can sleep like a baby and wake up refreshed and ready to take on the new days trials and tribulations". Theo asks, "where in the world did you ever come up with such a contraption?", as he looks at several wooden pipes and what looks like a fireplace with a metal box over the fire pit, with two pipes coming out of it. Cuss tells him the idea comes from the Japans, and then proceeds to tell Theo how he first came across the idea.

"Theo, several years ago before becoming a miner, I shipped out on a merchant ship that was bound for the Orient". Theo interrupts, and asks "where is that?" "Cuss asks if he had ever heard of China?" Theo said his mother had once read him a story about China. "China and the Japans are what are known as part of the Orient". "Now back to my story. The captain of the ship was a Portuguese man from the country of Portugal". "I've heard of them, they were supposed to have been some of the first sailors to sail around the world". Cuss say's "that's right". "Well we sailed from Savannah down the coast of South America, stopping at several ports to off load cargo and take on new cargo, we sailed around Cape Horn, where we got lucky with only a small storm to keep us busy keeping the ship afloat, I've heard that the most terrible storms on earth are in those waters around the Horn". "Anyway where was I?" "Oh yes, after getting around the Horn, we sailed up the coast of Chile, Peru, and Ecuador, from there we sailed west to the Sandwich Islands, and then on to the Philippines, from there to the Japans, all of this taking several months", "When we reached Japan we were only allowed to anchor in a bay off the port city of Nagasaki". "This is the only port that the Japanese will let white barbarians as they call us land and do business with them",

"While in port the captain took the whole crew and treated them to a Japanese Bath house experience", "We were taken to a very large building that had a red tiled roof that turned up at the corners". "In the building there was a very large hot pool of water". "We were asked to undress and these Japanese maids made us sit in these small tubs while they washed us with sponges that had a flowery smelling soap in them, then they rinsed us off and we were told to go to the big pool and get in". "The pool had benches that went around the perimeter of the pool that you sat on". "And you were in hot water up to your neck". "The hot water was so relaxing that you didn't have a care in the world". "After soaking for awhile the maids would ask you if you would like a massage, whereupon they helped you out of the pool and onto small tables where a husky maiden would give you a rub down, she massaged the muscles with such dexterity that you felt like you would never have the strength to get off that table". "When she finished the massage she told you to rest and nap if you liked". "After a short while it was back to the big pool again for a final soak". "When it was time to get dressed they brought your clothes back all cleaned and pressed". "I tell you Theo it was the greatest experience I ever had". "So that's why I have my version of a Japanese bath house".

"Now let me show you how it works, as you can see up there, there is a wooden pipe that brings spring water to the tubs and the furnace, that's what they call the fire place with the water box". "The water enters the metal box and then it is heated by the fire under the box, as you can see there are two pipes going to the big tub with branches to the smaller tubs". "When the water gets hot it raises up into the upper pipe and dumps into the tub, at the same time cooler water is dropping into the furnace box and is getting heated and then travels up the pipe into the tub, it's a continual cycle when the furnace is burning. "Now to keep the water from getting too hot I can turn a valve on that pipe over there and dump cold water into the tub until I get the temperature just right",

"The small tubs are for washing yourself clean as you do not want to get into the large tub dirty". "So I use one small tub for washing me and the other one for washing my clothes, which hang on that line over there". "That way I'm clean and relaxed and have clean work clothes the next day". "You'll see how much better you'll feel once you get into the habit", "But Cuss, you don't expect me to get into that habit do you?" "I'm used to taking a bath on Saturday night whether I need it or not". "That's up to you son you do what's best for you, but I guarantee once you try it you'll like it so much that you'll never stop doing it". "Now let's go up to the mine itself",

CHAPTER TWO

The Mine. After a quarter mile walk up the canyon that leads into the upper end of the meadow where Cuss has his cabin, we come to the actual diggings. It is a small ravine that leads off to the right of the main canyon, and you can see where Cuss has been digging away at the gravel and moving it down to a bin that sits over the sluice boxes. There is a flume that brings water from a small dam up the main canyon. When the dam gets full Cuss has a gate which he opens and let's water down the flume and into the sluice boxes. The gravel is dumped from the bin into the sluice box and the washing process begins. As the gravel and water move along the sluice boxes, the gold which is ten times heavier then the rocks and gravel drops down to the bottom of the sluice boxes and gets lodged behind the riffles, where it stays until it's time to clean up the boxes.

"To clean up the boxes I take a small shovel I made and shovel out the concentrates into a bucket then go down to that tub you see down by the end of the sluice boxes and put the material into a gold pan and pan it down till I have nothing but gold left".

"The gold then gets dried and weighed and put into a leather pouch.'" "When I get twelve ounces of gold in the pouch it is then stored away in a secret place that only I know about." "Why twelve ounce's?" asks Theo. "Because that equals a Troy pound."

Turning to the actual diggings Cuss shows Theo the spot where he left off, there is a very large boulder sitting on the bedrock that has to be moved before they can proceed with the digging. "Theo, tomorrow we will bring the black powder up here and the small sledge hammers called single jacks and the star drills and drill holes in that boulder and see if we can't blow it up into small enough pieces with the black powder, so that we can then move the pieces by hand out of our way.

"Theo, I want you to look at this piece of ground, can you see that there is an old river bed here that has dried up." "And that it is sitting in a U shaped ravine that is of slate bedrock."

"My theory is that at one time a good size river ran across this section of land, and through erosion and floods brought this assortment of gravel here, and with it gold and probably other minerals?' "Look at the rocks and boulders; they are all rounded from being tumbled down the river." "Look at the slate bedrock, and you notice that it is worn smooth like it was sanded by the river moving tons of material over it" "Now look up the hill about 50ft. and you'll see where the slate is jagged, then becomes smoother below like the rocks and boulders, to me that means that the river was up that high at one time, and has eroded down to what you see now." "As you saw we have big boulders and rocks in this digging, we also have fairly large nuggets here compared to the digging's closer to town."

"If you were to look at some of the diggings around Dahlonega you would find the gravel to be much smaller in size, most of the rocks can be moved by hand without any problem, and the gold recovered there is finer in size?" "Whereas here we will get bigger nuggets on the average." "I have recovered nuggets as big as your thumb at least once a week here." "But alas this good thing is not going to last forever, for I have traced this gravel up the ravine only about another four hundred yards." "So some day it is going to run out." "Hopefully by that time I will have enough gold to take it easy the rest of my years."

"Well Theo, that's the tour, it's time we go back to the cabin and get our rifles and see if we can get a deer for supper."

At the cabin they pick up their rifles and powder flasks and some extra shot and head out, going back up the canyon they follow the tree line around the meadow keeping inside the trees, and upwind of the lower part of the meadow. Cuss whispers to Theo that he has seen a small herd of deer come out of the woods and start browsing in the meadow several times when he is not working up at the diggings. So they set up a watch about midway down the meadow inside the trees, and hunker down to wait to see if the deer show up. About an hour later they spot movement in the trees along the lower end of the meadow, and sure enough here come the deer. The deer being very cautious take their time in walking out into the meadow. Slowly they move up the meadow to almost within rifle shot. Theo whispers to Cuss. "I can crawl out to that hummock I see out there and probably get a clear shot from there." Cuss whispers back "it's worth a try, do you think you can be quiet enough to get to the hummock?" "I think so; I've done it before when Dad has asked me to get some fresh meat for the family."

So off Theo goes, it takes him fifteen or so minutes to get to the hummock, during which time Cuss never sees him moving through the tall grass, and neither do the deer..

Once at the spot Theo headed for, he saw that the rise of the hummock was just right for a clear shot at a four point buck. Carefully laying the rifle on the top of the hummock, he cupped his left hand over the hammer of the rifle and slowly cocked it. The click of the mechanism was muffled enough by his hand that the deer with their keen hearing did not pay any attention to the sound. Taking careful aim, and a deep breath, which he let half of it out, he slowly squeezed the trigger like his pappy taught him. He shot the deer. The small buck dropped, the rest of the herd fled for the safety of the trees, Theo meantime started reloading the flintlock, and Cuss was running up to him, yelling, "you got him Theo, you got him." As soon as Theo finished reloading they slowly approached the deer, ready to shoot again if the deer was playing possum. The deer was dead with an almost perfect heart shot. Cuss pulled out his hunting knife and went over to the trees and found a stout branch to use as a carrying pole, he cut the branch off the tree, an returning to the deer, he and Theo tied the deer's legs together with the rope they had brought for that purpose. Then they slipped the pole through the tied legs and hoisted the deer between them and headed back to the cabin.

Back at the cabin Cuss had a tripod already set up, so they could hang the deer and butcher him into the cuts of meat they wanted. They took one of the hunches an put it on a spit over a fire that Cuss had laid out and started roasting it. It was to be supper and breakfast too. The rest of the meat was cut into strips and hung in the smoke house that Cuss had built and a low fire was started, when it became a good bed of coals, Cuss got some Hickory chips and soaked them in water and put them on top of the coals to make a lot of smoke to smoke the meat. This not only dried cured the meat but gave it a great flavor along with the salt and pepper that was rubbed into the meat before it was hung.

Meantime Cuss dug out a couple of potatoes and boiled them up, then he cut them up and adding onion, salt, pepper and a couple of cloves of garlic, fried the potatoes up to go with the roasted deer meat. When supper was done you were looking at two overstuffed men. Cuss said if we keep eating like this we will be the fattest two miners on the earth.

Theo burped, and then groaned, "You're right, I ate too much."

With supper done and the plates and utensils cleaned, it was time to settle in for the night, so Cuss said good night, and Theo put his bedroll into his new lean-to home and settled in. Out of his possible bag Theo took out a small candle and his blank journal book and pencil and put down in his journal the days doings and experiences as his

Mother suggested he do. Finished writing he blew out the candle and immediately fell asleep.

Next morning, up at dawn, breakfast of roast deer, coffee, and some pan bread that Cuss made up, some for breakfast, and some to have later at midday with the last of the roast.

Packing the donkey with a pack board that would hold the small keg of black powder, fuse, star drills and the single jacks, Cuss and Theo start for the mine, upon arrival they unpack the donkey, and Cuss has Theo take the donkey back to the cabin and stake him out on grass.

Cuss tells Theo when he got back, to stop at the bottom of the sluice boxes and bring up a bucket of the clay he will find there. While Theo is gone Cuss starts drilling the boulder, his plan is to put five holes in the big rock, one on each upper corner, and the same for the lower corners, and one in the middle deeper then the others, in the hopes that the boulder will break into small enough pieces to be able to be moved by the two. miners.

By the time Theo gets back Cuss has the two upper holes drilled. Cuss turns to Theo and tells him it's time for him to learn how to use a star drill and single jack. So he starts the center hole explaining how you hit the drill and turn it after each stroke of the sledge. This action keeps the drill bit from getting stuck in the hole.

Theo takes the tools in hand and proceeds to drill the center hole, after a few strokes he gets the rhythm of striking the drill then turning a quarter turn and hit it again, within a few minutes he has got the drill almost all the way in the hole. Cuss then takes the drill from Theo and gives him a longer one with which to finish the hole. When Theo finishes the hole, Cuss starts one of the lower holes. Finishing it, he gives the tools to Theo who does the last hole. Cuss then has Theo remove all the tools from the area so they are not covered by the blast. Then they bring up the blasting powder, fuse, and bag of tools with which to set up the charges. In the bag is a special wooden spoon to spoon the blasting powder into the holes they drilled, then Cuss got out a long wooden rod to use to tamp down the powder very carefully. When the holes are full he installs the fuses into each hole making them long enough so they will have time to get too safety. Then he packs the clay over the holes.

Cuss checks everything over to make sure that he didn't overlook something and sends Theo down to the bin and sluices where they can be safe from the blast, but also be able to watch. When Theo is safe Cuss takes out a lucifer match and lights the fuses then walks down to where Theo is hiding behind a part of the bin, after a couple of minutes the charges go off making a loud boom that echo's down the canyon. Theo is amazed at the loudness of the blast and the resulting dust cloud, plus the small pieces of rock that are falling out of the sky. They both duck under the bin until the rocks stop falling.

Cuss remarks. "I think we used a little more powder then we needed to, oh well, no harm done I hope." "Come on Theo the dust is clearing; let's go see what we did to that boulder." When they get up to where the boulder was, they found they had broken it up into smaller pieces then they were expecting. Cuss, shouting hooray and I'll be dammed, "will you look at that we did it son, we did it." "Let's go get the shovels and wheelbarrow's and muck this out and see what we can find."

They get the tools and go to work, moving the pieces of the boulder into the barrows and running them down to the end of the boards that is over the tailings pile, they make trip after trip, at midday they stop for something to eat, and a refreshing splash in the pond of dammed up water, then go back to work. About another ten trips with the barrows and Cuss is jumping up and down doing a jig. "Theo come here and look what we found." Theo comes running, and stops in awe at the site of a crevice about three feet long, just solid yellow with gold nuggets.

Cuss tells Theo to run down to the panning tub and get Molly and a clean bucket and we'll clean this crevice out. Theo hesitates, and asks "who is Molly?" Cuss laughs and says "that's right you haven't met Molly yet." "Come on we'll go get her and the bucket together." When they get down to the panning tub Cuss grabs a clean bucket and a funny looking tool. It has a spoon hammered into one end and a three quarters of an inch square handle that goes back to a tapered rod somewhat like a pick head which is bent at an angle. "Theo, meet Molly." "This is a special tool I had the blacksmith in town make for me." "I use it to clean out crevices like the one we just opened up." "Come on, I'll show you how slick it works."

They go back to the crevice and he gets down on his knees on a thick pad and starts scraping the gold out of the crevice with the tapered end. Then he turns the tool around and picks up the nuggets in the spoon and dumps the material into the bucket. "Notice the tool does not twist in my hand like a round handled tool does, that's why I made it square." He then hands Theo the tool and tells him to try it, while he takes a rest from all this excitement. Theo gets to work and scrapes that crevice as clean as he can get it, and we are looking at a pretty sizable amount of gold in the bucket. Cuss asks? "Do you think you got it all?" "It looks like it." With that Cuss tells him, "I'm going to show you one of the most important parts of cleaning a crevice,." He grabs a six foot long iron bar that has a point on one end and a wide flat spade on the other end, and he starts breaking down the sides of the crevice, and prying out pieces of the slate bedrock. After several minutes of doing this he has deepened the original crevice about a foot, and low and behold Theo can see more gold. When Theo had cleaned out the crevice, he was down to a hairline crack in the bottom, with no more gold showing. After Cuss broke it open deeper, there was more gold. Then Cuss explained to Theo, how the slate was in constant movement with the weather changes. When it was warm like today the rock expanded, allowing the crevice to open up a little, and gold being the heaviest material around would sink to the bottom of the crevice. When the rock got cold it would contract and close up that crevice, thereby hiding the gold. "So always break into a crevice deeper then you think is the bottom so you get all the gold." "That said, I think we have had enough work and excitement for today, let's take our bucket of dirt and gold down to the panning tub and wash the dirt away and see what we've got."

At the panning tub Cuss took a metal gold pan off a shelf and proceeded to show Theo how to wash the gold out of the dirt that they had put in the bucket. Filling the pan about half full, he dipped it into the water in the tub an shook the pan very vigorously and at the same time he was rotating the pan to the left. After several moments, he stopped, and let the material in the pan settle, then he tipped the pan away from him, and began sloughing the dirt off into the tub, using a wave action similar to the waves on an ocean beach. When the dirt started turning black on top, he dipped the pan back in the tub again, and again shook it vigorously, repeating the same process over and over till the dirt was gone and there was nothing but gold in the pan.

While he was doing this he explained what he was doing. "The gold, as I told you earlier is ten times heavier then anything else in the pan, so by shaking the pan real hard, and rotating it at the same time you are causing the dirt to be suspended in the water allowing the gold to drop to the bottom of the pan, then by sloughing off the dirt you are getting down to the gold," "Now that you seen me do it, it's your turn," "So take the pan and fill it with the dirt from the bucket and let's see if you can pan it down, as they say." Theo takes the pan and puts dirt from the bucket into it, then dips it into the water and shakes it real hard, while rotating the pan as he saw Cuss do it, being that he wants to be careful, he doesn't shake the pan hard enough. So Cuss tells him to shake it harder until you can feel everything in the pan is kind of floating. So Theo shakes it harder and loses almost half the dirt out of the pan, He looks at Cuss in a panic and exclaims, "I've lost some of the gold we worked so hard to get."

"Don't worry about it, it can't go anywhere, but to the bottom of the tub." "That's why I use the tub for clean ups." "When I get ready to take the dirt out of the tub, I take that small tin bucket over there hanging on the wall and dip the dirt out and put it on that table over there and run a very slow stream of water over it, you can watch the gold concentrate in a line on the slate surface of the table, while the dirt and black sand washes away." "Let's finish panning out the bucket and I'll show you how the table works." Cuss grabs another pan and they both start panning again, by the time Theo is working on his third pan he is starting to get the hang of it, and says to Cuss "This is kinda fun once you get used to it." Cuss gives Theo a big smile.

When they finish panning, they look into the tin cup that they were putting the gold in and Cuss guessed there might be twenty ounces of gold in the cup. Theo exclaims, "That's a lot of gold." "Yep, if it weighs out that much it will be the best day I've seen from these diggings."

"Now let me show you how the slate table works," Cuss goes over to the head of the table and turns on a water valve, adjusting it so there is an even flow of slowly moving water moving over the table, He then grabs a sieve and dips it into the tub and fills it with dirt, then while it is under water he sifts the dirt through the sieve into one of the gold pans, this brings the material size down to around an eighth of an inch. As he is doing this he explains, "that what we have been doing all day is what the miners call classifying the material." "We started with a big boulder that we made into smaller boulders then dug up small rocks and gold out of the crevice, and by panning the dirt we eliminated the dirt and left only the gold." "So now I'll show you how we will do the same thing on the table." With that he slowly pours the dirt from the pan on the table and the water starts washing the lighter dirt away leaving a trail of fine gold and black sand on the table of slate. Theo watches in amazement as the process takes place, and asks Cuss where he learned how to do all this and where the ideas for the different equipment came from?

"The slate table idea came from a tin miner from Cornwall England, the man said that he worked in a tin mine and this was how they concentrated the tin ore." "The gold pans came to this country from the land of Mexico and before that Spain, the same for the sluices." "I just took all these ideas and put them together, and so far it is working."

"Now let's finish up, I'm getting hungry, and I haven't had a bath and a soak for days." So they packed up for the day and headed down to the cabin. When they got there, Cuss showed Theo how to get a fire going in the hot tub furnace, and then they went to Cuss's cabin to weigh the gold.

Taking a small gold pan off a shelf they dumped the gold into it washing all the fine gold out of the cup and into the pan. Putting the pan on the stove he got a cooking fire going and dried the water out of the gold pan leaving the gold dry. While the pan was cooling he put on a pot of water to boil, stating he was going to have a cup of tea to help relax with. By the time the pot was boiling the gold had cooled off enough to be handled and weighed. Cuss poured himself a cup of tea, asking Theo if he wanted one, Theo said he had never drunk any tea but after today he was game for anything.

So Cuss got another cup down and made two cups of tea, it was green tea which has a sweet dry taste to it. Cuss said try it with sugar, when he saw Theo's face scrunch up at the first taste. So Theo added a spoonful of sugar and found that the tea was much better that way, so good that before they finished weighing the gold he had another cup.

Taking a gold scale and small box of scale weights off a shelf, Cuss sets it up on the table. On one side of the scale there is an adjusting screw that he turns until the balance beam pointer is at the middle of the scale that's on the vertical upright that the beam is positioned on. Cuss then takes a small spoon like tool, that has a handle at right angle to a V shaped copper trough, by dipping the large end into the gold Cuss can funnel the gold onto the pans of the gold scale.

So he starts weighing. Having only five ounces of gold weights he puts them on the scale pan on one side than starts putting the larger nuggets on the other pan. The first two nuggets weigh over five ounces, so Cuss takes one off and adds smaller ones till he has five ounces.

He puts the gold into another small gold pan and repeats the process. After weighing out twelve ounces he puts it into one of several leather pouch's that he had made up for him. Again more gold goes on the scale, another pouch is filled, and still there is more gold to weigh, the gold left does not weigh five ounces so Cuss starts to remove some of the small weights until the beam is balanced. He looks at the weights left and reads the numbers on them and announces that they had recovered twenty seven ounces, seventeen pennyweight, and eleven grains: Theo is all eyes and excited.

"Cuss, how much money does that come to?" Cuss takes down a writing tablet off the shelf and makes some calculations "Theo, we have had the best day I've seen from our hole in the ground, at sixteen dollars an ounce, which is what the gold buyers are paying." "We recovered " Theo bursts out, "that's four hundred and thirty some dollars, why that's almost as much as pa and I make in a year on the farm, and you made that in one day." Cuss looks at Theo, and asks how he comes to that number so fast? Theo flushed, and said, "ma taught me numbers and I found out I could do them in my head faster then most people can on paper." "That's amazing, you know Theo you are going to make the best partner I have ever had, you work hard, learn fast, and brought me luck on our first day digging together." Theo flushed again and because he was at a loss for words, quietly said, "thank you." After a pause where the two just looked at each other, Cuss said, "it's time to eat, I'm hongry". So they put the gold and scales away on the shelf, and start to make supper. Cuss had put some beans to soak before breakfast, so he rinsed them off, put them in a pot of water, and started cooking them, he had Theo go out to the smoke house and get a couple of deer steaks. While Theo was gone Cuss whipped up some pan bread and started it cooking. When Theo got back with the steaks, Cuss coated them with a homemade sauce that he made from tomatoes out of an airtight, and molasses, vinegar, salt and pepper and dry mustard, and then he put the steaks on a spit. He told Theo to go out to the hot tub furnace and stoke it up. Cuss took the deer steaks, put them on a holder he had made, to go over the open fire of the cook stove after a burner cover was removed. This allowed him to flame broil the meat, while coating it with the sauce. The only problem was it smoked up the cabin so bad that Theo thought it was on fire. So running back, he saw what was happening and opened the windows and door and started waving a coat of Cuss's to get rid of the smoke. "That happens every time I want steaks cooked over an open fire." They both laughed so much they got tears in their eyes.

Meantime the beans are almost done, except for some seasoning that Cuss puts in, salt, pepper, a couple of cloves of garlic, something called cumin, that he got in the islands off Florida, and ground chili pepper for a little heat, he told Theo. By now the pan bread was done, so he takes it off the stove and shakes cinnamon on the bread, and then adds honey to cover the bread.

Now the steaks are done, so are the beans and bread, so without any fuss they grab their tin plates and fill them, going outside where Cuss has a sturdy table, they sit and eat, almost wolfing down the first helping, then they both go back for seconds. This time they take their time, and talk a little. Theo said he has never had such interesting different flavors in the food he was eating, and where did Cuss learn how to cook like he does? "It's a long story Theo; tell you some of it while we take a soak in the hot tub." Theo looks at Cuss and thinking to himself, *oh no! Another new experience, he knows that Cuss is proud of his hot tub and enjoys it as often as he can, but he is leery of taking a bath before Saturday night, as Saturday night baths are almost a religious thing in his family.*

CHAPTER THREE

So Cuss and Theo clean up the plates and utensils, and get ready for what Theo thinks is the dreaded bath. Cuss tells Theo to grab a change of clothes and a pair of boots and come with him to the bath house. Cuss laughing, tells Theo that they don't have to adhere to the Japanese ritual of having a maid wash them seeing as how they don't have a maid. Theo says, "Oh!"

When they get to the tub, Cuss stokes up the fire in the furnace, and goes over and checks the tub to see how hot it is, and exclaims it feels just about right. Theo timidly puts his hand in the tub and declares, "I don't know Cuss, it feels hot enough to boil the hide off a tough old steer". Cuss just laughs, The two smaller tubs are also hot, so Cuss tells Theo, do as I'm going to do, and with that he shucks his dirty clothes, and standing there naked puts them in one of the tubs and scrubs the dirt out, and then plunges them into the tub to rinse them, then wrings them out and hangs them on a rope that is strung across the platform. He tells Theo, "now I will have a clean set of clothes for the next day or day after depending on how long they take to dry".

Now Cuss goes over to the other tub and taking a bucket, he dips some of the hot water out and puts the bucket next to the tub so he can reach it. He tells Theo to get one of the other buckets over there and dip out a bucket full for himself. "Now watch what I do". Cuss takes a bar of lye soap and climbs into the tub and washes himself, when he's done he grabs the bucket and pours the water over himself to rinse off. Now that he's clean he walks over to the hot tub and climbs in, and with a big sigh he settles himself on a bench that is built around the inside of the tub. Cuss hollers over to Theo, "It's your turn, youngster". Theo not being used to disrobing in front of other people, especially a, up to a couple of days ago more or less stranger, hesitates, trying to get up the courage, he slowly starts to take off his clothes, first his shirt, which he puts in the wash tub and scrubs the dirt out of it, following Cuss's example. After he gets the shirt hung up he takes off his boots and socks, and washes the socks and hangs them up.

Now comes the moment of truth, can he, with his shyness, get his pants off, washed and hung up without turning red with embarassment. So turning his back to Cuss he manages to get his pants off, washed, and hung up. "Come on boy; get in the tub before it cools off too much". So Theo slowly emerges himself into the water, thinking to himself, that he going to be boiled alive

After a minute he is getting used to the hot water and finds that Cuss was right, the hot water starts to relax him in a way he has never experienced before, "Well Theo, was I right?"

"Isn't this just about the most relaxing thing you can ever do". Theo shakes his head yes and sits back and he swears he can feel the soreness being washed right out of him.

"Now I can tell you about the life of yours truly Chastain Castle". "I was born in England to my father Chastain and mother Agnes". "My father was a master carpenter, building anything from houses to fancy tables, chairs, or cabinets". "Unfortunately there were more carpenters than work, so making a steady income was very hard to do". "One day after a fruitless day of trying to find work my father asked my mother, what she thought of going to America and live". He had been hearing in the pubs that there was so much work there that the Colonials were paying boat fares for any craftsman that was worth his salt to come and settle and work. Agnes looks at her husband and wonders if he has gone daft,

So Chastain spends the rest of the evening talking Agnes into the move. The next morning he goes to the docks and inquire about a ship that is going to the Americas. He finds two that are leaving within a week, and a couple more that will be shipping out about a month later.

He finds the ships and talks to the captains about sailing to America, and the fact that people in America will pay the passage. The first two captains said they had not heard of such a proposition, and told Chastain the fares for him and his family. Alas, the fares were out of reach even if Chastain had been working steady. The third captain said, yes he had heard of the offer, but that there was a problem with it, He told Chastain that he would have to indenture himself to the patron for a minimum of five years. Chastain was shocked, but not overly surprised as he had heard of others doing this to get away from England. He told the captain thank you and started to turn away, the captain put a hand on Chastain's shoulder, and asked him what it is he works at? Chastain tells him that he is a master carpenter. The captain asks Chastain if he has ever worked on a ship. "No, but I have worked on parts of ships, such as making spars and blocks for the tackle, and once I replaced the entire railing on a small packet boat". "Good enough, how would you like to work as my ships carpenter for your fare to America". "Really?" "Of course I would, but there is a problem, I have a wife and eight year old boy that would be going too". "The captain thinks for a moment and tells him, I could give the job of galley slave to your boy, and if your wife can sew, she could help the sail maker keep the sails repaired". •Chastain looks at the captain, and tells him you have a new carpenter. "When do we leave?" "Within the month, but you can start work tomorrow as there are a myriad of repairs to do, plus we are taking on a cargo that will require special crating to keep it steady in the hold". Chastain said, "I will see you in the morning" And takes his leave.

At home he tells his wife of his good fortune, and the roles they would play on this now grand adventure. He tells Agnes about her being the sailmakers helper, and I was going to be the galley slave, I looked at my pa and said very defiantly, "I was not about to be anybody's slave". My mom looked at pa and they both laughed, and proceeded to tell me that galley slave was just a sailing term that meant, he would be the cook's helper. I said, "Oh!"

A month later we sailed, my pa had made the ship, shipshape as they say. " I settled into the cooks helper job and soon found out why they called me the galley slave, washing the dishes and pots and pans, taking out the left overs and giving it to the half dozen Yorkshire pigs we had on board, and on and on, it seemed like I could never stop working", "The cook was a slave driver to coin a pun". "Course mom and dad worked hard too".

"At last America, we docked at Wilmington, Virginia and unloaded the special cargo, Pa had to take the crates he had built apart, so they could get the cargo out of the hold". "While in port my pa asked around about work, and found that Wilmington did not have much to offer, he spoke to the captain about the lack of work, and the captain told pa to stay on board until they reached Savannah Georgia, where he knew of a man that was looking for furniture makers".

Pa looked at the captain and said, "again you have given me an opportunity that I cannot pass up, as furniture making is what I enjoy the most in this trade I have chosen for myself'.

"Savannah, the captain takes pa to the furniture factory and introduces him to his friend, and tells him of his talent with wood. The man tells my pa to bring his tools and go to work tomorrow if you can? Pa asks if he can start the day after, as he needs to find a place for mom and me to live in. The man tells pa, That is not a problem, as he has housing for his workers that he rents to them a lot more reasonable then the usual landlord, plus they are much cleaner. Again pa says a silent prayer for his good fortune.

CHAPTER FOUR

"Follow me Mr. Castle, and I'll show you the house that I think you and your family will find adequate". So they walk down the street about a block, and approach a small house, with a number 11 on the door, going inside the owner shows Chastain the house, it has two small bedrooms, a. large kitchen with a table and chairs, pots, pans, and utensils to cook with, plus a small living room to just sit and relax in. Chastain looks in awe at the small house and again says a small prayer. The owner then takes him out back and shows him the privy, it is a two holer with a partition so there is privacy between each side. The factory owner explains that Chastain and his family have to share the privy with the family next door, which is why there is a partition, one side for womenfolk and one side for the men.

Chastain tells the factory owner that the house is a castle compared to the hovel they lived in, in England. He then thanks the man, and tells him he will get his family and move in right away so he can start work in the morning. So they part ways and Chastain runs down to the docks to get his family and belongings.

When he finds his wife and son they are sitting on the toot chest guarding the rest of their belongings. "Agnes, I have the most wonderful news, I have a job in the furniture factory and we have a house to live in, and I start work in the morning". "All we have to do is get our belongings to the house and settle in, the place is completely furnished and you will think it is a castle compared to our home in England".

"Wait here while I find a Drayer to haul our belongings to the house and factory". Chastain is back in a few minutes with a small cart, horse, and a tough looking Irishman who is going to haul them and their belongings to the house and factory.

"Agnes, this is O'Brian". "O'Brian this is my wife Agnes and my son Chastain". O'Brian says, "Good day to you, ma'am, and what a bonny looking lad you have here". "Let's load up and be on our way, times a wasting". So away they go on another adventure. Taking their personal belongings to the house and unloading them there, Chastain and O'Brian take the tool box to the factory and deposit it there on the loading dock at the rear of the building. The factory owner comes out and tells Mr. Castle, "come and I'll show you your work station". They enter the factory and walk down a long aisle to a very large work bench with two wood vises and holes for bench dogs. Again Chastain is in awe of the amities that have been given him to work with. He gets a handcart and proceeds to bring in his tool box, setting it beside the bench that is now his new working home.

Chastain then takes his leave, and rushing home to his new house, sees what he can do to help Agnes and Chastain junior. Upon arrival he finds that with the help of one of their new neighbors that the house is in order and all they need to do is get some food so they can eat, it's then that Chastain realizes that they have not eaten all day in all the excitement. The neighbor invites them to have supper with them and meet our family; this will save you trying to find a shop that is still open where you can buy food. Chastain is again flabbergasted at the good luck and friendliness of the people he has met today

"So life in Savannah begins, Pa to work. I have to go to school; mom takes care of the home and such". "At age ten Pa gets me a job at the factory as a cleanup boy". "I don't realize it, but it's the first step in my apprenticeship". "I soon find out I went from galley slave, to furniture factory flunky, as the older men called us with a smile on their faces". "Hey flunky,

Come and sweep over here. or hey flunky come and help me carry this lumber to the work bench".

"As time went by, I learned how to recognize the different woods they used, and how to use a saw to rough cut the boards to length for the woodworkers, then came the use of the planes, there were long planes to smooth the rough boards, and bring them down to the thickness dimension they required". "Then there were the molding planes which gave the boards different designs, then the augers and small drills". "And so on, till at age eighteen I was a carpenter, not a master like my Pa but good enough to build a house if need be, or simple cabinets, etc". "Theo, look around you at the joinery in this platform and tub, etc. and you will find it to be more sophisticated then most of the building you see in town". "Yes, I've noticed".

"Anyway back to my story". "About this time in my life I was noticing the young ladies in town, and had started thinking I might like a relationship like my ma and pa". "One lady in particular caught my eye". "I tried to start a courting relationship with the young lady but she was having none of it, as I was a couple of stations in life under her". "She came right out and told me that she intended to marry a rich man", "She broke my heart, and she did marry a rich man, who proceeded to squander his inherited fortune, by gambling it away". "The last I heard she had turned into an old harpy, always berating her husband, and giving him a bad time of it".

"Just when I was going through this rejection, I was also having second thoughts about being a carpenter". "I wanted to do something else but didn't know what", "Along comes the captain of the ship that brought us from England". "He had kept in touch with us, stopping to visit every time he would dock in Savannah". "Upon hearing my tale of woe from ma and pa, he suggested maybe a trip at sea would be just the ticket to let me see things clearer",

"So he offered me a job on his ship as a carpenters helper", "So down to the sea in a ship I went". "The captain had a new ship that was larger, and he was going to the Orient, to help with the opening of trade with the Japans", "I've already told you about the Japans".

"But to answer your earlier question about my cooking", "As I told you I was a galley slave, and I learned a little about cooking then, but it was the trip to the Japans that I really learned a thing about the finer aspects of cooking", "You see we had a very good French chef in the galley, not just a ships cook" "And every chance I got I would help him prepare meals for the captain and his mates". "Now the French love to put a sauce on everything, so I became the sauce maker, which taught me how to enhance the flavors of any dish I wanted to make". "By the time the ship made it back to Savannah, not only was I a ships carpenter, I could also cook like the Frenchman".

"After three years at sea I felt it was time to spend some time on the beach as the sailors called it when you were not sailing". "So I spent some time with ma and pa catching up on their lives which hadn't really changed that much, except that pa was now foreman and a percentage partner in the factory".

"Course I had changed, I had learned to chew, plus drink the grog, and hang out in pubs which were a source of gossip, and information about everything". "That's where I learned about the gold strike at Dahlonega and decided to become a gold miner". "So having the better part of three years pay in my pockets I headed for the gold fields". "Upon arriving here I found that most of the good ground was already taken up, and not knowing anything about prospecting, I needed to become friends with the best miners around and get them to teach me about mining".

"I found out that there weren't any good carpenters around, so I started doing carpenter work to keep from having to delve into my ships pay". "This led me to the best miners around as they were the only ones who could afford to hire a carpenter to build whatever they needed",

"So I learned about sluice boxes, and bins to store ore while waiting for the ponds to fill behind the small dams". "I also learned how to make an automatic water gate that would let the water into the sluices when the dam is full". "But most important of all how to find and recover gold". "So here we are, I have a good paying gold mine, and a hand that is going to help make me a rich man, while he learns the trade so to speak". "Can life be any better then this?"

"Well that's my story Theo". "Got any questions?" Theo looks at Cuss and says, "yes, a thousand of them, but the one that has me the most perplexed is how did you become to be called Cuss?". "Since I have been here, I've only heard you use cuss words twice". "Oh! That". "That's part of the act I put on for the town folks", "It keeps them on their toes if they think I'm an ornery old cuss". "Now it's my turn, how did you get the name Theolonius Raphael?"

"From ma, she read about a Greek hero called Theolonius, and in another book she read about an Italian artist named Raphael, she put the two names together and said it rolled off her tongue like a song, so here I am, Theolonius Raphael Calhoun, the heroic artist as ma likes to kid me".

"Well son the water is getting cold and it's getting late, so I think it's time to get out and dry off. an head for the sack, tomorrows going to be another day".

Back in the lean- to Theo gets out his journal and puts down the events of the day, then goes to sleep.

CHAPTER FIVE

Thursday morning, up at dawn, breakfast, pack lunch then off to the diggings. Cuss tells Theo that today he is going to learn how to use a slick sheet when mucking out the ore. Theo asks, "What is a slick sheet?" "Remember yesterday, the two sheets of metal that were just down from the boulder?" "Yeah, I wondered what they were for." So Cuss proceeds to tell Theo how a slick sheet is used. "You put the sheets up against the face of the gravel bank we are working on, then with your pick, you break the gravel loose and let it fall on the metal sheet; when you have a sizable pile of gravel, you bring up one of the wheelbarrows and shovel the gravel into the barrow." "The sheet of metal makes shoveling, or mucking out as they call it, much easier." "The smooth surface lets the flat nosed shovel slide under the gravel just as slick as grease, that's why it's called a slick sheet."

"Also remember the wheelbarrows, there was something different about them, wasn't there?" "Yes, they had two wheels in front, instead of one." "I was so excited over the boulder and the crevice that I forgot to ask about the wheels." "Well son, the reason they have two wheels is for stability." "With one wheel, I was always tipping the barrows over on their side and losing the load." "So one day I had the Blacksmith make me a set of side by side wheels and axle, then I took a borrow apart and spread the handles, box, and axle supports, so the new wheels would fit in." "That stopped the barrows from tipping on their sides, then the only problem I had was to make sure the boards that are on the ground were wide enough for the wheels."

"Well here we are, let's start by finishing up where we left off yesterday, then we can start picking and shoveling." So with molly and the bar, they finished cleaning the crevice filling two buckets full of ore. Then they got one of the slick sheets and placed it against the face of the gravel bank, then the other one beside it and proceeded to pick away at the bank.

Fortunately the gravel deposit was only about ten feet wide, and six feet on average high, so they did not have to pull the gravel down in steps in order to reach the top of the deposit, the slick sheets were four by four feet, so they covered the area quite nicely.

"By the way Theo, the idea for these sheets came from that same tin miner I told you about, they used the same idea when mining tin ore." "These fellows from Cornwall England are called cousin jacks, and they are the best miners around." "Almost all of the fixtures and tools we are using originated with the cousin jacks."

"So picking and shoveling, and wheel barrowing we go." The gravel was placed in the barrows and wheeled to the top of the bin, there the gravel was dumped into the bin. On top of the bin was a screen that Cuss had put together, by laying three quarter inch thick square bars over the top of the bin and securing the bars with baling wire so that it formed a screen with four inch square holes. By placing the screen over the bin on a forty five degree angle, we would dump the gravel on it and the bigger rocks would fall off the side of the lower end of the screen. While the smaller gravel with the gold in it fell into the bin. As Cuss said, we are classifying that material so we don't have to wash rocks that don't have any gold in them. Soon we had the bin full, so we ate our noon meal, then got ready to wash some gravel.

Cuss tells Theo, "Now we have a new thing for you to learn." "Look up at the dam, and you will see a gate." "In front of the gate is a flume that leads down under the bin, then into the sluice boxes." "What we do is open the gate, and let the water into the flume and sluices then we feed the gravel into the flume so that the water washes over it and moves it down the flume and sluices." "As I said before the gold drops out of the gravel and gets caught behind the riffles, while the gravel washes away to become tailings down the hill." "Now the important thing is to feed the gravel steadily and at the same time not over load the sluices, so you want to put about the same amount of gravel as a bucket holds in about a minute's time in the flume."

"At the bottom of the bin is a hole about a foot square, up into that hole I have installed a couple of rods, they are attached to a handle that can be moved back and forth, thus allowing the gravel to fall on the flume, so the idea is to shake the gravel enough to fall, like I said about a bucket a minute."

"You see that rope that goes up to the gate." "I use it to open the gate and let the water into the flume." "I've got the gate adjusted so that the right amount of water is released in a constant stream down the flume and sluices, when the water reaches the level of the bottom of the gate, the gate automatically closes and shuts the water off." "Then we wait for the dam to fill and start washing again." "Fortunately there is, enough water in the dam to wash a full bin of gravel, so while we are waiting for the dam to fill, we can refill the bin and start all over again." "The timing is such that we can wash a bin a day."

"So let's start." "I'll open the gate and you can work the gravel feed handle, then I'll watch the sluices and let you know if you're feeding too much or too little." Here comes the water and I start moving the handle back and forth, Cuss hollers at me to slow down a might, which I do.

He then yells, "That looks good, keep the feed going just like that." After about an hour Cuss comes up and tells me he'll take over. "I want you to watch how the sluices work." "There will be days when you will be working the wash plant by yourself, so I want you to be able to judge whether the system is working properly." "Work the plant by myself?" "Sure I set it up so one man can do it without any help." "With you here, I can be cleaning out crevices, or chopping wood for the hot tub furnace and the cook stove, moving boulders with the mule or any number of chores that need to be done."

So I watch the sluices and move some of the larger rocks out of the trough, and generally get the hang of how the process works. Another hour passes and I notice that the water is clearing up, and that there doesn't seem to be any more gravel coming out of the bin. Cuss hollers, "The bin is empty, we will let the water run another five minutes or so, then shut the gate."

"I want you to go over on the other side of the flume and grab the rope you find there and when I yell, pull on it and it will release the gate, so it will close." Cuss walks down the sluice removing some of the larger rocks, and watching the flow of the water and material, shortly he hollers, "now Theo, pull hard." I do and feel a click on the other end of the rope, and the gate closes.

"Come on down here and take a look." As the water recedes in the flume and sluices, I begin to see yellow lines of gold behind the first four or five riffles. Cuss tells me, "that's what it's all about, I would say we had another fair day." "Get a couple of buckets and the small shovel I showed you and we'll clean up the first section, about ten riffles." I get the buckets and shovel and we start to clean out the sluice box, there's enough concentrates to fill both buckets, then down to the panning tub and pan out. Cuss being much faster, finishes much sooner then me, so he takes some of the gravel in my bucket and helps me pan. Shortly the panning is done, and we look at the cup of gold and see about third or half of what we had recovered the day before. Cuss exclaims, "Another good day at the mine."

So we close up for the day and head for the cabin to dry and weigh the gold, get the hot tub furnace going, fix and eat supper, another bath and soak, which Theo is beginning to really enjoy, and off to bed to sleep and dream of what tomorrow will bring,

CHAPTER SIX

Friday morning, up, breakfast, on the trail to the diggings. "Theo, guess what son, we forgot to pan out those last two buckets from the crevice under the 'boulder." "That's right, we got so busy with the bin and sluice, that we plumb forgot." "I'll tell you what, Theo, when we get up there, we move the slick sheets back so you can clean the bedrock that we uncovered yesterday, and I'll take the buckets down and pan them out, then I'll come up and help you with the bedrock." "We are going to quit early today so you can get back to your folks before nightfall." "Cuss, I don't have to leave early, I'm not afraid of the dark, and I can find my way, home after dark, I've done it before." "I know, but my mule that you will be riding is afraid of the dark and he doesn't know the way to your house." "Oh!" says Theo.

So they finish cleaning the bedrock, pan out, and head back to the cabin about noon. They have a noon meal, and then pack Theo up to go home. Cuss gives Theo a list of supplies to pick up on Monday when he comes back to work, and gives him instructions to bypass town on the way home in case there are some other fools like Arnold around. "Monday when you ride into town for the supplies, go back the way you came like you were going back to the farm then when it is safe double back around town and come out here." "Stop and take a pee once in a while so you can watch your back trail without being obvious." "When you know no one is following you come on up to the cabin." "I'll be chopping wood for the hot tub and cook stove."

So Theo takes off, being cautious, he gets home way before nightfall, and the family is waiting full of questions.

After taking care of the mule, letting him roll and giving him a rub down with a gunny sack, graining and watering, Theo goes up to the house. Setting down at the kitchen table, the family cannot hold back their questions, and they all begin to talk at the same time. "Whoa! let me talk and I'll tell you everything." So the evening was spent with Theo telling his family all about his experiences of the week at work and especially about the hot tub, and kiddingly asked his pa why they did not have a hot tub. Amos asks him if he wanted to spoil his Saturday night ritual bath whether I need it or not, I should say not, with that everybody has a good laugh.

Weekend filled with farm chores. Sunday Beatrice makes fried chicken, and asks if Cuss might like to have some. "I bet he would, since you make the best fried chicken in the area." "Go on with you, there are plenty of ladies that can fry chicken." "Not like yours, ma, not like yours."

Monday before daylight and Theo is off to town to take care of picking up the supplies, putting them on Cuss's account at the general store and doing as Cuss told him, back tracking towards home, and then the roundabout way to the mine, checking his back trail. With no sign of anybody following, he heads up the trail to the cabin. Upon arriving, Cuss asked if there were any problems. "None that I could see, the store owner put the supplies on your account like you told him, and there wasn't anybody lurking around

43

that I could see, and nobody on my trail." "That's great" remarks Cuss.

So unloading, and taking care of the mule, they head up to the diggings, back to the old grind. Moving the slick sheets in place, picking and shoveling, mucking up the ore, and taking it to the bin, turning on the water, washing the gravel, cleaning up and panning out, back to the cabin for supper, wash clothes, take bath, hot tub, up the next morning to start it all over again. Occasionally taking a break from the mine to hunt for game, or cut wood for the stoves. And so it goes.

A couple of months later Theo informs Cuss that his seventeenth birthday is this weekend and the family is going to have a small party for him, and Cuss is invited to come. Cuss wants to know if Theo's mom is going to make fried Chicken? "That and a glazed ham and a chocolate cake." "You couldn't keep me away." "What time's the party?"

"Sunday afternoon." "Good exclaims Cuss, that will give me time to go to town and get a shave, and haircut, and make myself presentable, also I need to stop at the notions store and get some more leather pouches." "The lady there makes them up special for me, and with you helping me I'm filling them up faster then I would usually do.

So Friday at noon they take off for town, Theo on the mule, and Cuss on the donkey, because he is smaller then Theo. Before they left, Cuss gets out his brown twill pants and frock coat, white collarless shirt and flat crowned hat to wear to the party.

When they get to town, Cuss heads for the notions shop to get his pouches, as they tie up the animals out front, Cuss notices that the sign above the door has changed; it has been freshly painted to say Sara's notions, instead of Mrs. Olson's notions. "Strange says Cuss, "I didn't know Mrs. Olson's first name was Sara." As they walk into the store Cuss notices how it has changed since the last time he had been there,.., what four or five month's ago. He steps up to the counter just as a very handsome woman in her middle thirty's steps up to the other side of the counter. "May I help you?" she asks. And Cuss with his mouth agape, just stares. He has not seen a woman so lovely, and he feels an immediate attraction to her. He finally gets his voice to work, and says hello. "I'm Cuss, and I'm here to get a dozen pouches that Mrs. Olson makes up special for me." "So you're Cuss, I've heard a lot about you, are you really as mean an ornery as the town folk say, according to Mrs. Olson the former owner of this store, you were always a perfect gentleman when doing business with her." "Well Cuss, I'm the recently widowed Sara Winston, and I just bought this store from Mrs. Olson a month and a half ago and I will be more then happy to keep supplying you with the leather pouches that Mrs. Olson made special for you, as a matter of fact I have been expecting you and have the pouches right here on this shelf waiting for you." "The price is the same, as is the quality of the workmanship." With that said she gets the pouches off the shelf and starts to hand them to Cuss, as she does Cuss tenderly takes, Sara's hand in his, and asks? "My lovely lady may I kiss your hand, and tell you how handsome I see you are." "Why Mr. Cuss, how nice of you to say that, as for kissing my hand we haven't been properly introduced yet." "Cuss turns to Theo who has been taking in the scene in front of him with surprise, and says, "Theo will you please introduce the lady to me and I to her." "Sure." "Mrs. Sara Winston this is Cuss." Cuss interrupts and tells Theo to please use my given name. "Oh!, I'm sorry Cuss, I'll try again." "Mrs. Sara Winston, please let me introduce you to Mr. Chastain Castle, Mr. Castle let me introduce you to Mrs. Sara Winston." "How do you do Mr. Castle, I'm charmed to make your acquaintance." "And I am more than happy to make yours, now may I kiss your hand", and with that he does, and they all have a friendly laugh."

Cuss turns to Theo, "Theo why don't you head for home now and I'll see you Sunday at the party." So Theo says goodbye to Mrs. Winston and Cuss, and heads for the farm, thinking to himself now what was that all about.

After Theo leaves, Cuss turns to Sara and tells her, "I'll take those pouches now, and while you are wrapping them I would like to know if you would do me the extreme honor of having dinner with me this evening, at say the Hotel dining room at whatever time is at your convenience." Sara looks at Cuss. "Why Chastain, I would be more then happy to, but I must say that with your reputation for being mean an ornery, I will have to be on guard at all times so as not to rile you up and therefore cause scene." Which they both laugh at. It seems to Cuss that Sara has seen through his act, and therefore is not intimated by his gruff behavior.

Cuss asks her. "What time should I pick you up?" "About six thirty would be fine, that will give me time to freshen up after closing the store, just come here, as I live in the back, and I'll be waiting with bells on." Again laughing.

"I'll be here, but I caution you to look for a stranger, as I am about to get a haircut, shave, bath and a change of clothes." Sara suggests that Cuss just trim his beard, as she likes him with a beard, and he would not be such a stranger at her door.

Dinner, the hotel serves the best meals in town, and Sara and Cuss enjoy the dishes they order, along with a decent bottle of wine. The conversation is lively and informative, Cuss learns about the tragic death of Sara's husband during a fierce storm,' while he was out fishing with friends in the bay off Savannah. The wind came up so fast that they couldn't get to safety before the boat capsized, and since Tom, her husband couldn't swim, he drowned, along with one of his friends. They found the body's washed up on shore two days later.

As Sara couldn't run their business by herself, and needing a change of scenery, she sold the business and loaded up a small freight wagon and came to Dahlonega to buy Mrs. Olson's store. Cuss asked how she knew the store was for sale? Sara told Cuss that Mrs. Olson was an aunt of hers and had been wanting to sell the store for about a year now. "So here I am, having dinner with the infamous Cuss of Dahlonega."

"So Chastain, what is your story?" "Besides the act you have been trying to put over on the people around here?" Cuss looks at Sara and exclaims, "you sure know how to read a fellow don't you?" "Well as you probably know, I have a small mine a few miles from town, where I eke out a modest living, and I too left Savannah to come up here to make my fortune." "By the time I got here all the best ground had been spoken for, so I went to work as a carpenter for the various miners, making a decent wage, and learning all I could about the finding of gold and the recovery of same."

"When I wasn't working at my trade, I would roam the hills in search of a place to mine gold." "A couple of years ago I found the piece of ground I'm working now." "It has taken me a lot of years to find this mine."

"Sara, you said you came from Savannah, isn't it funny that we are both fugitives from the same town." "I left because I wanted a new trade, and came here to mine gold, instead I spent most of my time working as a carpenter, the very trade I was running from, life sure is funny."

"Tomorrow I want to find a present for Theo," "He has been the best worker, companion, and good luck charm for me." "The very first day we worked together, we recovered almost a year's income that his father makes on their tenant farm, and we have been doing quite well since." "So I was thinking of getting him a horse to ride back and forth to work, plus a side arm to protect himself with." "It seems there are certain rough characters around here that would do foul deeds to find my mine and the small amount of gold I have accumulated."

"So a good horse and saddle and a revolver would make a great birthday gift, plus it would ease my mind to know he could protect himself in case of trouble."

"Chastain, I have just the horse you're looking for." "When I came here I drove a team of matched Morgan's to pull my small freight wagon, as I was carrying a considerable amount of books, plus my clothing, china, silver, etc. I needed a team of strong horses to pull the heavy wagon," "The pair were foals from the same mare and sire, a year apart, I want to keep the mare as she is a delight to ride when I want to go riding and be alone."

"The gelding is slightly larger and well trained for both harness and saddle; my husband and I got them as colts and had them trained by a wonderful trainer just out of Savannah." "The man had the uncanny ability to talk the horses into doing his bidding, without using the normal harsh methods so many horse trainers do."

"The owner of the stable where I keep the horses makes saddles, and I have not seen finer, I have seen fancier ones, but for practical everyday riding, you could not ask for better, plus they are reasonable in price." "So why don't we meet tomorrow for, breakfast and you can take a look at my horse, and the stable owners saddles; and as for a revolver, I heard that the gunsmith has a new shipment of Colt Dragoons, that all the men are salivating over." Cuss tells her, "That is the best idea I have heard." "What time would you like breakfast?" "I have eaten here before and again there is no place finer for a good meal."

"How about eight o clock, that way we can look at the horses and take care of the other business, and maybe have time for a ride and a picnic, and while riding you can check out the horse for yourself." "Chastain, I know I am being bold asking you to have a picnic with me, but I have a feeling we are about to embark on a relationship that both of us are going to enjoy."

"And now kind sir, If you would be so kind as to escort me home, I will get my beauty sleep and be refreshed for tomorrow, as we have a busy day in front of us." At Sara's home they said goodnight, and went their separate way to await the dawn and another new beginning.

CHAPTER SEVEN

Saturday morning, Cuss picks up Sara for breakfast, after which they walk down to the stable to see Sara's horse. Upon arriving at the stall where the horse is kept, Cuss for the second time in two days is speechless; finally he manages to blurt out, "What a magnificent animal." The horse is solid black with a blaze on its face, about sixteen hands high, deep chested, and heavily muscled, obviously built for stamina, and speed.

Cuss exclaims, "I'm flabbergasted." "I never expected such a beautiful animal, if I can afford him, I must buy him for Theo." "Chastain, I know you can afford the price I want for this horse, now come look at the saddles I told you about." So they go into the tack room, where the stable owner is working on some harness repairs. "Charlie, I believe you know Cuss." "Why yes, we have met." "Charlie could you show Cuss a saddle that would fit my gelding, one of your good practical, ride all day specials." Charlie takes Cuss over to several new saddles and tells him to look at that one there.

"It is built for the gelding or another horse of his size." "It has a double cinch, metal rings to use to tie down a

The sun is waning and it is time to head back to town. Cuss asks Sara if she would like to have dinner with him again. "I really shouldn't, how would the town folks take to our being together so much after just meeting yesterday? "They would be jealous, and full of gossip, and spread awful rumors about you being the towns shameless hussy and all.

"In that case, Chastain, I except your dinner invite." "But you must let me freshen up and change clothes if we are going to become the talk of Dahlonega." So off they go back to town.

After a leisurely dinner, Cuss asks Sara if she would like to go to Theo's birthday party the next day? "I would love to, but would it be proper, after all I hardly know the people." "It not only would be proper, I know that with your love of books coupled with Beatrice's love of books, the two of you will be the best of friends by the end of the day."

Sara asks, "What time are you expected to be there?" "Around noon, so we can eat all afternoon, and josh with Theo. "It's about two miles from town, so if we leave here around eleven thirty we can arrive just in time to eat." "We can have breakfast at nine at our usual table, and that will leave us plenty of time to saddle up and ride out to the farm.

Sara looks at Cuss and says, "Another breakfast in the company of old mean and ornery, you are really going to cause a riot of gossip in this town." "How am I going to ever live down the reputation that you are causing me to get, why the next thing I know the Sheriff is going to have to bring you to the alter with a shotgun to make an honest woman out of me." With that Sara laughs , and laughs.

Cuss looks at Sara and very seriously tells her, "That a shotgun would not be needed to make me walk down the aisle with you." Sara exclaims, "Oh my!, What have we started?"

Next morning after breakfast, Cuss and Sara ride out to the Calhoun farm. Theo is excited to see Sara with Cuss, he had told his folks about the strange behavior of the two when they had just met. Amos and Beatrice looked at each other and remark, "remember our first meeting? it sounds awfully familiar".

After introductions, Cuss says to Theo, "youngster since you have come to work for me I have had the best of luck with the gold recovery, you work hard and never complain, and you have become like a son to me with your companionship." "So I have brought you a present that you will enjoy, also a present that will protect you in time of danger", and with that Cuss gives Theo the Colt Dragoon revolver, "and son I want you to take extra good care of this horse that you now have."

Theo is speechless. Finally he says, "Cuss I can't accept such a great gift." "Oh yes you can, if you don't take the horse and gun I'll cry and tell everybody in the county how mean you are to me." With that Theo goes over and gives Cuss a big bear hug, and says "thank you, but I'm going to get even with you for this."

"Time for food" says Cuss, so out comes the fried chicken and glazed ham. Mashed potatoes and chicken gravy, sweet potatoes and red eye gravy made from the ham juices, corn on the cob boiled in sweet sugar water, and a fine chocolate cake. Cuss pipes up after seeing the cake and says "life is short, let's start with the cake first." this gets , everybody laughing.

And so the party is a great success, Beatrice and Sara hit it right off, promising to exchange books. Theo can't wait to ride the beautiful Morgan, and go out and practice with the new Colt Dragoon revolver. Then it's time to say goodbye for the day, Sara and Cuss go back to town. "Cuss asks Sara, do you think we can sneak in an early breakfast before Theo gets here to go up to the mine?"

"What again, that would make the third breakfast in a row, what are the tongue waggers going to say?" "Why they could all have fainting spells, from talking about our outrageous behavior." "What time did you say we would meet at the restaurant, dear Chastain?" "Oh, ah, around eight I guess." And so it goes, the courting of Sara has begun for Chastain "Cuss" Castle.

CHAPTER EIGHT

Promptly at Eight, Sara and Cuss meet for their third breakfast together. The waiter is surprised to see them together again so soon. They order steak and eggs with fried potatoes and toast, and a pot of coffee to wash it down with.

While waiting for their breakfast to be served, Cuss asks Sara, "If you don't mind, why don't you tell me more about yourself?" "There's not that much to tell you Chastain." "I am the daughter of a merchant in Savannah, who arranged my marriage with my husband Tom." "Tom's parents owned a couple of merchant ships and the two fathers thought that a merger of the two businesses would be beneficial to the two families." "As it turned out it was a financial success."

"As for the marriage, it was civil." "Tom started out by paying lots of attention to me, until we found out I couldn't have children." "Then his ardor towards me cooled, and he started spending more time with the business then with me." "This of course left me with lots of time on my hands, so I spent my time reading everything I could get ahold of, and riding my horse."

"We lived in a modest two story house, with a stable where we kept the two Morgan's, and a buggy." "Tom entertained business client's quite often, and I was required to entertain their wives, most of them were too prim and proper for my tastes, and quite the boor's."

"Anyway life went on until Tom drowned." "He had always treated me very well, and life was comfortable." "When he died I found out he had provided for my future quite well, so that I would not have to be beholden to anybody for my income." "I had been made a silent partner in the business, and upon his death was given a monthly stipend on which to live." "A very generous one I might add."

"Anyway, being more of a country girl, then the social butterfly my so called peer's thought they and I should be, I decided to move here to Dahlonega, and take over my aunt's store and live a more simple life." "So here I am, and so far it has been more then I had hoped for."

"Since I have been here, I have met more down to earth people, then I think Savannah has in that city." Cuss interrupts, and tells her, "You probably didn't travel in the right circles to see the honest working people of the city, the so called salt of the earth." "You're right, I was told they were beneath my station and I should ignore them." "What a loss." replied Cuss. "I know now what you're saying is true," says Sara.

"Chastain being a miner, I should tell you of my mining experience." "Shortly after I got here I was introduced to a man called Cousin Jack, and he invited me out to his diggings, as he called it, too give me a first hand look at the mining process."

"Upon arriving there, this Cousin Jack handed me a clean set of work clothes and a pair of gum boots that were way too big for me, and told me to go in his cabin to change, and then we would get down to the actual diggings and I could experience first hand, what mining was all about."

"This Cousin jack?, was he about 5ft 7inches tall and had very large muscles in his arms and shoulders, and a twitch in his left eye when he talked to you?" "Why yes, do you know him?" "Yes, his name is Jocko Alwin and he is the man who taught me more about mining than all of the other miner's I know."

"Go on with your story Sara." "Well I went into his cabin and changed into the work clothes, and put on the oversize gum boots and went outside feeling like the perfect fool in the boots and clothes that were too big, but Cousin Jack did not even crack a smile in jest as I expected him to do." "We went down to the place where two miners were picking and shoveling away at a gravel bank." "And Cousin Jack told me how the gold was in the bottom layer of the gravel and how they would pick the gravel apart and move it down to a bin, and then wash it in these long boxes to separate the gold out." "We walked down to a big tub and got two gold pans, and some small digging tools that looked like garden trowels and went back to where the two men were picking away at the gravel." "Cousin Jack had the men clear off a space of what he called bedrock, and then had me grab a thick pad to kneel on, and put it down on the bedrock and told me to scrape the gravel up from the rock and put it in the gold pan." "When we had about three quarters of the pan full, we went back to the big tub and he showed me how to run a pan as he called it." "So shaking the pan very vigorously, and then stopping to tip the pan in the water he sloughed off some of the dirt, repeating the process over and over until we could see a fine line of gold in the pan."

"Then I tried it, it took me awhile to get the idea of what I was supposed to be doing, but Cousin Jack was very patient with me and finally I got the pan run down." "There were a few specks of gold in the pan, and I told Jack that it seemed like a lot of work for those few pennies worth of gold." Jack told me, "yes it is, that's why we shovel the gravel into those Longtoms, that way we can wash a hundred times more gravel in the same time and get more gold that way."

"So he told me to get more pans of gravel and see how much gold I can get in a day."

"Let me tell you, I was covered from head to toe in dirt and mud, my back and arms ached, I almost had blisters on my hands from all the digging, and finally I was down to my last pan when low and behold I had a small nugget in the bottom of the pan, one I could actually pick up with my thumb and forefinger." "I was so happy that I started jumping up and down. I almost dropped the nugget out of the pan."

"Anyway that was my gold mining experience." "Jack or Jocko as you called him, let me use his cabin again to wash up and put my own clothes back on." "When I got back outside, he had put my gold in a glass vial with clean water and a cork to keep the water and gold from falling out." "And' said little lady you made about two and a half dollars today, how would you like to come to work for me?" "I could use a good worker like you." "I looked at my sore hands and felt my sore back and shoulders and said to Jack, "I don't think so, my poor body is built more for sewing then dirt digging." "So thank you kind sir for the job offer, but I have to decline." And with that we had a good chuckle.

CHAPTER NINE

"Then Jack took me home, exclaiming what a good miner I was, and how lucky some man would be to hook up with a woman like me" "Chastain, do you think he was hinting that he and I should become a couple?" Cuss looks at Sara and asks "now what would make you think that?" and laughs.

"Chastain, why don't you tell me some more about yourself'. "Ok, I will, but **I** see Theo arriving, so it will have to wait till later, say dinner Friday evening, after you close shop" Sara looks at Cuss and tells him, "yes that would be wonderful, but will we be able to wait that long before seeing each other again?" At that they look at each other and wonder.

They leave the restaurant to meet Theo, who is riding the Morgan gelding and looking as proud as a peacock. In a sack he has his new Colt Dragoon revolver. Hailing Sara and Cuss, he tells them he has to stop at the gunsmith and get instructions on how to load the gun, as he has not had any experience with revolvers before. Cuss tells Theo, "I'll join you as soon as I walk Sara to her store, as I can use some pointers too".

Sara and Cuss say goodbye in front of her store, and Cuss heads down to the Gunsmith's. When he gets there, he finds the gunsmith showing Theo how to load the weapon. Cuss asks if he can have a lesson too, as he is not all that familiar with the new weapon himself.

But of course says the gunsmith, and proceeds to show the two men how to load and care for the guns. He than asks how the fellows were going to carry their weapons. Cuss remarks, "I hadn't thought of that, how do you carry them so they are at hand when you need them". The gunsmith shows them several holsters and belts, and the different ways to carry the guns, "this is a shoulder holster that is popular with drummers and business men who wear frock coats most of the time". "This is the common holster that most working men wear, it is worn on the hip like so, and is easy reach". "Then there is the so called cross draw holster". "It is worn on the opposite hip with the butt of the gun facing forward, and you reach over your belly and grab the gun and pull it out to use"

"Now Cuss since you and Theo are miners digging in the dirt all day, I would suggest the military style of holster that has a flap over the butt of the gun that keeps dirt out of the weapon" "The gun is still within easy reach, but kept clean by the holster completely covering the gun, also I would suggest an extra pouch for the extra cylinder that goes on the belt, and probably the most important thing to remember is to only load five chambers when carrying the gun on your hip, and keep the hammer down on the empty chamber, that way the gun, cannot go off if you should accidently bump or drop the gun and possibly shoot yourself in the leg or elsewhere".

"Good advice gunsmith, we'll take two of the right hip holsters with flaps and the pouches for the extra cylinders and belts". Cuss again pays for the goods with gold dust, and then they leave the gun shop.

Next stop the general store, for some food and other supplies to tide them over the week ahead. Then on to the mine and work. Pick, shovel, wash, pan, eat , bath, hot tub, sleep, and then start all over again, only this week is different in that Cuss does not seem to have his mind on the work as usual. When Theo asks him what he was thinking about? Cuss would say "Oh! nothing, just daydreaming". And so it goes until Friday when Cuss tells Theo, "we have to knock off early as I have an appointment for this evening". Theo exclaims, "Oh! So that's where your mind has been all week". "Now son, you just mind your manners and beeswax or I'll have to cuss all over you", then he laughs and says, I guess I've been caught". "now don't go blabbing all over the place about me and Sara". "Yes sir! Cuss, yes sir".

So it's clean up and off to town, Theo taking the bypass route to home, telling Cuss he will see him Monday morning. Cuss off to his dinner date with Sara, and another weekend of talking , eating at the restaurant, taking sight seeing ride in the country side and getting to know each other better. Monday comes all too soon for Cuss and Sara. Theo comes riding in and tells Cuss come on, we have lots of work to do. Cuss turns and waves to Sara, and rides wistfully out to the mine.

And so it goes. Work all week, weekends in town for Cuss getting to know Sara, Theo doing chores at home on the farm. Theo is accumulating a nice nest egg of gold even though he gives half to his mother to help the family. Six months go by and Cuss and Sara announce that they are going to get married, the wedding to be in six months, and Amos and Theo both stand up for Cuss, and Beatrice and Amelia for Sara. It's agreed, and the couple wants to keep the wedding small. So just a few friends are invited, course you can't keep the engagement a secret, especially when the whole town has been gossiping about the courting going on between Sara and Cuss.

The wedding is held in one of the small churches in town with just the couple and their close friends. Upon leaving the church Cuss and Sara find the whole town has gathered very quietly outside and when they step outside there is a shout of congratulations that is deafening, and the bride and groom are whisked off to a reception and dance the likes of which Dahlonega has not seen in a long time.

After the reception is over Sara and Cuss retire to Sara's house in the back of the store and spend their first night together in the same bed. The next morning at breakfast in the hotel, there are people coming up and congratulating them again and wishing them good luck.

Cuss has planned to take Sara away for a couple of weeks so they could be alone. Meanwhile Theo was to help his father with the harvest, as it was that time.

When Cuss and Sara got back, the harvest was done and Cuss and Theo went back to work at the mine again resuming their routine with one exception. Sara would come out to the mine every weekend to be with Cuss and her new love, the hot tub. After Cuss introduced Sara to the joys of the hot tub soak, she couldn't get enough of it. So every weekend they would stay at the mine and relax.

CHAPTER TEN

So the mining progresses, and the marriage settles down to a nice routine, Cuss, knowing that the mine is going to play out in a couple of years, asks Sara what she would like to do with some of the money they are accumulating, and she asked, "have you ever thought about raising horses, maybe Morgan's, this is good country for a horse farm, and there is good money in good animals". "That's not a bad idea, maybe we ought to look into it Sara, since you know more about horses, and especially Morgan's, then I do, why don't you make a project out of learning just what it would require to set up a farm". "How much land would we need? How many horses to make it profitable, and so on, and if it looks like something we can handle, we can start the ball rolling, as they say". So Sara has a new interest and project to keep her busy when Cuss is off at the mine.

The mine is paying very well, for now, But Cuss can see the end in a couple of years, as they are about half way through the gravel deposit. So they keep working away, Theo saving half of his wages, Cuss salting away the gold that is recovered, over the expenses of the operation.

One night after Theo and Cuss had retired, Theo was awakened by a strange noise, carefully looking around, he sees Cuss kneeling by the hot tub furnace fighting to get a stone loose at the base of the furnace, between the scratching of the tool Cuss is using and his swearing at the stone it woke Theo up. Theo doesn't say or do anything but watch, and he sees Cuss stashing the gold they recovered that week, in behind the cantankerous stone. "Ah ha!" Thinks Theo so that's where Cuss hides the gold". "Good spot, now just go back to sleep and forget about it".

Time passes, and the mine recovery is slowing down, not only is the gravel running out, but so is the gold, plus they are pushing the wheel borrows almost a quarter mile one way to fill the bin.

So one evening after weighing the gold, Cuss looks at Theo and asks, "What do you think son? "Are we about done with this piece of ground?" Theo says "it appears so, the gold has really fallen off, plus we are working much harder for what we are getting". "I would say it's time to button the operation up". "Cuss, I sure hate to quit as we've had some great times here, not to mention what I've learned about mining and the great friendship we have made between us". "Yeah! it's going to be real hard to walk away from this spot, after putting in almost five years working here, but that's progress, and besides Sara has found a farm we can buy and set up the horse farm she has her heart set on". "Theo how would you like to learn how to be a horse trainer and stay working together, only at a different job?" " I will have to think about it, as you know I've always had the dream to go to California to see if I can strike it rich out there, and now with what you have taught me I have a better chance then most people of finding a good piece of ground like you did to work"

"Theo, you're young and full of life's dreams, so far be it by me to try to talk you out of your dream, and as you say with what you have learned here the last few years, you have a hella've better head start then most people". "So let's close up this operation and let your folks know what it is you would like to do, and see what they say". "Now that you're 21, and full growed, you should be able to set your own course in life".

So the two of them start shutting down the mine, they clean up the fines from the sluice boxes, gather up the tools that can be used on the farm or the new horse farm, and start packing the equipment out. Meanwhile, Arnold is back in the neighborhood and is not only up to no good , he has two friends that are with him to help him with his plan.

After Arnold was run out of Dahlonega he eventually ended up in Athens where he met up with the Blackburn half brothers, two of the worst cuthroats to inhabit the confines of Georgia.

Arnold had told them how Cuss, Amos and Theo had humiliated him and had him run out of Dahlonega, and how Cuss had this well paying gold mine, that Arnold was caught trying to locate by following them. When the Blackburn brothers heard about the gold they were only too glad to hook up with Arnold in the attempt to get even with the three men and steal Cuss's gold.

So while Cuss and Theo were shutting down the mine, Arnold, Rufus, and Buford were camped outside Dahlonega not far from Theo's family's farm. Rufus was a big man with a black shaggy mane and beard, scared knuckles from too much fighting and very little teeth in the front of his mouth. His half brother Buford was a head shorter with eyes that seem to dart everywhere as if trying to see everything at once. Both were known for their cruelty, especially to the women they visited in the various red light districts.

Now Arnold had talked Rufus and Buford into robbing
Theo's family after the harvest had been sold, and if they
wanted to, have their way with the two Calhoun women.
Rufus and Buford got this evil gleam in their eyes at the
mention of the women, and Arnold was playing up to their
obvious cruel streak.

Rufus and Buford spent a week watching the Calhoun
farm, to see the comings and goings of the family, they soon
learned that Theo went to work at the mine early Monday
morning, and that Amelia, like to go to the pond in the
small woods behind the cabin and go swimming, in the heat
of the day. Seeing this beautiful young female swimming
in the nude was getting to Rufus. He told his smaller half
brother that she was his, and that he could have the mother.
They saw that they would have to probably kill Amos to
get to the women and the money. So they planned to have
Rufus attack Amelia at the pond and when she screamed
Amos would come running out the door, where Buford
would be waiting with a shotgun and shoot the farmer. Then
Buford would take the mother and ransack the house, while
Rufus was busy with the girl.

They told Arnold of their plan and he agreed it was a
good one. Arnold said that the next day being Friday, that
Theo would be home just before dark for the weekend, so if
they were to get the deed done in the afternoon they could
ambush Theo when he rode into the farm yard. Rufus and
Buford said, yeah, "that way we can get all of them in one
day, and when we are done with them we can get Cuss and
his ole lady and find their gold and split". So with that,
they break open a bottle of rot gut whiskey and get drunk,
waiting for tomorrow.

The next day being Friday the two half brothers take
up their post at the farm waiting for the girl to take her
afternoon swim, and Amos and Beatrice to take a break

in the coolness of the cabin, Arnold, meantime is skulking around town to see if Cuss is coming in this evening for the weekend. Knowing what the Blackburn's have planned for Theo and his family, Arnold does not want to be there. He wants to see Cuss suffer as he was the one who caused Arnold so much humiliation.

Meanwhile Cuss and Theo are packing in their first load of tools from the mine, they plan to take them directly to the farm and store them in an extra shed that Amos had built. They figured they could go back out to the mine the next day and with Amos's and Sara's help bring in a substantial load on Saturday.

Rufus and Buford are at the farm, waiting for Amelia to go for her swim. Rufus is hiding in the bushes next to where Amelia normally disrobes and Buford is near the barn where he can watch the girl go, and then he can sneak up to the house and wait for Amos. Presently Amelia walks out of the house carrying her towel and heads for the pond, when she arrives there, Rufus attacks her letting her scream, Buford is waiting beside the door for Amos, Amelia's scream brings Amos running right into Buford who pulls the trigger and almost blows Amos's head off, Beatrice comes running and at the door she runs into Buford, who shoves her back into the house and into one of the bedrooms, ripping off her dress, he throws her on the bed and proceeds to take her. Beatrice knowing she was going to probably die decided to fight for her life, she scratched the left side of Buford's face with her nails leaving four bloody scratches, and at the same time she tried to knee him in the groin, at the pain from the scratches Buford went berserk and dodging the knee to the groin he pulled out his knife and stabbed Beatrice in the throat, and while she was bleeding to death he finished raping her.

Meantime Rufus has Amelia down on the ground and is tearing her dress off, Amelia is fighting with all her might, kicking and screaming, she manages to poke Rufus's left eye out. Rufus screams and taking his right fist he hits Amelia so hard in the side of her face he snaps her neck and kills her, still screaming he takes the girl and rapes her dead body over and over until he is completely exhausted. When he finally calms down and gets his wind he rips Amelia's dress into a pad to cover his eye, tying the pad with another piece of the dress. He then gets up and staggers to the farm house to see what Buford is doing. Upon arriving at the house he finds that Buford is just finishing ransacking the house, he has a necklace that belonged to Amelia that Theo gave her for her eighteenth birthday, a locket that belonged to Beatrice, a box of money from the harvest sale and a pouch of gold dust that belonged to Theo.

Looking up from the loot, and seeing the patch over Rufus's eye, Buford asks, "what happened to you?" "That she-cat took my eye out". "Yeah, I almost lost mine to her mother"

They looked at each other and groaned. "I hope there is enough loot to make this pain worth while". Buford gives the pouch of gold to Rufus and says "feel the weight of the gold in there, there must be over three hundred dollars there". Rufus feels the weight of the pouch and agrees, Then he says "we better get out of here, I need to see a doctor". "Me to".

They leave heading straight for town, and right at the outskirts they run into Cuss and Theo. Cuss seeing how rough these two are, tells Theo "have your pistol ready in case there is trouble". Stopping in front of the rough pair Cuss asks "what happened to you two?" "Those are some pretty bad cuts on your face". "We ran into a she lion and before we could kill her she marked us pretty good", "Where is the animal asks Cuss?" "The hide is worth some money". Rufus says, "Oh we left it behind, as hurting as we are we want to find the Doc and get patched up, besides the horses were too skittish to load the cat on one of them". "That makes sense; Well we won't hold you up any longer". So they each proceed to their destinations.

CHAPTER ELEVEN

So Theo and Cuss head for the farm, while the Blackburn brothers head for town and the doctor. Arnold watches as the brothers rein up in front of the doctor's office and go in. He sees the patch over Rufus's left eye and wonders what happened? Soon enough he should find out, have patience he tells himself, Meantime Cuss and Theo get to the farm and seeing Amos on the ground in front of the house, Theo hits the ground running up to his pa. "Cuss! he screams someone killed my pa" Cuss looks at Amos and then into the house, and sees Beatrice sprawled on the bed in one of the bedrooms, with blood all over the bed.

"Theo don't look in the house, your ma is dead too, and as she is naked, it looks like someone raped her". Theo screams "Amelia! Where's Amelia?" "I don't know I don't see her in the house" says Cuss. Theo gets up and runs toward the barn, and that's when he notices the buzzards hovering over the small woods where the pond is. "Cuss! Cuss! She must have went for a swim, and they got her there by the pond".

They run down to the pond and find Amelia, lying on the ground naked and bloody, with a couple of buzzards starting to tear into her flesh. Theo yelling at the top of his lungs chases the foul birds away from Amelia. Cuss tells Theo to go up to the house and get a blanket so we can put her in it and carry her up to the house. Theo runs to the house and trying not to look at his naked dead mother finds a blanket and runs back down to the pond,

"Look here Theo, your sister fought the bastard pretty good, and she's got his eye in her right hand". That's when they both realize that the pair of rough characters they met outside of town are the murderers They roll Amelia's body into the blanket and carry her to the house, lying her on one of the beds, still clutching the eye. Cuss then tells Theo to take a fast look around and see what is missing, then let's get back to town and tell the Sheriff what happened here and get him after that pair of animals.

Theo finds that the money box is gone, his leather pouch too, and he cannot find the gold chain that he gave Amelia, and his mother's locket and chain.

Cuss and Theo mount their horses and running them as fast as they dare, get back to town. Stopping in front of the Sheriffs office they bolt through the door to find the deputy there. "Where's the Sheriff? There's been a killing out at Theo's farm". The deputy tells them, the Sheriff is having coffee and pie over at the cafe with Doc. So the three of them run over to the cafe and burst through the door. "Sheriff there's been a killing out to the Calhoun place, and we know who did it", The Sheriff looks at Cuss and Theo and asks "who are they?' Theo describes the big guy who had a bandage over his eye. Doc tells them, "I just came from patching them up, I thought that something was funny when they said they were attacked by a Cougar", "Cougar's usually go for a horse, not the riders". "Anyway they said they were going to the saloon to get a couple of whiskeys to kill the pain and then leave town". "They are still there, as

I haven't seen them ride out".

The five of them head for the saloon. The Sheriff has his deputy go and cover the back, while he and the others go in the front doors. The Blackburn's are standing at the bar in the middle of putting away a whiskey, when the Sheriff tells them to put their hands in the air and don't move. Seeing as there are four guns pointing at them, they slowly put their hands up. Doc and Theo get their guns and knives and then Theo puts his Dragoon in the big guys face and yells, "you killed my sister, and I'm going to blow your head off". Cuss grabs Theo's gun and tells Theo to let the sheriff handle these animals, as soon as we prove they did the killing they will hang.

The Sheriff takes the two to the Jail, and searches them, then puts them in a cell. Meantime the deputy brings their horses to the Jail, and going through their saddle bags, they find Theo's pouch of gold, the locket and chain of his mothers, and the gold chain of Amelias. plus a large sum of cash.

Cuss tells the Sheriff that if he goes with them to the farm, they will find Rufus's eye in Amelias dead hand. The Sheriff exclaims, that clinches the fact that these two did it.

Deputy go tell the Undertaker to bring his wagon out to the Calhoun place, we need to bring the victims bodys in for a decent burial.

Cuss tells Theo, "I think it would be best if you go stay with Sara until the Sheriff, I and the undertaker get back". "You are about to collaspe son, so go do as I say". Sara standing outside the Jail door hears Cuss and takes Theo's arm and tells him, "come on Theo, You need to sit down, the shock of today is about to make you fall down, come on son it's just a little ways to the store".

Meanwhile Arnold is taking in all the goings on, and while nobody is paying attention to him, he sneaks around to the back of the Jail and gets Rufus's attention, and tells him not to worry that he would find a way to get them out. Arnold then goes hides in the loft of the livery until long after dark.

The Sheriff, Cuss and the undertaker are taking care of the bodys. The Sheriff almost looses his pie, when he sees the eye clutched in Amelia's hand, he turns to Cuss and says, "what a brave, tough thing to do". "Amelia pointed out her killer even after she died".

Back in town, shock is setting in on Theo, so Sara has the Doc come over and give him a dose of laudanum to put him to sleep, so he can get over the shock of losing his family in such a cruel way. It's going to be a long time before he gets over the nightmares.

It's after midnight when Arnold climbs down from the loft, the town is quiet, except for the saloon. And it is not as boisterous as usual because of the murders. Arnold walks into the saloon and orders a beer, and since he hadn't eaten all day he makes himself a sandwich from the free lunch. Wolfing down the sandwich and the beer, he then orders two whiskeys, after drinking them, he leaves the saloon and heads for the Jail. Knowing that the old man who watches the Jail is the same one who used to let Arnold sleep off his occasional drunk, he has a plan. He staggers up to the Jail pretending to be drunk and bangs on the door, waking the old man who is snoozing, "who is it he asks?" "It's Arnold, I'm drunk and need a place to lay my head down till I sober up". "Arnold, what are you doing back in town, I thought they run you out". "Yeah they did, I'm just passing through and I drank to much, come on let me in so I can sleep this off". The old man opens the door and lets Arnold in, as he turns his back on Arnold to lock up again, Arnold cold cocks the old man in the back of the head, knocking him out, he hits him a second time to make sure he doesn't come too before he lets the Blackburns out. Taking the keys from the old man, Arnold unlocks the cell door and lets the boys out, Rufus angrily starts to shout, "it's about time". "Arnold tells him to be quiet, does he want to wake up the town, and get caught again?" Rufus shuts up. "Come on find your guns and lets get out of here, they get their guns and a couple of shotguns and shells that belong to the Sheriff, and leave.

Sticking to the shadows they walk down the side of the building and into the alley. "Come on said Arnold, the livery is just down the street, and the horses are saddled and ready to go".

They get to the livery and get their horses and quietly walk them to the end of town down the same alley, then mounting the horses they still walk them until they are out of earshot of town. Then putting the spurs to the mounts they lope down the road to the southwest towards Alanta, where they figure they can get lost in the large town, and also get a grubstake by waylaying drunks and stealing their money. Now that they are wanted for murder, the idea is to get out of the country. So Atlanta, and pick up enough money to get to Savannah and a ship out of Georgia.

Back in Dahlonega, dawn breaks and the Sheriff arrives at his office and finds the door unlocked, strange? When he gets inside he finds the old man on the floor, dead from the two blows on the head. Seeing that the prisoners are gone he gets up a posse to go and find them.

He has to break them up into four groups, as there are four ways out of town, and not knowing which way the Blackburn's went, he has to cover all four routes.

Arnold and the Blackburn's knowing that they will be chased are trying to play it smart by hiding out in a woods and traveling only by night. With Atlanta about a hundred miles away they can be there in three days without having to push their horses too hard. Meanwhile the posse not finding hide nor hair of them have given up, and gone back to Dahlonega.

The Sheriff tells Cuss about their bad luck in not finding the culprits, so he is going to get word to all the law in the state he can. First he is going to send a rider to Atlanta and put the descriptions of the murderers out on the new telegraph, which will cover all the big towns and Citys in the state in a matter of hours once we get to a telegraph. From there we can pass the word faster to the smaller towns by riders. I'm bound and determined to bring these animals to the gallows.

As luck would have it, the rider to Atlanta runs into an ambush that Arnold and the Blackburns had set up to rob someone. After killing the rider and searching him for loot they discover the wanted posters that the Sheriff had made up for the telegraph people. So the telegrams never got sent, giving the owlhoots a better chance of getting away. Their plan eventually works, and they end up on a ship to California.

Meantime Theo is having a hard time coping with his loss. He has taken to drink to blot out the murders. Cuss and Sara are very worried about Theo and try to do everything they can to stop him from destroying himself in a bottle of booze. Finally they get the Sheriff to lock him up till he sobers up enough to talk some sense into the boy. Cuss tells Theo it's time to get over the tragedy and get on with life. Now he had a dream to go to California to find a gold mine and get rich, now is the time to do it. "Tell me you are ready to go and I will help you".

Theo is still angry about being tossed into Jail, but he realizes it has been for his own good, so being sober for the first time in weeks, he agrees with Cuss and says he will try to get it together. He asks Cuss to give him a couple of more days to dry out and then he will be ready for the new adventure

So after a couple of days, Cuss takes Theo home and fills him full of Chamomile tea to calm him down and Sara feeds him good meals. In between, Cuss has Theo chopping firewood to build his strength back up. While Theo is working, Cuss is building a pack frame for his mule, which he is going to give to Theo for his trip. That way Theo can pack enough supplies for about two weeks at a time, between towns and villages. And if he supplements his food by getting game he can go longer between towns.

So the day comes for Theo to leave on his new adventure, he is still bothered by the loss of his family, but be realizes he must go on. Cuss has gathered up the necessary supplies, and packed them on the mule with Theo's help. Theo has gotten a good supply of powder and shot for both his Dragoon and the Rifle, He is finally ready to go. Cuss hands him a leather pouch full of gold coins, and tells him that, that is the bonus he earned while working at the mine. Theo is beside himself, "what bonus?" "You never said anything about a bonus".

"I know, it was to be a surprise, and so here it is, take care of it, there's a thousand dollars in there". "A Thousand dollars!" "I can't accept this exclaims Theo". It Son you earned it and you're going to take it or I'm going to get mean an ornery and show you how to pummel a man with my fists". And laughing, Sara gruffly says, "and that goes for me too", as she makes a couple of fists and strikes a fighters pose. "Ok! I know when I'm beaten, don't hit me, don't hit me"

So its farewell and Theo rides off leading the pack mule to see the Elephant.

CHAPTER TWELVE

Theo stops at the Sheriffs office on the way out of town to see if he had heard anything about the Blackburn brothers. The Sheriff tells Theo that he hasn't heard anything, and worst of all the rider he had sent to Atlanta had not come back, he should have been back days ago. Theo asks if something could have happened to him on the way there or coming back?. "That is what I'm wondering". "Theo could you stop and see the Sheriff in Atlanta on your way through, and give him the information I sent with the rider". "Of course Sheriff, be only to happy too". So the Sheriff gives Theo a packet of wanted posters and a letter to the Sheriff in Atlanta.

Theo makes Atlanta in three days, and finds the Sheriffs office, talking to the Sheriff he finds out the rider from Dahlonega never made it to Atlanta. He has disappeared. So Theo gives the letter and packet to the Sheriff and explains the heinous crime the two pulled on his family.

The Sheriff is really upset, and promises to get the descriptions of the culprits on the wire and the posters passed out to the surrounding towns. If they are in Georgia we'll catch them.

"And son I'm so sorry to hear of your family". Theo says thanks, and goes on his way.

Stopping at a general store he replenishes his supplies and heads out of town to find the Natchez trace which will take him west to the Mississippi river where he can catch a riverboat to St Louis, and then a wagon train to California. At least that's his plan.

Two weeks later Theo finds himself in a forest in Alabama, and being it is towards the end of this particular day he starts looking for a place to camp, rounding a bend in the trail, he sees a funny looking wagon, with another flat bed wagon attached to the rear. The first wagon has what looks like a small cabin built on it, with a door in back, and windows on the sides. The flat bed has what looks like a blacksmith shop on one side and a load of iron of various shapes on the other side. As Theo gets closer he sees lettering on the side of the first wagon, proclaiming that the owner is Brutus the traveling Blacksmith. At a campfire sits the biggest man Theo has ever seen, he thinks to himself that the man must weigh three hundred pounds and be as tall as an oak tree.

As is the custom, Theo calls hello the camp, is it alright to come in? The man at the fire turns and in a booming voice asks, "is that you Theo?" "Yes please be my guest and come on in".

Theo is shocked, how did this person, a perfect stranger know my name? And as if reading his mind the blacksmith tells Theo he will explain everything over supper, "meantime take care of your animals, while I fix a special repast for us", Bewildered Theo removes the saddle from the Morgan, and the pack from the mule and puts them down where the Blacksmith points. He then lets the animals roll and rubs them down with a gunny sack, then hobbles them near the creek so they can drink and graze on the grass.

"Come Theo". "I know you have many questions, the first of which is how I knew your name", "I can only tell you that the voices told me your name and that you would arrive today, I have been camped here two days now to make sure I didn't miss you".

"But! but! nobody knew I would be here today, and why would you be waiting for me, is this some kind of joke or worst yet a trap to rob me, at which his hand went to his pistol"..

Brutus tells him, "the voices told me of your coming, and of your recent tragedy and sent me to be your friend and new mentor". Theo asks, "What voices are you talking about and why do I need a new mentor?"

"Theo, you are going to have bad nightmares about your family, and I will be by your side to help you over them, also with your dream and final destination of California, you're going to need a trade to see you over the slim times before you find your mine".

"How do you know all this asks?" Theo more confused then ever. "I know because the voices on high have told me and entrusted me with your fate for the next few months". Theo is speechless, he has never heard anyone talk like this before, or know so much about him, he is dumbfounded. "it will all become clear in good time my son, now let us eat, here is a plate and fork, hold on to them while I dish up the special meal I made that comes from the old country".

Theo asks what old country is that? And Brutus tells him, "Sweden, Theo! Sweden". Theo looks at Brutus and says, "you must be Swedish then, my mother read me a book about the north countries and the Viking sailors and fierce warriors, and how they invaded the north of England".

Brutus exclaims, "ya! that was my ancestors, a pretty mean bunch of guys he says laughing, but seriously, my ancestors were Seers or as the Indians here call them Shaman, they could see into the future on occasion and predict the outcome of battles, or bad storms at sea, or whether the King would have a son or daughter by his new wife, and so on", "I have the gift Theo, that is how I know so much about you". "Here, hold your plate still, and gives Theo a big spoonful of noodles, then a spoonful of meatballs in a light colored gravy, and pointing at the dish, tells Theo, they are Swedish meatballs and noodles, very good".

Theo looks at the dish and wonders what this new dish is going to taste like, having spent many years with Cuss, he is not afraid to try anything, as Cuss was always coming up with a new dish to eat. Theo takes a forkful and is chewing on a meatball, which is delicious, and just then Brutus say's, "I bet Cuss never made this dish for you". This surprises Theo so much that he almost chokes on the food. "The answer to your question is, the voices told me of your friend and his cooking". "The voices again," says Theo, "You're driving me to distraction with your voices", "Yes I know, it's to make you so curious, that you will stay with me until we get to Vicksburg, where you will proceed with the rest of your journey".

"How did you know I was going to Vicksburg?" And waving his hand at Brutus to stop him from answering," he said' I know the voices told you". "You are learning fast Theo my friend, we are going to have a great time getting to know each other in the next six months",

"Six months Theo exclaims why it shouldn't take more then a month and a half to reach Vicksburg". "I know, but you are going to be my new apprentice, and we will be doing all manner of blacksmithing work before we get to Vicksburg". "But why should I be your *new* apprentice?" "Because the voices told me you will need a trade with which to make a living as I said before".

Theo gives up and finishes his meal, and asks for seconds, which Brutus is only too glad to give him.

And so starts the apprenticeship. Brutus, whose real name is Lars Holman, starts Theo out by explaining how Iron is made and worked in the forge to make any object that will help man with his work and travel. There are shoes for the horses, mules, and oxen. Iron rims for wagon wheels. Iron fittings for the harnesses to pull the wagons with, Iron strapping to hold the wagon boxes together. Iron collars to hold the wagon hubs together so they won't break from the load• they have to carry over rough ground. Iron picks and shovels, Iron pots and pans to cook with, lanterns made from iron, by which we can see with after darkness falls.

"Son there is Iron everywhere you look." "While gold is pretty and you can make a lot of money with a small amount of gold, it's Iron that holds the world together.

During the next six months, they travel to every farm and small village that are along their route to Vicksburg, and get work making or repairing all sorts of objects and hardware to help their customers. Theo has learned much and finds he likes working with the hot metal, the satisfaction of seeing an object come together from his own hands is exciting to him. He has also become quite expert in handling the six up set of mules that pull the wagons down the trail

Brutus or Lars as Theo has been calling him, even taught Theo how to put up food in canning jars, a process developed in France to feed the troops of Napoleon. That was how Lars always had a supply of sweadish meatballs on hand, The noodles he made fresh as long as he could get ahold of eggs, which went in the recipe.

Reaching Vicksburg, Brutus starts looking for a place to set up a blacksmith shop, with a couple of blacksmiths in the town already, Brutus figures he needs a specialty line to offer the public. Looking around he discovers that the richer homes do not have wrought iron fences like they do in Georgia, so he makes up some small models of different styles and starts going door to door to interest the home owners in having a fancy fence around their properties.

He has immediate success in selling a number of fences, now all he has to do is set up a permanent shop and go to work, Theo meantime has found a building suitable for Lars to open his shop in, When Lars sees the building he says yes, and he rents the building and he and Theo set up the equipment and go to work. They are so busy that they have to hire helpers.

Lars talks Theo into staying with him until the next spring, by that time Lars will have trained new helpers and it would be the right time for Theo to head for St Louis on a steamboat,

Meantime Theo is building quite a nest egg for himself again, he hasn't had to touch the money that Cuss gave him, so with the wages and percentage that Brutus was giving him, the bankroll was growing nicely.

Spring, steamboats arriving almost daily going up or down river. Theo making his plans to leave. Lars helping and giving him advice, his voices are telling him it's time to let Theo go.

The horse and mule are in excellent shape. Theo has his possibles bag ready, all he needs now is a steamboat that will take his animals and him to St Louis.

Chapter Thirteen

The River Princess steamboat docks, Theo finds the captain and asks if he can get passage to St Louis for him, his horse and pack mule. " You're in luck son, it just so happens that I am equipped to handle live stock". "As you can see I am captain of a side wheeler, that gives me room to have a set of stalls to keep horses, mules, oxen or other animals on the aft deck of the boat". "You take a stern wheeler, with the paddles making so much commotion on the rear of the boat, animals are scared and uncomfortable, and therefore hard to control".

"To get your animals aboard we will use that derrick or gin pole as we sailors call it, and with the proper harness hoist them aboard". "You will need enough feed and grain for about six weeks of travel, and you will be in charge of caring for the animals". "Done, do I pay you now or after we are aboard". "I can take your money now" says the captain. "We will leave first thing in the morning at seven bells, oh that's seven o'clock to you landlubbers". "Fine, I'll go and find the feed and have it brought aboard". The captain tells him to bring the horse and mule around at six and we will load them last,

84

Theo finds, and has delivered, the feed and grain. Then gets his pack and possibles bag ready. The next morning he is at the dock at six with the animals, and watches how the harness is put on the horse and then the horse is picked up by the winch on the gin pole, then swung over the boat and gently put on deck. Theo is there to help unharness the horse and put him in a stall, and to quiet the horse down as he is quite nervous after flying through the air. The mule is next and he seems to handle the loading much easier, That done, Theo gets his baggage aboard, then goes to say goodbye to Brutus. Brutus gives Theo a big bear hug and tells him the voices told him to help the Card Man, and that a man called Cougar would be his new mentor and the woman would have inner beauty that will astound and captivate you the rest of your life. "May the gods go with you Theo and think of me once in a while", "I'll never forget you and what you have done for me, and with the threat of tears overcoming him he turns to board the boat".

So with the whistle blowing and the side wheels starting to turn, the River Princess leaves the dock to carry Theo on his way to new adventures. Theo waves to Brutus and then goes to see about his animals. They are quite nervous with the movement of the boat, so Theo talks to them to calm them down and then he grains the two and waters them. After cleaning up the horse apples and tossing them overboard, he makes sure they have good straw bedding, then goes to find something to eat.

The Salon is the center of activity on this boat, it's where Theo will eat, drink, and socialize, while his small cabin is where he will sleep. This particular boat can carry about twenty passengers, the rest of the boat is built to carry freight of all kinds.

Theo finds the salon and a breakfast spread, and for a nominal price is able to chow down, and have coffee to chase the food down with.. After eating he decides to walk around the boat to get familiar with it. He finds the engine room is on the first deck under the salon, there are crew quarters in front of the engine room and behind it, the passenger cabins are on the second deck behind the salon, and above the salon is the wheel house from which the captain guides the boat up the river. There are several other passengers on board, and they seem to be resting on deck chairs on a porch in front of the salon. Not wanting to intrude on these people, Theo climbs up to the wheel house and asks the captain if he can observe how he runs the boat. The captain being a friendly sort, says."sure lad, come on in and I'll give you a lesson on how a river boat is run". "First this is the wheel or as we call it, the helm, that steers the boat, that stanchion there with the handles is called the telegraph, with it I can send signals to the engine room to get more steam to go faster or less to slow down, or to put the engine in reverse". "The box on the pedestal holds the compass, which is rarely used, as we can normally see both shores". In running up or down the river, the object is to stay in the deepest part of the channel to keep from running aground, so we have learned to read the river and it tells us where we should run the boat". "We have to watch out for snags of logs that could get in the paddle wheels and break the paddle boards, sand bars that we can get stuck on, rocks and log snags that can rip a hole in the bottom before we know it", "It's a full time job to steer a steamboat on this or any river". "So lad sit and watch and we will enjoy what's left of the morning and afternoon together".

That evening the boat tied up at a small dock for the night, and to take on more fuel, as the river is hard to read at night the captain elects to travel only during the daylight hours.

Theo, goes to check on the horse and mule and sees they seem to be doing fine, they have calmed down quite nicely, so Theo being hungry goes to the salon and has a fine supper, the chef takes pride in serving food as good as he can make in his small galley. After supper Theo takes a stroll around the boat to kill some time before going to his cabin and turning in for the night.

As he passes the salon, he sees that it is now full of people, more then he had seen on the boat during the day, being curious he goes in and orders a beer and turns to survey the crowd.

Turning back to the bartender, he asks where all these people came from? The bartender tells him, some are passengers that come out at night, others are some of the crew, but most of them are from the small town just up the road. They come to gamble. "Oh! said Theo, I wondered what was under the covered tables I saw earlier. I see now that they are gambling tables and devices". "Can I go and watch, as I haven't seen this much gambling before?" "The town where I lived near had a saloon with one poker table, and a faro table, neither of which did I ever see played". The bartender says "sure, if you go over to that table over there you will see how the Card Man teaches these locals how to play poker". Theo looks at the bartender, and asked "that man is known as the Card Man?" "That's right" said the bartender, "he looks old and decrepit, but he can handle the cards better then most of the riverboat gamblers that ply their trade on the muddy water, he wins more then he loses and does so without cheating".

So Theo goes over near the poker table to watch, and looks at the gambler. He looks to be sixty years old, but his nimble fingers tell Theo he is probably younger. His hair is white, his complexion is pasty from not being in the sun, he's wearing black as Theo has heard most gamblers do.

As Theo watches the play he notices that the Card Man is winning more then the other players, one in particular. This fellow is obviously a poor poker player and he is not only getting angry about his losses, but he is drinking too much to keep a clear head, When the gambler wins the next hand, the poor player explodes, and accuses the Card Man of cheating, and goes for his gun that he is carrying. As he pulls it out, Theo jumps up and grabs the mans wrist, pushing the gun up to point at the ceiling just as it goes off Theo punches the fellow with his free hand, while pulling the gun from him. The guy goes down, knocked out by Theo, Just then the captain bursts into the salon and yells what is going on? The Card Man tells the captain, this yokel tried to shoot *me* and this young man stopped him with his fist. The captain looks at Theo, and tells Theo, "It looks like you have had some excitement on your first night aboard my boat".

"Yes sir, the kind of excitement I don't need". "Amen to that" said the captain. The captain tells a couple of his crewmen to take the unconscious man and throw him off the boat; we don't need his kind here. The Card Man tells the other players, that he thinks it's time to close down the game, as he wants to buy this young fellow a beer for saving his life. So Theo meets the Card Man.

CHAPTER FOURTEEN

The Card Man, tells Theo to take a seat at the vacated poker table, while he goes and gets two beers for them. While he is gone Theo picks up the deck of cards and is studying them when the Card Man gets back, "play poker?" he asks "No, in fact this is the closest I have been to a set of playing cards, working on the farm, and at the gold mine my friend Cuss had, I didn't have time to learn how to play card games". "Well now", says the Card Man, "we'll just have to remedy that; every man should know how to play poker". "Why?" asks Theo, "what good would it serve to be able to play poker or any other card game, besides maybe winning a few dollars, then getting someone mad enough to want to shoot you". "Ah! That's the down side of the game, but otherwise it is a way to study people, for instance, every man who plays poker has a giveaway". Theo asks "what is a giveaway?" The Card Man tells him, "It is a twitch or raised eyebrow or blink, or some other mannerism that gives an astute player opposite him the message that he is holding good cards, and will be hard to beat". " Oh!" exclaims, Theo. "Anyway let me introduce myself, they call me The Card Man, my real name has been lost over the years, so I don't use it". "I heard the captain call you Theo", Theo nods yes, "it's short for Theolinous". "Theolinous Raphael Calhoun, at your service sir". "That's quite a moniker for a Georgia farm boy, so Theo what brings you so far from home?" Theo tells the Card Man about his dream and plan to go to California and find himself a small but rich placer gold mine to work and recover enough gold to be well off.

"Well that's a noble dream, but you know that the rush to the gold diggings is over, and most of the men went back home broke". "Yes, I know, but the majority of the gold rushers knew nothing about finding a gold deposit worth working, and the ones that made fortunes stumbled into their finds, with a certain amount of good luck involved"

"I on the other hand have almost five years of work experience, working with one of the best gold miners in the area where I lived". "This man taught me how to find a good placer deposit, and how to recover the gold". "So I think I have a better chance of doing good then most men."

"Now that is good logic and sound thinking, as it's the same thing I use to make my living at cards". "I learned from the best many years ago, and practice everyday to keep from losing the edge that I have over the other players of the game"..

"Back to why I bought you a beer, I want to thank you for stopping that idiot from trying to shoot me, you saved me from having to kill him". Theo looks at the Card Man, "but he was going to kill you". "He was going to try but I had him covered, and you saved him from being shot to death". "But how were you going to kill him?, when he had the only gun that I saw".

"Watch my right hand Theo, he puts his right hand out in front of himself, and with a flip of his wrist a two shot 41 caliber Derringer appears in his hand from out of nowhere, you see Theo, I was about to shoot him, when you grabbed his wrist, and shoved it toward the ceiling, like I said you saved him from being killed, and me a lot of explaining to the authorities". "While you punched him, I put the gun back up my sleeve, and acted like I was unarmed". "In the excitement nobody saw my gun". "So everything turned out alright, nobody was seriously hurt, although that yokel is going to have one sore jaw from the way you knocked him out, what did you have in your hand to have hit him so hard?" "Nothing, I guess I have an extra hard fist from being a farmer, miner, and just before I got on this boat a blacksmiths helper". "Yes, that would explain it", remarks the Card Man.

"Theo, how would like to be my helper for the rest of the trip?, all you have to do is sit and watch the card players and do what you did earlier, if there is any trouble", "Gee! I don't know, I just got lucky then, I don't know if I could do it again on purpose like". "Sure you could, because you acted out of a need to prevent a shooting without thinking about it, those kind of reactions are what most men lack, and they get themselves into all kinds of hassles because they take time to think before reacting to a situation, so by the time they do the moment is gone and lost"

"Theo, I'll tell you what, I'll teach you to play poker with enough skill that you will be able to hold your own in any man's poker game, and you will find the skill will give you enough edge over most players that you will be able to make a grubstake, if and when you might need it".

"I guess learning how to play poker won't hurt, just by watching you earlier, I could see the skill you have over the other players that were here, besides, my Blacksmith friend told me to help the Card Man just before I got on the boat".

Now it's the Card Man's turn to look at Theo and ask, "what do you mean the Blacksmith said to help me?"

"Yeah, my friend told me to help the Card Man just before I got on the boat, he also told me my new mentor will be a man called Cougar, and that I would meet a lady whose beauty within would astound me". The Card Man looks at Theo like he may be a little short of a few cards in his deck, but he knows the youngster is telling him the truth as he sees it.

"Tell me more about this Blacksmith". "So Theo describes Brutus, and tells the gambler how he is descended from a long line of Seer's or Oracles from the Vikings of the north countries of Sweden, Denmark, and Norway, "Oh! That explains it", exclaims the gambler. "I've run across Indian Shaman who had the gift of foresight or the ability to tell the future". "Theo I think we are going to have an interesting trip together, I'll teach you the cards and you can watch my back, and I know of the Cougar man, he hires out as a scout and wagon master to folks that are heading west, and my guess is he will be in St Louis when we get there, getting a wagon train together".

"By the way, the reason people call him Cougar is because he has a large Par`fleche made from a mountain lion skin that has the head of the lion on the front as a decoration". "The story goes that Cougar killed the lion with his hunting knife, as that was the only weapon he had on him at the time". Theo asks, what is a Par`fleche? The Card Man, tells him it is a large bag or purse that the mountain men carry their possibles in, usually made from buffalo skin by a squaw that the mountain man is living with, in the case of Cougar, his squaw made his from the lion he killed. While most Par`fleche's are decorated with beads and porcupine quills, Cougars has the addition of many scalps that he has taken from his enemies. "Scalps!" Theo asks? "Yes, the gambler tells Theo, many an Indian and white man has tried to kill the Cougar killer, but he has bested them all so far". "Back to the Par`fleche, it has a wide belt that goes over a shoulder so it can be carried while walking, and it also has ties on it so it can be tied to the back of a saddle while riding a horse, much like a set of saddle bags". "Anyway that is Cougar's Par`fleche, and he got his name from the Indians, they call him Cougar killer, who has counted many coup". "I see" says Theo

So Theo is learning about the game of poker, meanwhile spending his evenings watching the gamblers back, and learning how to read the different personalities that come and go at a poker game.

Ten days up river from Vicksburg, the captain tells Theo that he is going to dock over two days at the port of Memphis, unloading cargo and taking on more cargo for St Louis, and that it would be a good idea to offload his horse and mule and give them some exercise. Theo agrees that it would be a good idea, plus it would give him a chance to see another big town.

He asks the Card Man if he would like to join him, but the gambler declines as he is not very good when it comes to riding, most of his traveling is done by boat or buggy.

Memphis turns out to be similar to Atlanta, lots of people, some in a hurry to take care of their business, others just strolling in the park along the river, saloons, restaurant's, merchantile's of all sorts, general stores, gunsmiths, saddle shops, blacksmiths, banks, and a slave market.

Theo did not hold much with slavery, but he was raised not to question it. After a day of exercising the animals, he heads back to the boat. The captain tells Theo to put the horse and mule in a livery there on the dock until tomorrow, he will have them put back on board the next morning after all the cargo is loaded. Theo puts up the animals, giving the livery man and extra dollar to wash and curry them, plus he buys some more feed and grain. Then it's back to the boat for supper, as he realizes in his excitement of sight seeing the city, he had forgotten to eat a noon meal.

On the river again, it's beginning to feel like home. The captain lets Theo take the wheel once in a while, while he smokes a pipe and tells Theo stories of the river. Lessons from the Card Man. Watching his back while he is earning his keep. and so it goes, a nice routine to while the hours away.

CHAPTER FIFTEEN

The steamboat makes a fuel stop just about every night, occasionally people come on board to gamble and have a few drinks. Theo watches the poker play, and the Card Man's back as agreed He is fast becoming a good poker player himself, and sits in on the games that don't have a full table of players. He is winning more then he loses as he has been taught by the Card Man. Theo has one problem with the game, and that is handling the cards, because of his large work hardened hands he does not have the dexterity to handle cards like his teacher, so he has to rely on his ability to cipher numbers rapidly, and therefore have the edge to play better then most of the card players that come aboard to gamble. The Card Man recognizes early in the card lessons, Theo's cipher ability and coaches him to use it as an advantage over the other players, especially since he doesn't have the hands to handle the cards with finesse.

Every few days the boat stops long enough to unload the Morgan horse and the mule, so Theo can exercise them, by now the animals have been hoisted on to shore and back to the boat so many times that they are getting used to it and don't put up any fuss. So they are staying in good shape despite the long trip.

The weeks pass, and one day the captain tells Theo that they will be in St Louis in two days, Theo is beside himself, at last the end of one journey and the beginning of a new one. He is a little depressed that he will be leaving behind the captain, the Card Man, and others that he has made friends with, but he is also excited that the jump off city to the west, is so close.

They dock in St. Louis around noon time. Theo gets his belongings on shore, while the crew hoists the horse and mule onto the wharf. He saddles the horse, and packs the mule, and says his last goodbyes to the captain and Card Man. The two tell Theo of an outfitter who might be able to put him in touch with Cougar if he is there. Theo tells the two that he is positive that he will find the scout, as Brutus's predictions have so far come true. So it's off to see St. Louis and the outfitter.

Riding through the city, he sees the opulence of some of the homes that belong to the more affluent citizens of St. Louis, he also sees the seamier side of the poorer sections of the city.

Soon, following the captain's directions, he finds the wagon train outfitter, and tying his horse and mule to the hitching post, he enters the large building that is stacked to the ceiling with goods. Approaching the large counter Theo enquires of the owner, and is told to knock on the door over there in the back of the store and ask for Mr. Allen.

Theo goes to the back of the store and knocks on the door the clerk pointed out, a man's voice says come in, and he looks at Theo as he enters, "what can I do for you son?" Theo introduces himself, and tells Mr. Allen that the captain of the steamboat River Princess said that, he, Mr.

Allen could probably put Theo in touch with a scout and Wagonmaster called Cougar.

Mr. Allen asks where Theo heard of Cougar? Theo relates the story of the blacksmith who told Theo that Cougar would be his new mentor and together they would escort a wagon train to California. Mr. Allen sits back in his chair with a look of amazement as just that morning Cougar was in ordering supplies for a wagon train going to California, and he needed a helper who could handle a six up team of mules and have some knowledge of how to repair the wagons when they eventually broke from the rigors of the long trip across the plains and mountains.

Theo tells of his months of working with the blacksmith, and driving his mules and wagon with its trailer full of equipment and iron, and how the smith taught him to work the iron and make any object he needed. He was also a good shot with rifle and pistol, and had been hunting game since he was a child big enough to hold and fire a rifle, Mr. Allen asks Theo if he has a horse, and Theo says "yes, plus a pack mule, they are tied up out front". "Good" says Mr. Allen, "come with me and we'll go down to the livery and get my horse and ride out to where the great Cougar is putting together a wagon train". So they walk to the livery and saddle up Mr. Allen's horse and head out of town to a prairie lot where there are many large wagons parked and waiting to leave to head west.

Mr. Allen hails the Scout and introduces him to Theo, and tells him he is the fellow that he was looking for this morning. "Is that so", Cougar says, "Why he looks like he just got off the boat after leaving the farm". " That's right Mr. Cougar, I just got off the River Princess this noon, and the captain and the Card Man told me how to find you, so that you can become my new mentor" . Cougar looks at

Theo, and asks what is a mentor? Theo tells Cougar that a mentor is a friend, teacher, and all around protector of the apprentice who is in his care until such time he is smart enough to take care of himself. "Allen", Cougar growls, "I got no time to look after a snot nosed youngster, I've got a wagon train to finish putting together, and hopefully be on the trail at the end of the week". "Now look here Cougar, this morning you were looking for a mule skinner, and someone who could repair wagons when they break down, this farm boy can do both, plus he is a good hunter, now what more can you ask for?"

Cougar looks at Theo hands, and remarks, he has the look of a man who has worked with his hands." What experience do you have son?". Theo tells Conger of his recent experience working with Brutus, the traveling blacksmith, and before that the almost five years working with Cuss at his gold mine, where Cuss taught him mining and also wood working, and how he worked on the family farm since he was old enough to walk. And how he has been around mules all his life, and has no trouble handling a six up team. "Plus with the lessons I got from the Card Man, I bet I can beat you at poker any day of the week". "Now that sounds like a challenge to me" says Cougar . "Everybody knows I'm the best poker playing mountain man this side of the Rockies", "Theo you're hired, just so I can beat the britches off you in poker".

Mr. Allen tells Theo," it looks like you have a job son, and Cougar you look out after this young one, as I have a feeling he is going to be your salvation", "Salvation!" yells Cougar, "I don't need no saving, I'm the Cougar killer remember". "Just the same, Cougar, the boy is going to be a big help to you, wait and see". With that Mr. Allen heads back to his store.

So begins the new adventure and apprenticeship. Cougar tells Theo to find a place to put down his bedroll, and picket his animals, supper will be ready soon.

Theo gets the horse and mule taken care of, fed, watered, and curried, then puts his bedroll and saddle down where he expects to bed down for the night. Then it's off to find Cougar and supper, wending his way through the camp he finds Cougar at a fire that has a pot of stew simmering over it, and also a large pot of coffee. The smell of food reminds him that again he had forgotten to have a noon meal, he had gotten so busy with unloading off the boat, and then finding the outfitters store, then Cougar, that he forgot to eat.

Cougar tells Theo, "Come, sit son and meet the folks whose wagon you are going to be driving". "This is Ethan Winslow and his niece Amy". "Ethan is taking three wagon loads of merchandise to Virginia City, Nevada to set up a store there, and Amy is going on to Auburn, California to take a teaching position there". "Folks this is Theo, I didn't get the last name Theo". Theo tells them, it is Calhoun, and "I'm from Dahlonega, Georgia, and I'm pleased to meet you". Ethan says "likewise I'm sure". "Can you drive a six up mule team Theo?" "Yes sir, like I've been doing it all my life, sir". Theo looking at Amy, says "Miss Amy, my ma was a school teacher before she married my pa, and she taught me how to read, write, and do numbers." Amy says to her uncle, "what luck uncle, a mule skinner that has an education, unlike the crude men who have been applying for the job". "Welcome Theo". "Now get a plate and spoon and we'll eat". So it's stew, pan bread, and coffee, so good that Theo has seconds.

After supper Cougar tells Theo to get some sleep, as he would like to be up just before dawn to go hunting for some deer meat for the stew pot, "plus I want to see if you can shoot that old rifle you carry". "Yes sir, and "I'll wager we can both bring down a deer apiece, me with my pea shooter, and you with that cannon you carry around". "Cannon, is it, why you young whippersnapper, have you know that this Hawken rifle can outshoot any gun you have had the privilege to shoot." Theo tells him "I don't doubt it, but can you hit anything with it" ." I mean you're so old that you probably can't see a deer at a hundred yards." "Why you! you how dare you insult me that way." "Mr. Cougar, I'm just funning you, I know your reputation, and I have no doubt you can outshoot me any day of the week, and that's saying a lot, because I was the best shot in Dahlonega". "Not to brag, but I would win the turkey shoot every year, so I could bring home a turkey for ma to cook for thanksgiving dinner."

"Well son, it looks like you have gone and challenged me again." "We'll just see who can bring home the meat tomorrow" "Meantime get some sleep, because you're going to have a hell'va time out shooting my cannon with your pea shooter". "Yes Sir Mr. Cougar, yes sir." and so they part friendly, waiting for the contest on the morrow.

CHAPTER SIXTEEN

The next morning at daybreak, Theo and Cougar saddle their horses, and put the pack saddle on Theo's mule, after a cup of coffee and a couple of biscuits, they head out to find some meat for the camp. Cougar tells Theo that he had some luck the other day about five or six miles southwest of the camp, so we will head that way and see if we can pick up some spoor.

Theo asks Cougar what kind of horse he is riding, as he has never seen one marked like it is.

Cougar tells Theo that he is on an appaloosa, they are a breed that the Nez-Pierce Indian tribe has developed, they are a tribe that live in the north part of the Rockies and plains, sometimes ranging into Canada.

The horse was bred to be at home in the mountains and the prairies, their stamina is almost unrivaled by any other horse breed. The spotted blanket on their rump is the trade mark of the breed, and I think it's the best horse around. "I don't know about that, this Morgan was bred not only for riding but to pull the light buggies of the well to do, and therefore has a tremendous amount of stamina too exclaims Theo"

"Sounds like another challenge to me, do you want to *see* who has the better horse in a horse race asks Cougar?" "No" says Theo, "that would be a foolish waste, we have a long work day ahead, and to exhaust the horses in a race would jeopardize the hunt". "And besides I can see the horses are pretty evenly matched, I mean look at their builds, both are deep chested, with strong withers, and the same height." "No, I say it would be a waste of good energy to run the horses". "You're right son", says Cougar

So they proceed to the place where Cougar saw the deer on his last hunt. Cougar tells Theo that he got the last deer on the other side of the small copse of woods up ahead. "It might be a good idea to dismount and tie the animals on this side of the woods and walk through quietly and see if there are any deer on the other side". "Good idea Cougar".

So they dismount and secure the animals, and keeping the wind in their faces they creep through the woods. When they get to the other side, they can't believe their luck, for there in the meadow is the small herd of deer that Cougar ran into the other day. Keeping back in the trees, they survey the herd and pick out two of the bucks to try and kill. Theo looks at Cougar "Cougar with your Hawken you can get the one on the left from here, but my rifle does not have the range to get the other buck from here, so here's what I'm going to do, I'll crawl through the grass and get close enough for a sure shot, when I raise up to take my shot, you take yours at the same time." "Theo, what makes you think you can sneak up on those deer, their hearing is far greater then our's, and they will spot you before you can get close enough for a shot, better I get the one buck, then to run off the whole herd". "Trust me Cougar, I've done this many times before back home, just be ready to shoot when I do". "Ok, but don't say I didn't tell you so when the herd runs for it."

Theo starts his crawl, telling Cougar to be ready in about ten minutes. Cougar watches for sign of Theo crawling towards the buck he is after, and to his amazement he cannot see or hear Theo making his way through the tall grass, after what seems like an hour, Theo raises up and takes careful aim an shoots his buck. Cougar being ready with his Hawken squeezes his trigger and instant later, and when the smoke clears, sees that his buck is down as is Theo's.

Cougar sees Theo reloading, waiting for Cougar to join him, and Cougar is also reloading while walking up to Theo. Then they both go to look at the two deer, coming to Theo's first, Cougar sees that the deer is dead with a clean shot to the heart. "Nice shooting son, now let's go see if the old man did as good." Upon reaching Cougar's deer they see it is another killing shot to the chest.

Cougar tells Theo that since he is the youngest and his official apprentice that he can go get the horses and the mule, so they can pack the deer back to camp. " Ok old man, I guess all the excitement has worn you out so much that you can't walk back to your horse".

Cougar growls at Theo and starts to chase him, they are both laughing at the joke Theo has pulled on Cougar. Cougar hollers at Theo, "one of these days son, I'm going to get even".

While Theo is getting the horses and pack mule, Cougar is gutting the deer and getting them ready to take back to the wagon train camp. When Theo gets back, Cougar walks over to his horse, and reaches in his Par`fleehe and gets out a large piece of oiled paper, which he uses to wrap up the hearts and livers of the two deer. Then the two lift the deer onto the mule and tie them down. When they are ready to go, Theo asks Cougar if he could shoot Cougar's Hawken, as he was impressed with the accuracy and the long range the rifle just displayed in downing Cougar's deer. Cougar had shot his deer at twice the distance that Theo did on his kill.

Cougar hands the rifle to Theo and shows him how it works and especially the rear sight, that flips up to give him the correct amount of elevation to make long distance shots much easier to hit, he tells Theo that he still has to use Kentucky windage as they call it, to compensate for the wind

So Theo picks out a tree about three hundred yards away, and checking the wind he puts the rifle to his shoulder, takes aim, and after a deep breath, that he lets half of out, he squeezes the trigger. The gun goes off, and the recoil knocks Theo back a foot, "wow! I wasn't expecting that much kick, my rifle is a thirty six caliber and does not kick like this one, just how big are the bullets in this gun?" Cougar laughs, and said I knew I would get even, as Theo rubs his shoulder. "Well son you just shot a fifty four caliber ball, with probably three times the powder your pea shooter uses". "Let's go and see if you hit any thing but sky." They walk over to the tree Theo had aimed at and found a hole where he had hit the tree, and on the back side of the six inch around tree they found a very large hole where the ball had exited the tree.

"My god! Theo exclaims, that's the most powerful rifle I have ever seen and now shot", still rubbing his shoulder. "And to top it off the accuracy is fantastic, I got to have me one of these, where can I get one Cougar?"

Cougar tells Theo, "you're in luck as the Hawken brothers have a large shop in St. Louis where they make these rifles, usually on custom order for the owner". "They fit each rifle to the buyer, so that the owner will get the most out of shooting the gun." "Can I go in and order one of these rifles, and have it before we leave?" Cougar tells him, the only way to find out is to go see the

Hawken's this afternoon and ask.

Having gotten the deer early in the day, Cougar and Theo have time to take the deer back to camp and let the wagon folks do the skinning and butchering, the skins are salted down for future processing, and the deer is made ready for roasting for that nights supper.

After taking care of the mule, Theo and Cougar head for St. Louis and the Hawken brothers shop. Upon arriving at the shop Theo looks at the sign above the door, it says Jacob and Samuel Hawken, Gunsmiths, and makers of fine rifles.

Cougar enters the shop with Theo right behind him, and upon seeing Jacob he blusters out a greeting, and Jacob steps out from behind a counter and gives Cougar a big bear hug, and declares. "How the hell are you, mountain man, who still stinks like a goat?" "Why I'm just fine you old reprobate." And they both slap each other on the back and laugh. "What can I do for you Cougar?" asks Jacob "Well I need to replenish my powder, ball, and caps, and my new apprentice here would like to buy one of your fine rifles", " Well now" says Jacob, "let's just see what we have to offer this fine looking young man."

"Now don't go putting ideas out that this mongrel pup is handsome, I've got enough trouble with his cocky behavior, let alone letting him think he's good looking too", says Cougar

"Young man, what did you have in mind for a rifle?" Theo tells him, one like Cougars.

Jacob steps back behind the counter and looks at the rack of rifles on the wall and picks out one and sets in on the counter. "Now what we have here is a fifty four caliber long gun, with our new riffling technique, it will hold shot groups at around six inches at two hundred yards, it has the new percussion type action, wherein you just shove a cap into the nipple and cock the hammer and it's ready to fire", "Now let's see if this gun will fit you". "Take hold of the gun, and bring it up to your shoulder smartly as if you are making a quick shot without time to settle the butt into your shoulder, and be ready for the recoil". So Theo does as Jacob says and finds this rifle is a little short in the stock. Jacob takes down another rifle and has Theo try it, this one fits just right, but it is the wrong caliber. Jacob tells Theo, "What we need to do is lengthen the stock on the first rifle, so it will fit you young man". "Theo asks, how can you do that?" Jacob tells him, "we have some rubber pads that we use on shotguns all the time that will take up the space, plus it cuts down on the recoil pain from the gun going off." Theo says, "Now that is a good thing, I still have a bruise from firing Cougar's rifle this morning."

Jacob steps over to a doorway to the back and calls his brother to come up front and measure Theo for the correct length of pad he will need for the fifty four caliber rifle he is looking at. Samuel steps out of the back room with a tape measure and has Theo pull both guns to his shoulder again, while measuring the difference in the stocks. He looks at Jacob and says, it looks like an inch and a half should make it fit. So Jacob goes to another counter and pulls out a rubber pad and hands it to Samuel , along with the rifle and asks his brother to mount the pad. Samuel takes the gun in back stating to Theo and Cougar this will take a few moments. Theo says, "That is just fine, meanwhile I will need powder, ball, and caps". "Cleaning kit, maybe a scabbard to carry the rifle in when I am on my horse". "The rifle comes with a cleaning kit, and a good portion of powder, ball, and caps, but since you will be traveling with Cougar you will ' need to stock up on plenty of extra ammo" . "You're right, with the way Cougar shoots; I'm going to need extra ammo to back him up when he misses".

"Cougar yells, why you! you! there you go again, just wait till we get back to camp, I'm going to show you what Injun wrestling is all about, and give you the licking of your life", Jacob pipes in and says Cougar! "You still can't take a joke can you?" With that, Theo and Jacob laugh. Jacob tells Theo." Son I like you, anyone who can get old Cougar's goat is a friend of mine." Cougar growl's, "Just you two wait, 1'11 get even". And they all laugh.

So Jacob gets the supplies that Cougar and Theo need together, meantime Samuel brings out the rifle with the new pad mounted on it, and tells Theo to try it out. So Theo pulls the gun up to his shoulder several times and tells Samuel it fits like a glove. "Good, now come with me out back where we have a place to shoot". "We test all our rifles out there to make sure there are no problems".

Jacob leads Theo and Cougar through the shop where there are several men working on different stages of making rifles, Out in back Theo sees a professional shooting range, with benches set up to bench test the rifles at various ranges. Jacob takes Theo over to a spot where he can shoot offhand and shows him the loading procedure, and then hands him the rifle.

He tells Theo to bring up the gun natural into his shoulder and site on the target down range and squeeze off a shot, remember to keep the stock tight against your shoulder. Theo says," I will, I learned the hard way this morning with Cougar's rifle".

The target is a hundred yards, the site is set for that distance, checking the wind, Theo begins his squeeze, the rifle goes off with a roar, Theo feels the recoil, but it is much softer with the rubber pad, plus he was ready for the additional kick over his old gun his pa gave him so many years ago.

They go down and retrieve the target and find Theo had hit it exactly where he had aimed. Jacob tells Theo," that's very fine shooting son for the first shot, I think you have a rifle that fits you to a T, you'll know after you practice with it awhile". "I love it, it's going to take a little getting used to after shooting my old Brown Bess for so long, but I'm sure I'm going to be more then happy with this fine rifle."

So they go back up to the front, and conclude the purchase, it didn't come cheap, but Theo feels it was worth every penny, besides the money came from his poker winnings, which means that he still hasn't had to get into his bonus money from Cuss.

After they leave the Hawken's, Cougar says. "Now what you need are some trail clothes." "What's wrong with what I have?" "Son those clothes will be rags before we are a month out from St_ Louis, come on I'm going to take you to a store where you can buy some real buckskins, that will last forever".

So down the street they go, a few blocks later Cougar pulls up before a store with a set of buckskins in the window, plus other items made of Buffalo and Deer hide. Getting down off his horse and tying it to the hitch rail he goes inside, and again blusters, hello to an old friend. Turning to Theo, "Theo, I want you to meet the meanest, ornery, uncouth, old fur trapper that ever inhabited the beaver creeks of the Rockies". "Pierre, meet my new apprentice Theo Calhoun." "Glad to meet you Mon Dieu" , says the Frenchman, but when did this clumsy oaf get smart enough to get an apprentice?" "He hardly has enough sense to come in out of the rain", " Why you bearded little runt, why is it every time I come to see you I get insulted." Pierre, slaping his leg and laughing, tells him, "Because it is so much fun."

"But seriously Cougar, what can I do for you?" "This youngster needs a set of hardy buckskins if he expects to see California in anything but his scarred up skin." "Those country clothes he has on won't last a month on the trail" Pierre looks at Theo, and tells him, "what Cougar says is true lad," "I know from many years in the pursuit of the beaver that you need clothes that will withstand the wilds of the plains and mountains". "It is why I have this shop, when I got too old to trap, and at the same time the market for plew's fell off, I figured I could make a living making clothes for the few trappers left and the homesteaders going west". "So I set up shop with my Shoshone wives, and am now a modestly successful businessman." Theo asks? "Did I hear right, you have more then one wife". The old trapper tells him, why yes, "I have several, all good hard working squaws, who I hardly ever have to punish for being lazy". Theo is shocked by the candor with which Pierre talks about his several wives, like it is an everyday occurrence, and thinking about it I guess it is here in the west,

"Come Master Theo, we will go in back and get you measured up for two sets of my good buckskins". With that they enter the back room where there are several Indian squaws cutting and sewing on different sets of buckskins and Par`flechs, moccasins and leather hats. Looking around Theo sees hundreds of tanned skins, waiting to be made into an article of clothing or footwear, He's amazed at the activity in this shop.

Pierre calls one of his wives over and in French tells her to measure Theo up for a set of buckskins, moccasins, and hat. Then he turns to Theo and asks if he will need a Par`fleche? ""I don't think so, I have a very good set of saddle bags that I use".

Standing on a raised dais Theo is being measured by the wife of Pierre's who is telling one of the other wives Theo's measurements, when she comes to the inseam measurement she pushes her hand all the way up to the top of Theo's thigh and gives the measurement to the other woman, then makes a comment in her native tongue, and all the other wives giggle. Theo looks at Pierre, and asks, what did she say? Pierre said she told the others that you are much mucho man, and the ladies better watch out or they will have their hearts broken . Theo turns red as a beet, and is speechless.

CHAPTER SEVENTEEN

After Pierre's wife got through measuring Theo, Pierre said, "Come with me and pick out the style of buckskins you would like." So Theo picked out a set that was comfortable looking, with fringe hanging off the sleeves and middle chest. "Good choice lad, these are a good everyday working man's set." "Why the fringe?" Asks Theo. "It helps to keep the rain from soaking into the rest of the suit, plus gives you a source of leather thongs to tie things up with." So two sets of buckskins, a hat, and a pair of high boot type moccasins, and you are ready to go. "Do I really need the moccasins asks Theo?" Pierre tells Theo, "Once you get used to them, you'll wonder why you ever liked the white man's boot."

"Ok, how much is this going to cost me?" Pierre adds up the total and shows it to Theo. Theo reaches into his pocket only to find his money pouch gone. Pierre asks, "are you looking for this, as he hands Theo his pouch." "How did you get my pouch?" asks Theo. Pierre, exclaims, "my wives are all expert pickpockets, and sometimes they like to play a joke on my friends, sorry to scare you like that, but we are all a bunch of jokers, aren't we Cougar?" as they laugh at the joke they pulled on Theo.

Theo pays Pierre for the outfits, and asks when he can get them? Pierre tells him late tomorrow afternoon. "Good." So Cougar and Theo head back to camp with their new supplies and Theo's new rifle.

They get back in camp in time to put their things away and wash up for supper, while they were in town the wagon folk put together a feast, roast venison, with yams, corn on the cob, greens with salt pork, cornbread, and dried apple pie for desert. The whole camp ate like there was no tomorrow, everybody gorged themselves.

After supper Theo excused himself and went for a walk, after a while he went to his bedroll and dug out his journal and as it was starting to get dark he lit a candle and started to write.

"Well journal, we have come a long way together since I started you six years ago, and I see there are only a couple of blank pages left. So let me recap my adventures with you by my side."

"Mining with Cuss, getting the Morgan for my birthday, the terrible day I lost my family, the year with Brutus, the steamboat, and her captain, the Card Man and poker. It has been quite an adventure, and now a new one starting." "Tomorrow I'll get a new journal to start writing in, but tonight I am compelled to fill the last page with a secret I've kept all these years." "Cuss's hideout, I still marvel at the way he hid his gold in the base of the hot tub furnace." "I just hope that if I ever have enough gold to hide I can come up with as clever a bank as Cuss did." "Farewell old friend."

Just as Theo was finishing writing he spotted Amy walking his way, He closed his journal just as she approached him, and she asked if she could visit with him, as she was curious as to what he was writing. "Oh! This is a journal I have been keeping the last six years." "I see." said Amy, "I thought you might be writing a book about all your travels and adventures." "Come to think about it I guess that's what I have done, it is an almost day to day chronicle of my life since I went to work for Cuss, a gold miner back in Dahlonega."

Amy asks, "If it would be alright if she could read it, I would love to learn more about you."

Theo hesitated, and said, "I don't know, Amy, there are some very personal things in there that I don't know if I want another person to know about." "Oh, Excuse me, I shouldn't have asked, it's probably like a diary, and I sure wouldn't want someone to read my diary." "I guess I wasn't thinking." "That is quite alright, no harm done, in fact I take it as very high compliment that you want to know more about me." "I feel the same way about you, and as the journey to the west proceeds, we should have plenty of opportunity to have many conversations and get to know each other like brother and sister before the trip is over." Amy looks at Theo, "brother and sister! I was thinking along a different type of relationship."

"Oh! Exclaims, Theo, how dumb of me, you'll have to excuse me but my experience with women is very limited." Amy asks, "Don't you like girls?" "Oh yes." "it's just that I haven't had the time to spend getting to know about any women other then my ma, sister, and Cuss's wife, Sara." "Oh! I see," "well we'll have to work on that won't we," at that she turns and giving Theo a wink of her eye she heads back to her wagon.

Theo thinks to himself, "oh! oh!, I do believe I am going to have another adventure, that of learning about how the womenfolk think."

The next morning Theo gets with Cougar and they start discussing the trip in front of them. Theo asks about the trail they will be going over, and how rough it is going to be. Cougar tells him, the first couple of hundred miles aren't too bad, there is almost a road to follow up the Missouri river, it's when we leave the river and turn west that it starts getting rough. We will need extra wheels for each wagon, axles, and mounting hardware, Jacks, spud wrenches for the axle nuts and so on.

Theo tells Cougar that what we need to do is get everybody together and make an inventory of what everybody has and what they need to make sure that we can take care of the problems as they arise. Cougar looks at Theo and said, "now why didn't I think of that."

So they get the wagon owners together and make a list of what they have and what they need to handle the repairs that will eventually come up. By midmorning they can see the need for a simple blacksmith shop to take along with various pieces of iron with which to make wheel rims and axle shafts and any other part that might break.

Cougar takes up a collection to go into town and get the necessary equipment. Theo takes his mule along to pull a wagon full of iron and tools back to camp. Stopping at a hardware store they inquire as to where they can get a small anvil, bellows, tongs, hammers, and iron to make a crude blacksmith shop. The hardware man tells them of a man who has a scrap yard down by the river who might have what they are looking for, so getting directions they ride down to the yard. Getting ahold of the owner they explain what they need and ask if he can help them. "Boys, you're in luck, I have equipment from a couple of blacksmiths who either went broke or decided to go west and left their stuff here."

The Scrap man tells them to follow him and let's see what you can use. As they walk through the yard Theo sees tons of iron and pieces of wagons, and junk of every description. The man stops at a large open shed and said look in there. Theo and Cougar see several anvils, racks of tools, bellows of various sizes, even a hoist frame with which to pick up oxen while re`shoeing them.

So Theo tells Cougar, everything we need is here, now what we need is a wagon to haul what we buy back to camp. "I've got several wagons that you can rent to haul the equipment you want says the Scrap man." So while Theo is picking out the anvil, hammers, tongs, bellows, and other pieces, Cougar takes the mule and harnesses him to a suitable wagon and drives it over to Theo and his pile of tools. Theo is also looking at some iron and a couple of used axles that can be used for spares. "How much is this going to cost us?" asks Cougar of the Scrap man The man takes out a notebook and pencil and starts adding numbers, and coming to an answer, he declares it looks like around a hundred and ten dollars, plus five for the wagon. Cougar looks at the Scrap man "I'll tell you what, I'll give you a hundred even, and we'll load the wagon ourselves, and bring it back empty in about three hours." The Scrap man says done, "pay me and be on your way."

Theo starts loading as Cougar pays the man, twenty minutes later they are on their way back to camp. Getting into camp they unload the tools and iron, and start back to town. Theo tells Cougar, "we should be done with this chore in time to go pick up his new buckskins and he needs to find a store where he can buy a journal to write in." Cougar tells him, there is a store just down the street from the Frenchman's that handles paper goods.

After taking the wagon back and getting Theo's new buckskin's they go to the store where Theo gets his new journal. When they are all through with their errands, Cougar tells Theo, all this work has given him a mighty big thirst, "I know a saloon where we can get a cold beer and probably say hello to some of my old friends at the same time." "A cold beer does sound good, lead on o master of this apprentice."

At the saloon Cougar swaggers in the swinging doors and roars, "is there a mountain man bigger and meaner then me in here, if so I want to shake his hand." "Bartender set up two cold beers for me and my friend here." With the beer in hand Cougar drinks it down in one long pull, setting the mug on the bar he tells the bartender to pour another. He says to no one in particular, "I am really thirsty," and drinks the second beer down with out coming up for air, "another bartender." Theo is nursing his first beer, and looking at Cougar in amazement at how fast he is consuming the beer. "Cougar, take it easy or you'll be so drunk I'll have to carry you back to camp slung over the back of the mule." "Don't you worry boy, I can drink all day and night and still ride a horse like a mountain man, proud and upright."

Just then the doors of the saloon open and four of the roughest looking trappers come in. Upon seeing Cougar at the bar they come over and start insulting Cougar, calling him names that Theo never heard before, thinking it is another of Cougars friends, Theo is watching Cougar to see how he greets these fellows Cougar bellows out, "why you sumbitchin stinking Frenchie, I ought to break you in half for what you did at the last rendezvous." Frenchie says, "You ain't big enough to take me on." "Oh yeah! bellows Cougar," as he swings at the Frenchman and knocks him halfway across the room. The three trappers with the Frenchman grab Cougar and start beating on him. Theo is not about to see three dirty trappers beat up his friend and wades into the fracas, grabbing one of the trappers, he lands a solid right fist on the man's nose breaking it, and knocking the man out. As he is about to grab another one, Frenchie comes flying back, and throws a punch at Theo catching him in the ribs, and knocking the wind out of him.

Grabbing his side, Theo takes a step back and kicks the Frenchman in his left knee, causing the man to drop to the floor with a broken knee. The Frenchman is howling like a banshee at the pain, meantime Cougar is choking one of the trappers, while the other one is groping for his pistol. Seeing that the man intends to shoot Cougar, Theo grabs the trappers wrist and twisting around he gets the mans arm over his shoulder and pulling down breaks the mans elbow.

Cougar lets go of his trapper's neck and knocks him out with a hard right to the jaw. The Frenchman is still howling and at the same time reaching for a large knife to throw at Cougar.

Cougar ducks the thrown knife and dives at the Frenchman, grabbing his head he gives it a violent twist and breaks the Frenchman's neck. The fight is over; the bartender has gone after the law. So Cougar steps behind the bar and pours himself another beer and one for Theo.

The law shows up, and after questioning, find that the Frenchman and his trappers caused the fight and tried to kill Cougar. So calling it a case of self defense, the lawman told Cougar and Theo they were free to go, and that it might be a good idea if they left for their camp now. So they finish their beers and leave, Theo with sore ribs and Cougar with several bruises and a black eye that is getting darker and darker.

CHAPTER EIGHTEEN

On the way back to the wagon train camp, Theo asks Cougar "What was the fight all about?" Cougar tells Theo how Frenche' killed his best friend at the last rendezvous. "While I was cavorting with a Shoshone squaw, Frenche' and his pals were getting my best friend Louis drunk, then they picked a fight with him, Louis knocked Frenche' down, then two of his pards grabbed Louis and held him while Frenche' got up, took out his knife and stabbed Louis in the gut."" They left him there to die a painful death." "Meantime Frenche' and his men packed up and took off" "By the time I discovered Louis they were miles away." "Louis told me in his last breaths how Frenche' had kilt him, and begged me to avenge him". "I saddled my horse and grabbed my rifle and possibles and went looking for the bastards, but with all the trappers and Indians and traders coming and going, I couldn't find a set of tracks to follow."

"So I gave up then, knowing that some day I would cross trails with them and make things right with Louis's spirit." "That was five years ago, this is the first time I have run across Frenche' since then, and he won't be killing nobody again."

By the time they got back to camp, the word had got there of the fight. So the wagon folk were waiting and concerned. Amy ran up to Theo as soon as he got off his horse, and cried, "are you alright?" Theo blushed at the attention from Amy, and said." I'm fine, I just have some sore ribs where I got punched."

Amy grabs Theo's arm and tells him to "come with me, I want to check those ribs to see if they are broken" . At Amy's wagon she makes Theo take off his shirt, and examines Theo's side. It is black and blue, and Theo said, yes it hurts when he takes a deep breath. "you probably have a couple of cracked ribs," and with that, she climbs into her wagon and comes back with a roll of gauze cloth. Theo looks at the cloth and recognizing it as the cloth that women use for that time of month, asks Amy what she intends to do with it? "Hush, I'm going to wrap your ribs with it,so they will heal faster," "but, but, Theo exclaims, I can't be seen wearing that." "Nobody is going to see it under your shirt, now hold still while I get this wrapped properly" . When she is done and Theo has his shirt back on, Amy asks, "now doesn't that feel better?" "Yes, where did you learn how to do that?" Amy tells Theo how she used to help the Doc in the town where she came from, and how he had taught her to change bandages on his patients.

"Come on, let's go see how Cougar is doing", says Amy. Getting to Cougar's spot in camp, they find that he is holding a raw steak over his black eye, and telling the small crowd around him about the fight. "You should have seen it!", he says, "there I was being beaten by three of the dirtest, stinking trappers you ever saw, when Theo steps in and grabbing one of the men, he hits him in the face so hard that he not only broke his nose, but knocked him clean out at the same time," "Then as he is starting to grab another of the bastards, excuse me ladies, Frenche' comes off the floor and punches Theo in the ribs, Theo takes a step back and while holding his ribs he kicks Frenche' in the knee and breaks it, meanwhile I'm choking one of the B--- ah men, when Theo catches the other one going for his pistol, I see Theo grab the man's wrist and twisting around, put the man's arm over his shoulder, pulls down and breaks his elbow", "Then I let go of the sumbi---, I mean the neck of the man I've got ahold of, and knock him out. " Just then I see Frenche` pull his knife and throw it at me, luckily I ducked in time, and dove on to Frenche' and broke his neck," "That ended the fight, and let me tell you I. don't think there is a better man to ride the river with then Theo Calhoun." At that everybody looks at Theo and gives him a Cheer.

Theo turns red as a beet again from embarrassment. Amy is secretly beaming with pride, as she feels the attraction for this soft spoken man from Georgia increasing by the day.

Next morning, both Theo and Cougar are stiff from the punches of the fight, but life goes on, They gather up the wagon folk and tell them that they should be ready to leave on the morrow, make sure you have everything packed and secured so the load won't shift while on the trail, fill all the water barrels, and make sure all your possum belly's are filled with firewood, as it will get scarce along the trail.

Theo with the help of Amy's uncle Ethan shifts things around in the three wagons, so he can haul the anvil on the wagon he will be driving, and distributes the rest of the blacksmith tools to other wagons so as not to overload his wagon. He then checks all the harness for the three wagons, and the mules for loose shoes or any other problems. With everything looking good, it's time for a noon meal. Amy brings a plate of stew to Theo and they sit and talk of the journey ahead, After the meal, Theo asks Amy if she would do him a favor? "What favor do you need?" Theo wants to know if she had room in one of her trunks for his journal and two bibles he carries. Of course, they will be no trouble at all."

Theo goes to his saddle bags and retrieves his books that he keeps wrapped in a water proof wrapping and hands them to Amy. "My these bibles are heavy she says, come, you're going to have to help me unpack one of the trunks so we can put the books in the bottom of it" . Theo goes with Amy and helps her with the trunk she choses, and seeing some of the frilly underthings, blushes. Amy seemly ignoring his embarrassment goes on with the rearranging of the trunk as if nothing has happened. With the books in a safe place, Theo goes to find Cougar.

Cougar is saddling his horse, and tells Theo to go get his horse, we're going to ride out on the trail and see if there are any problems ahead of us for tomorrow, Theo gets the Morgan and they ride out, following the trail along the Missouri river, checking for excessive mud holes, gulley's made by erosion from the winter rains and snow melt, and any other obstacle that might impede the progress of the wagon train.

About ten or twelve miles out they spot a small herd of deer. Knowing that the camp is always in need of fresh meat they circle around the herd to get downwind, then dismounting they stalk the deer, keeping low in the tall grass they manage to get within rifle range. Cougar, whispering to Theo, "Now is a good time to see what the additional range on the Hawken can do, You take the one on the right and I'll get the left one" . So cocking the rifles as quietly as possible they both raise up, take aim, and as one, squeeze off their shots. Both deer drop, the rest of the herd take off for a woods nearby. Theo sees his deer get up and run a couple of yards then drop. Both men reload and start approaching their deer. "Cougar warns Theo to be careful, his deer might be playing possum," Theo gets out his Dragoon, and is ready to shoot the deer again if necessary; approaching the deer they find them both dead. Theo's shot was a little low, missing the heart, but taking out the lungs of the animal.

Cougar again sends Theo for the horses, while he guts the animals in preparation for the trip back to camp. They load up the deer and head back to camp. A couple of miles later they pick up a pack of coyotes, who decide that, they want the deer. Cougar yell's at Theo, "run your horse for about a mile to tire out the coyotes then stop, dismount and with your rifle pick off the leader of the pack on your side, while I get the one on my side, then with your pistol get as many as you can." That should scatter them enough, so that we'll be able to take our time back to camp.

Running as hard as the horses can with the load they are carrying, they go about a mile, stop, take aim at the coyotes, and fire, Theo not being used to the Hawken yet misses the running coyote, so taking out his pistol he waits until he has a sure shot, then lets the lead coyote have it, hitting him in the chest, the animal tumbles head over heels, and comes to a stop, dead,

Meanwhile Theo is shooting two more of the coyotes before they break off and retreat.

Cougar is having the time of his life shooting at the coyotes, yelling and screaming, come on and get it you bastard's. He kills four before they retreat. "Come on Theo, get on your horse and ride, and reload as fast as you can, in case they decide to attack again."

As they ride away from the dead coyotes the others start howling, and very slowly start to regroup to follow the horsemen. "Watch them on your side Theo, if one of them gets close enough for a rifle shot , take him down, after losing a few more they will stop their foolishness, and we'll be able to ride back in peace".

After about five miles the coyotes get wind of the wagon train camp and decide to stop following Cougar and Theo. So Theo and Cougar ride back into camp with fresh meat, and another story for Theo's new journal.

CHAPTER NINETEEN

When they get back to camp, they find Pierre waiting for them. " What's up Pierre?" Yell's Cougar. "I heard of the fight last evening, and I wanted to see how you are?" "We're fine, Theo has a couple of cracked ribs and I have a black eye and bruises" "We'll live to fight again, he brags".

"Theo, I have brought you something", says Pierre. "Here I have made you a Par`fleche, it's a gift for saving this old fart's life, we all have to die sometime, but I'm glad it was not at the hands of those scum that killed Louis". "I heard how you stopped the trapper from shooting Cougar".

"I don't know how to thank you Pierre, except thanks, this is awfully nice of you".

Cougar tells Theo, "let's get these deer over to the ladies, so they can skin them and get them ready for our last supper here, tomorrow we will hopefully be camping twenty miles from here".

"Pierre stay for supper, and you can take the skin's back with you, we have two from the other day, plus two from today," "It'll help defray the cost of my new buckskin's when I get back from taking these pilgrims west."

So another feast is prepared by the women of the wagon train, After supper Cougar asks for everybody's attention, "Folks I want to say a few words, the journey we are about to embark on is going to be fraught with new experiences." "Danger, boredom, exhaustion, hunger, thirst, that is the good part, then there is the threat of Indians, as we will be in their old hunting grounds, it's possible we might run into hunting parties, as long as they are finding game, they usually don't bother the wagon trains, except the Blackfeet, and the Piutes over past the great salt lake." "So we will set up watches, day and night, and practice placing the wagons in a circle, and setting up defenses in that circle". "Hopefully we won't have any trouble with the Indians, but we must be prepared for the worst."

"In the morning when we get going, I want Theo to be the lead wagon, Amy next, her uncle Ethan next, Hooper next since you have the majority of the blacksmith tools in your wagon, Carlyle, if you don't mind I would like you to ride drag, and have your two boys take the flanks on either side, far enough out to watch, but close enough to be in sight of the wagons," "The rest of you fill in the train as you see fit." "Draw straws for the positions." "Once the train is moving, keep enough distance between the wagons so you can see any obstacles in the trail and avoid them, but I want you to be bunched up enough to be able to circle the wagons in case of danger." "So with that said, everybody get as much rest as you can, I want to be on the trail and hour after daybreak."

"Theo, will you walk with me?" Asks Amy. "I'm so excited about finally leaving that I can't go to sleep just yet". "Sure", so they walk around the camp engaging in small talk, after a couple of turns around the camp, Amy stops at her wagon and thanks Theo, and tells him that she will see him in the morning, then quickly kissing him on the cheek, she turns and climbs into her wagon. Theo feels the flush in his face, and is glad it is dark so nobody else can see,

At his bedroll he takes out his journal and puts down the days events, closing with the strange feeling he is getting when he is near Amy. Putting the journal away, he rolls up in his blankets and tries to go to sleep, which comes slowly because of all the anticipation of what the morrow will bring.

CHAPTER TWENTY

Up before dawn, harnessing the mules to the three wagons, Amy fixing breakfast, Ethan making sure everything is secure, packing the possum belly's on all three wagons with firewood,

Hour after daylight, and Cougar yell's, "alright folks let's move 'em out." And so the journey begins. The trail is in good shape, Cougar expects twenty miles today.

The mules, and oxen are well rested, so they are eager to do their days work. Cougar is leading, staying within sight of Theo, the others following at good distances as Cougar instructed. The train stops for a noon rest and meal, then onward. The day passes; Cougar has the first camp site picked out, close to the river for water and graze for the animals.

Camp is set up, supper of left over venison, beans, coffee, biscuits with honey. Cougar gathers the wagon folk, and commends them for a good first day, let's hope we can keep it up, at this rate of travel we can be in Kansas in a week.

After supper, Amy asks Theo to walk with her around the camp to stretch her legs, and talk Theo is beginning to see a pattern developing, Amy wants his company for her walks, and of course the conversations, which are about their dreams and desires. Theo is becoming more comfortable around the girl, but he still hasn't figured out the strange feeling that overcomes him in her presence.

Then it's off to his bedroll, keeping his journal up to date, to sleep, and the dawn to start over again. Six days from St Louis and the train is making good time, the only mishap is when one of the youngsters of the Mayhew family falls off the tail gate of their wagon and comes close to being stepped on by the oxen from the following wagon. Other then a few bumps and bruises the youngster is alright. The father closes the tail gate and tells the youngsters to tie themselves to the wagon so they can't fall out again.

About time for the midday stop, Theo hears three loud shrieking whistles from the vicinity of the river. Cougar comes riding back to the train and tells Theo to stop his wagon, and get on his horse and come with him to investigate the whistles. "Ethan", Cougar yells, "keep the train moving, there is a grove of trees ahead where you can stop for the noon rest. "Theo and I are going to see what those whistles are about. Just then they heard the shrieks again. Theo looks at Cougar, and tells him "it sounds like a steamboat, and if I remember right, three loud whistles like that means they are in trouble".

"I think you're right. Jump on your Morgan and let's go find out." A couple of miles later and they are at the river, not seeing anything at first they wait for the next set of whistles, shortly they hear the shrieks, and it is corning from upstream around a bend. Being cautious they ride toward the sound, and around the bend sure enough is a steamboat, and it seems to be stuck on a mud bar. The rear of the boat is high and dry on the bar, making the paddles almost useless. Theo looks at the boat and realizes it is the River Princess. "Cougar, that's the River Princess, and it looks like they are stuck" So they get as close to the boat as they can and yell to get their attention, but nobody hears them over the noise of the engine, so Theo takes out his Colt and fires off three shots. The captain hears the gun, and looking at Theo gives the whistle a couple of toots. Then taking a megaphone he yells through it," Theo, Cougar is that you two up there?" They shake their heads yes. The captain yells "Wait, and I will be there in the small boat".

The captain comes ashore in a small boat and shakes Theo and Cougars hands and exclaims, "Am I glad to see you, as you can see my boat is in quite a predicament." "Last night when I Anchored, we thought we were secure, this morning we found ourselves adrift and before I could get up steam we ran aground, what makes it so bad is that it lifted the side wheels out of the water so high that we can't get enough power to pull us off the bar. What we need is a tug from your mules or oxen to help us get unstuck "

"We can do that captain", says Cougar. " Theo why don't you stay here and look the situation over, and I'll go get us some animals to pull the boat with. It will probably take a couple of hours." " Hurry back old man," Cougar looks at Theo, "There you go again, one of these days boy! one of these days."

The captain tells Theo he is sure glad to see him again, and I bet the Card Man will be too. "Meantime we need to figure out how to get the boat back into midstream". Theo looks at the boat and the way it is stuck and suggests that they need to take a line across the river and run it around a stout tree and then bring it back to the teams that cougar will bring back. The captain remarks, "that's kind of what I had in mind, except we will use a pulley block to run the hawser through for less friction on the line". So while they are waiting for Cougar, the captain has a couple of crew members take a small line across the river, which is attached to the larger hawser, and securing a large pulley block to a stout tree, they thread the hawser through the pulley and start back across the river to the other side, once there, they secure the line and wait for Cougar. Shortly Cougar shows up with four teams, two of mules and two of oxen. " Sorry I took so long sonny, but you know how oxen are, they only have one speed, slow" , "Yep!" "That's how I see you, say's Theo, just like oxen, slow". "Why you! you!" "Damm it, you did it again, just wait, I'll get even, Captain do you see what I have to put up with this sassy youngster, humph!"

Cougar, Ethan, Carlyle and Amy back their animals down as close to the river as they can, and hook up the hawser. Meantime the captain had the engine man get up steam, the captain went back aboard the boat and when everybody was ready, gave a couple of toots on the steam whistle, the wagon men and Amy got the oxen and mules pulling, While the captain started the paddle wheels turning. The boat started to move, very slowly at first, then it almost jumped into the river channel, it was free of the mud, with a loud shriek of the whistle, the captain maneuvered the boat into midstream, and had the first mate hold it there, while he came ashore in the small boat and thanked everybody. "Cougar, Theo" says the captain, "West Port Landing is only a day away, I'll wait for you there and we will have a celebration on board the boat for your wagon folks, to thank them for my rescue," "That's not necessary captain, said Cougar" " I know, but I want to." So next stop West Port Landing, at the foot of Kansas City, Missouri's main street.

CHAPTER TWENTY ONE

So Cougar, Theo, Amy, Ethan, and Carlyle head back to the wagon train to give them the news that they are invited to a party by the captain. Amy has Theo ride along side her as she takes the mules back. She asks how well he knew the captain? Theo tells her he spent six weeks aboard the River Princess, coming up from Vicksburg, and that the Captain often let him take the wheel and steer the boat, while he had a pipe and told Theo stories of the river. "Oh!" said Amy, "he seems like a very nice man",

Back at the wagon camp Theo leaves to go get the wagon he is responsible for, and about an hour later he is back, he unhooks the mules and gets all the animals watered, and grained, and then picketed where there is grass, then wash up for supper. After supper Amy is ready for her evening walk. Theo asks her about her teaching job, and she tells him, that the school is in Auburn, California, and she will be teaching all grades, and that she will also be tutoring two children in French. Their parents are going to France to learn about the making of wine and champagne, it seems the area around Auburn has the ability to grow excellent wine grapes, and they feel that it could become a good business to be in. So I will teach the children to read, write, and speak French, as they will be there a year or more

Theo looks at Amy "I didn't know you could speak French". "Could you teach me enough to be able to talk to and understand the French trappers and miners that I might encounter?" ""Of course I can", says Amy, "it would be my pleasure to teach you Theo." So without realizing it Theo has committed himself to spending an hour each evening learning how to speak French, and Amy is looking forward to spending more time with Theo, as again she feels the spark of attraction growing larger.

The next day and everybody is excited to get on the trail, and proceed to *West Port Landing for the party aboard the River Princess. Arriving midafternoon, everybody hurries to take care of the chores, feeding and watering the animals, and getting cleaned up for the party.

The evening arrives and the wagon train members are boarding the steamboat. The Captain greets everybody and sends them to the salon, where he has set out a. sumptuous buffet. After everybody has eaten, three crew members take up their instruments, a fiddle, guitar, and squeeze box and start playing music, and so the hoedown begins.

Now West Port Landing being at the foot of Kansas City, which a fair size town, has an ice house, the Captain has obtained enough ice to cool off two barrels of beer, so with cold beer and music the party is really moving along. Amy is standing next to Theo, and she turns to him and says," lets dance Theo." Theo stammers, "Aw! Amy I never learned how to dance." "Come on, I'll teach you", and with that she drags him onto the floor, and begins to show him the steps of this dance, Now Theo is usually light on his feet, but he finds that for dancing he doesn't know his right from his left, and try as he might he cannot seem to get the hang of the movements.

When the music stops, they head to one of the beer barrels and get a beer, standing next to the barrel is a fellow who is about Theo's size, who says to Amy, how about you dancing with me little lady? I can waltz rings around this rube, what calls himself a man, and with that the music starts and the rude man grabs Amy's wrist and starts for the dance floor. Amy tells the man, "take your hand off me you rude clod, I wouldn't dance with you if you were the last man on earth". The man tells Amy, "lady out here you would do well to do as a man tells you, or suffer, and he continues to drag Amy out on the floor, Amy's had enough, and she kicks the clod in his knee". With the sudden pain the man starts to slap Amy, only to have his wrist caught by the iron grip of Theo, Twisting the man's arm, Theo gets it behind the man's back, and tells him the lady doesn't want to dance with you. "And I may be a rube, but at least I have better manners then to go around insulting people". "Now I think it's time you leave this party", and grabbing the man's collar and holding his arm behind his back he escorts him to the gangway. "Leave and don't come back" Theo tells the guy as he lets go of him.

Now this guy is not going to let a rube tell him what to do, so as Theo lets go of him, he swiftly turns and hits Theo with a solid left hand to the jaw, knocking Theo up against the cabin of the boat, as Theo is shaking off the blow the guy is coming in to hit Theo with a right to the side of the face, Theo blocks the blow, and manages to land a hard right hand to the guys gut, doubling him up and knocking the wind out of him, then he kicks the man's knee, breaking it and putting the man down for good, still the guy won't give up, he reaches under his coat and pulls out a small pistol and starts to point it at Theo, just then there is a shot from behind Theo, that kills the man. Theo turns and sees the Card Man holding a smoking derringer. Theo looks at the Card Man and says thank you, "It looks like I owe you one now". The Card man says no son, "I think we are even now".

At the sound of the shot, Amy, the Captain, Cougar, and the rest of the people in the salon come pouring out the doors to see what happened. Amy runs up to Theo and cries, "are you alright?" "Yes, but this idiot isn't, he pulled a gun on me, and the Card Man shot him, lucky for me he was behind me and saw the gun,"

The captain looks at the guy, and states, "I know this guy, every time I tie up here he comes on board and gets drunk, loses a lot at poker, then accuses the Card Man or one of the other dealers of cheating". "I've had to throw him off my boat more then once". "So there is no loss here".

"Everybody go back to the party, and I'll have the crew take care of this problem". As they all go back inside, Theo turns to Amy and introduces her to the Card Man. "Card Man this is Amy, Amy is teaching me how to speak some French, he tells the Card Man". "Do tell says the gambler, I speak a little of the Cajun patois, which is a mixture of French and other common dialects of the New Orleans area, said the gambler to Amy". "Why don't we go find a quiet corner and catch up on the events that have been happening since I last saw you Theo, and bring your lovely lady".

So they climb up to the top deck away from the music and revelry, and find a place to talk "So, Theo how goes the apprenticeship with Cougar? and what brings this dear lady to the wilds of America?" "The learning is going good, Cougar has a lot to teach me, sometimes I josh him a little to much, but he has given back as good, and Amy has a teaching job in California that she is going to."

The Card Man tells Theo, he sure is glad that Theo and Cougar showed up yesterday, to rescue the River Princess, "I sure wouldn't want to be on another boat that sank on the

Missouri, like the Arabia did three years ago". "Oh!" says Theo, "I didn't know you were on a boat that sank". "Yes, I'll never forget it, It was September fifth, 1856, we were heading up river from here to Parkville, Missouri the next stop, we were just sitting down to supper, when we struck a large snag, the boat hit with such force that it knocked everbody down, within minutes the first deck was under water, the Captain said we just lost 222 tons of cargo". "As the boat hit the mud bottom it slowed the sinking, the Captain launched the one life boat and started getting everybody ashore, the only loss of life we had was a mule that was on the aft deck tied to some lumber mill machinery". "As we watched from shore we could see the boat slowly sinking into the mud, by the next morning only the two smoke stacks and pilot house were above water, it was quite a loss, the steamship was only three years old"*

"Well Theo how does the poker playing go?" "I really haven't had time to play, what with driving the wagon for Amy's uncle Ethan, and helping Cougar, plus doing all the blacksmithing on the wagons, so far we have been lucky in that department in that there haven't been to many breakdowns". "Anyway the journey has been pretty good so far, Cougar says we are in the easiest part, when we get to the other side of Kansas is where it starts getting tough"

"Well youngsters I hear the party winding down," "It's probably time to say goodnight, I imagine Cougar will want to get an early start in the morning". "You're probably right, but I bet there are going to be some nasty hangovers tomorrow the way some of the men were into the beer". So they part, Theo escorts Amy to her wagon, where she tells Theo," she had a great time, despite the rude gent". "And Theo we have to work on your dancing." Theo blushes, and is glad it is dark so Amy can't see his red face; again Amy kisses Theo on the cheek, which only deepens his blush.

At his bedroll, he gets out the journal, puts down the two busy days, and ponders the feelings that are getting stronger when he is with Amy. He rolls into his blankets and is soon asleep.

Footnote:
* West Port Landing is renamed Kansas City, Missouri
* The Arabia steamboat sank on Sept. 5th 1856, attempts to salvage it were futile. The ship remained buried for 132 years. Bob Hawley, his sons David and Greg rediscovered the ship in July of 1987, a half mile from the present course of the Missouri river in a corn field, using magnetometers. The ship was 45 feet deep in the soil. 18 months later they began the painstaking recovery operation. It took twenty wells to dewater the dig site. They recovered all of the cargo, one paddle wheel, and the stern, all of which can be seen in the Arabia Steamship museum in Kansas City, Missouri.

CHAPTER TWENTY TWO

The next morning, practically all the men were hung over from too much beer, even some of the women were not feeling too good. As Cougar was one of the worst, Theo could not get him up, he just lay in his bedroll and moaned. He did manage to tell Theo to take over, and that they could use some fresh meat for the camp. So Theo got ahold of Ethan and Carlyle, and told them he was going to go hunting, and that they should hold down the camp as best as possible.

Amy overheard the conservation between Theo and her uncle, and asked Theo if she could go along on the hunt? "I don't know Amy, can you ride a horse and shoot a rifle?" "Of course I can" , "You should know by now that I'm not one of those city wallflowers who only know how to flirt behind a fancy fan".

"Ok, I'll get my Brown Bess, powder, and shot, and you can use it, we'll need a horse for you to ride", Amy asks Theo if he thought Cougar might loan her his Appaloosa, since he isn't going anywhere. "I'll ask him" says Theo." I'll go change into something to ride in and meet you over by the horses". So Amy borrows a pair of jeans and shirt from her uncle, and a hat from one of the youngsters who wears the same size hat as she does, and changes into the clothes,

The jeans and shirt are a little big, as she expected, but confortable, the hat fits, and her heavy boots are just right for riding.

As Amy approaches Theo, he can't help but laugh at the sight Amy makes in her hunting outfit, she tells him "laugh, but just you wait and see if I don't get the first deer for our supper". So off they go, Theo on the Morgan, with the pack mule on a lead, and Amy on the Appaloosa, which is almost to big for her to handle.

After about ten miles, they come to an area of low hills, woods and small meadows, just the kind of place where deer like to inhabit. Theo had borrowed a telescope from one of the men in the train, and points to a hill that overlooks most of the area, and tells Amy to head for it, stop just below the top, and we will dismount and creep up to the top and see if we can spot any game. "Ok" says Amy. Lying on the top of the hill and using the scope they survey the area and found just what they were looking for, about two miles away there stood several deer browsing in a small meadow. Theo tells Amy, "we'll circle around the herd and get down wind of them and see if we can get a shot". So they ride a couple of miles around the deer, then picket the horses and mule, then start the hunt in earnest, creeping through a wood, they come up down wind of the herd, but are too far from them to get a shot even with the Hawken. "Darn" whispers Theo, "we are to far away, and there isn't enough cover to crawl closer to get a shot"

Amy asks Theo," have you got a piece of white cloth?" Theo looks at Amy, and asks her whatever for does she need a white cloth? Amy tells him, "it's a trick I learned from my father", "Deer are curious, and if you hang a white cloth on a branch, where it can be seen by the deer, they will come closer to see what it is, Pa used the trick all the time, and never came home with out a deer".

"The only white I have is my under shirt". "That will do" Amy said, So Theo takes off his buckskin shirt, and then his under shirt and hands it to Amy. She takes the under shirt and carefully ties it to a branch of a small oak tree in plain sight of the deer, then they crawl back in the woods and wait.

Soon they see that the deer have seen the white cloth, and are slowly coming toward them, while still browsing. Theo has his eye on a large buck, which seems to be the most curious, and is getting closer. Theo whispers in. Amys ear, "I'll get the buck, and you get the doe over to the right of him, wait for my signal, and we will fire together". Theo crawls over to the right a few yards and waits for the deer to get within range. Then with a small movement of his left hand, he signals Amy, on the count of three, they both fire. Both the deer fall, the rest of the herd {scramble, and Amy being excited, jumps up to go look at her deer. Theo yells at her, "reload first Amy", she yells back, "it's alright, the doe is dead, and there is no danger". But as she approaches the doe, the buck staggers to his feet and makes a run at Amy. Theo sees the buck get up, and as he yells at Amy to hit the dirt, he is running and firing his Dragoon at the buck, it takes three shots to bring down the buck, and he falls so close to Amy that she feels his last breathe on her face.

Theo is running up to Amy as she rolls away from the buck, and as she gets up, he is gathering her into his arms, and asking her if she is alright? "Yes", as she starts to cry.

"He was so close Theo, I thought I was a goner". "It's alright Amy, I'm here and I'm not going to let anything bad happen to you, come on, we'll go get the horses and the mule, and you can calm down". "It was a close call, but everything is alright now".

A few minutes later they are back with the horses and the mule, and as Theo guts the deer, Amy gets the rope to tie the two deer onto the mule, then together they get the deer loaded and tied down, before getting on her horse to head back to camp, Amy walks over to Theo and gives him a hug and another kiss on the cheek, and says "thanks for saving my life once again, you know Theo, you are becoming my knight in shining armor, except you don't have a white horse". Again Theo is blushing at the complement Amy is giving him, while she is pleased with herself for the little joke she made about the horse's color.

Back at camp, all is well; the hangovers are slowly going away, Cougar is up and checking with everybody to see if there are any problems that need attention. As he looks to the south he sees Theo and Amy coming back with the mule loaded. He shouts to the camp, "here come Theo and Amy with our supper, get the fire going, and let's make this a feast". So once again the wagon train is eating a great meal.

The next morning everybody is feeling better and eager to get back on the trail, so after a hearty breakfast, they are on their way. Cougar has already told them they are following the Oregon trail, and that the next sign of people will be Fort Kearney. The next two weeks pass without to much in the way of mishaps, a broken wheel on one wagon, spilled water from a barrel that the cover had not been secured on, Cougar scouting out further, and getting a deer for the people on the train just about every other day. Theo leading the train down the well marked trail. Each camp site is near water and grass, as it is still spring and the grass is still growing. Fort Kearney. The fort commander directs them to a camp site within sight of the fort, where there is water and grass for the animals. The wagon people make camp, then head for the Sutlers store, the military usually let civilians buy goods at their store, so it's extra Arbuckles coffee, bacon, beans, and hard candy for the sweet tooth. The commander gives Cougar the news of the trail ahead. His patrols state that the trail is mostly quiet, the Buffalo are moving, so be aware of a possible stampede, especially during a thunder storm. So far the Indians have been quiet this spring, but you never know.

Cougar thanks the commander, and takes his leave, back at camp he fills in the people about what to expect on the trail. After a good nights sleep they are on the way again, day after day they keep moving, one day after another, sometimes the boredom is overwhelming. Theo and Amy are progressing in his French lessons; the wagon people are seeing the two as a couple, although Theo still hasn't figured out that he is in love with Amy.

One day Cougar hears a distant rumble, and having seen Buffalo on the run before, he rushes back to the wagon train, " Theo!" he yell's, "turn your wagon and head for those woods over there, and get the wagons into the woods". Theo asks "why?" "Do you hear that rumble?" "Yes" says Theo, "I thought it was thunder, but I noticed it didn't stop". Cougar tells him, "it is Buffalo on the run, and they are heading this way, so hurry into the woods," with that he drops back to Amy and tells her to follow Theo and do as he is doing. He then proceeds to warn the whole train. The mules which can run faster then Oxen, make it to the woods in plenty of time, but the oxen are too slow, and the Buffalo are almost upon them. Cougar starts shooting his six gun at the Buffalo to try and turn them. Theo sees what Cougar is trying to do and yell's at the rest of the men to do the same. Theo jumps on his Morgan and rushes out to help Cougar, with his gun added to Cougar's the Buffalo are starting to turn, and as more guns are being added to the fight , the wagon people get the Buffalo turned in time to save the wagons being pulled by the oxen. As soon as the Buffalo are turned, Cougar pulls out his Hawken from his scabbard and takes down a large bull. Theo asks Cougar what he is doing. "Camp meat Theo, go get one," So Theo takes out his Hawken, and rides close to the side of a big cow and takes his shot, the cow goes down, and Theo swings his pony away from the herd, to wait their passing.

After the Buffalo are gone, Cougar gets a team of oxen to pull the dead Buffalo into the camp that is being set up next to the woods. After the excitement of the stampede, the wagon people decide to call it a day, and get ready for a meal of Buffalo meat and potatoes that they got from the Sutlers store at Fort Kearney, plus corn bread, coffee, and dried apple pie.

Cougar asks Theo, "how he liked his first encounter with Buffalo?". Theo tells him, "it was exciting , but knowing the danger we were in, I don't think I want to see another stampede of those brutes again".

After supper it was time for Theo's French lesson, but Amy was too excited over the event of the stampede to concentrate on the lesson, so she suggested they walk and talk. They started to walk around the outside of the woods and shortly came upon a small stream coming out of the woods, turning into the trees; they followed the stream until they came to a small pool.

Amy said to Theo," what I wouldn't give to take a bath in that pool". Theo blushing said "me to, after the dust of today I could use a bath". "Then let's do it", as she starts to disrobe, Theo asks Amy "what are you doing?" "I'm going to take a bath" says Amy, "But you're going to be naked, and that's not proper" exclaims Theo. "Now how can a person take a proper bath with their clothes on asks Amy?" "Come on my knight in dirty buckskins, the last one in has to scrub the others back." Theo throwing caution to the wind, races

Amy in taking off their clothes, and almost at the same moment run into the pool. Now both happen to be good swimmers, and Amy says, "I bet you can't catch me and swims away from Theo". Even though Theo is embarrassed with being naked, he isn't going to let Amy's challenge go unanswered, so after her he goes, being the stronger of the two he catches her, and after a silly little struggle, Amy puts her arms around Theo's neck and kisses him on the lips. With the intimate closeness of their wet bodies, and the passion that is in their kiss, Theo is experiencing the natural arousal that two people in love do to each other, Amy says, "Come Theo it's time".

And so in the grassy glen next to the pool, Amy and Theo discover the age old thrill of being in love. Afterward they silently dress, and slowly walk back to the camp holding hands. Back at camp, the wagon people notice a different look about the couple, and good manners prevent them from saying anything, but in their wagons, or common bedrolls, the married folk whisper to each other, remember when we looked like that, or love is blind but the neighbors ain't. And so a new chapter has opened up in Theo's life.

Because of the amount of meat in the two Buffalo, the train takes a day off from traveling and make jerky out of the meat. Since Theo had lots of experience with smoking deer that he and

Cuss shot, he showed the wagon people how to make a smoke house which would cure the meat faster, plus give it a better flavor, so by midday the next day the process was done enough that they could get in half a days travel.

Following the Platte River, and still on the Oregon trail, they soon find they are approaching Scottsbluff. The bluffs which suddenly rise out of the plains are an awesome sight after miles of prairie land. Cougar explains how the bluffs are named after a fur trapper who died here after being deserted by his companions, as you can see the trail goes up the bluffs, at a place called Mitchell's pass, now we start to get into some of the difficult part of the trail. We'll camp at the base of the bluffs and start up in the morning. We'll have to double up the teams on each wagon so they have enough power to make the climb, more than likely it's going to take two maybe three days to get everybody over the top. From there it is easier going till we get to the base of the pass over the Rockies.

CHAPTER TWENTY THREE

So camp is set up as usual, Cougar calls a meeting after supper to explain how they are going to climb the 'bluffs. We will start with Theo's wagon. We will take the team of mules from Amy's wagon and hook them to Theo's team. Theo you will ride your Morgan and lead the mules, Amy will handle the lines and the brake when needed. When you get to the top, you will find a large flat area, pull your wagon over to the side and set the brake, and chock the wheels; you'll find large stones to use, left by the previous trains. When the wagon is set, unhook the teams and start back down the hill, halfway down you will find a pull out where the teams and a wagon can pass each other. When you start down I will fire a shot as a signal for the second wagon to start its climb. With this method we should have a wagon going up, while a team is coming back down to hook up to another wagon.

Ethan, you have your wagon ready to go after Theo's, Hooper you next, by that time Theo and Amy should be hooked up and ready to take Amy's wagon, the rest of you be ready to go, make sure you hook mules to mules, and oxen to oxen.

Carlyle as usual I would like you to ride drag and have your boys keep watch, those of you who will be the second half, rest up, feed and water your animals with extra portions, they are going to need extra energy for this climb. Also make sure everything is tied down securely in your wagons.

So you will know what to expect on the climb, it is almost two miles to the top, and it usually takes and hour if nothing breaks, the trail is bumpy and narrow in places, so let the animals set their own pace, if the mules balk, stop and take a look to see what they are unhappy about, and try to correct the problem, with the oxen, the lead rider will have to be very watchful, as the oxen will keep going, even if there is a problem.

Theo be ready at first light, I'll be scouting the trail ahead of you to make sure we can make the climb. When I reach the top, Ill fire a shot to let you know it's safe to start, two shots, means there is a problem, don't start up, three shots means I need help, come quickly, and be ready to fight. Alright everybody get lots of rest, tomorrow is going to be a rough day

Theo and Amy take their usual walk, steal a few kisses and head for their separate bedrolls, Theo writes in his journal, then goes to sleep.

Morning, Theo is up before dawn and getting the mules hooked up, Amy is fixing breakfast, Cougar has left on his scouting of the trail, about a half hour later the camp hears a shot from Cougar. Theo is ready, Amy climbs onto the wagon seat and takes up the lines, and they start.

The first part of the trail is fairly easy, after a quarter mile the trail starts to get steeper, the mules slow down, pretty soon they are just barely moving, then the trail flattens out somewhat but gets so narrow that Theo is very cautious about keeping the wagon on the trail. Amy is trying not to look down, as they get higher, presently the trail widens again, and goes into another steep portion, the wagon is swaying from side to side because of the bumpy surface, Amy is on the verge of screaming with the rocking of the wagon, but she hangs on, after what seems like an eternity, they finally reach the top. Cougar is waiting for them, and asks Theo, "How did it go?"

Theo says. "It was a piece of cake." Amy cannot contain herself any longer, and screams, "piece of cake! Sure you were on your sure footed horse while I'm on a rocking wagon watching the canyon trying to swallow me on one side and the cliff walls trying to crush me on the other".

"On the next trip, I'm going to ride the horse and lead the mules, while you drive the wagon".

Theo looks at Cougar, then Amy, and says to her, "calm down honey, we made it and you were marvelous, you handled the teams better then any man I know." Amy looks at Theo, and asks "really?" "Yes really, you were fantastic".

Cougar tells Theo, "now look at what you've done, there's not a manjack in the train that's going to be able to do a better job than Amy has and be able to brag about it, you've gone and given her a swelled head". With that they all laugh.

"Ok get the wagon pulled over and chock the wheels, I'll signal the other wagon to start up, while you take your team down". So they set the wagon, and unhook the mules, and with Amy on the Morgan behind Theo they start down to the pullout. They get there several minutes before Ethan and his wagon. Hooper is on the seat, with the lines, while Ethan is leading the mules. As they pass, Ethan asks Theo how was it? "A piece of cake", meanwhile Amy is watching Hooper, who has a grimace on his white as a sheet face, and she feels better about the way she handled the trip up.

Theo and Amy lead the mules down, and as they reach the bottom they hear Cougar's signal to start another wagon up. So the next wagon starts up. Theo and Amy stop to take a drink and a quick bite, then hook the mules to Amy's wagon. They are ready to start up the trail when the next signal is given, this time Theo is on the wagon seat and Amy is on the Morgan leading the mules, several times the wagon swayed so severely that Theo got a scared lump in his throat, and Amy secretly laughed to herself, as she saw Theo's face turn white during those moments.

Finally they reached the top, Theo tells Amy, "lady you have no idea how much I respect how you handled that first trip up". "I thought I was going to be thrown off the wagon and die trying to learn how to fly before getting to the bottom of the canyon." Amy laughs.

Cougar comes up and tells the couple to hook up their mules to the other wagon and follow the trail about a half mile and you will see a place to camp, there is a stream, and good grass. So far we are doing good We should have half the wagons up by nightfall.

So Theo and Amy go to set up the camp, soon Ethan and Hooper join them, then two more wagons show up. By nightfall there are ten wagons and their owners in camp, as Cougar predicted. As everybody is exhausted, supper is warmed up left over beans, fresh pan bread, and coffee. Then too sleep.

The next morning, they are up before dawn again. Cougar has Theo and Ethan hook up a double team of mules to start down the trail, when it's light enough at the bottom, the first wagon starts up. Theo and Ethan are waiting at the pull out, as the uphill wagon approaches, it gives a lurch and the woman on the seat screams, "please husband I can't do this anymore", hearing the terror in her voice, Ethan tells Theo to finish taking the mules down. I'll help drive this wagon up , by this time the wagon has stopped, and Ethan walks over to the lady and tells her to come on down and walk, "I'll take it from here". The woman is so relieved she bursts out crying, and runs up to her husband, who hugs her and tells her it will be alright. So they start up again.

Theo gets to the bottom with the mules and hooks up a wagon, and with the man driving and Theo leading they start up at the next signal. And so it goes, a wagon up, a set of mules down, then it's the oxen bringing up the wagons, as they are slower the lurching of the wagons is less, but they have to be guided more carefully. The only mishap with the oxen was when one of the lead oxen got too close to the edge of the trail and fell, luckily the driver was able to stop the wagon and the rest of the oxen before it took a tumble over the cliff. From then on the man leading kept the oxen as close to the bluff wall as he could.

The Carlyles being the last wagon, pulled into camp just as it was getting dark, and the wagon people had a nice welcome for them, supper, with dried apple pie for desert was waiting for them, and while they ate, the men took care of their animals for them. And so Scotts Bluff trail was conquered, without any major mishaps. Cougar tells the wagon people they did good, tomorrow will be much easier, and we'll only travel a half day so as to let the animals recuperate from the hard climb.

CHAPTER TWENTY FOUR

The next day the train gets around to moving out after the noon meal, stopping just before dark they've come about eight miles. The usual routine of taking care of the animals, supper, an eventually sleep.

Three days later they pull into Fort Laramie. Cougar goes to see the commandant of the large fort, to see what to expect of the trail ahead. The fort commander tells Cougar, he has good news and bad news, the Sioux are making noise, and have hit a few settlers. The good news is, I have a patrol going out in the morning that can escort you as far as Fort Casper.

There you should be able to get an escort to Independence Rock. After that you're on your own, and you should be alright, as there hasn't been any trouble that far south, Plus you will be getting into Shoshoni country, and they have always been friendly to white folk, preferring to trade then to fight.

Two days later they come to a set of ruts worn in the sandstone, that is called Signature Ruts, they were made by the hundreds of wagons that were trying to get to California, during the gold rush several years earlier.

Two weeks go by and they are in sight of Fort Casper. The Calvary escort has enjoyed their mission, as they have been getting dried apple pie, to go with their hard tack and jerky rations, plus fresh meat when Cougar can get a deer or buffalo, of which there are a goodly number.

At Fort Casper they take a days rest, while the next patrol is getting ready to leave. The next day they cross the new thousand foot long log bridge over the Platte river and head southwest down the trail. Ten days after leaving Fort Casper they spot Independence Rock, and as is the custom, they camp there for two days while the wagon train people climb the rock and carve their names, and leave messages for others to see

With the escort gone, the train proceeds down the trail, they are following the Sweetwater river in fairly high country. Several days later, one of the Carlyle boys comes galloping into the train, and tells Theo that he just saw some Indians. Go get Cougar, Theo tells the boy, as he pulls off the trail and waits for Amy and Ethan to pull up along side. We have Indian company, he tells them. "I see a small stream ahead, we'll circle the wagons next to it, so we have water, and get ready for what ever is going to happen."

As the train finishes getting into the circle, Cougar and the Carlyle boy arrive, "Theo", Cougar yells, "get on your Morgan and let's go see these Indians, I have a hunch that the Chief of this bunch is an old friend of mine." "What makes you say that Cougar?" "The boy said the fellow he thought was the chief was wearing a large war bonnet, and had a very shiny chest, like a mirror." "There's only one Indian I know who that can be." "His tribe calls him Ironbelly." Theo exclaims, "What an odd name for an Indian." "Yeah!" "But wait until you meet him and you will find out why."

Heading back to where the boy saw the Indians, they come to a small rise, and about a quarter mile away they see the Indians on another rise, taking out his telescope. Cougar looks at the Chief through it, and sees his old friend, who by the way is looking at Cougar through his scope. Recognizing each other, they put up their right hand, palm forward in greeting. Then slowly at first they head for each other, as they get closer they start to gallop, then Cougar is yelling, and Theo can hear the Chief yelling, as they approach each other they count coup by striking each other with their hands, turning their horses, they dismount and start to wrestle, all the while laughing and yelling at each other. Shortly they stop, and Cougar motions to Theo to come on down, the chief does the same to his small bunch. While the others are converging on the pair, they sit down and start to pass a pipe in friendship.

When Theo gets close enough, he sees the chief is wearing a metal front torso piece of armor, and while it shines from being well cared for, it looks like an old Spanish Conquistadors armor piece that Theo saw a drawing of in one of his mothers books a long time ago.

" Theo" get down and come meet my friend lronbelly." "Chief this is Theo Calhoun, my apprentice and second in command of our wagon train" " Theo, meet Chief Ironbelly." The Chief puts out his hand to shake Theo's, and Theo does likewise, as they shake, the Chief says in almost perfect English, "pleased to meet you master Theo". Theo is stunned by the mans words, and getting his wits about him, he returns the greeting.

Before Theo can ask The Chief where he learned to speak English, the Chief says, "I'll explain later". Cougar tells Theo to ride back to the train and tell the wagon folk that we are going to have company for supper. Turning to the Chief, he asks "how many are you?" Chief Ironbelly tells him, twenty five with the squaws and a couple of youngsters. Turning back to Theo, he tells him to ask the wagon folk to start to prepare a feast Ironbelly and I will find a couple of deer for meat, and be there as soon as possible. So Theo heads back to camp, and when he gets there he relays Cougars message and tells the folk that they are about to meet the most unusual Indian Chief he has ever heard about.

CHAPTER TWENTY FIVE

Over the next couple of hours the Indians arrive and start to set up camp, meanwhile the wagon folk are putting together a feast. The men have gathered firewood and have several cooking fires going; the women are preparing beans with salt pork, cumin, mild chile peppers. and canned tomatoes. Mrs. Carlyle is putting together numerous dried apple pies, which the other ladies are baking, and there are also canned peaches for more desert.

Shortly Cougar and Chief Ironbelly show up with two deer slung over the backs of their horses. Theo notices that the Chief is now riding an Appaloosa, that could be the twin of Cougars horse. The Chief takes his deer to his squaws, who quickly skin and butcher it, getting it ready for the roasting. Cougar does likewise with the wagon women, and shortly both deer are being cooked. The cooking aromas are soon making everybody salivate in anticipation of the upcoming feast. Soon all is ready, Chief Ironbelly asks for silence from the gathering, and says a prayer of thanks first in his native dialect, and then in perfect English, he gives thanks to the white man's god, to the amazement of the wagon folk.

The Chief asks Cougar, Theo, Amy, and Ethan to sit with him, and then he has his wives serve them. Theo tells the Chief, "we can get our own food, it is not necessary to have your wives serve us" The Chief looks at Theo and tells him, it is alright son, while the squaws are fixing our plates, I can answer some of the questions you have.

First, the Appaloosas are rare twins from the same mare. "How did you know I was wondering about the two horses." "It was obvious", says the Chief. "Next I was taught English by an Episcopalian minster and his wife, shortly after I met Cougar the first time". "Ah! here is the food, eat and afterwards I will tell you of the first meeting of myself and the great Cougar killer."

The feast begins. As the meal is eaten, there is mostly silence, then it is time for desert, and the Chief is handed apiece of dried apple pie. "Ah!" he says "I haven't had apple pie since leaving the minster and his wife." Finishing the pie, he asks for seconds. Mrs. Carlyle says to the Chief, "I'll be right back with some more." When she returns, she brings the Chief a whole pie fresh out of the oven she has improvised for baking pies and bread. The Chief thanks her, asks her if she would like to become one of his wives, as none of his squaws know how to bake pies.

Mrs. Carlyle blushes, and tells the Chief. "I'm already married to Mr. Carlyle, but I can teach one of your wives how to bake pies if you would like" The Chief tells his number one wife to go with the kind lady and learn how to bake pies. The squaw says, "Yes Robert, I will do as you say".

Theo, looks at the Chief, "your wife called you Robert." "Yes". "She likes to use her English whenever she can, and Robert was the name given me by the ministers wife".

"And now to the story of the great Cougar killer and my meeting." "1 was on my teens warrior vision quest, high up

155

in the mountains, when I came across this cave". "Entering I could smell the scent of bear, but looking around I saw that it was not there." "So I gathered wood for a small fire, and pine cones to make a torch with." "I then began my fast and the quest for my vision. "After three days of fasting, with only water for my thirst," "1 had my vision, in it was a great grizzly bear, a dead soldier, with a shinny chest, Cougar, and the minister and his wife, and that I would become a chief someday."

"After I awoke from the vision, I took water and pemmican and ate, then slept," "The next day I explored the deeper part of the cave. "That's when I came upon the skeleton of the dead soldier, still wearing his armor." "I tried on his head piece, and found it too heavy and uncomfortable, then I removed his torso piece and put it on, and found that it fit, and did not resrict my movements." "Lying alongside the skeleton was a war lance with a metal point." "I picked it up and found it to my liking." "I then proceeded to leave the cave for my trip back to my village, and that's when the grizzly of my vision showed up." " It seems that I was in his cave, and he didn't like it." " With a great roar, he stood up and attacked". "As I only had the lance for a weapon, I thrust it at him, and managed to pierce his thick hide just below his chest." "He kept coming at me while still roaring, and swung his right paw at me." " He hit me so hard that I was knocked back several feet landing on my back." "The armor saved me from serious harm,"

Cougar interrupts at this point, and says. "This is where I come in to the story" ." I was passing under the cave when I heard the first growl of the grizzly." "looking up I saw it attack this young Indian, who was screaming at the bear." "I saw the boy thrust the lance, striking the bear." "I was off my horse and running up to the cave, getting there just in time to see the bear strike the boy with his paw." "As the boy was hitting the ground I raised my Hawken and shot the bear in the side of his head." "As he died, he fell forward on top of the Indian boy." "It was all I could do to roll the bear off of the youngster." "I reloaded the Hawken and then saw to the boy." "He was alright except for having the wind knocked out of him." "I was amazed at the armor the boy was wearing, and I noticed claw marks on the iron where the bear had hit him." When he was able to hear me. I said "The lron Belly saved your life, look at the claw marks where the bear hit you." "As he looked down he saw the marks I showed him, then he told me of his vision quest, and that the great Cougar man was in his vision, and he thanked me for saving his life, and invited me to his village for food and a gift for helping him."

"So that's how Cougar and I met, and where I got the name Iron Belly" . "And that's how I got the Appaloosa horse", says Cougar, "Iron Belly's mare had the colts about a year before we met, and because they were twins they were considered something special by the tribe."

Iron Belly then tells of the vision he had several days ago that told him that his friend Cougar would soon be here and that he was supposed to meet him and his new friends. "The vision also told me that I am to perform a marriage ceremony for his friends Theo and Amy". Theo and Amy both exclaim, "What did you say?" The Chief says, "That I am to marry the two of you tomorrow as the sun comes up." "but! but! We haven't decided to get married yet exclaims Theo" Amy turns to Theo, "but we have talked about it, and since the Chief has been sent here to perform the ceremony we don't want to insult him by refusing him that right, do we?" Theo looks at Amy, "I guess you're right, I just didn't expect it to be so soon."

The Chief tells them that it will be a glorious ceremony, and just to let you know, it will be legal in the eyes of the mighty spirits, and the white man's god also, second wife, show them the marriage papers from the white minister, and the head of the Mormon church. The squaw hands the papers to Amy and Theo and they see that Iron Belly is a marrying minister for the Episcopalian church and that he is an honorary bishop of the Mormon church with the right to marry folks. Signed by Brigham Young, head of the Mormon church.

The Chief stands up and raises his hands and says "let me have your attention wagon folks, we are going to have a wedding at sunrise." "Theo and Amy are going to tie the knot"

With that the wagon folks give a cheer, and the women come up to Amy, and congratulate her and rush her off to help her get ready for the wedding. The men do the same with Theo. Cougar says to Iron Belly, "there you go again, always marrying people off, you've been hanging around with them Mormon's too much, that's all they think about is marrying."

With the anticipation of the upcoming wedding there is not much sleep gotten that night. The grey light of dawn, just before the sun shows its face, the wagon folk and the Indians are gathered in front of the Chief. Ethan is bringing Amy to the front of the crowd. Cougar is standing up as best man for Theo, and just as the sun starts to peek over the mountains to the east in one of the most spectacular sunrises ever, the Chief starts the ceremony, first in his native tongue, then in English, he finishes the marriage vows just as the sun clears the peaks, as Theo and Amy kiss, the wagon folk give out with a loud cheer, and the Indians start whooping as is their custom.

As the couple and the crowd start walking away, the Chief asks Ethan, if he could have a word with him in private. "Of course" says Ethan, "what is on your mind?"

The Chief tells Ethan, that in his vision the other day, he was told by the spirits to give Ethan this letter, as he hands it to him, "you are to deliver it to Brigham Young, and after he reads the greeting from me, he will put you in touch with a Mr. Green, who will make you a business proposition". "I am asking you to accept it, so that you can go on to the Auburn place and be there for Theo and Amy." " They are going to have need of your strength in the future". Ethan looks at the Chief, and asks, "why?" The Chief tells him that is all the spirits told him. Ethan is perplexed, but agrees to do as the Chief asks.

After a wedding breakfast, the wagon train gets ready to get back on the trail. Theo and Amy walk up to the Chief and thank him for the beautiful ceremony, and that they hope to see him again sometime. The Chief tells them that it is unlikely that they will meet again until they see each other on the other side. "Oh!" says Amy, "well in that case happy hunting." And Theo says, "for me too." The Chief has one last thing to say to Theo. "Brutus says hello, and good luck, and enjoy the beauty within." Theo's mouth drops, "when did you see Brutus?" The Chief tells Theo, "we speak to the same spirits son". "Oh!" says Theo. Amy looks at Theo with questioning eyes, and asks him what that was all about? Theo tells her, "I'll explain it later, it's time to go". So it's back on the trail, the Indians remaining in the camp, while the wagon people wave good bye.

As the wagon train goes out of sight, the Chief turns to his number one wife, "Winona, did you learn how to make pies?. "Yes Robert, I have, and knowing you, you will get so fat from them that you will not fit into your shining iron any more". With that they both laugh.

CHAPTER TWENTY SIX

That night, after supper, and chores, Theo and Amy take their bedrolls off away from camp so they can have some privacy, and after an intimate interlude, they are lying there looking at the stars. Amy props herself up on her elbow, and asks, "Ok, now tell me what that was all about this morning between you and the Chief." So Theo tells Amy about Brutus, the blacksmith, and his ability to see things, and how they met, and now the Chief, who has the same powers, and is in touch with Brutus, through the same guiding spirits.

Amy looks at Theo, and asks him if he believes in what he has just told her? " I have too Amy, I've seen too much of it come true, not too." "Oh!", exclaims Amy.

"Anyway here we are, can you believe, we are a married couple, I don't feel any different, but at the same time I do." "Amy, have I told you I love you?" "This is the first time in words, but I've known for a long time your feelings toward me, probably longer then you yourself have." " Now hold me and go to sleep, we have another long day ahead of us".

A week later they are going through South Pass, everybody was kind of expecting a narrow passageway, so they were surprised to find South Pass was almost twenty miles wide, at an elevation of over 7500 feet, then it was down to cross the Big Sandy river, then five days later they arrived at the Mormon Ferry that would take them across the Green River.

When Ethan showed the letter he was delivering to Brigham Young, to the Ferry owner, he agreed to let them cross for half price, which made the wagon folk happy. Two weeks later they were approaching the Wasatch Range, Cougar tells the wagon folk, we are going to have to be very careful going through these mountains, there are steep trails, worse then Scotts Bluff, we will have to double and triple the teams at times for some of the climbs. We are also going to hook up a team or two to the back of the wagon to act as brakes, they will be facing backwards to hold the wagons from going down too fast, in other words we have a lot of work ahead of us. It takes three weeks to go fifteen miles, and they are only half way through, there are mishaps, such as broken axles and wheels, a mule that goes down with a broken leg. Cougar puts it out of it's misery with a shot to the head. Theo's mule takes it's place in the team, meanwhile Cougar has a couple of men butcher the mule for fresh meat, against the objections of some of the wagon folk. With fresh meat scarce here Cougar convinces everybody that the mule will be put to good use, so roast mule for supper, and it wasn't too bad.

Finally they get through the worst of the mountain range, and it's down hill to the Great Salt Lake City. As they get near the city, they find a place to camp. The next morning Cougar, Theo, Ethan, and Amy ride into the town and go looking for Brigham Young, Cougar thinks he knows where to find him this early in the day. Riding into the center of the city, they find Mr. Young, sitting in the church square, giving instructions to some of his followers. Seeing Cougar and the others coming down the street, he excuses himself, and walks to meet Cougar,

"Cougar, to what do I owe this visit from you?" "It's been too long since you graced us with your presence." "Ah! Brigham, that it has." "I've brought you these friends of mine to meet with you". "Ethan Winslow, this is Brigham Young". "Brigham, Ethan here has a letter from an old friend of yours, Ironbelly." "That is good news" says Brigham, "and who are these two fine looking young folk?" "They are Mr. and Mrs. Theo Calhoun, recently wedded by the Chief." "Amy here is Ethan's niece, and Theo is my apprentice, so he says" Brigham tells the couple he is delighted to meet them. "Now where is this letter from our Ironbelly?" "Here sir" said, Ethan,

Brigham reads the letter, and says to Ethan, "I see here that you have three wagon loads of goods that you intend to use to set up a business with in Virginia City, And that the Chief wants me to put you in touch with Mr. Green, as he will have a much better offer for you". "The Chief further states that he has a more important job for you to do". "That's what he told me Mr. Young".

"Well then we had better do as the Chief wants, or he will bring down his spirits to chide us for not listening to him" , "Now it just so happens that Mr. Green is here at our meeting, so come with me and make the introduction." "Meanwhile, Cougar, why don't you show these young newlyweds our fair city, and then come by the house for lunch, at say twelve thirty". "Ok Brigham, we'll see you for lunch,"

"Now then Mr. Green, I want you to meet Ethan Winslow, our old friend Ironbelly says you should look at Ethan's goods and make an offer for them that Ethan cannot refuse, it seems the the Chief has a more important job for Ethan to do then be a store keeper in Virginia City,"

So Ethan and Mr. Green ride out to the camp site and look at the goods that Ethan has, after the inspection, Mr. Green tells Ethan the goods are just what he needs to fill out his emporiums inventory. "Do you have an inventory list he asks?" "Why yes I do, excuse me while I fetch it." A few moments later Ethan hands Mr. Green the list, "Are all the goods here as the list states?" "Yes, we were lucky in that Cougar and Theo were able to get us here without any major problems; none of the wagons lost any of their loads". "Good, says Mr. Green, now give me a moment to add this together," A few minutes later Mr. Green has a figure for Ethan, "here is my offer". Ethan looks at the number, and states," why that is more then I expected to get in Virginia City." "Yes, I know" states Mr. Green, "but that's my offer, take it or leave it".

"I'll take it, I'll take it, exclaims, the now excited Ethan." "Where do you want it delivered?" "Come, we'll go to my place, so I can show you where it is". "And then we should be just in time for lunch with Mr. Young."

CHAPTER TWENTY SEVEN

Riding into town, they meet Cougar, Theo, and Amy. Ethan tells them the good news about the purchase of the goods. "That's great" says Theo, "but what about your plan to open a store in Virginia City?" "I don't have to go there now, I figure I will go with you and Amy to Auburn, and see what develops there". "Meanwhile 1 am going with Mr. Green to his store, to see where I have to deliver his goods, we'll meet you at the Beehive house for lunch."

At the house, Mr. Young welcomes his guests. " Come and meet the family'. Upon entering the large house, they are ushered into a large dinning room where there are many women, and children, busy preparing for lunch, the lunch is going to be buffet style. Mr. Young, explains that they usually have lunch this way, and a regular dinner in the evening, when most of the family can be together. Ethan, Theo, Amy, and of course Cougar, meet my wives, Ethan says "wives?" "Cougar has explained that you have many wives, but may I ask why so many?" Mr. Young explains, that do to the fact that we have more women then men, the Prophet told us to take as many wives as we can afford, so that our ladies do not want for a roof over their heads, or food, an especially so they do not have to become homeless and have to turn to tawdry means to support themselves. "Oh!" says Ethan, "well that sure makes good sense."

During lunch Brigham asks Ethan what his plans are now. Ethan tells him, "I'm going to go to Auburn with my niece and Theo", "That's good, they will have need of your strength later on remarks Brigham". Ethan looks at his host, "that's the same thing the Chief told me." Brigham says "yes, I know". Ethan's eyes are wide with astonishment. "Now as to your trip to the west, after you leave the city, you will be entering a great desert, and for over a hundred and sixty miles there is little to no water, by this time of year most of the streams have dried up, until it rains or snows next winter"

"So since you have three almost empty wagons now, I would get as many barrels of water as you can carry, plus grain for the animals that should get you to the Humboldt River, where you can replenish your water, and supplement the grain with grass along the river"

"The only problem with that route is the possibility of running into the Paiutes, so to help you with them, I will give you a flag with the angel Moroni pictured on it, if you fly it on a standard on your lead wagon it will help you". "We Mormons have an understanding with the Paiutes." "That sounds great" Ethan said.

"Cougar, how far are you going with the train?" asks Brigham. "I'm thinking of going all the way to the Sacramento valley with some of these folks, and then on to San Francisco, to see the big city, and partake of the pleasures there," "From there I might take a ship to Panama, and cross the isthmus and catch a ship to New Orleans, and eventually back to St Louis." "That sounds like an interesting adventure" says Brigham.

"I've never been to Frisco, and the other places, except New Orleans remarks Cougar"

"And Theo, what are your plans, now that you are married to the beautiful Amy?"

"I haven't thought about it". "Originally I was going to California to find a good gold mine, and see if I can recover enough gold to live on, but now that Amy and I are together, I guess I'll find a job and try to make enough to set up a home for us." Brigham, asks Theo, "may I offer a suggestion?" "Please do" says Theo. "Knowing that you have the skills of a blacksmith, and the knowledge of gold mining, why don't you put the two together and start your own business, I'm sure that there is a need for mining equipment that you can make and sell". Theo asks, "how did you know of my mining and blacksmith experience?" "Brutus and the Chief let me know." "Oh", says Theo, "I see you're one of them too." "Yes", says Brigham.

"And now my new friends I must beg your forgiveness, as I need to go take care of my duties to my people, one more thing Theo, please give my regards to the Mustanger, when you see him." "Who or <u>what is a</u> Mustanger <u>asks Theo?"</u> <u>"You'll</u> see when the time comes" Says Brigham. Theo thinks to himself, *"Now what am I getting into?"*

That evening at supper, Cougar announces the plans to get back on the trail, and that Ethan's wagons will be hauling extra water and grain, for the arduous trip across the great desert.

Several of the wagon folk want to know if they could stay here, as they see a great opportunity for farming here. Cougar tells them, he will ask the Mormon council in the morning if they would object to having you join them.

The next morning Cougar meets with the council, and explains the wishes of several of the members of his wagon train. The council has no objections to more farmers settling in the area, as long as they can accept our way of living and doing business. Cougar tells them, I think they have already reconciled themselves to that. "Fine" says the leader of the council, "have them come see us and we will find places for them to settle on." "Good" says Cougar.

Cougar goes back to camp, and gives the farmers the good news, and where and who to meet about places to settle on. "Meanwhile the rest of you start getting ready to leave, if all goes well, we can be on the trail in the morning".

Ethan, Theo, and Amy hitch up their wagons, and head to town to find the cooper and get as many barrels as the two wagons will hold, and a wagon load of grain for the animals, plus a Mule to replace the one that they had to put down. When all is ready, they find Mr. Young and say goodbye, whereupon he wishes them Godspeed, and hands them the flag with the angel on it. That night after everybody is down for the night, Theo takes out his journal and brings it up to date, then crawls into the bedroll that Amy and he share.

The next morning they are back on the trail heading for their destination of California.

Twenty days later they have reached the Humboldt river, during the twenty days they have buried the wagons hub deep in sand, crossed dangerous arroyos, climbed mountain passes, and negotiated the down hill sides, plus crossed several dried river beds. Cougar showed the wagon folks how to dig for water in the dried river beds, therefore helping to conserve the water in the barrels. The river showed up just in time as the water was down to about two more days rations. Camping close to the river, the women found a pool where they could bathe, as twenty days without so much more then a wipe down with a damp cloth was getting to them. Then the men were made to take their baths.

With everybody clean and in good spirits, they decided to have the best feast they could have with the supplies they had.

Cougar motions to Theo, "come with me", and grabbing a package out of his Par`fleche, they head up river, until they find a pool with a set of rapids in front of it. Cougar finds two stout willow branches and takes the package he brought along and unwraps it. in it Theo sees several long strings, with fish hooks tied to them, Cougar asks, "do you know how to find bait?" "Yeah, there should be some worms here, and maybe some of those ugly water bugs that the fish love to eat". So digging up some worms and rolling rocks in the shallow water they get the bait they need. After about an hour they have enough fish to feed the camp. So back to camp they go for a fish fry. When the women see the fish they grab them and get them ready to cook. Again Cougar and Theo supply the wagon folk with the makings of a feast.

The next day after replenishing the water barrels, they head down river on the trail. That night they camped near the river again, and Cougar and Theo caught another fish supper,

This time one of the ladies showed the others how to make a fish chowder, using some wild onions they had come across, potatoes, and carrots they had gotten in Great Salt Lake City, the meal was yet another feast,

On the trail again, fairly easy going with the river next to them. And then it happened, The Paiutes showed up, with their war paint on they looked very fierce and menacing. Cougar took the Mormon flag, and waving it slowly approached the Paiutes. The leader of the Indians recognizing the angel Moroni on the flag gave Cougar the sign of peace and rode out to meet him, They parleyed in sign language for some time, then gave each other the peace sign, and rode back to their respective groups. Theo asks Cougar "what did they say?" Cougar tells him, "they wanted to know how the Great Chief Brigham of the many wives was doing? So I told him he is doing just fine and sends his greetings. So this young Chief says they must go see the Great one and make trade with him soon, and after a little chat about nothing, he said go in peace, and turned and left."

So another Indian encounter that has ended well. Back on the trail again. Following the Humboldt they cross many miles of otherwise desert country. One day Theo see's something shining from the sun reflecting off it, being curious, he stops the wagon and goes over to pick the object up, and low a behold it is a good size gold nugget, looking around he finds two more, just lying on top of the ground, he can't believe it, all the gold he helped Cuss to mine was buried deep. By now the whole wagon train is stopped and the folks are getting down and walking up to Theo to see what he is doing. Amy asks Theo, "what are you doing?" He looks at her and tells her, "why I'm mining gold nuggets right off the top of the ground". "What?" "Let me see". So Theo shows Amy and the other folk the three nuggets he has found. All of a sudden, everybody is looking for more nuggets. "I found one", says one of the men, and then there are more exclamations of discovery, soon everybody is finding nuggets, as they expand the area they are looking in. Amy has found four nice sized nuggets. Theo a half a dozen more, and all the folk are finding them. Just then, Cougar comes riding in to see why the train has stopped,

"What in tarnation is going on here?" he shouts One of the men shouts back, "we found gold, look here, real gold nuggets". Cougar looks at Theo, "this is your doing, ain't it, I should have known". " Ok folks, stop what your doing, let's get the wagons set for camp. and we will stay a day or two and let you have some fun," Yea, cry the crowd, we're going to be rich. "No" says Cougar, "but you will have some extra money in your jeans".

By the second afternoon the pickings have fallen off to nothing, so while the folks all have about three or four ounces of gold each, they are disappointed that there isn't any more to be found, One of the men asks Theo if it would pay to dig for the gold? He says no, most of the gold was found on a hard rock surface, and in all probability there is no more to be found, as it cannot sink into the rock. "Oh, I see" says the man. So it's off they go down the trail, with a story of gold they can tell their children and grandchildren

Two weeks later they come to the end of the Humboldt river, it seems to have gone underground in a large area called a sink. Cougar tells them," water will be scarce for the next few days, we'll have to relie on the water in the barrels, so ration it carefully".

The next day as Theo tops a ridge, he sees a cloud of dust heading his way. Cougar comes back to the train, and tells Theo," stop here until the dust storm goes past". As the dust comes closer, Cougar and Theo see that it is being caused by a stampede of wild horses, as they come closer, Cougar tells Theo to get out his colt and be ready to shoot into the air if they don't turn away from the wagons. "Now! Theo, shoot and hope they turn". At the sound of the guns, the horses turn away from the wagons, and run into a canyon to the left of the wagons, soon they slow, and then stop, as they have gotten into a box canyon. As the dust clears, Cougar sees three riders at the tail end of the horses. While two of them keep the canyon closed off to the horses retreating from the canyon, the third rider comes up to the wagon train," Howdy folks, thanks for the help". "I'm Nash Bingston, top mustanger in these parts". "Who might you folks be?" "I'm Cougar, trail boss of this wagon train, and this is, "Theo!" Says the mustanger, "I've been waiting for you." "The Chief said that Brutus told him you were coming." "Oh not another one." " That's right Theo", "I'm another one of the chosen".

"But come folks, set up camp at the opening of the canyon, that will keep the horses from getting loose, and we can share a meal and some tall tails", So Cougar leads the wagons down to the opening of the canyon, and they set up camp.

As supper is being prepared, Cougar and Theo make introductions, and Nash introduces his two compradres, Manilito, and Roy, the best two wranglers a fellow could have for partners.

After supper Nash asks Cougar and Theo if they could help him and his partners build a brush fence over the front of the canyon to keep the wild horses in, once they are contained like now, we can start breaking them to ride. "Sure" says Theo, "if it is alright with Cougar and the rest of the train". So Cougar and Theo ask the wagon folk if they would mind staying here for a day, and help the Mustangers, everybody agreed it would break the monotony of the trail, plus give them an insight into these strange men who chase and catch wild horses.

Next morning after breakfast, the wagon men gather brush and build a fence about six feet high to keep the horses in the canyon. Nash asks Theo if he can shoe horses? Theo says sure, "I've got everything I need in the wagon." Nash then tells Theo that he will pay him for shoeing his and his partner's horses as they are about due. So Theo gets out his tools and goes to work, meanwhile Nash and Manilito, are looking over the herd to see which horses are worth keeping and which ones will be let loose. Roy is taking care of the tack, that they will use to break the animals into riding stock. Nash says to Manilito., "see that pretty little black mare there, that horse would make a good horse for Theo's wife, why don't we work on it first and use it to pay Theo for the work he is doing". "Good idea" says Manilito. So he goes over to Roy and tells him Nash's idea. Roy says "sounds good to me, let's start". So the two of them get a rope on the mare, and while they are holding her, Nash slowly walks up to the mare and starts to talk to her, When she lets him get close enough, he gets an arm around her neck and suddenly hoists himself on to her back, for a second the horse stands there, then it's black powder going off, the horse goes straight up then twists to the right, Nash is almost unseated, but manages to hang on, the horse goes the other way, then starts to buck, coming down on stiff legs, Nash is hanging on for dear life now, after several minutes, the mare starts to tire, and slows down, finally coming to a stop. Nash talks to the mare and rubbing its neck, he gets her to walk slowly around the camp, then he lets her trot a ways, then a short run, next he tries to get her to turn, left then right , but she's not ready yet. So he guides her back to the camp and puts a bridle on her and ties her to the back of Amy's wagon. "Amy, he says, if it's alright with Theo, we'll pay him for his blacksmithing with this horse, and I think it would be a fine horse for you". "So I'm leaving her here so she can get used to you". Amy looks at the horse and falls in love with her, "I'm sure that Theo will agree with you, I know I do".

Nash tells Amy to approach the horse slowly, and if she has some sugar, or maybe a carrot or two, she can start the horse getting used to her being around her. Eventually she will let you touch her, talk to her in a soothing voice, and she will respond. In no time at all, you will be riding her.

So Amy has a new mare. Theo is delighted with the horse as payment for the shoeing work he has done, and tells Nash and the boy's thank you. Later Nash is telling Theo all about mustanging, and how it is feast or famine, money wise, but they love the freedom of being their own men, and the excitement of the chase. Theo says "I can understand that, I get the same feeling when I'm making something new at the forge, or out hunting for deer or Buffalo."

Nash, then tells Theo, why he was sent to meet him, "I'm supposed to let you know that the men who caused you your greatest tragedy are in California, somewhere, and you should watch your back trail as we say out here, also when you get around to prospecting, you should be looking at the area north of Downieville". "A gravel bed such as you worked with Cuss, is there somewhere". "I wish I knew how you and the others know all this stuff, and why I am being given this insight to the future". "Nash tells him the gods don't tell us that, we just go where they occasionally tell us to, and relay the message they give us." "Well I really appreciate what you and the others have done this past couple of years, and if you're ever in touch with any of them, give them my thanks, and a hello". "Will do Theo". "Now I'm hungry, do you think the ladies have supper ready, I could eat a horse".

The next morning, the wagons are loaded, and ready to leave, Amy has her new horse tethered to the rear of her wagon, Nash is giving Cougar locations where he can find water, Theo and Ethan have snugged down their loads, and the rest are anxious to go, so it's head' em out yell's Cougar, and a new day starts.

Ten days later, Lake's Crossing*, a small supply town for the ranches and miners that are in the area, situated on the Truckee river, Mr. Lake has a toll bridge over the river. It's a stop over for the coming and goings of the miners that are mostly working at Virginia City. Ethan, finds out from one of the local merchants, how wide open Virginia City is. There is a shooting over the most trivial arguments everyday, it's a tough place to do business and stay alive. Ethan silently thanks his stars that he sold his goods to Mr. Green in Great Salt Lake City.

Following the Truckee river they start the climb over the infamous Donner summit, having gotten to this point at the end of August, they do not expect to run into snow like the Donner party did. So slowly they climb up what is now a stage road between Lake's Crossing and Sacramento, they push on, near the summit they run into a rain storm that stops their progress for a day, because of the mud. They camp near Donner Lake for the night hoping the rain doesn't turn to snow. It doesn't, but the mud is bad enough to cause them to stay another night The next morning the sun is out, and drying the trail, by noon they start to move out, watching the road very carefully to keep from getting stuck. All goes well, until a wagon wheel slips off a rock and breaks, so they stop, jack up the wagon and replace the wheel, then onward, slowly they make it over the pass, and start down the other side. Several times they meet stages going to Lake's Crossing, and some coming back, in each instance the wagons are asked to pull over and let the stages by. Ten days after leaving Lake's Crossing, they pull into Auburn, California,

Lake's Crossing becomes Reno, Nevada, Named after a famous solder of the times,

174

CHAPTER TWENTY EIGHT

Setting up camp just outside Auburn, Amy, Theo, and Ethan get ready to ride in and locate the city fathers that hired Amy for the teaching job. Stopping at the general store they ask the owner if he can direct them to the men who hired her for the job. The owner said, "I'm one of them, and I'm so glad you are finally here, If you will wait a few minutes, I'll get some of the others, and we can give you a proper welcome". With that he leaves, while his wife introduces herself, and engages the three in conversation. Shortly the store owner comes back with several men, "this is the mayor, Mr. Parker, the feed store owner, Mr. Owens, and Mr. Stark, who runs the land office, there are several others, but they are out at their ranches, farms, or mines".

Amy, tells them she is pleased to meet them. "This is my husband Theo, and my uncle Ethan". The mayor looks at Amy, and said " we understood you were a single lady", "I was, till I met, and fell in love with this wonderful man here, at which Theo blushes.   "Is there a problem with my being married", she asks? "No! no! says the mayor, except that the house that goes with the position is rather small, and I don't know if the two of you will be comfortable enough in it".

Amy tells him, "After living out of a wagon for the last four and a half months, I'm sure it will be fine".

" Mayor! if the house turns out to be too small for the two of us, I'm prepared to rent, buy, or build a larger house, so that is the least of our worries" said Theo "Fine, then let me show you the quarters, and the school house we have built" says the Mayor.

Ethan, tells Amy, "while you are doing that I'll find a livery, and put up our animals, then a hotel or rooming house for myself". The store owner tells Ethan, "my sister has a nice clean rooming house up on the street behind the store, with a stable behind it for your horse, let me take you up there and introduce you to her".

So the two groups go their separate ways. The mayor takes Amy and Theo to the school house, and the small house behind it where they will stay. The school is a fairly large building, for a one room school, built to hold at least thirty students from first grade through twelfth, there are two separate rooms, one for the lower grades, and one for the upper grades. The mayor tells Amy, 'I'll introduce you to the other teacher tomorrow, after you have settled in,"

Meanwhile Ethan is being introduced to the store owners sister, Maggie, who is a right handsome woman, and Ethan is immediately attracted to her. She shows Ethan a corner room on the second floor, which is airy, light, and spacious. There is a large bed, wardrobe, dresser, mirror, and the usual pitcher and bowl, plus the chamber pot under the bed. She tells him the outhouse is out back. "I serve breakfast at seven and supper at six". "The room and meals are a dollar a day or twenty five dollars a month, if you want a monthly rate". "I'll Take it", and reaching in his pocket, he retrieves enough money for three months in advance. Maggie is delighted, as normally she has to wait for the rent until the first of each month from her regular tenants.

So meeting back at the store, the three ride back out to the wagon camp to get their wagons, and say goodbye to the others and Cougar. There are tears of sadness over the parting of the wagon folk, and Cougar takes Theo aside, and tells him, "despite his being a sassy brat, he has been the best friend on a wagon train he could ask for, and if he got this way again he would look him up". "You do that" Theo tells him, "you're always welcome, and stay out of trouble, you're too old for it without my help to get you out of the tight spots your big mouth gets you into" And laughs '. Cougar growls, "why you! you! you had to do it again, didn't you", and laughing with Theo, he gives him a big bear hug, and tells him he is going to miss him.

Theo and Amy drive their wagons and horses to the house behind the school, while Ethan goes up to the rooming house, and gets settled in, it's the first night in four and a half months that any of them has slept in a real bed.

The next morning, after breakfast, Amy is anxious to get her stuff moved into the small house so she can get the house organized, So Theo unloads the wagon, and stacks the belongings in one corner so they can sort it out, Meanwhile Ethan is enjoying a breakfast at his new home in the rooming house, after everybody else leaves, Maggie and Ethan are having a cup of coffee together, and getting to know each other. Maggie tells Ethan how she is a widow because of her husband being shot in a holdup, while working at the bank. Ethan tells Maggie how he became a widower, when his wife died of cholera back east. So when Amy was offered the teaching job, he decided to come west with her and start a business. "I had three wagon loads of goods that I was going to sell in Virginia City, but I was offered a better deal in Great Salt Lake City, so I took it and came with Amy and

Theo to Auburn". "I'm sure I can find a business to invest in here", "I think you're right, the area is slowly building from a mining boom town to a more stable farming community". "There are lots of orchards going in that will eventually pay good incomes for the owners". "Also the underground hard rock mines are said to be rich and will last for years, unlike the placer mines which are mostly worked out by now".

"Auburn will be a supply center for those mines and the people who will work in them, plus there is talk of the railroad going through here". "There is plenty of opportunity for a man of vision to invest in", "Maggie I'm glad we had this little talk." "I can see where I can find something to invest my money into, which will give me an excuse to stay in Auburn". "Now if you will excuse me, I need to see to my animals, and then go help Amy and Theo".

So the day is used to settle in, Amy and Theo in the small house. Ethan finds a place to store the wagons, and keep the mules. He doesn't want to sell them just yet, as he can see where they might come into good use. One thought is to freight supplies to the mines, or bring goods from Sacramento to Auburn until the railroad is built, even then there will be a need for wagons to transfer goods from the railroad to the surrounding area. He must look into this opportunity that seems to be presenting itself to him.

The next day Amy wants to find the couple who want her to tutor them in French, so while she is doing that, Theo and Ethan are looking the town over, Ethan has paid Theo the money he promised him for driving the wagon from St Louis, plus a hundred dollar bonus as a wedding gift. So again Theo has money in his pocket, and still hasn't had to get into the money that Cuss gave him before he started his journey.

As they are looking the town over, they come across a blacksmith shop that does not seem to be open. Walking up to the place, they see a for sale sign on it. The sign says to contact the banker Mr. Woods for information. Theo looks at Ethan, and 'asks "what do you think?"

"Could I make a living as a blacksmith in this town?" "Let's check it out, the big question is why the shop is closed", states Ethan, "Certainly there must be enough work for a blacksmith here in this town".

So they head for the bank, and when they get there ask for Mr. Woods. The Banker introduces himself, and asks, "What can I do for you gentlemen?" Theo and Ethan introduce themselves, and ask about the blacksmith shop that is for sale, and why? Mr. Woods tells them of the terrible fire out at the Jones place that killed the whole family, Mr. Jones was the blacksmith, and was killed. As the bank had a mortgage on the business and the large lot next to it, they became the owner of the property.

Theo asks if there is another blacksmith in town? "No" says the banker, "we have need for a good man to take over the business". "We've been without a smith for a month now and people are already complaining about things that need repairing and new items to be made. Some of the folks have had to make trips down to Newcastle to have things done",

Theo asks how much does the bank want for the property? Mr. Woods tells him a thousand dollars, and that would include the lot next door, plus all the tools and supplies there in the shop. Theo looks at Ethan, and asks, "What do you think Ethan?" "We should look at the business and take inventory, and if you're still interested, make the banker an offer". "Ok, lets go look at the shop says Theo". The banker tells them to go to the back door of the shop and knock loudly on the door, "Swamper Sam will answer, tell him you're there to look at the shop". "Who is Swamper Sam? Asks Theo". The banker tells Theo, he is the town drunk, who earns his keep by mopping out the saloons, and is caretaking the blacksmith shop for me. "He's a drunk as I said, but he's fairly reliable, so the town takes care of him"

Theo and Ethan go to the blacksmith shop, and going around back, knock on the back door, shortly a slim fellow with unruly hair answers the door. Theo introduces himself and Ethan, and tells Sam that they are there to look at the shop. Sam invites them in, excusing his appearance, and proceeds to show them the shop. There are the usual tools, forge, foot operated bellows, anvil, a good assortment of iron, hoist frame for shoeing oxen and unruly horses. Sam shows them how two of the shop sides slide open, so a breeze can blow through, and also access for larger pieces of equipment that need repair. Theo notices that there is also a skylight in the roof that let's in the light from outside. They also look at the lot next to the shop. Sam tells them that the blacksmith, god rest his soul, was going to expand the shop when the railroad started to come through, and the hard rock mines started to need equipment repairs, that they couldn't handle themselves. He was even thinking about getting one of the new steam driven forging hammers, so he could increase his production capability, During this discussion, Theo is noticing , that Sam is articulate, and sounds well educated, I wonder, thinks Theo, what causes this man to drink?

Theo turns to Ethan and asks him what he thinks of the shop? "It looks good to me, but you are the smith, and know better then me what is needed here to make it work". Theo tells Ethan, "customers, just customers". Sam tells Theo, "that's no problem, I have the list of customers, that the previous blacksmith had, plus the potential new ones that he was going to contact". Ethan asks Sam how it is he has this information. "Oh! that's because I kept his books for him, the bank has them now, but I have my own copy, never know when a copy is needed, the smith could have lost his in the fire, if they hadn't been here at the time", "Good thinking" says Theo.

"Sam, if I buy the shop, would you like to stay here, and keep books for me?" " Yes, if you can overlook my, umm, sickness". Theo tells him," we can probably work out something". "Good" *says* Sam.

"Ethan, let's go see the banker and see what kind of deal we can make". Ethan looks at Theo, and said," "From what I can see, this could work into a successful business, would you like a partner?" " But of course, with your business sense, your wagons, and my blacksmithing, we should have enough business for four partners". "Come on; let's go buy a blacksmith shop".

So they make a deal with the banker, and are now the proud owners of the newly named T&E Blacksmithing and Freighting Co. With Sam's help they get the shop in shipshape order and start spreading the word that they are open for business. The repair work starts to pour in, Theo finds himself working from sunup to sundown trying to keep ahead of the work load.

Ethan is kept busy picking up and delivering some of the bigger repair jobs, even Sam is kept busy keeping the books and occasionally helping out in the shop, when it takes two men to do a job.

After a couple of months, Theo asks Sam, if they can afford to hire a helper, for the shop, Sam tells him, "if the workload stays the same, you can afford two helpers". "Good, why don't you get out the word that we are looking for help".

Meanwhile Amy is teaching her classes at school, and tutoring the Augusta family in French, the father has been planting grape vines that have been shipped from France and

Italy, the weather and soil conditions seem to be suitable for the vines as they are healthy and starting to produce grapes. Mrs. Augusta and the son and daughter are getting along in the learning of French. Mr. Augusta is pushing himself to learn as quickly as possible, as he plans to be in France the following year, where he will learn to be a vintner, so he can start his own wine company.

From Amy's association with the Augusta family, Theo finds out that they are going to need oak barrels to keep the wine in while it ages, so he contracts with Mr. Augusta to make the barrels for him. As there are plenty of oak trees in this area, Theo finds he can kill two birds with one stone, he needs oak to make charcoal for his forge, plus heat the rest of the shop in the Winter time, and also their small house. So he finds a cooper and a woodcutter to start cutting the oak they need, Since many of the farmers are clearing their lands of trees, so they can plant whatever crops they want, there is a more than an adequate supply of oak.

One day Ethan tells Theo that he should go with him to Sacramento to check out the new steam engine he has seen at one of the dealers he has done some business with. Theo said, "I have been thinking of the same thing, with a steam engine, we could get one of those forging hammers, and I bet we could run a timber cutting saw off one of those engines too".

So Theo tells Amy, he and Ethan are going to Sacramento to look at equipment, she asks if she can go too. as she hasn't been there and she might be able to find some new clothes, and other things So the next day, being Friday they close up the shop, and Amy takes the day off from school and they head for Sacramento.

Arriving that evening, they get a hotel room, where there is a dinning room, after having a good supper, they take a short walk around the area down by the river, where there are shops for just about everything, then off to bed.   _ -

Next morning they are up having breakfast, and getting ready for the day. Ethan tells the couple that the dealer for the steam engines is less then a quarter mile away, so they can walk there and look at the equipment. Arriving at the equipment dealer, Theo is shown several engines the dealer has in stock. Theo explains to the dealer what he has in mind as to what he wants the engine to do, one to run a timber saw, and also run a forging hammer. "Come and look at the catalogs I have, as I can supply you with all the equipment you need, for a package price".

After Theo and Ethan go through the catalogs, they find just what they think will do the job, so getting a price from the dealer, they ask him how soon can he deliver the equipment? The dealer tells them as soon as he has a down payment of half of the purchase price he can start delivering, the engine and timber saw I have in stock here, the forging hammer has to come from our warehouse in San Francisco. "Good" says Theo, "I can give you the money now for the down payment." "When will I get delivery?" The dealer tells him, we can start tomorrow; it will probably take a week to get the engine and saw to you, and another week for the hammer.

Theo concludes the deal, and he, Amy, and Ethan leave to see if they can find some stores for Amy to shop in. Amy soon has an arm load of new dresses, hats, shoes, underthings, and even a bottle of French perfume. So back to the hotel they go, to rest up for supper, and the trip back home.

A week later the equipment starts arriving, first the boiler for the engine, then the rest of the working parts, two days later the saw parts arrive. Now comes the hard part, figuring out where the engine will sit, so it can run the saw, and the forge when it arrives. Knowing the dimensions of the forge, Theo figures out where to set the engine. He finds a mason who can start making a foundation for the engine. After it is made they start to mount the steam engine on the foundation, meanwhile the first of the forging hammer arrives, it is coming in pieces, unfortunately, the base is coming in last, so they have to wait to make the foundation for it.

After a month everything is in place, and they are ready to fire up the boiler to make steam, and test everything. Pretty soon they have a head of steam, and slowly letting in the clutch affair, the saw is running. Then they start the hammer, the noise is terrific as the hammer strikes it's anvil in the base of the hammer. Theo looks at Ethan and the others and says it's a good thing, that machine is in a building, the noise would be deafening if it were outside, . Ethan tells Theo," let's go outside and listen to it", after walking a half of block away, they decide to insulate the building to decrease the noise.

So after getting everything fine tuned they are cutting wood, the saw dust is going into the walls of the shop to act as insulation for the hammer noise. The cooper is getting his barrels made. Theo is making the barrel strapping. Ethan is hauling wood from the farmers, and delivering repaired equipment. Meantime the hard rock miners are starting to bring in orders for star drills, single and double jacks, and other equipment used daily in the mines. Both Ethan and Theo have to hire on additional help. Drivers for the freight wagons, wood workers to make handles for the sledges and shovels. Sam is kept so busy with the books, and coordinating the ordering of supplies, and delivery of the repaired pieces, that he has virtually stopped drinking. Theo is pleased with that development, for he always felt that there was no need for Sam to drink. One afternoon after the work for the day is over, Theo gets Sam aside and asks him if he can ask him a personal question. Sam says "sure, as long as it doesn't concern why I was drinking so heavy." "Oh! that's precisely what I was going to ask".

Sam tells Theo he has been waiting for the question for a long time, but he is not yet ready to confide in someone as to the cause of his becoming a drunk, "but let me say this, if it hadn't been for you coming along and giving me this job, and the responsibility, I would probably be a dead drunk by now, so I want to thank you, and some day soon I will tell you my tale of woe". "Ok" says Theo, "I can live with that".

With the business doing so good, Theo asks Amy if she would like a bigger house to live in? "Why yes, a couple of more rooms would be nice". So they start looking for a bigger house, not finding what they want, they find a nice lot and have a nice two story with basement and attic built for them.

Meanwhile Ethan is courting Maggie, and they are getting ready to announce their engagement, So life is good for the group that met in St Louis so long ago.

The business is doing so good, that between Theo and Ethan they have a dozen men working for them, Theo has found a blacksmith who can do everything that he can do, plus make dies for the forge, so they can stamp out different products. Theo tells his new smith about the tool Cuss had made, that he called molly, and asks if he can make a die to make a production run of the tool, "I bet there are still enough placer miners out there that could use this tool". So they tool up and make a couple of hundred, and Theo gives a dozen away to get the miners to see what the tool can do. It's not long before he is sold out, and people are asking if he is going to make more, So he has the smith make up a couple of hundred more. Then one day a drummer comes into the shop and inquires about this tool he had heard about called a molly.

Theo says "sure we make that tool, why?" The drummer tells him, "I can sell them up and down the mother lode for you, plus up in the Trinitys". "I'm guessing I could move a couple of hundred a month if you can make them that fast". Theo tells the drummer, "we can make a couple of hundred a week if you can move them that fast". The drummers eyes widen, and he says "a couple of hundred a week, I don't know, that's a lot of selling." "Theo asks, what kind of deal do you want?" " I don't rightly know, how much do you sell them for?" Theo tells him normally a dollar apiece around here.. The drummer asks?, " can you sell them to me in lots of fifty or more for seventy five cents apiece?" "Yes" says Theo. "Good, then I can retail them for a dollar and a half apiece away from your local market, and make some money on them"

"That sounds fair to me" says Theo, "let's figure my local market is within a twenty five mile radius of the shop, and you can have the rest of California". "Done" says the drummer. Theo calls Sam over to tell him of the deal he just made, and to write up a contract with the drummer, and to get paid up front for the goods. So the drummer is delivered his first lot of fifty Mollys.

Within a week he's back for more. And so a new line of product is being introduced to the world of miners.

Theo and his new smith then go to work and develop some more tools that can be forged on the Hammer, and give them to the drummer to sell. It's not long when the drummer has to hire help to move the products that T&E Enterprises is making.

Time passes, Theo and Ethan are pleased at their business success, Ethan is now married to Maggie and is now her partner in the rooming house. Ethan has been trying to get Maggie to sell the house and take it easy, but she resists, by telling him she wouldn't have anything to do, and would get bored as all get out, So they continue to run the boarding house. Ethan has insisted that the linens be sent out to the Chinese laundry to be done, so Maggie doesn't have to work so hard.

The Augustus's have been to France and back by now, and are taking delivery of the wine barrels, and lumber to make racks to hold the barrels on. The lumber mill has expanded, They are making mining timbers, soon the railroad is going to need lumber for rail ties and storm sheds. Ethan has organized a lumber company, to go out and cut timber, and bring it to the mill, to be cut into boards.

Theo's blacksmith is running the shop well enough that Theo doesn't have to be there. Sam has the books under control, he has two helpers now, a shipper and receiver who keep the iron coming in and the finished products going out.

So Theo's mind has been wandering, he has been thinking about the reason he first came to California. One evening while sitting on their porch after supper, Theo approaches Amy with the idea of him going prospecting. "If that's what you want to do, then by all means you should," "Really!" says Theo "I thought you would be against it". "No my love, I have felt your restlessness these last few months, I think you should go out and chase your dream for awhile, after all that's why you came to California". "It's not your fault that we fell in love and got you sidetracked for these many years, what's it been now? "Three and a half years since we got here." "Yes" says Theo. "All right then, it's obviously too late in the season to go prospecting up where Nash told you to go, so why don't you plan on next spring when the snow leaves the high country, meanwhile you can make sure the shop can get along without you". "Sam and Ethan can run the business just fine, and you can find that rich gold mine that you have been dreaming about for all these years". "In the meantime you can be getting the necessary supplies together, and getting your horse and mule back in shape for the rugged trails you will have to travel, and when's the last time you shot your rifle and pistol?" "Yes my husband you have a lot to do to get ready for your adventure."

CHAPTER TWENTY NINE

Theo is now getting excited. Amy being the understanding woman she is, has given him the go ahead to go prospecting. So during the remainder of the fall and into winter, which are mild in Auburn, Theo is getting ready for his new adventure. He takes the horse and mule out for almost daily exercise, Amy goes along when she can on the mare she was given by the Mustanger. The mare is still a little wild, but training nicely. Theo is also shooting his Hawken and Dragoon, to keep in practice. At the general store he finds a good. pocket compass, and a telescope, thinking that a small gold scale might come in handy, he finds one that comes in a case small enough to put in a shirt pocket. Knowing how tough buckskins are in the wilds, he has a new set made, along the pattern of the old set, except for more pockets.

Theo is spending enough time in the shop, working at the forge to keep his muscles in good shape. Ethan and Sam are almost as excited about Theo's new adventure as he is. They are making every effort to relieve Theo of the day to day problems, so he can leave in the spring and not worry about the business.

For Christmas Amy and Ethan buy Theo one of the new Henry repeating rifles, its a lever action, fifteen shot, 44 caliber saddle gun. It doesn't have the long range of the Hawken, but is better suited for shooting in the forest, where most game is closer to the hunter because of the cover trees afford the animals. And so it goes, Theo is refining his supplies, and now practicing with the new Henry rifle, The horse and mule are in fine fettle, spring is to Theo slowly approaching. All is in readiness.

But far to the south all is not well. Three desperate rough looking men with southern accents are trying to outrun a posse of twenty men. It seems they have been preying on the miners around the Placerita Creek area, north of Los Angeles, stealing their meager pouches of gold dust, and then robbing a stage coach, and killing everyone aboard, but not before raping the two women aboard the coach.

The Sheriff and the citizens of the area have vowed to bring these bad men in to hang. So they are hot on the trail of these owlhoots, Arnold, Rufus, and Buford have been on the run before, so they know how to throw the posse off their trail and get away. Finding a hard rocky area they cross it, then double back through an arroyo, and get behind the posse. While the posse is trying to find their trail, they head west up to the pass that will take them to the valley south of Sacramento. Finding a remote ranch on the way to the pass, they stop and steal six horses, this gives them the advantage of fresh mounts and they can relay between the six horses.

Soon they have outrun the posse, who have no hope of catching them.

Staying to the east side of the lower Sacramento valley, and traveling at night, they soon find themselves near a mining camp called Course Gold. There they camp for several days while taking a good look at the prospects of continuing their robbing, and killing.

Back in Auburn Theo is ready to take off on his prospecting trip, kissing Amy goodbye, and waving to the others he is off. Sticking to the foothills he heads for the Yuba river east of Marysville, where he knows he can cross the river safely, the spring run off is through, so the rivers are low enough now to cross.

After crossing the Yuba River he heads east towards Downieville, the country is rough, steep Canyons, forested mountain sides, but there is a stage trail that goes to Downieville, and the La Porte, St Louis, Brandywine area, so this is what he is following. Having spent the winter pouring over all the maps available of the area, he almost knows the trails by heart.

A week after leaving Auburn, he is in Downieville. Taking a room in the hotel, and putting up his animals in the livery, he spends a week in Downieville, talking to those miners who are willing to talk about what is going on in the mines. He learns that the placers around Downieville are according to the locals, pretty much worked out, or that the good ones are under claim and being worked with some success. So remembering what the Mustanger told him, he replenishes his supplies, and heads north. Now to get over the mountain to the north, there is a trail up the Downie river, then on into the Poker Flat area, and finally into La Porte.

Again he hangs around the area getting the lay of the land from the locals.

Now he starts the painstaking process of prospecting, going back the way he came, he checks every small ravine from La Porte to Poker Flat to find what he is looking for. A small piece of gold bearing river bed that hasn't been worked, like the one that Cuss had found.

Remembering that Cuss had told him it took years before he found his mine, Theo is not discouraged after ten days of looking, but he is running low on provisions. So he heads back to Downieville, to get more supplies. While there he listens to the gossip, to see if there have been any new finds. After two days he heads out again, going back to where he left off, he again begins his systematic search for the elusive channel he is looking for. Week after week he continues his search, keeping his journal as a means of recording his efforts, each time he goes back to Downieville, he sends a letter to Amy and the others to let them know he's alright, but so far no luck in his search. The summer is passing, and still he hasn't located the spot he is looking for. He has found considerable color in different places, but not the rich mine he knows is out there. Continuing his search into the fall, he still hasn't given up. Then on one of his re-supply trips back to Downieville, he is taking a different route then normal. Using his compass to keep from getting lost he is approaching the town from a different direction.

Traversing the side of a mountain, he hasn't been on before; he comes across a small ravine. Looking up the ravine he sees river rock. Tying off the horse and mule, he takes his tool pack and starts up the ravine, reaching the gravel, he begins to remove gravel off the bedrock, after an hour he has exposed the bedrock under gravel that hasn't been moved in eons, there in front of him is a crevice lined with gold nuggets, using his molly tool he cleans out the crevice, placing the material in a canvas fold up bucket to be panned out later. Moving more of the gravel, he finds another crevice, using the molly he cleans this one up also. By now he has a bucket full of material that needs to be panned down. He then climbs down the ravine, and taking the horse and mule he heads down the mountain side to a small stream at the bottom, whereupon he pans the material out. After cleaning all the gravel and black sand from the pan, he looks at the gold.

He has several large nuggets, possibly going over an ounce in weight, plus lots of smaller nuggets. Gathering some small dead wood, he makes a small fire, and places the pan on the coals to dry the gold. After the water is gone and the pan is cooled off, Theo gets his small gold scale out to weigh the gold. The scale can weigh four ounces at a time, so using the small flat funnel that comes with the scale, Theo begins pouring gold on the scales until there is four ounces in the scale pan, then he repeats the process until he has weighed all the gold.

According to his figures that he has been writing down, he has just recovered eighteen and a half ounces of gold.

Is this the place he has been looking for?. As it is getting late in the afternoon, he decides to camp here, and in the morning take a better look at his new diggings. So getting the animals taken care of, he tries his luck at catching a fish or two from the stream for supper. After about a half hour, he has two nice trout, just big enough for his frying pan. After supper he sets up his bedroll, and starts to write in the journal. "I think I have found it he writes, "after tomorrow I will know if it is the right one". "The gold I recovered today shows me this could be a rich patch of gravel". "Tomorrow I will map out the extent of the gravel, and locate this piece of ground according to the local mining law". "Then with my compass locate this ravine in relation to Downieville".

After putting his journal away and lying there in the dark, he thanks all the friends and spirits who have guided him through the last years. And in honor of Cuss, he decides to call the mine, the Deja-vu, because of it similarity to the gravel bed that Cuss had discovered. Then thinking of Amy he drifts off to sleep.

The next morning, after a breakfast of boiled oats, and coffee, he begins his mapping of the gravel bed, It seems to be about four hundred feet in length, average six to eight feet wide, and about three feet deep. The nearest water is down the hill side, which is about a hundred feet.

He can either fill buckets with the gravel, and carry them to the stream, or dig a ditch along the hill side to bring the water to the gavel. He will have to think about which will be the most efficient, way to mine this spot.

After he has the location notice posted, and the spot mapped, so he can find it again, he decides to dig some more, and see what he finds on this day. So taking his tools and repeating the process he used the day before he again fills the canvas bucket with gravel and gold nuggets.

This time his total comes out to twenty five ounces, and a few penny weights of gold. Theo is overwhelmed with the richness of the ground so far.

With his supplies running low, he knows he has to get back to Downieville, to restock. So with the afternoon waning he packs up his tools and stashes them near the gravel bank, leaving them here to be used when he gets back. After a supper of more boiled oats, a piece of jerky, and coffee, he again settles in for the night. Tomorrow he will head back to Downieville.

During the night he feels a chilling drop in the temperature. He realizes that a storm is going to come soon, I hope it waits till I get down to town, he thinks to himself. The next morning the sky is gray, and the clouds are building up for a good one, so hurrying as fast as is safely possible Theo gets down off this mountain and into Dovvnieville. As he gets into town the storm breaks, rain is coming down in sheets, he makes for the livery so he can put up the animals, and then gets himself a room at the hotel. After getting dried out, he goes down to the dining room and orders dinner, seated by a window overlooking the Downie river, he can see the river rising. The next morning, as he looks out the window of his room, he can see that it snowed about a thousand feet up the mountain, this is going to make getting back to Auburn difficult. After breakfast he is checking on his horse and mule, when the stage comes in from Sierra City up the road a few miles. Talking to the driver, Theo learns that they will go on to Marysville, despite the weather, and he is welcome to follow along, or ride in the coach if there is room. Theo asks "when they are leaving?" "About an hour from now, we change horses here and eat, then push on". Theo tells the driver, "Ill be ready to go with you, all I have to do is check out of the hotel and get some supplies, and I'll be ready". The driver says "ok, meet us here, and we'll be off".

So Theo rushes back to the hotel and checks out, then to the general store for his supplies, then to the livery to get ready for the trip down to Marysville. Shortly, the driver is back, with two passengers, a miner, and a drummer, who want to get down to the valley before they are snowed in for the winter.

So off they go. The driver has Theo tie his animals to the back of the coach, and ride with him on the seat. Leaving town they follow the trail down river to Goodyears Creek, then up the creek trail to the top of the ridge, where the stage trail follows the ridge line down to the valley. On top they run into snow about a foot deep, which slows them down. For a good twenty miles they fight the snow, the driver cusses his horses the whole time, keeping them moving. Theo is hanging on for dear life, as the driver is going faster then he thinks he should.

When they break out of the snow, Theo breathes a sigh of relief, only to find the mud that they are encountering is just as slippery as the snow, the coach is slewing from side to side on the wet road. Theo starts to say something, when the driver looks at him, and tells him, "don't worry so much, me and them horses have been doing this for a couple of years, and we haven't lost a coach yet". Of course fate steps in just then and one of the wheels hits a big rock and starts to break. The driver hears the crack, and hauls in on the reins to stop the horses. The wheel collapse's just as the coach stops, and the coach tilts to the right rear.

Theo asks the driver "if he has a spare wheel?" "Yes" says the driver, "it's hung under the coach." So Theo and the driver get down and tell the two passengers to get out and help.

The driver gets the jack out of the rear boot, along with the spud wrench, meanwhile Theo is under the coach unhooking the spare wheel, the passengers are getting some brush to put under the jack, so it won't slip in the mud. Then loosening the axle nut, they get the coach jacked up and change the wheel. Theo tells the driver he better slow down, so he don't break another wheel, as he doesn't have another spare. Theo checks his animals and sees they are alright except for spatters of mud on them, and then they are off. They stop for the night at the next stage stop, changing horses in the morning, they are off again. The sky has cleared, and the sun is drying out the road, so they are making good time. One more over night stop, then on to Marysville.

Theo is amazed at how fast they got to Marysville. He took almost a full week getting up to Downieville last spring, course he wasn't in a hurry, so he didn't push his animals like the stage driver did. Theo and the driver part friendly, with the driver thanking Theo for the help, and invites him for a beer if he is in the area again. Theo tells the driver, "He will probably run into him next spring when he comes up to prospect again".

CHAPTER THIRTY

After leaving the stage driver Theo heads for the livery stable, he asks the hostler if there is someone there who can wash down his animals, then curry and comb them, plus give them an extra bait of feed and oats. The hostler calls for his son, a strapping teen, and tells him what Theo wants done. The boy looks at Theo and says that will cost an extra dollar for the two animals. Theo tells the boy, I'll pay you a dollar apiece for the job if it is done right. Yes sir! says the boy, for that much, they will be the best looking horse and mule around.

Theo then heads for a hotel, with his saddle bags, Henry rifle, and possibles bag. He wants a haircut, shave, hot bath, steak dinner, and a real bed to sleep in. Which he gets in that order.

The next morning he retrieves his animals from the livery, paying the boy an extra dollar as a tip. Then he packs up and leaves, heading for Auburn, going the way he came in the spring he arrives in Auburn on the third day. Going straight to the house, he finds Amy just getting home from teaching school. They hug and kiss, and both start asking questions at the same time.

"Let's slow down, my lovely woman". "I'll tell you all about my trip as we take care of the animals". In the stable, Theo unsaddles the Morgan and let's him roll, taking the pack saddle off the mule, he also rolls in the dirt, then Theo gets a brush and rubs down the horse, then puts him in a stall with fresh straw and a bit of feed, the mule gets the same treatment, all the while he taking care of the animals, he is telling Amy about the prospecting trip.

How he spent day after day looking for the right spot to mine and how about ten days ago he finally found a good spot. Then he told her of the snow storm, and the wild ride on the stage, and the new friend he made of the stage driver, "Now let's go in the house and get a dinner plate to set on the table, and I'll show you some gold". Taking his saddle bags into the house, and setting them on a chair, he opens one and pulls out a leather pouch.

Amy has gotten a plate down and put it on the table, Theo opens the pouch and pours the gold nuggets on the plate. "My word! will you look at all those nuggets, Theo that's wonderful, why I've never seen so much gold all at one time". Theo tells Amy, there is a little over forty three and a half ounces there, "And the best part is there is a lot more where it came from."

"This pile only took me two days to recover, so with the right equipment, and system, I can probably average this much on a daily basis, providing the gravel and bedrock stay this consistent". "Knowing how placer ground is I don't expect it to stay this rich daily, but it is definitely worth working, which I plan to do starting next spring". "Oh!" exclaims Amy, "you mean you're going to leave me here alone again all summer?". "I think you should take me with <u>you, so I can have</u> some fun finding gold too"

"Theo looks at Amy, an tells her, "honey, I figured after the trip across the country, that you would never be interested in roughing it again, the area where I found the gold is really rough country, there are grizzly's, catamounts, rattlesnakes, plus all the other small creatures that women usually hate". "But Theo think of the adventure we could have together, after all that is what marriage is all about, sharing the continual surprises that life brings, enjoying the good, and working through the bad". "I'll have to think about it" grouses Theo.

Later Ethan comes over to check on Amy, and finds Theo has come home. " Theo! when did you get here?" "Just a little while ago", says Theo, "Come and look at what I found." Ethan looks at the gold on the plate, and whistle's, "Now that looks impressive", says Ethan. "Did you find the mine you were looking for?" "I think so, between running out of supplies, and the weather turning sour, I didn't have time to do a thorough evaluation of the gound, but from what I have seen, it is worth mining",

"So I take it you will be going back next spring?" "Yes!" says Theo, "I have to spend at least one summer there". Amy tells Ethan, that she might be going too. " What?' says Ethan "The wilds of those mountains are no place for a woman." "I know, I tried to tell her that, besides Amy, I told you I have to think about it". "Well think faster Mr. Calhoun, because I have to make plans if I am to be allowed to go". Theo can see that there will be no peace in his life if he tells Amy she can't go, but he is not going to give in just yet

A week later on his way to the shop, Theo comes across a man beating a good size dog with a stick. "Here now fellow, that's no way to treat an animal", said Theo. The man looks at Theo and yells at him to mind his own business, and turns back to hit the dog again, as he is swinging the stick at the dog, Theo grabs his wrist and twists it to stop the stick from hitting the animal.

"That's it, I told you to mind your own business", and proceeds to take a punch at Theo. Theo_ ducks the left hook the man ˉthrows at him and plants a solid right fist to the man's jaw, with devastating effect. The man's jaw is broken, and he collapses on the ground out cold.

Meanwhile the dog comes over to Theo and. licks his hand, then turns to the man and growls at him. Theo reaches down and pets the dog, "Come, we'll leave this fellow here, and see if we can <u>find</u> something for you to eat". <u>The dog gives what sounds like</u> an <u>agreeable bark,</u> and turns toward the direction that Theo is walking in. Theo thinks to himself, and asks, *"Now what have I got myself into this time?"* And from deep inside his mind, a spirit tells him this is a good thing you have done, and to except it for what it is. -

So Theo has a new companion, the dog goes wherever he goes, he makes friends with Amy, Ethan, and Sam, right off, the other people he is a little cool towards. As he gets to know Amy better, he is her protective companion, especially when she takes the mare for a ride, Amy notices that the mare has a kindred spirit in the dog, and is behaving much better now that the dog is part of the family.

Theo meantime has given in to Amy's wish to go mining with him, with the dog being part of the group, he has a better feeling about Amy being with him, as the dog will try to protect either of them from harm. So they make plans for the new adventure to be had in the spring.

Since Amy has to teach school until the first of June, Theo will go up to the mine in the spring after the snow melts and start mining and also build a small cabin for them to stay in. He also has to figure out the best way to mine the gravel deposit, and what equipment to use for the gold recovery. After work and supper each day he sits at the table, drawing a map of the area, as he can remember it. If only he had a source of water above the gravel deposit he could use a Longtom to shovel into, similar to Cuss's operation. Maybe move the material down to the creek on the back of the mule and then shovel it into a sluice box. He needs to look at the area more thoroughly, before he can decide which way to go.

So instead of worrying about the mining, he makes a plan for the cabin, and a list of tools he will need for its construction. He soon sees that he will need several mules to get the equipment, and all the supplies he will need for the summer up to the mine. He then remembers the stage road; he could use a wagon, with one or two mules at most to haul the stuff up there.

Getting out the latest map of the area, he notices that where he has figured the mine is, he is only five miles from where the stage road drops off the ridge into the Goodyears Creek road. If he were to keep going east instead of down the Goodyears road he would end up close to the mine. So he continues to plan.

Meanwhile the eastern part of the country is involved in the war between the north and the south, the shipping of some of the materials that are used in daily commerce is erratic, the small Placer mines are being depleted of their gold, but with discovery of very large gold bearing ancient river channels and the use of large ditches and pipes, the hydraulic mining industry is starting up. There are channels at San Juan Ridge, Iowa Hill, Table Mountain near Oroville, The Klamath, and Trinity rivers way up north, plus many more. The telegraph is being installed to the major towns of the west, even Auburn has a telegraph office now, and Ethan has shown Theo how using the telegraph has given their business more efficiency by its use in ordering supplies for the business. This news gives Theo an idea," I wonder if I can telegraph the stage office in Marysville and get in touch with the driver of the stage to Downieville?"

Ethan tells Theo, "that he couldn't see why not, but why?" Theo tells Ethan that the stage runs winter and summer, and the driver could tell Theo when the snow is off the ridge route so he could safely drive a wagon up to the vicinity of the mine with the supplies and tools he will need. "Oh!" says Ethan, "you know that's a good idea". So Theo goes to the telegraph office and checks with the operator about his need to contact the stage company in Marysville. The operator says sure, "we have an office in Marysville so it won't be any problem". Theo then writes a message to send to the stage office, requesting the stage driver to contact him. The telegrapher sends the wire, and tells Theo he will have his runner bring the reply to him when it comes.

Theo decides to make a rocker and a Longtom to take up to the mine, so he designs one of each that can be hauled up there in pieces, then put together on the spot. He also remembers the pleasant hours spent in Cuss's hot tub, and decides he wants one for the mine. So he gets with the cooper that works for them and has him build one that he can put together at the mine claim?. The cooper suggests using redwood, as it will not rot from the hot water, plus it is not a heavy' wood like oak, so will be easier to haul. Theo's list of supplies and tools is getting bigger. He decides that a small freight wagon and two mules will be what he will use to transport the stuff.

Meantime Amy is getting her own supplies together, she goes to the mercantile and gets several pairs of jeans and some men's flannel work shirts, work gloves, gum boots, and so on.

She takes the jeans and shirts to her seamstress and asks her if she can alter them to fit her better. "Yes" says, the woman, "let's take your measurements for the pants and shirt, as they will be different then the ones I have for your dresses". Amy also gets a work vest, and fleece lined denim coat to wear when it is cold.

She then goes to the local gunsmith, and buys a new Colt 36 caliber Sheriffs model hand gun, the gunsmith suggests changing the grips to fit her hand better, and shows her a gun belt and holster that he can modify to also fit her. Amy then asks the gunsmith if the Henry rifle comes in a smaller caliber then the 44 caliber that Theo has. The gunsmith tells her, "I can get you one in the same 36 caliber that your Colt shoots, it won't have the stopping power that the 44 caliber has but, it will be a touch more accurate". "Fine: I'll also need a scabbard to go on my saddle for the rifle"

So the two of them are getting ready for their adventure. A week after he had sent the telegram to the stage company, he heard back from the driver, saying hello, what can he do for him? Theo sends a telegram back requesting the driver to let him know when the snow is gone off the stage road, so that he can bring a wagon load of supplies to his mine, and get started mining for the season. A few days later the driver answered, that he would be glad to, and is waiting to see Theo so he can buy him the beer he owes him

And so it goes, Theo and Amy getting excited over the prospects of next summer, meantime business is still going good, they have had to expand the shop again, The Central Pacific Railroad had started laying track in Sacramento that summer, and one of their representatives had approached Ethan about handling some of their blacksmithing needs, and occasional freighting for them. So new business for T&E enterprises, as they call themselves now.

Meanwhile, down south at Course Gold, Arnold and the Blackburn stepbrothers are in trouble again, they have been stealing gold pokes as usual, which the sheriff has been suspecting them of. But what got the citizens really upset was when Rufus beat up one of the popular soiled doves. As the word got around the next day, a posse of miners, ranchers, and town folk went after the trio. Arnold ever vigilant caught wind of the posse and made it out to where they were staying in an old cabin at a worked out mine, and got them out of there just in time. They managed to cover their tracks again and get away. This time they headed for the coast figuring the posse would look for them to go up or down the mother load in search of more mining victims. Arnold, now the leader of the trio, convinced the Blackburns that they should go to Monterey, and catch a coastal steamer to San Francisco, then up to Marysville, the jump off place to the northern mines. So once they eluded the posse, that's the way they went, robbing people whenever the opportunity presented itself.

Getting to Monterey they found a coastal steamer to take them and their horses to Frisco. Upon landing there they found they had to wait a day before they could get a steamer going up the Sacramento River to Marysville. Rufus and Buford, being drinking men couldn't resist going into one of the saloons on the Barbary Coast, the roughest place in Frisco. When after a few drinks they start getting boisterous and insulting. Now two owlhoots in a saloon full of sailors, is like a match being lighted in a room full of kegs of black powder, there is bound to be an explosion.

Sure enough, Rufus says the wrong thing, and the fighting starts. Rufus being the larger of the two manages to deck a couple of the sailors before being dragged down and beaten to unconsciousness. Buford on the other hand has taken on a burly seaman a head taller then himself, and finds he is being overwhelmed by the man's large tough body, and is soon out cold with his stepbrother. The bartender has his bouncers drag the boys out back, and dump them in the alley, whereupon two goons who work for the Sidney Ducks, figure they can rob the pair and then shanghai them onto a ship bound for the Orient. Arnold looking for the two miscreants sees the end of the brawl through the window of the saloon and the pair being dragged out the back door. He goes around to the back of the saloon through a gangway between the saloon and the building next door, and gets there just in time to see the goons starting to go through the Blackburns pockets. Drawing his revolver and cocking it, he tells the goons in a quiet controlled voice, to stop what they are doing, or he would blow their heads off. The pair not being armed with nothing but clubs and knives back off, and with a wave of Arnolds gun, they take off running down the alley. *Arnold thinks to himself again I'm saving these two, I'm really getting tired of their stupidity, but then again life would be pretty dull without them.*

Finding some water in a large can, he splashes it on them and wakes them up sputtering. "Come on you two idiots, let's get out of here before the goons come back with their friends and finish the job they were about to do on you". "What goons are you talking about" asks Buford? "The ones who were about to rob you while you were out cold". "Come on, get to running". The next morning they were on a steamer to Marysville.

CHAPTER THIRTY ONE

Back in Auburn Theo and Amy are refining the supplies they are going to need at the mine, Theo is making sure he will have all the necessary tools needed to put up the cabin, stable and corral for the animals, mining tools, oil lamps for the cabin, even special hinges for the door.

Amy has got her own list, besides her special work clothes, she wants to have a confortable bed, so it's blankets, comforter, and a couple of sheets, pots, pans, coffee pot, eating utensils, the lists seem endless, but they are paring the items down to a manageable load for the wagon Theo plans on using.

The dog senses something different is going to be happening soon, so he is constantly underfoot so he won't miss out. Amy looks at the dog one evening, and asks Theo if he ever gave the dog a name? "Yes, I think he should be called beans." "Beans!" says Amy, "where in the world did you come up with that name?" "Haven't you noticed how much he likes your

Beans?" "Beans with bacon, beans with salt pork, beans with ham, so why not beans for a name, besides haven't you also noticed how the beans effect him like some humans

I know, phew!" With that Theo slaps his leg and gives out with a horse laugh, Ha, Ha, Ha. Amy looks at the dog and then Theo and said," I see what you mean, like father, like son, and give the two of them her best laugh". So the dog has a name.

Spring has come to the foothills, Auburn is all a-bloom in wild flowers, the weather is warm enough for just shirt sleeves. Theo is anxiously waiting for the telegram from the stage driver which will tell him the snow is gone off the stage trail. Then mid April the wire comes from the driver, Theo immediately sends a reply that he is on the way, and will meet the driver for that beer they talked about.

The wagon is loaded, except for the food supplies, which only takes a short time. Next morning Theo takes off for Marysville and his meeting with the driver, then on to the mine. Heading towards the town of Marysville, Theo passes through and area where they have discovered an extensive deposit of clay, he finds several small mines that are working the deposits, and shipping the clay to Sacramento to be made into different clay products. He must tell Ethan about this deposit, as it would behoove them to get the freighting contract for the mineral.

Reaching Marysville, and the stage office, Theo is told the driver should be in that evening, and he is looking forward to seeing Theo again. So Theo goes to the livery to put up the wagon, mules, and his Morgan, then the hotel with the dinning room, and settles down to wait for the driver.

That evening the two meet at the hotel, and Theo buys the driver supper, as thanks for the telegram. After supper the driver invites Theo to his favorite saloon for a beer, since it is too early to turn in for the night, the two elect to sit in on a poker game for a while. Now Theo hasn't played for quite some time, so he is rusty. After losing a few hands, he starts to remember the Card Man's lessons, and starts to get into the game, and begins to win more then he loses. After about three hours, he is now ahead by quite a considerable sum. Noticing the time he tells the other players that he has to quit, as he has to take off early, all the other players groan, but you have to give us a chance to win some of our money back. "Ok" says Theo, "one more hand, and to make it interesting I'll give you two to one odds, who ever beats me I'll pay two dollars to your one, and the dealer deals the cards, and the game is five card stud."

Everybody agrees. The dealer shuffles and starts dealing the cards. The other players are getting face cards, while Theo is getting low numbered cards, his friend the driver has a pair of Aces showing, there is also a pair of Kings, a pair of Jacks and a pair of Tens, meanwhile Theo has a pair of deuces showing. So far the driver has the winning hand, it will depend on the hole card of the rest of the players. The driver raises on the pair of aces, everybody sees his raise, and the dealer, deals the next cards. Theo is watching the other players and can see that none of them can beat the drivers pair, so one by one they fold, when it comes to Theo he surprises everybody by raising the driver. The driver sees him and raises again. Theo calls. The driver tells Theo, you can see them, a pair of aces. Theo turns over his hole card, and he has another duece, three of a kind beats your two aces he says to the driver. The driver looks at Theo, and asks," How did you know I didn't have a third ace?" Theo tells him " You have to pay attention in this game."

"Look at the other Players hands, the fellow with the pair of Tens had an Ace showing in his hand, likewise the guy with the pair of Kings, so unless there are five Aces in the deck, you couldn't have had three of them." "With the others folding on your pair, I knew I had you beat with the three deuce's." "Well gentlemen, I do have to go as I have a long day ahead of me tomorrow."

So the next day it is off to the mine over the stage trail, since the trail is mostly going uphill, he is taking his time so as not to overwork the mules, it takes him three days to reach the spot where the trail drops down Goodyears Creek. Planning to proceed straight ahead on the ridge, he looks at the terrain ahead of him and sees that by careful driving through the trees he should be able to get considerably closer to his destination. Leaving the stage trail, he drives into the trees a little ways, then stops and sets the brake on the wagon. Walking back to the trail he gets some brush and removes the tracks he just made all the way up to the wagon. Again walking back to the stage trail he checks for his tracks, seeing that they are not visible, he proceeds to drive on the ridge toward his mine site.

Theo manages to get around a mile and a half before he has to stop the wagon. The ridge angles away from the direction of the mine, plus it starts down at a gradual grade, too steep for the wagon and mules, so it's time to stop and transfer the load to the mules to continue to the site.

Parking the wagon behind a line of bushes, so it will be out of site, Theo unhooks the mules, then gets their pack saddles out of the wagon, and proceeds to load the first mule with food stuff, and utensils, then the second mule gets a load of tools to be used to build the cabin. Putting some small items in the saddle bags of the Morgan, he takes off down the mountain towards the future mine site. It takes an hour to get to the ravine where he will be mining, and on the way he finds a small spring with clear water up the hill from the ravine. He had not noticed it last year because it flowed away from the ravine and disappeared on the hill side above the trail he had used when he had discovered the ravine with the gold bearing gravel.

Having come across the spring, he now knew how he would process the gravel, he would dig a ditch to bring the spring water to the ravine, and making a pool, he would *use* the water to work the rocker, not as fast as the Longtom, but more efficient, since he wouldn't have to transport the gravel down to the stream, it might prove to be just as fast. Time will tell.

Taking the mules down the hill further, he finds a place where he can put the cabin, it's a niche in the hill side that is almost flat and big enough for the cabin and stable. There is brush and several trees to be cleared, otherwise a very good spot. Close enough to the stream for water, but up above the high water mark so there is no worry of being flooded.

He unloads the supplies here, and heads up the hill for another load, this time he brings his bedroll and a small tent that Amy insisted he have for the chance of rain or snow, more food, and tools. By the time he gets to the mine, it is getting late in the afternoon. Unloading the animals, he lets them roll, then rubs them down with a gunny sack, takes them to water, then cross hobbles them so they can graze on the spring grass that is coming up. Setting up the tent, and his bedroll, he gets a fire going to make supper, and coffee. By the time he is through eating and cleaning up it is getting dark, so after checking on the mules and horse, he goes over to the tent and crawls in. Taking his journal out of the saddles bags, and a candle to see by, he brings the journal up to date. Finishing his writing, he yawns and crawls into his bedroll, blows out the candle and falls asleep.

The next morning, He's up at first light, and after a breakfast of coffee, bacon and hardtack, he puts the pack saddles on the mules, and saddles the Morgan, and heads up the hill for more supplies. He is able to make four trips that day, the last load being mining tools and the rocker, which he leaves at the head of the gravel he will be working.

After the last trip, and taking care of the animals, he takes stock of what he has here, and what he may need from the wagon yet. Looking at the flat where he plans to put the cabin, he sees he will need tools to remove several stumps, after he has cut the trees down, he is thankful! the trees are small in size, as he will be able to use them in the cabin. Then he goes looking for suitable

rocks to use for the foundation for the cabin, About a hundred yards from the flat he finds a slate outcrop that is just the thing, by using his long bar, and a sledge and wedge, he will be able to gather enough flat slate rock to make a foundation for the cabin. After eating supper and cleaning up the dishes, he finds he still has some daylight left, so he gets his bow saw out and finds a small tree to cut down that he can use to make a stone sled with, The sled will be the easiest way to move the rock to the flat. Working until almost dark he is well on the way to having the sled built, seeing he can finish it in another hour, he gets a coal oil lantern out and lights it for light, an hour later he has a sled. Its two feet wide, about four feet long, with side rails about six inches high. Tomorrow he can get the last load from the wagon, and start the cabin foundation.

CHAPTER THIRTY TWO

The next morning he heads up the mountain for the last load from the wagon. Theo had built a wood stove from sheet iron for the cabin, keeping the design simple, he made it so it could be hauled flat, then bolted together once on the cabin site. The stove pipe was also built for easy transport, to be assembled on the spot. Loading the mules with the stove and pipe, and the last of the supplies he heads back to the cabin site.

That afternoon, he starts clearing the site for the cabin, hooking the mules up, he proceeds to pull the brush out of the flat, then using his horse to stand on he hooks a chain around one of the small trees as high as he can, then with pick, shovel, and axe, he loosens the root structure under the tree. Hooking the mules to the chain he has them pull the tree over, and out of the hole the roots make, one down four to go. It takes him the rest of the afternoon to completely remove the trees and fill in the holes and levels the spot off

After a supper break, he hooks up one of the mules to the stone sled and starts bringing the flat slate rock he wants to use, up to the cabin site. Just before dark, he has a sizeable amount of rock to start the foundation with. He then takes care of the animals, rubbing them down and feeding them some grain, as there is still light he takes a little walk around the area to better acquaint himself with it, he finds several animal trails to the stream, and tells himself to set some snares for fresh meat. Back at the camp he climbs into the tent, and again writes in the journal, before falling to sleep.

Next day is spent building the rock foundation for the cabin, as the flat area is almost flat he only needs about a six inch high foundation, finishing just before supper time, he is pleased with the progress he is making. After supper he sets some snares in the hopes of getting some fresh meat for a change of diet.

The next morning he checks the traps first thing, and finds he has caught a rabbit in one, a possum in another, and signs of a coon having gotten away from the third snare. Breakfast of rabbit, pan bread, and coffee, the rest of the day cutting trees, and laying down the log courses of the cabin. As he wants a wood floor, he is selecting small pines that he can split into twelve feet long halves. Then taking his long jointer plane, he smooth's the inside of the tree for the floor's surface, the edges are squared for a tight fit against each other. Laying the pines on the log joists with the smooth side up he spikes them down, since the wood is green, he can butt the boards right up against each other, and as the tree halves dry they will shrink. Later he can caulk the cracks as needed Possum for supper that evening, with a can of peaches for desert.

And so it goes, the cabin is taking shape, a door with real hinges made by Theo in the blacksmith shop, three windows, one by the door, and one on each end of the cabin for light and ventilation.

A steep roof so the snow will slide off in the winter. Making shingles was a new experience for Theo, Taking rounds of clear cedar or clear pine, he would split the rounds into quarters, then using a froe and wooden mallet, he would split shakes off the rounds, then the shakes had to be tapered with a draw knife so they would lay on the roof right to shed rain or snow. The shingle process was more time consuming then any other part of the cabin.

After a month he had a livable cabin with a loft under the steep roof he then built a shed for the animals, plus a small corral. Checking his calendar he sees it is getting close to the time to go get Amy. He has a couple of days to play at the diggings, so he moves some gravel, and filling his collapsible buckets he does some panning down at the creek, again he is rewarded with a sizable amount of gold nuggets. He puts the rocker together, and walking up to the spring, he starts to dig a trench down to the diggings for the spring water to run in. Seeing he will need a tub of some kind to contain the water for using in the rocker, he makes a mental note to have his cooper make one for him to bring up to the mine.

The morning he has to leave to go back to Auburn, he has a fast breakfast of bacon and coffee, puts the pack saddles on the mules, saddles the horse, and they are off to get the wagon and head for home. Arriving at the wagon he finds that nobody has been there to bother it, so he harness's the mules to the wagon and putting the mule packs and the saddle in the wagon, he is off

When he gets to the stage road, he stops and removes his tracks from the ridge he just drove off from, and then it's down to Marysville. Stopping at the stage station overnight, he says hello to the wrangler who changes the stage horses, and asks how the driver is doing. The wrangler tells Theo how the stage was held up just outside of Marysville, the driver was wounded, and the passengers were robbed and beaten, plus they got the strong box and the mail pouch,

"How bad was the driver wounded?" asks Theo "Oh it was just a flesh wound in his left arm near the shoulder, he's back to driving already". The driver said that the weird part of the holdup was that the three owlhoots all wore masks, and had southern accents like his friend Theo. He said he would recognize them by their voices if he ever ran into them again. Theo asks the wrangler if the driver could describe the men? The man said all he saw was that one was big with long shaggy black hair and beard and one eye, one was a head shorter with eyes that seem to dart every where at once, the third gay was thin with long hair and beard.

That's all the look he got at them as they knocked him out before leaving. When Theo heard the description of the trio, the hair on the back of his neck stood straight up. It sounds like the two that killed his family, but who is the third one he pounders? After taking care of his animals, and supper, Theo hits his bedroll to try and get a good nights sleep, but his mind couldn't get off the holdup and the men the wrangler told him were the robbers, so he had a restless night.

Marysville. Theo stopped at the stage station and left a hello for the driver, then stopped at the telegraph and sent a message to Amy that he was on the way. Then the livery for his animals, and a room at the hotel and dinner. Next morning up and on the trail again.

He arrived home two days later, Beans came running up to the wagon a block from the house, and jumping into the back made his way up to the seat to lick Theo on the face. Theo put his arm around the dog and gave him a hug and said hello old fellow, let's go find Amy and see if she wants to lick my face too. Driving up to the house he finds Amy waiting for him, after a kiss and hug she tells him, I'm ready to go, and anxious to leave as soon as possible. Theo had to calm her down; we will leave as soon as I can get the cooper to make me a tub for the mine. Walking down to the shop, Theo said hello to Ethan, and finding the cooper he told him what he needed. The cooper said that would not be any problem, all he had to do is cut one of the wine barrels in half and add a strap to the upper part to hold it together. "How long asks Theo?" "I can have it for you tomorrow morning."

So Theo tells Amy they can leave tomorrow, after they get the supplies loaded on the wagon and say goodbye to everybody. Amy is so excited she can't sleep that night, and is up before dawn getting breakfast ready for Theo, and rousing him out of bed before he had intended to get up. Amy he says, you really have to calm down, the mine will be there when we get there. There's no hurry. "Yes! Yes! there is" says Amy. "I 've got gold fever, and there won't be any rest for you or me until I dig up my first nugget". "Speaking of which I forgot to bring in the gold I got the last two days before I left". Amy asks, "Where is it?" "I want to look at the pretty yellow rocks so I will know what I am looking for," "He tells her to go get it out of my saddlebags, it's in the right one". "I guess I better get your gold plate down so you can dump it out and take a good look". Amy hollers back, "you betcha my honey", Amy comes back with the leather pouch, and dumps the gold on the plate, and marvels at the warm glow that the nuggets have. " How much did you get this time Theo?" He tells her just over 27 ounces for two days of playing with the gravel. Amy tells Theo she has been learning all she can about gold, and what it is worth. She informs him that the price of twenty four karat gold at the mint in San Francisco is twenty dollars and sixty seven cents an ounce, but that the gold buyers here in town never pay over eighteen dollars an ounce, so they can make a profit when they send it to the mint. The average price is sixteen an ounce when they buy to compensate for the impurity in the nuggets.

"You really have done your homework, haven't you?" " Yes says Amy." "Now taking what you have recovered, around seventy ounces, and multiplying it by sixteen we get a value on the gold of eleven hundred and twenty dollars". "Oh my that's more then most working men make in two years of hard work and sweat", "Yes, that is one of the reasons I have dreamed of finding a gold mine." "The rewards can be fantastic, but the other reason is the treasure hunt so to speak, and the enjoyment of the great outdoors." "Nothing is finer then a summer night, a full belly, a pouch of gold, and the stars to keep a couple company",

CHAPTER THIRTY THREE

After breakfast Amy starts loading her stuff in the wagon. Theo is harnessing the mules, and tying Amy's Mare and his Morgan to the back of the wagon. Beans is underfoot and getting in the way, so Theo puts him on the wagon seat, and tells him to stay. Ethan and Maggie have come to help and say goodbye. Shortly they are ready to go to the shop and get the tub the cooper is making for the mine. Then on to the general store for more food, especially air tights of peaches, and other fruits, and lots of tomatoes, beans, bacon, jerky, flour, sugar, and hard candy, and grain for the animals. Amy said we have to eat good if we are going to work hard.

Then saying goodbye to everybody they are off Two and a half days later they are in Marysville. On the way they pass through the clay mines, and Theo tells Amy that he told Ethan to check into the freighting situation here, there might be a potential for more business.

Arriving in Marysville, Theo stops at the stage station, and says hello, and asks about the driver, the office man tells him, he will be in later. "Good, ask him to join us for supper at the hotel dining room, and tell him I'm buying."

Putting the wagon and animals up in the livery, Theo and Amy get a room, and clean up for supper. Beans is left in the room to guard it, he is told. Meeting the driver in the dining room they get a table and order steak dinners with all the trimmings, and fresh berry pie for desert.

During dinner, Theo asks the driver about the hold up. The driver tells him he was shot in the arm and stopped by these three hard cases. The big guy with one eye jumps up on the coach, and knocks me out, meantime the other two have dragged the passengers out and are beating them, while taking their possessions. The big guy was taking the strong box and mail bags, then they hightailed it as I was coming to. Theo asks if he can describe the trio?

"Yeah", says the driver, "even though they were masked." "The big one had one eye, and the skinny guy called him Rufus, the other guy said something, and the big guy told him to shut up Buford, then he turned to the skinny guy and asked Arnold did you get everything?" "And the man said yes". "The thing is even though they wore masks, I would know them anywhere as they have the same southern accent you have Theo". Upon hearing the descriptions, the hair on the back of Theo's neck stood up again. "I know those men" says Theo, "Rufus and Buford Blackburn who are stepbrothers, and Arnold who used to be a roustabout in Dahlonega until we run him out for stealing." " How do you know these men?" asks the driver. Theo tells him how the Blackburrns killed his family, and how we caught them and put them in jail, only to have them break out and get away. "Now I know who let them out, it was Arnold."

"Well it will be wise to be on the look out for them says the driver, although I think they are laying low now, they got a considerable sum of gold dust from the strong box, plus the mail bags always have letters with money in them that people are sending back home".

The driver tells Theo, that he should come and play poker with him and some friends in Downieville. "I've gotten much better at the game since you took all our money last year, you taught me quite a lot in that game." "We play almost every Saturday night in the general store's back room". Theo asks if Amy can come too? "Sure says the driver, it's a family game, there's Clem the store owner and his wife, the Preacher and his lady, Charlie the deputy, and a couple of others that show up on occasion." "The ladies would be glad to have your missus there, it would give them some new news and gossip to talk about". "We just might do that after we get settled in at the mine," So after saying goodnight it's off to bed, to get ready for the next day.

First light, they are up, breakfast in the dining room, then on to the livery for their wagon and animals. Then on to the stage road, Beans senses the tension in the two as they are being overly wary and cautious about their surroundings. At the first rest stop Beans gets down from the wagon and runs on ahead a ways looking for what might be bothering his friends. Theo has on his sidearm and the Henry rifle next to him, and Amy is wearing her new gun belt with her new Colt, and her new Henry rifle across her lap. Two days and no problems, and then they are at the turn off that Theo uses to traverse the ridge, pulling into the brush ahead; he goes back and removes their tracks, then on to the spot where he hides the wagon, and goes by horse and mules to the mine.

Loading the mules with their bedding and food and Amy's clothes, they head for the mine camp. On the way Theo tells Amy they will have to sleep on the floor, as he didn't build the bed yet. Amy asks why not? Theo tells her that the inside of the cabin is hers to arrange for her comfort. Well isn't that nice of you she says, what a perfect southern gentleman you are, as she laughs.

Arriving at the cabin, they unload the bedding, Amy's clothes, and the food, then taking the animals down to the creek, they let them drink, then up to the new corral, where they rub them down and grain them. While Amy sets up the bedding, Theo has the supper fire going, Coffee, canned meat, and sourdough pan bread. After supper they take a walk down the stream to the game trails, where Theo sets up the snares, telling Amy, if we are lucky, we'll have fresh meat for breakfast.

Then it's get ready for bed, Theo gets his journal out and by lantern light brings it up to date, Amy remarks to Theo," some day you are going to let me read your life story, won't you?"

Theo says yes, "it's time for you to know all my secrets, all the drinking, gambling, fighting, and whoring around I did before I met you, and got religion." Then he laughs, as she takes a swing at him. "Theo! I know better then that, I was your first, so there was no whoring around, the drinking, gambling, and fighting I know you did."

Then it's lights out, and snuggle into their blankets, to have the first of many intimate moments together in their new cabin at the mine.

Morning, Theo is up and checking the traps to see if they caught anything, two rabbits and a coon, not bad he says to himself. So it's roast rabbit for breakfast, along with sourdough pancakes, with apple butter on top, and the usual coffee. After breakfast, Theo gets busy and for the next two days he spends making a bedstead for them, and shelves and hooks for their coats. Amy wants to know if he is going to make a table and chairs that they can sit down and eat at. "Theo good naturely, growls, boy give her and inch and she wants a castle with that French King's fancy furniture in it." Amy starts to chase him with the towel she is using to dry the dishes.

All kidding aside, Amy you're right we need a table and chairs. So Theo goes out and cuts four rounds of pine into equal lengths then he takes a piece about three feet long and splits it the long way, then he nails the two boards on to the top of the four rounds. This gives him four legs with two cross pieces, then he splits enough pine into boards to make the table top and nails them to the cross pieces, countersinking the nails he takes his long jointer plane and smoothes the table top and rounds off the corners and edges. Then he cut two rounds about twenty inches wide and almost the same height to use as chairs. There your Highness, the finest dinning set our superb craftsmen can make on such short notice. And again they both have a good laugh.

It's time to start supper, so getting the coon down that has been hanging since yesterday, Theo starts skinning it and preparing it for the stew pot. He shows Amy how his ma told him to cut all the fat off the meat, otherwise the meat will taste bitter, then cutting the meat into chunks; he coated it with flour, salt and pepper and braised it in the frying pan, once the meat was browned he put it in the stew pot, and let it simmer for about and hour. Then added onions, carrots, potatoes and green beans, he let that cook for another half hour or so till the vegetables were done but still firm. Meantime Amy was busy making a dried apple pie, and sourdough pan bread to go with the stew. They both thought some tea would be good for a change from the usual coffee.

So dinner by candle light on their new fit for a queen table and chairs. After dinner they took their usual walk with Beans by their side. While walking Amy remarks to Theo, that if we keep eating this good we are going to get fat, Theo tells her, "Once we get to work mining, we'll work off any fat we may gain".

Next morning, breakfast, Then put the packs on the mules to go get the rest of the supplies. Theo has brought two bags of cement to put the hot tub furnace together with, plus a tank, copper tubing and a metal box with a door on its side, instead of the usual lid on top.

Amy asks what the metal box is for? "You'll see says Theo, that's going to be our safe for all the gold we get." Back to the camp and unload, then one more trip and they are through with bringing the supplies from the wagon. For lunch, left over stew, and pie, then it's up the hill to the Diggings.

Getting to the diggings, Theo shows Amy how they will dig the gravel up off the bedrock, then with the molly tools they clean the bedrock crevices, then take that material and wash it in the rocker to get the gold out. First we have to set up the tub and rocker, then bring the spring water down to the tub, so you'll have water for the washing of the gravel. So clearing off a flat spot on the hill side they set up the tub and rocker, then Theo goes up the hill and starting where he left off he continues digging the trench for the spring water to flow down to the tub. When he gets to the tub, he finds he is going to need a couple of boards to make a trough for the water to flow into the tub, so down to the cabin and looking through his left overs from building the cabin, he finds two pieces of pine he can use for a trough.

Meanwhile Amy and Beans are digging on the face of the gravel. Amy has cleared off a couple of feet of bedrock and is cleaning it with the Molly, and putting the material into the collapsible canvas buckets. Beans has been watching both Amy and Theo digging all afternoon and figures it's time to see what they are digging for, so he starts digging at the face of the gravel and in his exuberance is throwing gravel all over Amy. Beans she yells "look at what you're doing to me". Beans, looking back sheepishly sees Amy covered with dirt, as he starts to crawl away, Amy grabs him and gives him a hug, and tells him it's ok Beans, just watch, I don't need the help right now.

By then Theo has the spring water running into the tub, and goes and carries Amy's buckets of gravel over to the rocker. Then he shows her how the rocker works, you take a shovel full of gravel and place it on the top of the punch plate, then dipping water out of the tub, you pour it over the gravel and at the same time rock the rocker back and forth. This washes the gravel and separates the gold from the gravel to let it fall through the punch plate down onto the riffles in the bottom of the rocker box. When we are through washing for the day, we'll take the riffles out and then scrape the concentrates out into a gold pan, then pan it down to just the gold. Then we'll take it down to the cabin and dry it, weigh it, then put it in the leather pouches I brought for the gold. We'll keep track of the ounces of gold we recover, and see how rich we can become.

"Well what are we waiting for? I'll wash, You dig, and let's get some of that gold you have been talking about". So they spend the rest of the afternoon mining. They are so excited, that they forget about supper and feeding the animals before dark, until Beans starts to raise a ruckus. Theo realizes it's starting to get dark, so he stops digging, and goes over to Amy and stops her from putting more gravel in the rocker. Scooping some more water, he pours it over the rocker, and gives the concentrates a final washing, then he carefully removes the riffles, and with a wide

Putty knife he scrapes the concentrates into a gold pan. Then he takes the pan over to the tub and pans it out Amy is wide eyed at the amount of gold that is showing up in the pan. When Theo finishes panning they head for the cabin. Putting the pan on the table, they rush out to take care of the animals, and then get a quick supper ready. After supper they dry the gold and weigh it. Theo tells Amy her first day as a gold rocker was pretty fruitful, they have just over fourteen ounces of gold, "My god says Amy that is a fortune for one afternoons work". "Yes" says Theo. "I can Thank Cuss for teaching me how to find such a spot, and the spirits of Brutus for telling me that I would find you for a partner." Amy blushes at the lovely words that Theo has just bestowed on her.

Next morning, with Amy's help Theo puts the hot tub together, Amy has heard of the hot tubs of Japan from Theo and also a book she read once on oriental culture. So she is as anxious as Theo to get the tub working. Spending the morning on the tub, they now have to gather rock for the furnace, plus sand for the mortar to cement the furnace together. Hooking one of the mules up to the stone sled they go down to the stream and gather rocks with which to build the furnace, when they have a sufficient amount of stones, Theo levels off a place below the tub where the furnace is to sit. Then he starts the foundation, a layer of stones with mortar to hold them together, then he installs the metal box they are going to use as a safe, just like Cuss's,

Then building up the rocks around the metal box to the fire box. Using a piece of the slate, he makes a rectangular stone that will slide out of the foundation to give him access to the safe box. On top of the fire box he installs the tank he made in the shop that will be the water heater.

Then he hooks up the copper pipe he made in the blacksmith shop at home in Auburn to the tank and the hot tub. By this time it is late afternoon, so they quit for the day and take care of the animals, then make supper. Amy has brought a couple of new books to read, so they settle in for the evening and read awhile, then Theo brings the journal up to date, then off to dreamland.

Next day Theo starts making wooden pipe to bring water from the rocker tub down to the hot tub. He takes clear cedar and cuts pieces about three feet long and about three inches in diameter, then using an auger drill bit he drills down the length of the cedar. The bit can drill about twenty inches, so he has to start from the other side and drill to meet the hole he has already put in. Then he takes a special tool he made and tapers one end of the piece, then using another special tool, he makes a cone shaped hole in the other end. One piece done, he continues making more. After the second piece is done Amy understands the reason for the taper and the cone. Taking the two pieces you fit the tapered end into the cone end , and you have a pipe. Then using baling wire, you wrap the joint. When the water gets in the pipe, the wood will swell and make for a tight non leaking joint. By late afternoon Theo has enough pipe to get up to the tub. So they quit for the day, and after supper have time to go for a walk, and set some more snares. Then off to bed and some loving, then sleep.

Next day Theo hooks up the pipe to the tub and the hot tub, he has brought a bung hole valve to install in the pipe, so he can shut off the water or turn it on as they need it to cool off the tub if it gets too hot, Now it's time to fill the tub and start a fire in the stone furnace. Starting with a small fire at first, so as to eliminate all the moisture in the rocks slowly, they eventually have a good fire going, and the water in the tank is getting hot. Putting his hand by the outlet of the top tubing, Theo feels the hot water coming into the tub. It's working Amy, tonight we will have a soak, and get rid of all the little aches and pains from all our hard work.

So the camp and the mine are finally set up. Now it's mining in earnest as the gravel bank faces the east, it gets the morning sun, so Theo sets up the tent as a tarp to give them shade while digging, plus a lean-to covering the rocker. Then its sunup to late afternoon mining, according to their records, they are averaging over nine ounces a day, some days are really rich, then it falls off until they uncover another rich set of crevices. Theo and Amy are tickled pink with the recovery.

One evening while they are enjoying the pleasure of the hot tub, Beans starts to growl and the hair goes up on his back, then he starts barking as a black bear walks into camp. Theo jumps out of the hot tub, and runs for the cabin to get his rifle. Amy starts to scream, and Beans runs and attacks the bear. The dog circles the bear, then jumps on his back, grabbing a mouthful of skin at the base of the bears neck, the bear howls, and raises up on his hind legs shaking Beans around where he can swat him with a paw. As Beans goes flying through the air, Theo is pumping lead into the bear, it takes three shots to kill the beast, Meantime Amy is getting out of the tub, and putting her robe on and running over to Beans, The dog is hurt and laying on his side breathing hard. Getting down on her knees, Amy starts to examine the dog; she finds several claw cuts and what seem to be cracked ribs. Telling Beans to stay, she runs to the cabin for the first aid kit, and her roll of gauze cloth. She has to sew up the cuts and wrap the dog's ribs. The dog knows he is being helped, and does not move while Amy is doctoring him up. Theo is making a stretcher, so they can carry the dog up to the cabin. When Amy gets done, they slide the stretcher under the dog and take him into the cabin near the stove where he can stay warm while he heals. After the ordeal is over, Amy tells Theo, to put some clothes on, he looks silly killing bears while running around naked, at which they laugh so much they get tears in their eyes.

Later in bed they are discussing the event, and Theo tells Amy, that the whole thing lasted less then a minute. Amy asks Theo," How come she is always wrapping up the cracked ribs of the men in her life, first you, now Beans," The dog barks, and Theo shrugs his shoulders, and says, "That's what happens when you hook up with two no accounts like us".

It takes Beans three days to get up and move around. A week later he's pretty much back to his old routine.

Meantime they are going to Downieville every Saturday, to get supplies, mostly food, and have their laundry done at the Chinese laundry and to visit with the stage driver and the others and play poker. Amy is getting to know the woman folk real well, and Theo is winning more then he loses as usual. The driver and Charlie are getting lessons from Theo on the finer points of the game, so they eventually are playing almost as good as Theo.

As the summer goes fleeting by, it is almost time for Amy to go back to Auburn and her teaching duties, the mining has been very fruitful, until the last week. All of a sudden the gold fell off to less then an ounce a day. Amy is concerned, but Theo tells her not to worry, that's the character of placer mining, for some reason the gold did not deposit itself here, but is bound to pick up as we get deeper into the gravel. So they keep digging, until they are up against a very large boulder. Theo, tells Amy," Now I know why I named the mine the Deja-vu." "Cuss and I ran into the same thing when I first went to work for him." Working around the boulder they run into gold again, lots of gold. And as they get further into the gravel they see that there is a crevice under the boulder that is unusual, for it is running length wise with the old river channel

The up stream side of the boulder is loaded with nuggets, and the crevice is full of gold. Usually the gold deposits itself on the down stream side of a large boulder, "this is mighty unusual" says Theo. Theo then tells Amy the only way to get the gold is to blast the boulder into pieces, so it can be moved and the crevice cleaned out. As it's getting late, and it's Friday, they quit for the day.

Next day they go to Downieville, and get a small keg of black powder, pick up their laundry, and Amy says goodbye to her new friends, as she has to get back to Auburn. Sunday morning they pack up the mules with fifty pounds of gold apiece, plus Amy's clothes and possibles, then checking their weapons they take off up the mountain to get the wagon and head for Auburn.

After the stage hold up Arnold and the Blackburns, decide to a change of scenery. At Arnolds urging they head for Sacramento, where with the money and gold they got they can have a good time. Arnold decides that it is time to change his appearance, so he goes to a barber, and gets a haircut, shave and a bath. Then he goes into a mercantile and buys himself some new clothes, a modest suit and derby hat, and some jeans and shirts for the trail, And most important, a new pair of boots. As he rides back into camp, the Blackburns almost shoot him, he has changed so much that they didn't recognize him.

Arnold tells Rufus and Buford that they should do what he did and change their appearance, for sure the people they robbed have given the law their description, "and Rufus I have a surprise for you," "I happened across a shop that makes glass eyes." "For fifty bucks, you can look more normal, which will help us to evade the law." Rufus says "Your're kidding! After all these years, you want me to wear a glass eye?" "Rufus! it's for your own good, someone is bound to look at you and a wanted poster, and put two and two together". Alright Arnold, I'll go get the eye, and do like you did, haircut, beard trim, new suit and boots". "I'll get so dandyfied up, my own mother won't know me, same goes for you too, Buford." "Aw! Rufus do I have to?" "Yeah", says the big brute.

After taking Amy home, Theo checks on the shop and Ethan. "How is everything going, he asks?" Pretty good says Ethan, "I checked on the clay mines as you suggested, and found they did indeed need freighting help." "The outfit they were using was gouging them, plus they weren't getting the loads to the customers on time, they had a bunch of drunks driving, so they were always late." "So we have some new contracts." "Also the railroad is asking us to mill rail ties for them." "It seems we can beat the fellows in Sacramento on their prices by twenty percent, because of their transportation costs from their source of wood to their mill, then back here where they need the ties". "Sounds good" says Theo. "Are you going to need me for the next couple of months?" "I have some unfinished mining to do yet this season". "No" says Ethan, "we seem to have everything under control." "Good" says Theo.

So Theo spends a couple of days getting Amy settled back in, and getting supplies that he can't get in Downieville, and packs up to go back to the mine. Arriving in Marysville, he stops at the stage office and says hello as usual, then on to the livery and hotel, another good steak dinner. sleep, then off to the mine the next morning.

Back up at the mine he misses Amy and Beans, but he knows he will see them in a couple of months. So it's back to work, first thing that has to be done is get rid of the large boulder. So using the single jack and the star drills he brought from the shop, he starts drilling the boulder like Cuss taught him. When the holes are drilled, he packs them with the powder, and sets the fuses. Giving himself five minutes of fuse time, he lights them and walks around the hill side out of the way. Shortly there is a tremendous boom, and rocks flying all over, Theo remembers Cuss's remark, about using to much powder, and laughs to himself.

After the cloud of dust and smoke clears, he goes to inspect the result of the blast. The boulder is broken into small enough pieces that he can move most of them by hand, so getting the wooden wheel barrow he made earlier, he starts moving rock. Working later then usual, he manages to get the area cleared of the remnants of the boulder. Realizing it's getting late he quits for the day, and goes takes care of the animals, starts the hot tub fire, then fixes supper.

A hot soak, then off to bed, which is too big without Amy there. "Journal, I forgot to bring it up to date", so he climbs out of bed and gets the journal and writes in it, What a day, blasted the boulder, and mucked it out, tomorrow see if we did any good.

Next morning, Oatmeal, with butter, bacon and eggs, and sourdough bread for breakfast Good idea I had getting some eggs he thinks to himself. He laughs as he finds himself starting to talk to himself

Up at the diggings Theo is shoveling off the crevice, as he cleans the gravel off, he is seeing glints of yellow, taking a stiff brush, he starts to brush the dirt away, and finds that the crevice is solid gold nuggets, some are almost as big as his hand. My god I've hit the mother lode of this old stream bed. The next two days are spent cleaning out the crevice. After cleaning up the gold, and weighing it, he has a total of just over a thousand ounces. "I still can't believe it" he says to himself, "A thousand ounces in one crevice, what a find."

During the weighing he finds he has several large nuggets over twenty ounces, many ten and up, over a hundred one ounce pieces, and many in between. That Saturday he is still floating on a cloud when he goes to Downieville. His friends see the elation in him and ask why he is so happy? "Oh!" he says "I had a rather good week."

So a good poker game, and fellowship with his friends, Theo is up the next morning, getting a few things at the store, then off to the mine.

The gold keeps coming, forty ounce day, another crevice with a hundred ounces, some with only one or two ounces, but it keeps coming.

It's now the last of September and Arnold and the Blackburns have migrated to the upper Yuba river diggings. Camping outside Downieville a few miles, they are looking for another good robbery opportunity. With his change in appearance, Arnold is able to hang around Downieville and glean information about rich diggings, or what the stage is hauling, even the bank is being looked at.

On the last Saturday of September, Arnold spots a horse he knows. Watching it he sees Theo get on it and ride out of town down river towards Goodyears Bar. Going into the general store, he asks the owner if his old friend Theo comes in often? Clem says, "Oh! do you know Theo?" Arnold tells him, "Why yes, we grew up together in Georgia, near a town called Dahlonega." "I haven't seen Theo in ten or eleven years", "At first I didn't recognize him until he got on his

Morgan and rode away." "I remember when he got that horse from his friend Cuss, who he was working for".

Now Clem listening to Arnold thinks to himself, that this fellow must be an old friend of Theo's, or else he wouldn't know so much about him. So he tells him that Theo usually comes in on Saturday and gets some supplies and plays poker with me and some of the locals here.

"What is he doing here" asks Arnold? Clem tells him he has a diggings up the mountain, and like I said he comes in for grub and poker on Saturday. "That's really all I know about him, except he has a great wife who teaches school in Auburn." "She was up here for a couple of months, but is now back to work". "Who should I say asked about him?" Arnold tells Clem, "Oh! just say his old friend Tom Brooks from back home". "If I'm still here next week I'll be sure to look him up and sit and have a beer and talk about old times". "What time does he usually get here asks Arnold?" "Around noon" says Clem. "Ok, like I said if I'm still here I'll be on the look out for him," With that he leaves the store and rides up river back to camp to tell the Blackburn's who he just saw.

CHAPTER THIRTY FOUR

Back at the camp, Arnold tells the stepbrothers about seeing Theo in town. " Theo?", says Rufus, "isn't he the brother of the little gal I had in Dahlonega, that tore my eye out". " The punk who helped put us in jail." "Yeah!" says Arnold, "and he's got a mine up on the mountain somewhere, the store owner says he comes into town every Saturday for supplies and to play poker with some of the locals".

Now suppose, next Saturday,. I wait in town for him to show up, then follow him to his mine, when I find out where it is, we can go and kill the sumbitch, and take any gold he may have.

Sounds like a good idea says the pair. "Meantime I sure could use a woman, I need my ashes hauled" says Rufus. "Then let's ride up to Sierra City to the cathouse and do that, only you two behave yourself" "We don't want to draw any attention to ourselves till we finish robbing and killing Theo, and some others if we need too for the money."

Next Saturday, Theo rides into Downieville, and stops at the store for his usual weekly stock up of grub. Clem tells Theo about the clean shaven skinny guy with a southern accent, asking about him Theo asks. " Did he give you a name?" Clem said yeah! "it was Tom Brooks".

Theo thinks a moment, and tells Clem, "you know I didn't know any one with the name of Tom Brooks as a kid growing up." "You say he was skinny, and talked like me?" "Yes", said Clem, "and he sure knew a lot about you." "He said he remembers when you got your Morgan horse as a birthday present from Cuss the guy you worked for." "A skinny guy, you say, the only skinny guy I know who might be out here is Arnold, and he is a no good bum running with the Blackburn stepbrothers." "They're the ones who robbed the stage and shot the driver in the arm."

"Damn!" exclaims Clem, "I told him you come in every Saturday and play poker with us, so if he is up to no good, he knows how to find you". Theo asks if Clem could point him out in a crowd, if he had to? "You betcha", says Clem. "Ok, lets see if we can lay a trap for him".

"We'll go about our usual game, only we'll play later then usual, so it will be dark when we finish". "I'll decide to stay over night at the hotel, and put my horse and mule in the livery." "Then before daybreak I'll slip out of town, and wait up the trail a-ways to see if I'm being followed." "If it's Arnold? I'll know him when I see him, even though he has gotten rid of his beard."

Arnold meantime is in the barbershop across the street getting a shave and watching Theo through the window. After the shave he leaves out the back door, saying he has to use the privy. Having already scouted the town, he knows there is a ladder leading up to the roof of the building next door. Quietly climbing the ladder, he goes to the front of the building, and crouching down in the shade of the false front he spies on Theo and the town. He sees Theo take his horse and mule down to the livery, and come back to the store. He also sees the stage driver go in, plus a couple of others. This must be where they play poker, he thinks to himself.

The afternoon turns into evening, and then it's dark. Arnold is about to quit the roof, when he sees Theo and the driver walk out of the store. Theo heads for the hotel a couple of doors away, while the stage driver goes to the stage office to bunk out there, Damn! Thinks Arnold, he's going to stay overnight in the hotel, and I'm hungry as hell. I can either stay here and starve and watch for him to leave, or head back to camp, eat, get some sleep, then be here first thing in the morning and follow him to his mine. Arnold's hunger wins out, so he carefully leaves the roof and gets his horse and heads for camp.

The next morning he heads back to town, when he gets there he decides to put his horse in the same livery, as an excuse to watch for Theo from the hayloft. He finds when he rides into the livery that Theo has already left. "Damn it!, I missed him". To keep from arousing suspicion from the hostler, he puts up the horse, and then goes to the cafe to have breakfast.

At breakfast he overhears the stage driver, and another fellow talking about how Theo beat them in poker again. The other guy, asks the driver how come Theo stayed overnight, then left before dawn this morning? The driver tells the guy that Theo got wind of an old enemy from Georgia is hanging around these parts, so he was watching out for him. But he didn't see him in town yesterday, so he left early, he should be up on top of Goodyears Creek by now.

From there it is a secret as to which way he goes. Arnold has just got the information he needs to set up an ambush for Theo. Waiting until the driver and the other fellow leave, Arnold pays his bill, then heads for the livery and gets his horse and rides out to where they are camping.

Arnold tells the Blackburns what he has learned, and plans an ambush for the next Saturday.

We will wait for him on the Goodyears Creek trail, then stop and disarm him, then make him take us to his mine, you know how these miners are, they all bury some of their gold somewhere and I'll bet Theo has a good stash. The guy that taught him how to mine had the best mine around, back in Dahlonega. So they lay low the rest of the week, then ride through Downieville late at night so no one sees them, and prepare to set up their ambush the next day.

Meantime Theo is still getting gold at the diggings; he hits another large crevice, with several hundred ounces in it. He is still amazed at how rich this small old river channel is. Midweek he weighs the gold he has recovered, and added to the stash in the furnace safe, he finds he has over two hundred and fifty Troy pounds of gold, at twelve ounces to the pound that amounts to over three thousand ounces. As Amy says," my god, we have a fortune here". He multiplies the ounces by sixteen and comes up with forty eight thousand dollars, again he exclaims, my god!

As it is now the middle of October, the weather is changing fast, colder nights, already one day of rain. Theo tells himself, it's time to call it a season. So he starts closing down the mine, making Friday the last day he will dig, then only for a half day. The rest of the day he gathers up all the equipment and stores it in the shed. Drains the rocker tub, and the hot tub. Weighs up fifty pounds of gold to take back to Auburn with him, and generally gets ready to leave the next morning. He plans to go to Downieville and say goodbye to his friends, pick up enough supplies to get him to Marysville, then on to home.

Up just before dawn, a fast breakfast of jerky and coffee, he packs up to leave. Saying goodbye to the mine, he is off. By midday he is almost to the bottom of the Goodyears Creek trail, when he sees a flash of sunlight off a gun barrel, at the same time the Morgan snickers, and there is an answering snicker, grabbing his rifle, he slides out of the saddle and walks behind the horse out of sight of whoever is around the bend in the trail. As the horse comes into view of the trio of owlhoots waiting in ambush, Rufus yells, where the hell is he, the horse is empty.

Theo shows himself and says here I am you bastards. Everybody is raising their guns to fire. Theo puts a bullet into Rufus, then levering another shell into the gun, he shoots Buford, then again another shell and he gets Arnold, Buford and Arnold both get off shots, but too late, Theo had already killed them. Watching the three, Theo advances toward them, as he gets to Rufus he sees his gun come up and the two get off a shot at the same time, Theo gets Rufus in the heart and kills him this time , but Rufus gets in a lucky shot and puts a bullet into Theo's gut.

Theo goes down, but not out. "Damn! He got me" says Theo, "I've got to get to town and see if the Doc can do anything." So getting up, he stumbles over to the Morgan and painfully pulls himself into the saddle, come on horse get me to town, and he rides as fast as he can towards Downieville. The five or so miles seem to take forever; as he gets into town he is dizzy and just managing to stay in the saddle, he pulls out his Colt, and fires three rounds into the air. This brings the Sheriff and Charlie running, plus people are coming out of the stores to see what is going on. Charlie sees that it is Theo's horse, and takes off running as fast as he can, he gets to Theo just as he is beginning to fall out of the saddle, Charlie catches Theo and gently lowers him to the ground, seeing the blood on his shirt, he knows that Theo is hit bad. "Get the Doc," he yells, Theo is gut shot." Charlie grabs Theo's canteen and using his kerchief he splashes water on Theo's face to bring him around, as Theo comes around, Charlie asks "What happened?"

Theo in a weak voice tells Charlie about the ambush, and how he had killed the three, but not before he got shot himself. Just then the Doc and the Sheriff show up carrying a stretcher, putting it down beside Theo, they slide him on to it and Charlie and the Sheriff head for the Doc's office.

As fast as they can carry Theo. In the office, they put him on a table, the Doc cuts Theo's shirt off and proceeds to examine the wound. "It's bad he announces, he's lost too much blood and the bullet damaged too many vitals." "I'll be surprised if he makes it through the night". Theo is awake enough to hear the Doc. "Charlie" he whispers in a choking voice, "Get me to Amy please." "You bet Theo, what else can I do for you?" Theo whispers again in Charlie's ear," in my saddle bags, there is my journal, bring it to me please, I want to write Amy a note." Charlie runs out to Theo's horse, and gets the journal. Back with Theo, he helps him to write the note by holding the journal for Theo.

Theo writes, Amy I love you, I have killed the scum that killed my family, but alas they have killed me, I'll see you on the other side where we will be together forever. P.S. the gold is in Cuss's safe. Take care my love. Then he starts coughing, and spitting up blood. The Doc says that's enough Charlie, he's going pretty fast, it won't be long now.

The Doc turns to the Sheriff and tells him he better get Mort. The Sheriff goes over to the undertaker, and cabinet shop. "Mort, the Doc says you should come now". "Alright" says the undertaker, as they get back to the Doc's office, they barely hear Theo tell Charlie. "Take me home Charlie, take me home." "I will friend, I will." Then he's gone.

Doc tells Mort, "Get him ready for Charlie to take him home to Auburn". "Charlie go get your bedroll and possibles, Mort should have Theo ready in an hour," Charlie is almost in tears over what has happened to Theo, everybody is down. Here was a good man taken in his prime of life. It's not fair.

By the time Charlie gets back, Mort has Theo ready to go. He's been embalmed, and wrapped in a canvas, so they can tie him on his horse. Charlie puts Theo's journal back in his saddle bags, then mounting up he grabs the lead lines of the horse and mule, and heads for the Goodyears Creek trail. Shortly he gets to the scene of the shooting. He takes the time to unsaddle the owlhoots horses, and send them off. He pulls the bodies off the trail, and goes through their pockets. There is a considerable amount of money between the three that Charlie believes belongs to the stage line, so he puts it into one of their saddle bags with all their other belongings and tie's it to the mule pack frame to take back to the Sheriff, when he gets back.

Then making as good time as he can, resting the animals every hour or so he heads for Auburn. Riding day and night, he gets to Auburn in three days. He is exhausted when he pulls up to the T&E enterprises shop late in the afternoon of the third day. Climbing down off his horse, he ties the animals to the hitch rail and enters the building. Sam is the first person he see's. "Mr. He asks? "Is Amy's uncle Ethan here?" "I come from Downieville with very bad news." Sam knocks on Ethan's office door and pokes his head in and tells Ethan, come quick there's a deputy here, with some bad news from Downieville. Ethan jumps up and rushes out to see what is wrong. "Mr.Winslow" says Charlie, "I've brung Theo home as he asked me to before he died". "What?" exclaims Ethan, "Theo is dead'?" "Yes" says Charlie, "He was killed in a shoot out with the men that killed his family back in Georgia." "He killed all three of them, but got gut shot doing it, he lived long enough to get to Downieville, and told us what happened."

"Do you mind if I sit down?" "I've been on the trail for three days and nights and I don't know if I can stand up any longer", "I'm sorry, deputy, of course come sit in my office, and I'll get you something to drink and eat," "Thanks" says Charlie,

"Oh my god, I've got to tell Amy, and with her just finding out she is pregnant, this is going to go down very hard for her says Ethan". Ethan sends Sam after something for Charlie, while he goes and gets Maggie, then up to Theo's house to get Amy. Knocking on the front door, and then going in, he yells for Amy to come quick, something terrible has happened. Amy is in the den working on grading papers for the school children, when she hears her uncle yelling for her. Getting up and running to the hallway, she sees Ethan and Maggie, and asks what is wrong?

Ethan tells her to come down to the shop, "Charlie the deputy from Downieville has brought Theo home, he was shot in a shoot out with the three that killed his family, and he died from the wound." "What! My Theo dead, no! no! it can't be true, not now when I found out I'm carrying his child." Then, it's too much for her to fathom, and she faints. Ethan and Maggie manage to catch her before she hits the floor. Ethan picks up his niece and carries her into the parlor and places her on the couch, Maggie is running to the kitchen and getting a glass of water and a damp cloth. Placing the wet cloth over Amy's forehead, they finally get her to come to.

She looks into their eyes and sees what she just heard is true and breaks out crying. Between sob's she shakes her head, "Not now! Not now, not when everything has been going so good, Why lord? Why now?" The sobs are uncontrollable; finally she gets herself under control, and says," let's go get Theo."

At the shop, there is a crowd, all wanting to know what has happened, Sam is trying to get them to quiet down so he can explain, but they won't stop asking questions, then Amy shows up with her uncle and Maggie, Everybody quiets down as Amy has Theo taken up to the house. Ethan is leading the Morgan and Charlie has the mule. In front of the house, Amy asks if they can carry Theo in and put him in the drawing room for now, "I'll have to have the undertaker bring a coffin to put him in, before we bury him". Then she starts crying again. Ethan tells her, he and Maggie will take care of everything, "You need to go and lie down, I'll get the Doctor to come up and give you something to help you". Amy cries, "I don't need a Doctor, I need my Theo back." "Maggie stay with her while I get the Doc, she's going to need something to calm her down."

Meanwhile Charlie has gotten his second wind and is taking the horse and mule over to the stable and is unpacking them. He gets the animals unpacked and unsaddled, then rubs them down, puts them is their stalls with feed, grain and water. Then he takes Theo's saddle bags up to the house, and asks Maggie where he should put them? She tells him to put them in the room off the kitchen for now. Charlie says there is more stuff from the pack mule. Maggie tells him to put it in the same room, which he does, "Ma'am, he says, if you don't need me anymore, I'm going to get a room at one of the hotels and sleep for a couple of days." Maggie tells him to go up to her rooming house, and stay in the room just to the right of the stairs, "It's the least we can do for you," "When you get enough rest I'll fix you a special meal to help you get your strength back." "Thank you ma'am," says Charlie.

As he is leaving Ethan is getting back with the Doctor. Amy is still sobbing quietly, The Doctor tells her, "Here Amy, take this, it will help you calm down, and sleep". "Alright doctor, I obviously need something". So the Doctor gives her a spoonful of laudanum, which shortly puts her to sleep.

CHAPTER THIRTY FIVE

Maggie tells Ethan to go and tell the undertaker to make a nice coffin for Theo," Then come back, so I can go and start supper for the roomer's." " When I'm finished I'll come back and stay with Amy." " I'll leave some supper out for you, then you can come back here." "Amy's going to need all the help she will let us give her to get her through this". Ethan, agrees," Yes I know." "A long time ago Chief Ironbelly told me something was going to happen, that would call on us to be strong for Amy, now I know what he was talking about."

So the vigil starts, Amy is having periods of bad dreams, and is talking in her delirium, "Screaming at Theo to watch out for the bear, and telling him that the trio of owlhoots will be caught and hanged for what they did". "Beans is hurt, carry him up to the cabin so I can fix him".

Then in the middle of the night, she finally quiets down and seems to be sleeping more peacefully.

The next morning, she awakes feeling very groggy, "Its the effects of the Laudanum" Maggie tells her, "Otherwise how do you feel?" "Drained", Amy replies. "Is it true?" "It wasn't a bad dream was it?" "I'm afraid so Amy", says her uncle, "But we are here, and the Chief told me a long time ago when you two got married, that you will have our strength to help you get through this." "The Chief knew?" asks Amy. Ethan tells her of the Chief taking him aside after the wedding ceremony, and telling him to sell his goods in Great Salt Lake City, then go on to Auburn to be with you and Theo, and that a tragedy would befall you, and that you would need my strength to help you through it. Amy looks at her uncle, and tells him how Theo believed in the power of his friend Brutus and the others they encountered on the trail to California. "Now I wish they had been able to tell him how to stop what has just happened", then she starts crying again.

Shortly, with Maggie holding her she stops, and says, "I have to be brave now," "I have the child to think about." "Maggie, Ethan, help me get through the funeral, then I must get on with having this child and teaching the children at the school." "Theo would want me to carry on and be brave, but right now I feel like the whole world has forsaken me." "I know, I feel the same way" says Ethan. "Theo was my best friend, business partner, and brother all wrapped up in one person." "Amen" says Maggie.

The funeral was two days later, the undertaker had spent extra time on the coffin, plus there were some of Theo's business friends from Sacramento and San Francisco that wanted to attend, once they got word over the telegraph of the tragedy. Almost the whole town turned out, it seemed like everybody that Theo had done work for over the years, showed up. Even Beans was there alongside Amy. The dog seemed to suffer the loss as much as the humans. After the service, and everybody wishing their condolences, Amy asks Maggie and Ethan to give her a few moments alone. She and Beans stayed by the grave for several minutes, while she prayed and talked to Theo. Then she got up to leave, with Beans following her. He kept looking back, and whimpering. The dog knew he had lost his best friend.

The next month was very hard on Amy, between mourning the loss of Theo, and her morning sickness that seemed to last forever, she was unable to teach school. The school board hired a temporary substitute for her, and told her to take her time, that she can always come back to teach whenever she is ready. Finally the morning sickness subsided and she felt better, but she was big enough now, that standing in a class room for eight hours was too much for her, so she had to take a leave of absence. Fortunately the substitute had not left town yet, so they put her back to work. Meantime Beans is disappearing for an hour or more each afternoon, when Maggie comes over to take Amy for a walk, Maggie is acting under the Doctor's order to make sure Amy gets enough exercise. He's afraid Amy is going to have trouble with the birth when it's time. It's nothing definite he can put his finger on, just a nagging feeling. On one of the walks, they go by the cemetery; there they see Beans lying alongside Theo's grave. Now they know where Beans disappears too each afternoon.

It's cold this March day, Amy feels the baby is quieter then usual, she knows that the time is near. Maggie has the spare bedroom fixed up for the delivery. Ethan can't keep his mind on work, he feels the spirits of Brutus and the others, they are trying to tell him something, but he doesn't know how to let them in. Beans has not left Amy's side all this day. That evening Amy goes into labor. Maggie has come over after she has fed her roomers, and finds Amy on the couch having contractions. She runs back to the rooming house and gets Ethan, and sends one of' the roomers after the Doctor. Ethan and Maggie run back to Amy's house. When they arrive Amy is on the floor and having another contraction. Ethan waits till it's over, and then picks up Amy and carries her upstairs to the room Maggie has fixed up. Shortly the doctor arrives; he examines Amy, and tells her so far everything looks normal. But he suspects the baby is in the wrong position. "Amy asks why she hurts so much during the contractions". "That's normal during the birthing process, the Doctor tells her, all women have much pain when delivering." "I'll give you a little laudanum to help deaden the pain, and then we wait." "The baby will come when it's ready; meantime take deep breaths when you have a contraction." After a long time, Amy is having contractions every minute, and she's feeling the urge to push, and as the doctor suspected the baby is coming feet first. "Maggie!" says the doctor, "we have a problem, the baby is coming out feet first." "I'm going to have to help Amy by gently pulling on the baby." "Amy! push! push as hard as you can." "Take a few deep breaths, then push." "Maggie be ready to take the baby because I'm going to have to cut the cord and be able to try and stop the bleeding." "We are going to have to watch Amy closely for hemorrhaging." So he grabs the baby's feet and gently pulls the little tyke out with the next several contractions.

Maggie is there with a blanket and wet cloth to swab the baby off with, meantime the doctor is cutting the cord and trying to stop the bleeding, Amy is yelling, let me see my baby, Maggie brings the baby over, and presents him to Amy, "A beautiful boy she says, and listen to him cry, he's going to have a healthy set of lungs." Amy holds the baby in her arms, and looks up at Maggie. "Maggie, I'm going to die, I can feel it, take the boy and raise it as your own, and name it after Theo". With that she cries out in pain. "My god says the doctor, she's hemorrhaging, I can't stop it! I can't stop it! He cries out". Shortly the pain subsides, and Amy weak from the loss of so much blood looks up at her child and whispers, I love you my little Theo, then she fades away. Beans who has been in the hall, goes down stairs, and out the back door and starts to howl, soon all the dogs in Auburn have joined him. The town folk know that there has been a loss, that somebody has died.

Maggie is beside herself at the loss, but realizes she and Ethan have to take charge immediately, if the baby is going to live. "Doctor, we are going to need a wet nurse as soon as possible" "Ethan, get the undertaker, and make arrangements for the funeral." "Also we are going to have to hire someone to take over at the rooming house for me'. "If I'm going to be a mother at my age, I'm going to need all the help I can get". "Yes dear, I know what you mean, here we are at the age of forty, and we have just been thrust into parenthood." "I only hope we have the strength".

After the funeral, Maggie decides that she and Ethan should move into Amy's and Theo's house. That will give the new rooming house matron a place for her to live, fortunately they have found a widow lady that can run the house. Ethan, gives Sam more responsibility in the everyday running of the business, so he can spend more time in helping Maggie with the child.

Beans has taken it upon himself to stay with the baby, and to Maggie and Ethan's surprise, he becomes the best baby sitter they could ask for.

After things settle down into a reasonable routine, Maggie is cleaning and rearranging the house. One day she looks into the spare room off the kitchen and see's Theo's saddle bags, guns, and packs from the mule, She had completely forgotten about his belongings after the funeral. She gets Ethan, and shows him the things. "What do you think we should do with them?" she asks. Ethan thinks a moment, "I know, put them in one of Amy's trunks that she brought from back east when we moved out here."

"They're down in the basement". So he takes some of the things down to the basement, and finding the key for one of the trunks tied to one of its side handles, he opens it up. Finding it almost empty except for several leather pouches and two large leather bound Bibles, he knows he can get all of Theo's stuff in it.

Bringing all the things down into the basement, he starts to put the belongings into the trunk. He has already noticed that two of the bags in the mule packs are really heavy for their size. He examines the bags, and finds they are full of leather pouches full of gold nuggets. Also in the trunk are a like amount of pouches. So he puts them in the trunk, and makes a mental note to someday tell Theo junior of the gold. Maggie comes down the stairs carrying some more things, and asks if there is room for it in the trunk. She has brought Amy's rifle, handgun and gun belt, plus her mining work clothes. "Yes, there is room in the trunk, but I need to run down to the gunsmith to get some oil paper for the guns to keep them from rusting."

So Ethan gets the oil paper, and taking the stocks off the rifles, he wraps them and places them in the trunk; he also wraps the Colt of Amy's and the Colt Dragoon of Theo's and puts them in the trunk. Then he remembers the Hawken', and the Brown Bess that Theo had, and gets them and taking the stocks off them, and wrapping them, he puts them in the trunk. Maggie comes down again, and has Theo's buckskins, and asks if there is room for them? "Yes", says Ethan, 'just barely". So the trunk is full of Amy's and Theo's things.

With the help of the wet nurse and goats milk little Theo is getting bigger everyday, so it seems to Maggie and Ethan. As he starts to crawl, Beans is there to keep him from going where he shouldn't, soon he is hanging onto the dog and walking. The two are inseparable, this of course gives

Maggie much needed help. As long as the dog is there she knows the little tyke can't get into much trouble.

As the years pass, Theo is getting bigger, he is going to be as big as his father, remarks Ethan one day. Theo starts school, Beans is waiting outside for him. On his twelfth birthday Ethan gives him a sixteen gauge shotgun to go hunting with. After he teaches him the correct way to handle and clean the gun, they go hunting for dove. Theo, like his dad is a natural hunter and excellent shot. He and Beans fill the dinner table with fresh game quite often. Beans is getting up in years now and slowing down. Theo doesn't quite understand why the dog doesn't run like he used to. Ethan sits down with the boy and explains how dogs age faster then people, and that in dog years Beans is very old, kind of like old Jake in town, who is the oldest man around these parts, and who hobbles around with a cane. Another year and Beans is gone. Theo is heartbroken, but he knew that the day would come when he would no longer have Beans for a companion.

Theo is helping out at the shop after school and on Saturdays, again he takes after his real father, by having a natural ability for working with his hands. He enjoys working with the blacksmith, making iron do his bidding, and the cooper shows him the fine art of making barrels of all sizes. Even Sam has been showing Theo junior how the bookkeeping of the business works

Theo hasn't realized yet that Ethan is training him to take over the business. All too soon Theo is about to celebrate his twentieth birthday. By now he has grown to six foot one inch tall, he is second in command of the business by virtue of his ability, not because he is the owners son. And he is courting a certain young lady by the name of Becky. At the birthday celebration, Ethan announces that he is retiring, and that Theo will be in charge of the business. Everybody applauds Theo for his new title. He gets up and thanks everybody, and says "I have an announcement of my own, Becky and I are now engaged if she will have me". Becky blushes as she accepts the proposal.

And so the dynasty goes on. Theo and Becky get married, and have a passel of kids. The oldest boy takes over the business when Theo junior retires. The business now is primarily logging and lumber processing, with a very large saw mill. The younger boys are mostly involved in the business in some capacity. The original blacksmith shop has been moved to the huge lumber mill and is mainly involved in the maintenance of the facility. The freighting business is hauling logs and lumber products almost exclusively.

Ethan and Maggie have passed on; Theo and Becky live in the old house, enjoying their last years. And so life and death go on.

Chapter Thirty Six

The year 1994. Meet John and Sue Bowden. The middle age couple live in Newcastle, Calif. Just down Highway 80 from Auburn. John is a small engine mechanic, welder, truck driver, placer gold miner, and more recently learning how to be a bench jeweler.

Sue is a certified nursing assistant, specializing in the care of older patients. She is also a gold digger, having spent a summer dredging for gold, with her two teenage sons, in 1980.

Recently married, the couple enjoy spending all of their free time prospecting for gold nuggets. John has a gold claim on a river, where he dredges for nuggets. When he is under water, Sue will be metal detecting for nuggets in the exposed bedrock alongside the area John is dredging.

Sometimes she finds more gold then he does, most times not, the work is hard, but rewarding in so many ways. They both enjoy the outdoors; the thrill of finding gold is akin to a treasure hunt, the work of moving tons of gravel, rocks, and boulders under water keeps John in good shape. The same goes for Sue in her quest for nuggets.

During the week, they work at their respective jobs, John in a local repair shop, repairing everything from lawnmowers, chainsaws, to small tractors.

Sue is presently taking care of a lady who in now ninety years old, her body is getting frail, but her mind is as quick as any person half her age. Sue got the job shortly after she and John got married, three years ago.

Meet Melissa Carpenter, presently ninety years old, a direct descendant of Theolonius Raphial Calhoun. As the great granddaughter of the original owner of the large saw mill in Auburn, she has had a long and interesting life. She and Sue spend hours talking about the old lady's life and adventures, and the history of her family, When Sue relates some of the stories to John, he is fascinated, especially since he is a history buff, who enjoys early California gold rush history most of all.

Once a month, John and Sue will bundle up Melissa, and sometimes a picnic basket, and take her for a ride. She really enjoys getting out and marveling at the changes she has seen in the country where she was raised. One Sunday they went to the Empire Mine Museum, and touring the grounds, she related to John and Sue, how she used to come here for the lavish parties that the owners threw before the mines were shut down because of World War Two.

Another Sunday they went to the Kentucky Mine museum outside Downieville, and during their picnic lunch, Melissa, told them the story of the original Theo, having a small rich placer mine somewhere near here. The location of the mine was a secret, only Theo, his wife Amy, their dog, two horses, and two mules ever knew where the mine was, and the animals weren't talking, as she laughed at her little joke.

Melissa related to Sue how she met her late husband, he was a descendant of Sam Carpenter, the original bookkeeper for the company, back in the 1860's. When the original Theo was shot and killed, Theo's partner gave Sam the responsibility of the day to day running of the company, eventually making him a full partner. As the families grew, the Carpenters were still partners. I and Josh were almost raised together; eventually we drifted into other relationships. I fell in love with this young fellow and got married at the tender age of seventeen. The boy, who was a year older then I, got caught up in the war in Europe, volunteered for the Army, shipped overseas to France and never came back.

Josh, also was in the war, wounded in the trenches of France, he was sent home. "I was doing volunteer work at the local hospital when Josh was sent here for rehabilitation."

"Naturally being childhood friends, I was interested in his recovery." "The rest as they say is history". "After the war we got married, had a son, who when he became of age, ran off and joined the Navy, so he could see the world". "He was on one of the ships that was bombed in Pearl Harbor and was killed." "Unfortunately, Josh and I only had the one child".

"Meantime we were both involved in the family business." "Josh learned the lumber business from the bottom up working green chain, where everybody starts in a saw mill, on up to plant manager." "Eventually co-president of the company with me". "We were a good team, he could relate to all the problems of the day to day logging, transporting, and milling of the lumber, while I handled the paperwork end of the business". "We made a lot of money, not only for ourselves, but for the workers and the community as well",

"When Josh died of a heart attack in 1964, I decided that it was time to retire". "I was sixty three, and still in good health." "Not having any heirs to leave the business too, I decided to sell it and invest the money in such a way that I had income for the rest of my life." "I kept the old house, and hired caretakers to keep it up, while I traveled." "I saw the world my son wanted to see." "I made many friends while doing so; most of them are gone now". "It seems I have outlived them all". "But now I have new friends, Sue, you and your husband have become my new family."

"Well, Thank you Ms. Melissa,"says Sue, "I think of you the same way." "Both our folks are gone, so we think of you as our adopted mother",

Several months later, Melissa, asks Sue to help her go down to the basement, "I've got something to show you that I think you would like to have." Sue exclaims, "You don't have to give me anything, you're already paying me a good salary." "I don't need to be getting gifts from you too." "I know" says Melissa, "But I know how you like old trunks, and how you like to restore them, so I've got one I want you to have." " It's an old family heirloom, I've been told that Amy brought it from back east when she and her uncle Ethan came west".

So Sue helps Melissa down the stairs after turning on the lights in the basement. Lots of cobwebs and the usual junk a basement accumulates. There over against the wall stands a trunk, iron bound ,made of eastern pine, probably from Pennsylvania as the style of it suggests.

"There it is" says Melissa, "What do you think?" "It's gorgeous, despite the rust on the iron bands, it's in remarkable condition". "A lot of sanding on the iron, and some on the wood, and paint and I could have it looking like new," "Good" says Melissa, "Then it's settled, it's yours, there is only one condition, I don't want you to open it until after I'm gone." "Oh?" asks Sue, "Why?" Melissa tells her, it is loaded with junk, and old books, and "I don't want you cussing me out for giving you a bunch of junk until after I'm dead and gone." "Oh! I see", says Sue

The old woman, chuckles, "It's my way of getting rid of junk that the garbage people would charge me a arm and leg to haul away". " Ok, I'll play your little game" says Sue.

"When do you want it gone from here?" "How about this weekend, you can convince John to take it to your place, where you can store it in the shop building you have until I leave this mother earth." "Give him a cock and bull story that there are some valuables in there that I want you to have after I'm gone, but he can't open it until then as you promised." "Ok" says Sue. "One other thing, it's very heavy, John will need one of those handcarts they deliver refrigerators with to get it out of the basement and into his truck."

So that evening Sue tells John about the trunk, and can he make arrangements to move it this weekend? "Sure, and since it is so heavy I'll go down to the rental yard and get one of their new electric stair climbing handcarts to move it with."

So that Saturday, John rents one of the new handcarts, and taking a couple of stout boards along, he drives the old Dodge Power Wagon pickup he has, and goes after the trunk.

Upon arriving at Melissa's house, Sue goes in and says hello to the weekend lady, and Melissa. Melissa gives her the key to the outside basement door and tells her to have John take the trunk out that way, it will be easier. John opens the outer doors, and turns on the lights, and fighting his way through the cobwebs finds the trunk. When he tries to put the handcart under the trunk, he discovers just how heavy it is, "My god he exclaims it must weigh close to three hundred pounds."

"Sue, hold the handcarts while I get one end up, then push the cart under the edge." John gets one corner up and Sue gets the foot of the handcart under it, then he lifts the other corner, and she manages to get the cart twisted under the edge of the trunk. John then takes the strap on the handcart and secures the trunk, then with a mighty heave he gets the handcart tipped over to where he can move the trunk. Now since this is one of them fancy electric carts, John switches it on and the cart starts to move, it has wheels that move back so it will stay tipped, then moving to the bottom of the stairs, John turns on the stair climbing device, and it starts up the basement stairs, all John has to do is steer it. Once out of the basement, he takes it over to the truck, putting his boards in place, he again puts the cart in drive and steers it up into the truck.

That was almost too easy; I've never moved something on a handcart so easily. Taking the trunk home, John unloads the truck, and puts the trunk in a corner he had already cleared out for it. Then he took the electric handcart back to the rental outfit and got his deposit back. True to their promise. Sue and John left the trunk unopened.

Life went on, working, prospecting, taking Melissa out for drives when she felt up to it. As of late she was getting weaker. Sue came home one evening after work and said that she had to call the Doctor to come out and check Melissa over, She had weakened enough, that she felt she could not muster the energy to go to the Doctors office for her check up. After the Doctor was through, he told Sue, "That she will need around the clock care." "She is failing fast enough that she could go anytime now." Sue asks "What do you mean anytime now?" "Days, weeks, months?" The Doctor told her it's probably a matter of two or three weeks. "That's what I needed to know", says Sue. "I'll provide the care she needs till it's time."

The Doctor tells Sue, that they may have to hospitalize her. "Sue tells the Doctor that knowing Melissa as well as she does, she wouldn't stand for it". "If you put her in a hospital room, with life support tubes and wires on her, she would go mad." "She has made her peace with her maker, and she has told me that she will die in her own bed." "And anything else would be an affront to her dignity, and she won't stand for it."

So the next day Sue moved into the house with Melissa. She arranged for the weekend caregiver to come in, in the evenings so she could go home for a short time, for supper and see John. Then back to the big house to stay by Melissa.

Melissa had told Sue, that she had sold the house to a couple from the Bay area. They wanted to move to the foothills, where life was a little slower. Melissa's house was perfect for them as it was in good enough shape that the renovations they had in mind would not require rebuilding the whole house, Plus Melissa could live there until she died before they took over the property. So she gave Sue their phone number, and asked her to call them, and tell them the end was near.

John was coming over after work the last week before Melissa died. She told him to keep on prospecting, as she knew it gave the two of them much pleasure, and companionship. He kept asking her if there was something he could do for her, did anything need fixing or painted, just so he had an excuse to be there. "Son" she would say, "You and Sue are all the fixing and painting I need." "You are both here, and that's all I need for now." That weekend Melissa passed on peacefully in her sleep. After the funeral, Sue informed the house owners that they could now take possession of the property. Then she went home to mourn the loss of her friend.

CHAPTER THIRTY SEVEN

A week after the funeral, Sue got a phone call from a Mr. Hardy of Bascomb, Hardy, and Bascornb, attorneys at law. Sue recognized the name because she had taken Melissa to their offices several times. Mr. Hardy told Sue that she and her husband needed to come to the office and sign some papers. "What for?" asks Sue The attorney tells her that Melissa Carpenter has left her and her husband some money, and they need to come to the office and sign a receipt for the check. "Oh!" says Sue, "When do you want us to come in?" Mr. Hardy tells her, anytime it's convenient for you. "Let me call my husband at work and see if he can get off early and we can come in this afternoon". "That would be fine". "I'll be here until five thirty".

Sue calls John at work, and tells him about the phone call from Mr. Hardy, "Can you get off work early and go with me to the lawyers office?" she asks him " Hold on , I'll ask the boss", a couple of minutes later he tells her it's ok for him to come home early. John arrives home around three thirty, changes clothes real quick, while Sue calls the lawyer and tells him they are on the way. They get to the office by four thirty, and are shown in to Mr. Hardys office,

"Sit down" he tells them, "I've got some good news for you". "First Melissa Carpenter left you a sizable sum of money". "Just sign the receipt here and I'll give you the check". As they sign the receipt they noticed the sum printed on it, "This can't be right exclaims Sue, that's a lot of money". " It's right alright, here is the check, made out to the both of you for the sum of one hundred thousand dollars". The two of them are speechless, when she gets her speech back, Sue exclaims, "We don't deserve this kind of money from Ms. Carpenter". The attorney tells her, "That obviously Melissa Carpenter must have thought you do, because here it is". Now one other thing, she left you two a note here in this envelope, with instructions to me for you to read it in private.

By the way she wanted you to know that she left the bulk of the estate in the form of a foundation to help displaced timber workers, whose jobs were lost because of the Spotted Owl fiasco. She told me that for the Enviro's to believe that some five thousand owls were more important then sixty thousand loggers and their family's and the mill towns that are now ghost towns is ludicrous, and she was going to do something to help these people. So she has set up a foundation, to find other job opportunities for them including the training needed for those jobs. Both Sue and John say, "That is wonderful."

In the car, they open the envelope from Melissa. The note is short, and says "Dear Sue and John, knowing how much you enjoy prospecting and mining for gold nuggets, I want you to know that there is a gold mine out there waiting for you. The key to it is in the trunk Love Melissa."

John and Sue look at each other, and exclaim together, "The trunk, we forgot about the trunk", "I wonder what she means by the key to it is in the trunk asks Sue?" "I don't know, I guess it's time to open it and find out".

Since it's too late to go to the bank, they head for home. John tells Sue, we can both go to the bank tomorrow and deposit the check, Probably be a good idea to invest in CD's or IRA's or something to make the money grow. Sue agrees," I'm really curious now about what is in the trunk, Melissa said it was full of junk, that she didn't want to pay to have the garbage people haul it off'. "Tell you what, Honey, I'll see if I can get it open while you make supper". "Oh no you don't, we'll open it together, I want to be surprised just as much as you do". "Ok, then we'll do it together after supper, meanwhile let's stop for some Chinese take out, that way we won't have to cook"

After supper they go out to the shop and uncover the trunk, it has accumulated a pile of stuff on top. Then dragging it out of the corner, they try the key in the lock. Nothing happens; the lock is rusted and won't budge. John tells her, "I can saw it off'". " No, that would ruin the whole outside of the trunk". "There must be a way to open it without ruining the built in lock".

" Ok I'll try some penetrating oil, maybe that will loosen up the mechanism". Giving the lock a liberal squirt of the oil, they wait several minutes for the oil to do it's job. Inserting the key again, John tries to twist it again, still nothing, then he gets a pair of pliers out of his tool box. "Maybe with a little more leverage it will break loose". He twists so hard that he can feel the brass key starting to twist and break, still it won't budge. Giving it more of the penetrating oil, he takes a leather headed mallet he has, and taps on the locking mechanism, this time there is a little movement in the lock Twisting the key back and forth, gets it to move a little more, then twisting a little too hard the key almost breaks. "This is no good" says John, "we need a stronger key or just cut the lock with a saw". "No says Sue, the trunk is too nice to ruin it by cutting the lock out", "There must be a way to get the lock to work".

John looks at the lock, then the key, and tells her, "you know it started to budge", "If we had a stronger key made out of steel, we might be able to get it open". "Then make one", says Sue, "you're always making things to solve problems here and at work, there must be a way to make a stronger key". John looks around the shop, and spotting an old railroad spike they picked up somewhere, he says "that will work". "The spike end can be tempered enough to make it hard, a lot harder then brass, plus if I bend it just right it will give me a handle to twist with". "You're going to have to help me Sue". "Ok, what do you want me to do". "Let me get the OxyAcetlyene torch out". "We'll have to heat the spike hot enough, so I can forge the end into a close copy of the key, then I'll grind and file it to the exact shape of the key", "Then with the casite hardening powder I have we'll case harden the key end". "After that we'll bend the spike into a right angle to give us a handle to twist with".

"Sue, here wear these dark safety glasses and hold onto the torch". With a pair of locking pliers John grabs onto the spike, then placing it in the flame of the torch he heats it up till it is almost white hot, taking it over to the small anvil he has he starts to hammer the end of the spike into the shape of the key, when it cools, he again heats it and some more hammering, eventually he gets the shape he is looking for, then he heats the spike one more time to a bright cherry red, then lets it cool off in the air. "This will anneal the metal he explains to Sue, so I can grind and file on it". While the spike is cooling off they get a soda from the fridge and share a drink,

"This is getting to be hot work" says Sue, "Yeah , reminds me of when I worked for the Blacksmith who taught me how to weld".

Now that the spike is cool, John starts to grind it into shape, getting the basic shape, he then gets out his files and finishes the key. While he is filing, he tells Sue how he figured out that the one thing he learned in four years of high school enabled him to make a living as a mechanic all his life. Sue asks "what was that?" "What I'm doing now, my first year shop class teacher taught us how to use a file correctly, and I've been making a living with the tool since". "Look at the ring castings I do, when I cut them off the sprue, I have to file the sprue's off the shanks, so the ring is round, it seems like I use a file everyday in one way or another".

"Ok, the key is made, now let's bend the spike". So he lights the torch again. He has the spike mounted in his vise, then heating the spike in the middle, he again gets it white hot, then he takes a piece of pipe and slips it over the spike and bends it into a right angle. Taking the hot spike out of the vise he cools it off in water. Then heating the key end to a cherry red he dips it into the caseite. Letting it air cool, It is ready except for a wire brushing to get the fire scale off.

"Now let's see if it will work". giving the lock another squirt of oil, and a couple of taps with the mallet, John inserts the new key, gently at first he twists the key, he can feel the lock mechanism moving, twisting back and forth the lock breaks loose and finally opens. The top of the trunk pops up, Sue jumps up and down. "Yea! it's open, and the lock isn't ruined".

Pulling the top up on it's rusty hinges, they have their first look into the trunk. There on top is a set of buckskins, with a peculiar musty oil smell, but otherwise in remarkable condition.

Gently lifting them out, there is another set, Taking them out there is a pair of knee high moccasins. Next to the moccasins there is a pistol wrapped in oil paper, "that's where the peculiar oil smell came from" exclaims John. "It's gun oil, the paper was soaked in it", carefully unwrapping the pistol, he finds a small colt, "I'm not sure he says, but I would guess it is a Sheriffs model from the 1860's". "This pistol is worth a lot of money to a collector, it's almost new in condition". "Let's see what else we have in here" says Sue.

Next is a pair of small levi's, holding them up, Sue tells John, "These were altered to fit a woman close to my size". Then a levi work jacket, again altered to fit a woman. Under the levi's are two rifles. The stocks had been removed so they would fit into the trunk. Wrapped in the oil paper, and again in pristine condition. The Henry lever action looked like brand new, and was an unusual caliber. John found the caliber stamped on the receiver to be a thirty six, he looked at the small colt and found the same caliber on it. He told Sue, "That this was a set made for a woman, the small colt which fits your hand, and notice the stock, how much shorter it is over the stocks on my shotgun and rifle".

The other rifle is an old cap and ball muzzle loader, probably one of the old Brown Bess's that they made so many of, Then another set of small levi's and flannel work shirts also made to fit a woman, Under the jean's and shirts are two more rifles, again with the stocks removed, plus another colt pistol, this one being much bigger in size. One rifle is another Henry lever action, with a forty four caliber barrel, and the pistol is also a forty four, so another set only this one made for a man. The other rifle is a fifty four caliber Hawken.

The next layer is two journals and a row of leather pouches. Sue, opening the newer of the two journals tells John, "This was written in the 1860's," opening to the last page, she reads the note that Theo wrote to Amy, telling her how he has been killed and that the gold is in Cuss's safe. "Wow!" exclaims John, "I wonder if this is part of the key that Melissa was talking about?"

Taking one of the pouches out, John knows by the weight, that they are filled with gold; he walks over to his jewelry bench and grabs one of his small gold pans and empties the pouch into it. Nuggets, beautiful gold nuggets, "Sue look at this, isn't it beautiful". "I'll bet this piece that I'm picking up weighs an ounce or more". So he puts it on his gold scale and sure enough, an ounce, two penny weight and sixteen grains. Then he weighs the rest of the gold. "Twelve ounces even he tells Sue". "Let's see what the other pouches are holding". More nuggets as he opens several more of the pouches. He decides to weigh a couple of more of the pouches,

Twelve ounces, again. Each of these pouches have a Troy pound of gold in them. Then they start counting the pouches. One hundred and fifty they come up with. "My god, exclaims John, there is a hundred and fifty Troy pounds of gold here". "That's 1800 hundred ounces of gold, at today's prices that's a fortune". He gets a calculator from his shop desk and figures the gold at around 400.00 and ounce, as the gold has enough character that he knows he can get better then spot price for it. "Honey, I don't know if my heart can stand this, my calculator says we have 720,000, 00 dollars worth of gold here". Sue tells John, "We both better sit down and take some deep breaths". "Melissa said there was nothing but junk in the trunk, but she wanted me to tell you that there were valuable antiques in it so you would take it from her basement and get rid of it for her".

"We are not to the bottom yet, remarks Sue, I see another Journal and two large bibles. Taking out the journal. Sue turns to page one and tells John, this is the first journal of the original Theo that Melissa was always talking about, here on the first page he is relating his first day of working for Cuss at his mine". "Remember the last page of the other journal;

Theo mentioned the gold is in Cuss's safe". "I wonder what he really meant by that?".

John is taking out the bibles, and tells her, "These are the heaviest books I have ever seen or picked up". Putting them down on the work bench that they had been putting the trunk belongings on, he started to unhook the leather straps that the books were bound with, opening one of the books he is reading chapter and verse as any bible would have, leafing through the book he finds that there is a cavity in the center of the book, filled with twenty dollar gold pieces. "Sue, look at this, more gold". Quickly he opens the other bible and finds it is also full of gold. Each taking a book they count the gold coins, "I have twenty five says Sue". "I've got twenty five also". "That's a thousand dollars face value". "The last time I checked, 20 dollar gold pieces were going for over five hundred apiece". "I've got to sit down, this is too much to fathom all at once". "Do you realize that with the check, and what we could get for the guns and clothing, plus the gold, and twenty dollar gold pieces, we are sitting on a million dollars". "Just think, a million dollars".

Let's put the stuff back in the trunk, and shove it back in the corner, and cover it with the stuff you had on top of it, then go into the house, and sit and stare at each other until this sinks in". "Neither of us will be able to sleep this night, and tomorrow we need to get the check to the bank and set up accounts that will give us a good return for our money".

So they pack up the trunk, except for the journals, and then go into the house. As it is almost bed time, they take a shower and get ready for bed, not sleepy yet, they each take a journal and start reading it. Being avid readers it doesn't take long for them to get into the books. Sue has the first one and John has the second. Sue gets to the part about Cuss and his hot tub, then she finds the part about the safe under the hot tub furnace. Meanwhile John has gotten to the part where Pierre has made his buckskins, and the fight he and Couger were in, pretty soon he finds out how the bibles were put in the trunk By now it's past midnight and as both are used to being asleep by eleven twenty, just after the weather news, they decide to call it a night. Both of them are so exhausted that they fall asleep almost immediately; even John's usual loud snoring can't keep Sue awake tonight.

Next morning John calls work and tells his boss that he has to take care of some business that came up, and that he would probably be in the next day. Then he and Sue go to their bank and put the check in a couple of IRA's two CD's and some in their checking account, and a thousand each in cash for themselves. Then stocking up on groceries they head back home to talk about what they want to do with their new found fortune.

As they get home, they decide to get rid of their old Subaru station wagon and get something in a small Suv. Sue likes the Suzuki Samurai, but John has heard the stories that consumers magazine has been telling the public about the fact that they can flip over on their side real easy in a swift evasive maneuver. So he checks with some of his 4x4 buddies and finds that Suzuki America has a law suit against the consumer outfit that made the tests, claiming they were done erroneously. Then picking up a 4x4 magazine he finds an article about the great things the little 4x4 has going for it. So that weekend they go Samurai shopping. Finding one they like, they put down a deposit, and told the dealer that they would be in Monday to take it home. "The dealer asks if they need financing for the used car they want?" "No" says John, "We have a bank that does all our financing for us".

Meantime John's boss has noticed that John has had several days off, and when he is at work he is not concentrating on his work. He takes him aside and asks him what is wrong? "You don't have your mind on the job these days". "I know" says John, "Sue and I lost a very good friend, and I'm afraid I can't stop thinking about it", The boss says to John, "Tell you what, you have some vacation time coming, and the shop is not too busy, why don't you take a week off, maybe get away to your mining claim and get your mind straightened out". "Thanks boss, that's a good idea, I'll see you in a week", with that he cleans up his tools and puts them away and goes home.

When he gets home, Sue says "You're home early, how come?" "The boss gave me a week off, as I'm not concentrating on the work, he's afraid I might screw up one of the jobs, and he's probably right".

That evening he gets out the last journal, and reads how Theo finds the mine above Downieville, and how he built the cabin, and him and Amy spending the summer mining together. Their long soaks in the hot tub he built, and especially the amount of gold they recovered. "Sue, it says here that when Theo and Amy came home from the mine, they brought a hundred pounds of gold with them, that would account for two thirds of what's in the trunk" Reading further he is looking at the recovery numbers Theo is putting down. Getting a pen and paper he starts to write the numbers down, when he gets to the large boulder, he can't believe what he is reading, "Sue, it say's here that Theo recovered over a thousand ounces of gold in three days". "Let me see that" exclaims Sue, so she reads about the boulder and the crevice under it. Giving back the journal, Sue remarks, "That's amazing," 'We've heard stories of big finds, but to see one written by the person who did it". "It kind of makes a believer out of you".

Reading further, John learns about Arnold and the Blackbums, by this time he is adding up the gold figures. "Sue! Theo stashed over two hundred and fifty pounds of gold in the bottom of the hot tub furnace". "What?" say's Sue. "Look here for yourself, I've added up the gold they recovered, subtracting what they brought home, there is over two hundred pounds of gold still at the mine". "And Theo says on the last page, that the gold is in Cuss's safe". "Think about it, where did Cuss stash his gold?" "Why in the bottom of the hot tub furnace". "Right" exclaims John. "And did you read the part about when Theo built his furnace, he put a metal box in the foundation to act as a safe?" "Yes" says Sue, "I see! Cuss's safe". "Well how about that".

"This is the key that Melissa was talking about, there is still two hundred pounds of gold already recovered from the mine in the bottom of that hot tub furnace". "But John, surely in the last hundred and fifty years someone has stumbled over the mine and the furnace". "Not necessarily, and even if they have think of the adventure we can have trying to find the mine and cabin". "I'll betcha nobody has found it, and if we do, think of the additional amount of gold we can have, plus how about the bottle dump, you know how you can't resist a good bottle dig, especially if there are some cobalt's there". So a new adventure begins.

CHAPTER THIRTY EIGHT

John and Sue have decided to go look for the mine and the cabin site. "First I have to go and quit my job" said John. "Why?" Sue wants to know. "Because it's going to take a lot of time to do the research, then the actual hands on exploring", "Theo said he took three compass readings of the mine site before he left it the first time", "Those readings will give us a starting point with which to begin with". "We will have to find some older Topo maps on which we can plot the possible where'abouts of the mine, plus some newer Topo's, to see if there are any newer roads or trails into the area", "What's the present status of the area we will be hunting in". "It goes on and on Sue"

We're also going to need some more equipment for camping out, maybe an ATV to help us cover more ground faster like some of our friends have, who get into places in one day, that takes us days to hike into by foot". "You just want a new toy". "I can see it now, you racing around on your four wheeler", "That's not fair, I was thinking how much easier it would be for you if we had some way to ride into some of the areas we like to go, it definitely would be much better on your arthritic hip, then miles and miles of climbing up and down mountains". "Ok, I can't argue with that logic".

So the next day John goes into work and explains how he and Sue came into a little money, and that they have a project they would like to pursue, and so much as he hates to leave the boss, he is quitting the job. "You have been great to work for, John tells his boss, but this is something Sue and I have been dreaming of for years, even before we met and got together, and since we're not getting any younger we're off to find the wizard, so to speak". "I really hate to lose you, you have been the best helper I have ever had". "If your project doesn't work out, come on back, I'll always have a place for you here in the shop". John tells the boss thank you, "You don't know how much it means to me to hear you say that". So shaking hands, John packs up his tools, and heads for home.

That evening John and Sue sit down and start planning the expedition as they are starting to call it. "First we need to figure out the compass readings Theo put in his journal, that will require a trip into Sacramento to our favorite used book and map store". "Then we need to get a good compass, the kind the army uses to triangulate coordinates with". "Possibly one of those new GPS units I have been reading so much about". "More toys", says Sue, laughing. "Come on honey, give me a break, this is serious business". " Ok! Ok! I promise not to laugh anymore, but you should see you from where I do", "Ok, after we get the maps, tomorrow?" "Yes, we can go into Sac. Tomorrow" says Sue. "Anyway after we get the maps and sit down and get half an idea where we are going, then we need to go up to Downieville and check out the area more thoroughly, get some of the local Forest Service maps". "Maybe check with the newspaper to see if they have any information on Theo". "I'll bet it made the front page of the Messenger, about how he was shot". "And since we have the date in the journal it won't take more then five minutes for them to look it up". "Then we need to check out the road system, there might be a logging road that will take us right to the mine". "In which case we can probably use the Samurai to get there, or the Power Wagon, if we need something heavy duty". "At this point we don't know".

So the next day they run around Sacramento, looking and finding the maps they want, a good compass at a survey supply store, and looking at the GPS units available, and how intricate they are, and the difficultly in learning how to use one they decide to pass for now.

If Theo could find the mine again after almost seven month's, with just compass coordinates, then we should be able to too. After lunch they went to look at ATV's while they are in Sacramento. They find a lot to chose from, so getting brochures and prices from several dealers, they head for home. We can make up our minds later, said John. "Let's find out if we really need one, before investing that much money in a machine we might only use for a short while", "Good thinking" Sue tells him

The next day they get up early, and pack a snack, cold drinks, and water, they jump in the Samurai and head for Downieville. Taking 1-80 to Auburn, then getting off onto highway 49, it only takes them a couple of hours to get there. Pulling into Downieville, they spy the Grizz sitting on one of the benches in front of the store. Parking across the street in the cafe's parking lot, they walk over to their old friend and say hello. "Well I'll be, what brings you two up here on a week day'?" "Oh we have some time off, and we want to check out a story we heard about", says John. "What story is that?" asks the Grizz "It's about a miner by the name of Theo Calhoun that hung around here back in the 1860's".

"Oh! That story", exclaims the Grizz, "well if you go into the newspaper office, they have the front page of the story about how he killed three owlhoots who were trying to ambush him mounted on the wall in a glass frame". "The story is right up there with the hanging of Juanita, the Mexican gal who shot her boyfriend". "Is that so" says John "Yeah", says the Grizz, "you can even get a copy of the story, it's one of the tourist souvenirs you can get here". "Well in that case, I guess we will have to get one" says Sue. "By the way Grizz, why don't you meet us back here when we get done, and we'll treat you to lunch". "You bet! I never saw a piece of food I didn't like". With that they all laugh as they all know the Grizz likes to eat almost more then finding nuggets with his metal detector.

After going to the Newspaper office, John and Sue go to the Forest Service office and pick up the maps they want. Looking at the map from the F.S., John asks if there are any new logging roads in this particular area he is pointing to on the map. The receptionist tells him, "I really don't know, let me get the Road man out here and see if he can answer your question, he just happens to be in today",

The Road man comes out and asks if he can help? "Maybe" says John, "We need to know if there are any new logging roads or old mining roads in this area he is pointing to on the map?" "None that I know of" he says, "In fact that area is presently under study to be included in a wilderness area". "The present administration is considering this whole area be puts a circle around to be made into wilderness". "Oh!, well what is the status now?" Can we drive into the area and camp, then go for hikes?" "Oh sure says the Road man, the trail up Goodyears Creek is open to OHV's for the present, you used to be able to drive a Jeep up there, but after the 86 floods the road got washed out and we never fixed it, as hardly anybody used it".

"Back in the 1860's, there was a good stage coach road up the creek, but it is gone now". "Well thanks for the information" says John. The Road man asks if they are planning on going into the area? "Yes, my wife and I heard from a friend that there are some very big trees up there and we thought we would try and get some pictures of them before they disappear, plus we dearly enjoy a good Trout dinner, and the ones they plant are just not the same as a native trout from a cold mountain stream".

"Yeah, I know what you mean, but be careful, some of the streams are posted against fishing". "Yes I know, I've got a map of the posted streams, from the Fish and Game". "Ok, well good luck, and check in with us before you go, just in case there is a problem we will know approximately where to find you". "We'll do that" says Sue. "Thank you for the concern and advice".

At the Cafe, they meet Grizz. After ordering something to eat, they ask Grizz what is happening? "Oh! not much, getting a little gold, here and there, giving detector lessons". "I was getting ready to come down and visit with you and the others, like normal". "Had a decent winter in Arizona, got enough gold to make ends meet, picked up some extra money selling detectors for Bill, pocket sold some gold for Riffles, J and B, and Goose". "With all the catastrophes that have happened in southern California the last few years, the big money isn't there in Quartzsite like it used to be".

"Yeah, I know, says John, my wholesale jewelry business has really slowed down". "I used to make a bunch for Edna to take with her when she went there". "But she quit going, as she found out she could make just as much doing two weekend shows elsewhere, instead of twelve days there". "Oh well things are bound to pick up some day",

"So what are you two doing these days?" asks Grizz "Oh the usual, going out on weekends and detecting, dredging when the season is open." "I still haven't found a nugget with the detector", says John, "but since Sue does so good, I don't mind". "Besides I get more gold dredging then she does". "So it all evens out". 'Right now we have a new project we're working on, but we can't say too much about it just now". "Oh? it wouldn't have anything to do with Theo's gold would it", "Uh! no not really, why do you ask?" "Oh! Its just that there is a rumor that when this Theo got shot, he had a lot of gold on him". "And supposedly had more buried somewhere". "People have been looking for it for over a hundred years, even I took a stab at it one summer".

"Oh! you never told us about that" said Sue, "I thought I have heard all of your adventures". "No, not hardly says Grizz, some of them are not fit for a ladies ears". "Why Grizz, you've been keeping secrets from us' she says laughing. "Anyway you'll read in the paper how this Theo was shot coming down the Goodyears Creek stage road, and he had a large cache of gold on him, and the Deputy watched him write in his journal he kept, that the rest of the gold was in a safe somewhere, everybody figured he had buried a lot of gold up at his mine, and even if he didn't, that there was still the chance that the diggings could be found and mined".

"That's very interesting" remarks John, "whereabouts has everybody been looking for this mine?" "Oh! up Goodyears Creek, and over on the north side of the ridge, there are a lot of diggings up toward that way". "Some big mines and hydraulic operations". "I have done pretty good detecting in the old hydraulic pits". "Yeah we know, that's where Sue finds most of her nuggets". "Someday I'm going to find one, and when I do, I'll find that patch that Riffles has been telling me about". "Probably so" says Grizz.

"Well good to see you Grizz, we have to be getting home, stop by when you're there, and we'll put on the feed bag." "See Ya."

As they are driving out of town, Sue says, "You sure didn't want him to know what we are planning". "Of course not", says John, "Nobody is to know what we are doing". "If the word got out we would have half the miners in the country following us, trying to beat us to the mine". "You're probably right, but I trust Grizz", "Yeah, me too, but one little slip of the tongue and somebody will sink our ship as they used to say during World War Two".

CHAPTER THIRTY NINE

At home that evening, they started to put all of the information together into a note book, going over the maps, and triangulating the compass readings, they have narrowed the location down to the side of a mountain northwest of Downieville. Getting there is going to be a problem, there are no roads, or trails within at least five miles of the location they have picked out. And according to the Forest Service road man, the area is overgrown, one of the reasons it is being considered for wilderness designation.

"Well John, it looks like you were right about using an ATV to help us get there, but how about camping, you know how much I detest sleeping on the ground, not only is it hard, but my hip cripples up at the thought of it". "I know". "I'm the same way, ever since my first and only boy scout camp out, I hate sleeping on the ground, not only was it cold that night, but no matter what position I used, I ended up with bruises on my body from the hard ground",

"Let's go look at ATV's and see what kind of accessories they have for camping, since deer and antelope hunters use these machines all the time, I bet they have all kinds of comfortable camping gear". "If not, I'll make something up for us". So the next day they find a dealer who has a low mileage olive drab colored 4x4 ATV, that comes with a utility trailer. It is a trade in from a young couple who wanted a faster machine to run the sand dunes with. Telling the dealer that they intend to use the machine for extended camping trips, they asked him what kind of camping gear they might have that would let them sleep off the ground and as comfortable as in our own bed at home. "Ah!, I have just the thing, if you want to go first class". "It's a little expensive, but really the way to go". "Come, let me show it to you"....

"Here's the unit and the brochure, as you can see it is fully self contained, and drops right into the trailer". "Here's how it works, first you unsnap these snaps, and lift the top up and over on it hinges". "Inside is a double sleeping bag, with built in adjustable air pillows and canopy that goes over your heads to keep the dew and or frost off of you, and to go under the bag, a guaranteed not to leak air mattress with a refillable air bottle that fills the mattress at least two times on one filling of the bottle, plus a foot pump for emergency use, in case you have to fill the mattress and you're out of air in the bottle".

"Now by lifting this board and swinging it over the mattress compartment you have the platform the forms a seven foot long bed". Under the next board, that you swing out of the way, you have the lower compartment that holds a built in ice chest, with ice containers, that come out so you don't have to empty the chest of melted ice". "Next a removable port-o- potty, then a two burner camp stove with food storage under it and the small sink next to it, last but not least is the 20 gal fresh water tank, with built in electric pump and a manual override if there is no source of twelve volt electric power". "And there is one more accessory". "This shower wand that hooks to this five gal black plastic bag, that you put out in the sun to heat up, then hooking the wand to this valve and the bag, you have adjustable hot water for a shower". "This button on the wand controls the electric pump, and this mixer valve controls the water temperature".

"What will they think of next?" asks Sue. "What about a trailer to haul all this stuff with?" asks John. "Come out back, I have just the ticket for you".... "Ah yes!, here it is", "I took it in on trade a year ago, and nobody wants a long narrow trailer, they feel that no matter how they loaded it, they would have to unload both units to get at the front one, as Murphy's law would always put the vehicle you want to use up front". "Anyway I'll throw it in the deal if you take the camping unit along with the ATV and its trailer". John looks at Sue, she nods her head yes, so he says "I think you have a deal, let's write it up, and I'll give you a deposit now". "Tomorrow, I'll bring my big truck and a cashiers check for the remainder". The dealer is all smiles, this is a nice sweet deal.

The next day John and Sue go get their new used ATV, trailers and camping outfit. Pulling into the yard, their good neighbor Grouchy, has to come over and see what they have brought home now, "Wow! he says, that must have cost you a bundle". "Yeah", says John, "I'm going to have to bust my back for a month at the jewelry bench to pay for this". "Oh?" asks Grouchy. "You mean you made a trade?" "Jewelry, for all this", "Yep", says Sue, "I'm going to have to get out the whip, and make him work night and day to pay for this".

That night, they start making a list of food, tools, gas, water, clothes, etc. that they will need. "Where are we going to put all this stuff, asks Sue?". "In the Power Wagon, John tells her".

"I'll go down to the metal place and get some one inch square tubing and make a frame to fit over the bed, then close it in with galvanized sheet metal". "It will give us a camper shell, that people can't see into, therefore they'll leave it alone", "I've done this before on my first old pickup, and it worked like a charm". "With your help, I can put it together in a couple of days".

So the next day they start building the shell. Two days later, after welding the frame together, and covering the frame with galvanized sheet metal, and a thousand pop rivets, it's done. The back swings up, the tailgate down, so they can drive the ATV inside if they have to.

The next day, it's gathering up food for the expedition, checking out military surplus MRE's, they decide to get the new backpacking freeze dried vacuum packed meals. They found out if they buy a case good for a month, that the price break on the case was enough that they got almost a weeks worth of food free, over buying just three weeks worth. So a case of mixed breakfast's, a case of mixed lunch's, a case of mixed dinners, plus a case of deserts. "Then instant coffee for Sue, powdered milk, and hot chocolate for me, and we are almost ready to go".

"One more thing, we need some of those surplus metal boxes to keep the food in", "I've found out in the past that if you can keep the mice out of your food , then you don't have trouble with rattlesnakes". So they pick up four decent size boxes that they can tie onto the top of the camp trailer to take with them. Then it's packing the truck with extra drinking water, gas, small chain saw, and fuel for it, extra saw chain and sharpening file, tools, clothes, toiletries, couple of books each to read, lantern's, backpacks, it seems like there is no end to what they think they will need. Finally they are ready to leave.

The next morning, they are off. Grouchy is going to watch the house for them while they are gone, they tell him they will call if it takes over two weeks for their trip.

Goodyears Bar. There is a camp ground where they can leave the truck and ATV trailer, unloading the ATV and the camp trailer, they start up the Goodyears Creek trail. The trail is fairly good for the first five miles then it gets progressively worse, it takes two hours to go almost ten miles to the top of the ridge, from there they turn right to follow the ridge northeast as far as they can go. "This is probably where Theo stopped and parked his wagon John tells Sue",

"Let's set up camp here for the night and explore the area for signs of a possible trail in the morning".

Opening up the camp trailer they get it ready for sleeping. After making the first of their backpacking meals, they comment, this isn't too bad, for a dried meal that you reconstitute, and then heat, it tastes pretty good, plus they put enough in it. Getting dark, they light a lantern, and read for a while, then knowing they have a long day ahead of them they turn out the light and go to sleep.

Daybreak, first thing is Sue's coffee, heating up water, John makes instant coffee for her, and some hot chocolate for himself. Then the morning ritual, of s—, shower, and shave. Only there is no shower since the shower bag will not heat up at night, Getting into their work clothes, and packing the backpacks. John has the chain saw and extra gas, oil, and tools, plus drinking water. Sue has the lunch, more water, and the camera's, one 35 mm, and a small super 8 video camcorder. Plus the map, compass, and notes. Just before they start to leave the camp sight, Sue calls John's attention to a mark that seems to have been carved into one of the big trees that are there. The mark is about twelve feet up, and is so old it is almost indistinguishable. John takes out his monocular he carries in his shirt pocket and takes a better look at the mark.

"It's a T carved into the tree, he tells Sue, and below is an arrow pointing off in the direction we were going to go", "Wow, says Sue, all we have to do it follow the arrows". "Maybe says John, but some how I feel it isn't going to be that easy". So they start out, keeping and eye out for more T's and arrows. Within a few hundred yards they meet their first obstacle. Buck brush so thick there is no way through with out using the chain saw and pruning loppers they have brought. So taking off their packs, they go to work. An hour later they have made it through this first patch, only to encounter another within a couple of hundred feet. So back to work, by the time they get through this one, it's lunch time. After a lunch break, they start down the ridge again, only to encounter more Buck brush, here they also find their second T, carved into a large fir tree.

By now they know they are going in the right direction, follow the ridge and it will lead us to the mine, says John. Late afternoon they have progressed about three quarters of a mile from the camp. The Buck brush is so thick, that the only way through it is to cut a path with the saw,

"It's going to take forever this way" says Sue. " I know, but we have no other choice". "Look down the hill, the brush is just as thick on either side of the ridge, even if we could get down there, we would still have to cut through it". "At least this way we have the T's to follow".

Taking out his monocular he is scanning the large trees ahead, and finds the next marked tree. "Sue, look there is the next T tree, handing her the scope and pointing at the tree". "Yes, I see it too". "I say we quit for the day, the saw is getting dull, and I forgot to bring the extra chain".

"Now that we know what we are up against, we'll come better prepared tomorrow", "I'll take the chain off the saw, so I can sharpen it back at camp, and fill the gas and oil, then head back". "A good supper, rest and we'll be ready for tomorrow".

For the next four days, it's clear Buck brush and small tree growth to make a walking path. On the fifth day since making their camp on the ridge, they come to an old tree with a T and an arrow that points down hill almost back the way they have come so far. A little confused as to its meaning, they quit for the day and go back to camp. They reckon they have covered just over two miles of the ridge trail in their path cutting effort,. Theo's journal mentioned that he felt the mine to be four miles from where he parked the wagon. "That means we have only come half way" exclaims Sue. "Yeah, I know" says John, "plus we need to make a trip down to the truck for more supplies, gas, oil, food, and water". "Tomorrow we'll pack up and make a trip back to the truck". "Maybe go into Downieville, for a shower, laundry, real food at the cafe". "We need a day off". "I'll second that", says Sue. "Meantime we need to figure out what the arrow means". "The journal puts the mine down in the canyon far enough, that it wasn't to far from the stream in the bottom". "Maybe this is a switch back, we have been on the ridge all this time, and somehow we have to go down hill to the mine". "I'll get out the map, and our compass coordinates and see where we are in relation to the mine".... "Look here Sue, according to the map and Theo's compass readings, we have bypassed the mine, but it is down in the canyon, so that arrow is the turning point for a switch back, remember he had horses and mules, so he would traverse the mountain sideways to keep from hurting the animals". "Going straight down or up would be too hard on them and people too".

"When we get back, we will start down back towards the camp, there should be some kind of trail even if it is covered by the Buck brush".

Next day Downieville, motel room, shower food at the cafe, more water for their camp. That night a real bed. next morning breakfast at the cafe, then back to Goodyears Bar. Unload the ATV and trailer, then loading the new supplies; they are off to the camp site. Arriving late afternoon, they have time to set up camp, eat supper, then on to bed to start the next phase of the expedition.

After breakfast the next morning they hike down to the tree with the arrow, gas up the chain saw, and put on a newly sharpened chain. They start looking for the trail down the hill. Using the monocular they spot the next tree with a T. It's a couple of hundred yards down the hill back towards the way they have come so far. Cutting Buck brush in line with the two trees, they find that they are indeed on a trail that could be traversed by horses and mules. After a couple of hours, they break out of the brush, for over two hundred yards there is almost open space, and they can make out the old trail. "What a relief" says Sue, "Maybe we can get a second wind here. John checking his watch, tells her, "let's have lunch, and take a longer then usual rest before attacking this mountain again". "I'm all for that" Sue says.

Back at it again, it's yards and yards of Brush, then a break, then more Buck brush. Then another marked tree, then more brush, it's getting monotonous. Day after day, finally after four more days they break into another small clearing, almost tripping over the rocker box that Theo had used. The rocker was pretty well deteriorated, but still recognizable, next to it, the tub that was used for water had collapsed, the iron bands had rusted through, so the staves had just fallen where they could.

The small ravine where the diggings were is overgrown with trees, so that the face of the gravel was not visible. Looking at the tub, they found the remains of the wooden pipe that went down to the hot tub, carefully following the pipe line down the hill, they come on the remains of the tub, and the furnace. "Honey, here it is". Sue exclaims, "look over there, there's the cabin under all those vines, from here it looks in good shape". Getting out the cameras, John starts to take pictures of the Cabin, hot tub, and furnace. The corral and animal shed has collapsed from snow loads obviously. But remarkably the cabin is in good shape.

On the door is a sign that says Theo's Deja-Vu.... "Let's see if the door will open", says Sue. "Ok, but first get the respirator mask's out and put them on, we don't want to take a chance of Hanta Virus being in there".

So donning their masks, John unlatches the door and gives it a tug, surprisingly it opens fairly easily, except for the vines, clearing the vines they get the door open. Looking inside, they are surprised again at how little deterioration has occurred in here. The dust is light compared to other cabins they have been in, the cobwebs the same way. John remarks, that Theo built one hell've a tight cabin. "Look, there are his tin plates, cups, tea and coffee canisters". "And look at the canned goods, there is hardly any rust on the outside of the cans and bottle lids". "Get lots of pictures, John". "This place is remarkable for it's age". After taking several pictures, they close and latch the door, then go over to the hot tub furnace. "Ok honey, now's when it's going to get exciting". Locating the long rectangler piece of slate that Theo described in his journal, John takes off his backpack, and gets two small pry bars out and starts to pry the stone out of the furnace foundation. Taking pictures and video while doing this, He gets the rock out of the cavity, and there is the metal door of the box Theo said he had built into the furnace. Prying the rusted latch up John pulls the door open. Sue pushes John aside to get a better look, and a better set of pictures. "Oh! look, John, there they are, the leather pouches just as the journal describes them"

"Ok, get the pictures, and let's see what kind of shape the pouches are in". "They might be rotten enough, that they will fall apart as soon as we touch them". Getting out the box of heavy duty freezer bags John has brought along just for this purpose, he gingerly removes one of the pouches. The leather is pretty well rotted, but holds together enough so that John can get it into a freezer bag, " That's one". Proceeding he manages to get forty five of them out.

"We'll put fifteen in your backpack" he tells Sue, "and the other thirty in mine". "Then a quick snack, and we're out of here for today". "It's going to be almost dark before we get back to the camp, if we're lucky". So loading up the packs and replacing the slate rock, they start up the mountain,

"How come you put the rock back"? asks Sue. "To keep the animals out, all we need is for a pair of pack rats to find the leather pouches and we would have gold nuggets all over the place".

So up the mountain they go, it takes them two and a half hours to get back to camp. The extra weight plus what they had, slowed them way down. Extra food this night, to prepare for tomorrow. John checks out the food situation, and tell's Sue, "we only have enough for two more days, the water is alright but we are low on the backpack food". Sue asks if he has checked the emergency stash in the four wheeler? "What emergency stash?" he asks. "Check out the small plastic boxes on the fenders", says Sue, "I put a bunch of power bars in them". "How did you manage that without me knowing about it?" asks John. She laughs, "We gals have to be able to get one over on you guys once in the while". "Yeah, you always have to have the last word don't you, and laughs so hard it starts to hurt".

"Anyway thanks to you we can stay two more days if necessary to get the gold out". After supper they stash the gold under the cook stove where the food normally goes in the camp trailer. Then try to get a weather report on the portable radio, as the sky was clouding up over to the west.

Finally getting a Sacramento station, they hear that a storm is coming in, rain and snow down to six thousand feet. John looks at the map they have and see that they are close to that elevation.

"We better get an early start in the morning, it could get hairy here tomorrow". So they go to bed and try to go to sleep, but the excitement of the day keeps them awake talking. Finally Sue nods off, John a little later. During the night the temperature drops enough that there is frost on the sleeping bag when they wake up. "Brrr, it got cold last night" says Sue. "Yeah, I know, but look at it this way, it's better then rain, here's your coffee, let's get going as fast as we can".

Looking at the cloudy sky, John gets out the rain suits, and puts them in the backpacks. After breakfast they close up the camp trailer, and make sure nothing is out that would be harmed by rain. Then it's down the hill they go. Arriving at the mine, John looks at his watch, an hour and fifteen minutes to get here, not bad. Repeating the process of yesterday, they get another forty five Troy pounds of gold into the backpacks. Closing up the safe, they head up the hill, just about when they hit the corner tree at the switch back, two things happen, the rain starts, and Sue's hip is really hurting, and she forgot to bring her pain pills, stopping, and putting on their rain suits, they proceed to the camp

It takes all of Sues will power to get up the hill, John helps her every where he can, but the trail through the Buck brush is only wide enough for one person at a time, it takes them an extra hour to get to the camp. As they get there the snow starts coming down, quickly they stash the backpacks in the plastic carrying boxes on the ATV, and start it up, while it is warming up, John helps Sue onto the saddle, then checks to make sure they didn't leave anything behind.

Climbing onto the machine, he puts it in gear and they are off. Because of the snow and Sue's hip it takes them two extra hours to get to the Power Wagon, by that time there is three inches of snow on the ground. John helps Sue into the truck, then loads up the four wheeler and the camp trailer. Making sure they are strapped down and secure. He then puts the front hubs on the truck in. Starting the truck, he warms it up, scrapes the snow off the windshield, and putting it into four wheel drive, they head for home.

Getting the truck warm with the heater, and Sue taking her pain medicine, she is feeling much better. Because of the snow it is slow going till they reach the main highway going into Grass Valley, "Sue, would you like to stop for supper?". John asks "Yes, I'm hungry enough to eat the proverbial horse". So stopping at one of the restaurant's, they go inside for something to eat.

As they enter, people are looking at them, and whispering, the lady that seats them, gives them a seat away from the rest of the people. Sue goes into the ladies room, and when she comes out, she tells John, "I just found out why people were staring at us". "My face was filthy, and look at my clothes, they are ripped in so many places, I look like a ragamuffin".

John remarks, "Yeah, I noticed, the looks we were getting". "But look at it this way, I bet there is not a person in here who is as rich as we are right now, he says quietly". Sue, beams, and says "you're right, I didn't think of that, so poo on them".... Supper, then hit the road again, rain all the way home. Getting there, John opens the large shop door, and backs the trailer into the shop. Then puts the truck in the carport. And it's off to the shower and bed. Sue is already sound asleep. What a trip, is the last thing John thinks of before falling asleep.

CHAPTER FORTY

The next morning, Sue's hip is so stiff and sore, that John makes her stay in bed. He fixes her coffee, and a bowl of cereal, then off to the shop to unload the ATV and camp trailer.

Grouchy comes over to see how the trip went? "John tells him great, we wore ourselves out, got cuts and scratches all over, Sue's hip is really in bad shape this morning, but we had a great time". "Doesn't sound like great fun to me" growls Grouchy. "But you weren't there" says John, "We even got caught in a blizzard coming down off the mountain we were on".

Shaking his head, Grouchy remarks, "I'll never understand people, they think they had fun, while getting caught in a blizzard, getting cuts and scratches, probably hungry and thirsty to boot". He walks away, shaking his head and mumbling to himself.

John then starts to unload the ATV and the trailer, removing the backpacks, he empties them and puts the gold in a cardboard box for now, and then he gets all the dirty clothes rounded up and into the laundry room. The extra food he puts on a shelf, the chain saw on its shelf, with the gas mix, bar oil, extra chain, and tools. He empties all the water jugs, and the trailer tank and stores the jugs away. Swinging the camp stove out, he removes the gold stored under it, and puts it into the cardboard box. The sleeping bag is next; he takes it into the laundry room, telling Sue what he has done so far. She tells him that the sleeping bag will have to be taken to the laundry to be cleaned. " It will never fit in our machine". "Ok", he says.

Next is the port-o-potty. He removes it from the trailer and sets it in a corner to cook for a week or so, he has found out in the past, that it is easier to empty it when all the solids have turned to liquid, then clean it out, so it is ready for the next trip.

Lunch time. John goes in the house and asks Sue what she would like for lunch? She thinks for a moment, and asks, "how about our favorite Chinese lunch special?" "Ok! that sounds good to me" says John, "I'll call it in, and go down and pick it up". When he gets back, he finds Sue getting dressed. "I thought I told you to stay in bed, he admonishes her". She tells him," I need to get up and move around, otherwise my hip will lock up and I'll be down for days". "Ok, just don't over do it".

After lunch, John decides to go into Auburn, and stop at the mining and dredge shop and get a set of classifying screens. "What are you going to use them for" asks Sue? "I'm going to classify the gold into different sizes, so we can pick out what will be used in jewelry making, and what we will sell just as gold, or better yet send it into a refiner and have them turn it into 24 karat shot that we can then alloy into 14 karat and cast into jewelry". "Sounds like a good idea". . "We know from experience that we can make more money from the gold if we turn it into jewelry and sell it as such". "Yep", replies John.

So John goes to the dredge shop and gets a set of classifying screens, and says hello to his old friend Sully who owns the shop. Back home, he and Sue set about classifying the gold nuggets.

The screen set has a bottom cup, then a small screen about the size of window screen, then progressively larger holes till it reaches almost a half inch. They start to classify the gold.

Pouring each pouch into the screen, and shaking them side to side, the nuggets fall through the screens until they reach the screen that they won't go through. Then using all of their gold pans, they pour each screen into a different pan. When a gold pan is as full as they want it to get, they take that gold and put it into a sturdy freezer bag, then another bag for insurance.

It takes them all afternoon to classify the ninety Troy pounds of gold they brought home.

Marking the freezer bags with the screen size, they put them back into the cardboard box, all except the smallest screen size. "These fines are what we will send in to the refiner", says John.

Getting out the gold scales they begin to weigh the fines. As the scale can only weigh four ounces at a time, it is another tedious job, putting the fines into the freezer bags at a pound each, they come up with fifteen and a half pounds of fine gold. "Not bad" says John, "That will make enough 14 karat rings to keep me busy forever". "We still have to classify the gold in the trunk", Sue tells him. "Yeah I know, but not today", "I'm bushed, how about a delivered pizza for supper, that way we won't have to cook", "Ok" says Sue.

The next day John sends Sue to the store for more freezer bags, her hip is feeling much better today, so the drive and store walk does her some good. When she gets back, they start on the gold in the trunk, another all day session. The result is almost forty pounds of fines to send off to the refiners. John gets out his calculator and tells Sue, "that's, almost 480 ounces of gold, refined with a fifteen percent loss for impurities, will still give us over 400 ounces of pure gold". "Adding forty one and a half percent back in alloys to make 14 karat will give us approximately 564 ounces of 14 karat casting gold". "Figuring an average of seven rings per ounce, that gives us 3,948 rings to make and sell". "Well honey, you better get out the whip you told Grouchy you were going to use on me, because that is a lot of work, and we haven't even taken into consideration the rest of the gold that we will make into earrings, pendants, bracelets, necklaces etc". "Well John, you better get busy, at our age we only have twenty years or so to make our million, as she pokes him in the arm and laughs". Putting the gold back in the trunk, John tells her," I think we better look into a safe to keep this gold in, probably a floor safe would be best, that way we can conceal it from prying eyes". "Good idea husband, and while you're looking at safes in Sacramento, I can get some new jeans and shirts to replace the ones I tore up on our little adventure". "I'm free tomorrow she says, so we can go then".

John looks at Sue, "Any excuse to go shopping, my honey". "You bet".

New floor safe, big enough to put all the gold in, plus room for other valuables, a couple of bags of cement and two days of breaking concrete and the safe is installed. Grouchy hollers over the fence. "What in the hell are you making now, I never heard such a racket?" "Oh just breaking up some rocks we brought back from our trip".

Grizz shows up, to say hello and goodbye for the winter, I'm heading for Quartzsite for the season. This gives John an idea. "How is the selling down there he asks?" "Not too bad" says the Grizz, "if you set up in one of the shows and have a lot of stock, usually you can do pretty good".

John looks at Sue and tells her, "Maybe we should go down there and look at the potential, we might be able to make some money there with the little gold we got this summer". "When do the shows start?" "Middle of January to the middle of Febuary, Grizz tells him". "Well this is the middle of October, so if I went to work now I could have a decent display by then", "What do you think Sue, want to spend a month in Arizona?" "Sure" she says, "A vacation would do us good, after our last adventure". So getting some more particulars from the Grizz they plan on going to Arizona for a month.

The next day they contact the refiner and find out how long it would take to process their gold? "If you ship it to us one day UPS, we can have it back to you in five working days, the refiner says". "Ok look for sizable shipment of raw fine placer gold, we want some in 14 karat, and the rest in 24 karat, can you do that" asks John?. "Sure says the refiner, how do you wish to pay for it'?" "In gold" says John. "Ok" says, the refiner, "Will do",

"Alright" asks Sue, "Now what are you getting us into?" "Quartzsite, we've been wanting to go ever since we met". "Now's our chance". "And just what are we going to go in and stay in when we are there?" "How about a camper on the Power wagon, we ought to be confortable enough that way". "Here we go again", says Sue. "You just can't stop buying toys or tools". "Ah, honey look at it this way, we just came into enough money to take care of us the rest of our lives, so why shouldn't we enjoy ourselves with it". "That means some new toys as you put it, some traveling, which we both enjoy". "New sights to see, pictures to take, different foods to partake of, new friends to make". "So why not?"

"How can I argue with your logic", asks Sue, "You can come up with the best answers I have ever heard".

"Ok, we'll go, but while we are looking at campers, I think we should consider a small motor home, something big enough to be self contained, yet small enough that I can drive". "Ok", says John, "What are your plans for tomorrow?" "You know as well as I do that we are free everyday to do what we want to do, what time do you want to leave in the morning?"

"Oh, daybreak" says John. "Daybreak! I'll daybreak you, you'll leave when I'm ready to go, and not before", she says, "daybreak, one of these days Alice, right to the moon, as they laugh together".

After shipping off the fine gold, they go hunting for a camper or motor home. It takes them three days to find a motor home suitable for them, it's a used 21 foot El-Dorado, just the right name considering the outcome of their adventure. Self contained, everything works, super clean inside, and only three thousand miles on the rebuilt engine and transmission. And since the seller was motivated, as they say, the price was right. Bringing it home, Grouchy again, had to come over and ask what now? "Oh, we made another great deal" says John, "We are planning on going to Quartzsite and sell some gold nugget jewelry, and the owner of this rig agreed to loan it to us, if we make him enough jewelry for all of his family for Christmas". "We couldn't say no".

Grouchy, again goes back to his yard shaking his head, and mumbling to himself, "How does he do it?" "I have never seen anyone who can make such deals in my life".

The next three months are hectic; John is busy day and night making gold nugget jewelry. Sue has the job of cleaning the motor home, an varnishing the interior. John decides to tow the Suzuki behind the motor home, so he makes a tow set up for the car. Sue ask's, "What are we going to do for show cases?" "Hum", says John, "I almost didn't think of that, in the back of my mind, I knew we needed some thing". "I guess we better take a day or two and find out what other people are using, and where to get them, also we're going to have to figure out how to haul them", Getting ahold of Grizz through one of his friends, we ask him what most people are doing for cases and canopies with which to set up with. He said not to sweat it, there are venders down here, who specialize in selling canopies, show cases from simple to expensive, tables to set them on, you can get everything right here, "Ok, that takes a load off, when does the first show start?" The middle of January like I told you, come down a couple of days early and you can look at the various shows and decide which one you want to be in.

"Ok", says John, "Where do we find you?" "At the Golden Arches almost every evening, just let me know when you plan to get there and I'll be waiting for you". "Ok", says John, "We'll call your friends in two days and let you know when to expect us".

Quartzsite. We take four days to get there even though it can be done in one days hard drive. John wants to stop at a ghost town he had been to twenty years ago. Found a booming silver mining operation going, around the old town. Not much had changed in the town itself. but a mountain was missing behind the old town. The mining company had taken it down and ground it up for the silver and gold in the ore. From there to Vegas, spent a day seeing all the new sights and played the slots a little, plus ate some great food. Then an overnight in Laughlin, again some great food, a movie, and a little gambling. Next day Quartzsite. I had been telling Sue about the sea of R.V.s that we would see coming into the valley where Quartzsite is located, even though we knew what to expect, we still gasped at the amount of vehicles that were there, We were told during the show that a million people showed up during the month of shows there.

Finding Grizz at McDonalds, we found a place in the desert nearby to camp until we decided which show to do. The next day we looked at the different shows, and decided to get into the one south of the freeway, fortunately they had some spaces open. So we paid for a space and parked the motor home, then taking the Suzuki, we found the venders with the canopies, cases, and tables. At last we were set up, just in time for the show to start.

Friday the first day of selling, we were selling our jewelry almost as fast as we could take care of the customers. We were told that we had some of the best gold nugget jewelry there, and best of all our prices were great. We found out we weren't underselling anyone, but we had better workmanship, and quality in our goods. Now this didn't give us very big heads, did it?

By the end of the ten day show, we had sold enough, that we didn't feel we had to set up at another show. The last day a couple of competitor's showed up and asked if we would wholesale to them? Sure we said, why not? "If we can come to terms on the price, you bet". "Plus if you want more in the future, we'll be happy to make it for you". So we sold out, and made a couple of new friends and customers.

After the show we hung around for a few days and went detecting with the Grizz, said hello to some of the other miners we knew from up north, met some new friends. Since we were flush with money, we decided to roam around Arizona and see the sights, lots of old ghost towns, the Grand Canyon, other places to detect for nuggets, mostly found square nails, Sue found a couple of nice nuggets. At one place we found a large lead heart on Valentines Day, so that was kind of nice. Then it was time to start for home, we were missing the old homestead. So we meandered north towards home, stopping to see the sights on the way,

Home, "Oh! Its good to be home" says Sue. We spend the next week unwinding, putting a sizable amount of money in the bank. Telling Grouchy we did so good that we can buy the motor home from our friend. Then getting back into the groove of our life here in Northern California.

Back to the work bench to make another inventory of jewelry, plus we now have orders to fill for our new wholesale customers. Spring comes and we can finally get out and prospect a little. We check in with the Downie-ville Forest Service to see what is going on with the wilderness, and they tell us it will be dedicated in two weeks.

Since there is still snow up there, where we would have to go to get to the Deja-Vu, there is no way we can get in there for more of the gold. The new wilderness designation locks it up to anything but hiking. We thought of using a snowmobile, but were told it was illegal in that area, even before the wilderness. So we give up on getting more gold from the old mine, besides we have more then enough to meet and exceed our future needs and wants.

So we go back to our old ways, detecting, dredging, and exploring. One day I find another Suzuki Samurai in the wheels and deals. "Sue, listen to this, Samurai factory hardtop, new 1600 motor, rockcrawler transfer case, 3 inch lift, almost new tires, positraction in both axles.

Divorce forces sale".

Now this is just what I want to 4 wheel with, We can get into more places with this rig, I tell her. She throws up her hands, and exclaims, "Another new toy, Ok, but you have to build me a sun room off the living room". "Deal" says John, so he calls the guy and makes a deal over the phone contingent on driving it. The guy asks where we live, and says he will drive it over right now and let me take it through its paces. A half hour later, he is pulling in the driveway with a light blue Samurai, the same color as ours, right away Sue approves of the rig. A mile away there is an old abandoned gravel pit and quarry, where the locals can go and play, so we run the car over there and proceed to climb up and down the obstacles there. The car never misses a beat. Back at the house, I crawl underneath to look at any damage that might be there. I find this guy had installed skid plates under any part that was subject to breakage, plus all the seals were dry, which means there is no oil leakage anywhere. I ask him if he will take a check? He says sure, so we clinch the deal, and now I'm the proud owner of a new, used tricked out Suzuki. "I suppose, I'm going to become a rockcrawler widow now". "Now you know better then that Sue, there's room for you in the car when we go out on the Rubicon trail". "Not with my hip" she says, "No Rubicon trail for me".

The next day, John gets with a couple of contractors he knows, to find out what a sun room will cost to build? One of his friends tells him, he can do it for this sum, and since he is between jobs right now, he can start tomorrow. "That's great", says John, "but what about permits?" "Come on" the contractor says, "let's go talk to the building department, and see what's involved in a sun room". The building guy, turns out to be the contractor's brother in law, and he tells him he can start tomorrow, if he can bring in a plan first thing in the morning.

So off to the building supply, and got every magazine, and book with a sun room in it. Then back to the house so Sue can pick one out, The contractor tells her not to be too concerned with the plans in the books, just pick one out that is close to what you have in mind, and as we are building it we can change the plan to suit your idea and needs. Sue looks at the books and picks out a plan. "Ok we'll go with this one to get the permit, and then if you want any changes we can do them as we build".

Next morning the contractor gets the permit, and by that afternoon the footing is dug and the forms are in place. Now is the time to let me know if the room is going to be big enough or too big the contractor tells Sue. "It looks alright to me" she tells him. The footing is poured the next morning. Here comes Grouchy, Sue looks at John, and asks what story are you going to tell him this time. "I don't know he says, but something will come up". Two days later they start framing the sun room. The contractor and Sue are picking out the windows from a catalog from the building supply. These are in stock he tells Sue, those real fancy ones have to be ordered, and would probably take a month to get. Sue tells him, I don't like them, they definitely don't fit the rest of the house. The ones that they have in stock do, so let's go with them, "Alright!" exclaims the contractor, "We'll have you in your sun room within a week". True to his word, Sue is enjoying her first cup of morning coffee in her new sun room a week later.

CHAPTER FORTY ONE

The following summer, John and Sue are out at one of their favorite old hydraulic mines, checking out their new expensive Australian made gold detectors. They are actually finding nuggets in areas where they had worked before. The new detectors were locating the gold deeper then the old units they had. Even John has broken the ice, and is finally finding nuggets detecting. This is why they bought the new detectors. they were told by friends that these units would reach deeper, and locate gold they had missed with their old detectors.

All of a sudden Sue screamed, *"JOHN, HELP."* John looking around can't see Sue, normally he tries to keep her within eyesight. "Where are you?" he yells, "I can't see you." "Over here, I tripped and fell." "My bad hip feels like I have broken it." Following the sound of her voice, John finds Sue lying on her side in a small gully. Rushing up to her, he asks "What happened?" She tells him how she slipped on a rock, and fell into this gully, and "I hit on my bad hip." "I think I fractured it, I can't move, the pain is so bad when I try." "Ok, let's see if I can move you." As he tries to lift her she screams out in pain. John tells her, "I've got to get you to the Suzuki, so we can get you to a hospital." "But it hurts." "Let me think a minute." "Do you have your pain pills with you?" "No they are in the Suzuki." "Great"

"Ok can you manage to lie still here while I get the Suzuki up here." "But you can't drive it here." "Honey, remember this is the Rubicon rig, it'll make it up here close enough, so I can get you in it and then out of here." "Just lie still, it's going to take me a while." So marking the place so he can find it again, he rushes down to the rig.

Locking the hubs in , then starting the engine, he puts it into four wheel drive and starts back up into the hydraulic pit. It takes him about fifteen minutes to get close enough to Sue so that he can carry her to the rig. Reclining the right seat and propping the door open, he goes to get Sue. "Where are your pain pills, he hollers?" "In my purse." he rummages around in the purse until he finds her pills. Then he takes them to her. "Take one or two he tells her." "How, many will it take to almost knock you out, without overdosing," "Two." "Ok, if you feel ok about taking that many right now, let's do it, here's the water and the pills."

"While we are waiting for them to kick in, I'll get our stuff into the Suzuki." So he loads up their equipment, "How are you doing?" "The pills are starting to work, the pain is not as bad as before." "Ok let's see if I can move you." He tries to pick her up as gently as he can, but she screams. "It still hurts too much," So they wait a few more minutes, then he tries again, this time she can stand the pain enough that he manages to get her into the little truck.

"Ok let's get you buckled in, and see if we can get out of here." Putting the Suzuki into compound low, John crawls in and out of the small gullies, and around large boulders to eventually get back to the old mining road that leads them out to the highway.

The pills are working well enough that Sue is almost asleep, plus the pain has subsided enough that the rough ride is not hurting her too bad. Getting to the highway, John takes the rig out of four wheel drive, and heads for the hospital in Auburn, which is the nearest one he knows about.

It takes a half hour to get there, pulling up to the emergency entrance, he runs in and grabs the first staff person he sees and tells her he has his wife in the car, with a possible broken hip.

The nurse gets two orderlies, and a stretcher and proceed to get Sue out of the Suzuki. Seeing that there isn't any bleeding, they take her into the X-ray room and start to examine her.

Noticing that she is almost knocked out from the pills, they ask if she is under the influence of anything. John shows them her pill bottle, and tells the nurse, "She took two for the pain, before I loaded her into the truck." "She has an arthritic hip, and her doctor prescribes these pain pills for her." "Ok, as long as we know what she has taken, there isn't any problem."

The X-rays show that Sue had indeed fractured her hip, and that they were going to have to transfer her down to U C Davis in Sacramento, where they have the doctors and equipment to take care of her properly.

So they put her in the Hospital's helicopter, and fly her down to the hospital in Sacramento. Meanwhile John drives home and gets the other Suzuki, and drives to the Hospital in Sacramento. Sue's Suzuki is geared for highway use, so is much faster on the road.

Getting to the hospital, John talks to the really tall Doctor that is taking care of Sue, He explains what has happened to her hip. That the cartilage has separated from the bone, and it is going to be necessary to give her a hip implant. I tell him that her Doctor had told her it was only a matter of time before she needed an implant because of the arthritis.

"Well then now's the time to do it, the tall Doctor say's." "Ok, we have the necessary insurance coverage to take care of the bill, so let's do it." Checking with Sue, she also agrees now is the time to do it. So the next morning she is operated on. A week later, John is allowed to take her home. The Doc has given him instructions on how to take care of her. So for the next six weeks, it's helping her to bathe, learning how to walk, and just generally getting her better. After six weeks she is almost like new, there is still some pain in the hip, but not like before the fall.

While Sue has been recuperating, John has been talking to his contractor friend about adding on to the house again. He tells him, he would like a workout room, with a whirlpool bath, and a room where Sue can work on her crafts. They look at the space between the shop building and the back of the carport, and decide that there is enough room for the addition. Checking with Sue, who is all for it, they proceed to draw up the plans and get the necessary building permits, then when the contractor finishes the job he is on now, they start the addition.

Grouchy is right in the middle of things as usual. "Damn, John here you go again, the jewelry business must be pretty good, to be able to afford another addition." "Yes, it is Grouchy. It makes my old job seem like I was making nothing in comparison." "When I finish this project, I'm going to have a Ramada built for the motorhome." "Then I think I'll be done with any major remodeling here on the property."

After the addition is finished, life is getting back to normal for Sue and John. Making up a new stock of jewelry for the show in Quartzsite, taking care of their wholesale customers, detecting when they can get away. The new detectors are great, they get more gold with them then they did with their old units.

A couple of years later, in late summer, the nightly news show is showing a catastrophic forest fire burning up north of Downieville in the wilderness area. They look at each other, and wonder how Theo's mine is? The newscaster is interviewing a Forester, who is saying that this fire could have been prevented if the Enviro's had let them thin this area, instead of making it a wilderness. Now nobody will be able to enjoy it, not even the trees and animals they thought they were saving.

And so life goes on. For Sue and John, it is good, they are only a couple of years from retirement age, even with the drop in the gold spot price, they have enough gold to keep them in a nice income bracket for as long as they live. As for the rest of Theo's gold buried in the hot tub furnace, maybe some day someone will discover the treasure there.

CHAPTER FORTY TWO

That year the campaign for President of the U.S. was in full swing. Lo and behold, after a very close runoff, we have a new administration. After the swearing in ceremony the new President tells the country that he is going to look at all of the new wilderness, and national parks that the old President put into being by using executive order under the 1906 antiquities law, thereby bypassing the congress and the right of the people to chose whether they wanted these new closed areas.

The new administration and the country as a whole considered these designations illegal and therefore subject to reversal of their present state of being.

The day after the announcement on the T.V., the Sacramento paper had a big article on the subject, with a list of the wilderness, and parks that were being given back their old status. And there in the middle of the list was the wilderness where Theo's mine is,

"Sue come and look at this", I holler. "What is all the fuss about?" she wants to know "Look at this article, they have turned the wilderness where the mine is back into regular forest designation". "So!" she asks, "What's so important about that?" "Don't you see honey, that means we can legally go and get the rest of the gold hidden there, plus mine the rest of the ravine that Theo was working".

"John! You're crazy". "If you think that I'm going mountain climbing, pick and shovel swinging, searching for gold again with my new hip just getting to feel almost normal, I repeat you're nut's". "When do we begin?". "I can't wait to be involved in another adventure". "It's been too quiet around here of late". "Tomorrow", John tells her, "We can start by going down to Sacramento to the B.L.M. office and see if we can file a legal mining claim in the area where the Deja-vu is located". "Does that mean I can do some shopping while we are in the big city?" "Yes", he tells her, "We can go shopping too". "Oh goody, can we also stop at our favorite little bakery and get a Bee-sting for breakfast?". "Yes dear, you can get as many as you want ".

The next morning they get up earlier then usual, and take off for the big city just thirty miles away. They stop at the bakery and have a breakfast of sweetrolls. Sue gets several Bee-stings to go, and then it's off to the B.L.M. office.

At the B,L.M., they get in touch with the head of the mining claims division and ask if they can put a mining claim in the area where the wilderness designation was, now that it has been put back into regular forest again.

The man tells them that as far as he knows, that yes, the area is now open to exploration and that the new administration is going to push for new discoveries of minerals, as the country has fallen way behind in that area because of the Enviros, and the last administration trying to appease them by locking up everything.

"Good", states John. "It's about time somebody wakes up to the fact that this country needs all the minerals we can mine to keep the standard of living that we as a country have gotten used to". "If the extreme Greens have their way, we would all be looking for a cave to live in, an big leaves to wear to keep warm".

Leaving the B.L.M. office with this good news, they spend the rest of the day shopping, then a good dinner in one of their favorite restaurants, then home to collapse from their busy day.

The next day John gets copies of the mining claim filing papers, and starts to fill them out. He figures he should lock up 80 acres around the mine. So he calls Sue's sons and asks them if they would like to be part owners in a placer mine. They both jump at the chance, as they have seen how their mother and John have enjoyed the mining they do. They don't know of the contents of the trunk, or the recovery of some of Theo's gold, but they have seen how their mother and John have suddenly improved their financial well being since the death of Melissa Carpenter, figuring the old lady must have left some money to their mother.

So with four names that are needed to make an association placer claim, John has only to get the correct coordinates for the mine. That evening, he gets ahold of his neighbor Bryce, who he knows is a computer whiz and can operate a GPS unit exceedingly well, and asks him if he can map out eighty acres on a Topo map for him?

"Sure", says Bryce. "It's relatively easy once you know how, if you like I'll show you how to run one of these units, knowing how you and Sue like to explore you should have one with you everytime you go out in the forest". "Not only will they show you where you are at any given time, but also how to find a particular spot, then the way back home so to speak". "Plus the units can store many destinations in them, that you can look up any time you want"

"That sounds great Bryce, I figured you could help me", with that he unfolds the Topo map he brought and points to the general area of Theo's mine. "I have three compass coordinates that we used in the past to find this spot". "Would they be of value in locating the exact spot I'm looking for?"

"You bet" says Bryce, "let me have them and I'll be able to pinpoint the spot on the map for you" Using the compass readings, and the G.P.S. unit Bryce puts a dot on the map, and states," there it is". "Ok, says John, now what we need is to expand the dot to eighty acres so we can make a mining claim out of the area". Bryce takes the G,P.S. unit and punches in a few numbers and comes up with the four corners needed to make an eighty acre mining claim, then he transfers the corners to the Topo map, and shows John how to describe it in legal subdivision terms that is required, to file it with the recorders office in Downeville, and B.L.M.

"Bryce, this is great, I guess you're right, Sue and I should have one of these new fangled machines, I can see where it would come in very handy out in the woods".

So armed with the information they need to file a legal mining claim, John goes home and tells Sue, they will be going to Downieville to file the papers as soon as she feels like another small trip. "Tomorrow's Friday, the courthouse in Downieville will be open, we can go then, I'll pack a lunch for us". "How early do you want to go, she asks?"

"Daylight of course", knowing that neither one of them are early risers. "John! one of these days I'm going to get even". "Yes, dear", as they laugh at one of their favorite jokes they have between them.

CHAPTER FORTY THREE

The next morning they get up and get ready to go up to Downieville. Taking their time they finally get on the road about nine o clock. Using Sue's car they run up I-80 to highway 49, then on to Downieville. John comments, that even with all the improvements the state has made on this highway, it still twists and turns, and is slow driving compared to the main highways. "Oh well, that's what makes it a rural road and rural setting". " Talk about rural setting, have you noticed the number of logging trucks that we have been encountering asks Sue?" "Yeah, and did you notice they are only carrying fire charred logs twenty feet long instead of the normal forty footers we usually see", "I wonder what forest fire they were in?".

Getting to Downieville around noon, they stop in the cafe and have lunch, since they had to wait till one o clock for the courthouse to reopen for the afternoon, they took their time at lunch. After lunch they visited the small museum on main street. Then to the recorders office to file the mining claim.

The woman who took care of them questioned the validity of the area in which the claim was being put in.

John had to tell her that the wilderness designation had been lifted from the area in question, and that the B.L.M. had given him a statement to that fact. So the claim was recorded, and extra copies made, one to send to the B.L.M., the others for Sue's sons

On the way back home they noticed that there was a large crew of loggers and equipment staying at the Goodyears Bar campground. Being ever curious, John decides to stop and find out where they are logging. The first logger he talks to, tells him he should go talk to the 'Side rod over at that trailer with the canopy room off its side. Sue asks John, "what is a Side rod?" Don't you remember your son Dan telling us about the foreman on his last job, and what a lousy Side rod' he was", "Side rod is a nickname for a logging foreman"

"Now I remember, Dan complained the guy drank to much and was lazy". "That's the one" John said.

Going over to the Side rods' trailer John and Sue find the man relaxing on his veranda. Introducing themselves, they ask him if he can give them any information on the logging operation that is going on? "Sure, what would you like to know?". "Well let's start with where the logs are coming from, as we noticed they all seem to be burned, and why are they only 20 feet long, instead of the normal forty?".

Hank as he had introduced himself, said "come on in and sit down, and I'll tell you what is going on here". After sitting down, John and Sue are getting the lowdown on the operation. First Hank asked them if they knew of the forest fire in the wilderness area last year? Yes they said. "Well, after the new administration took a look at all the lumber and bio-mass fuel being wasted by the wilderness designation where the fires hit, they decided to rescind all of those that had burned and have them salvaged logged and then replanted as soon as possible".

"The new boss of the Forest Service was given orders to start immediately on the process and to have it completed before any of the burned trees would become useless from rot".

"So here we are, logging as fast as we can". "We are only one of many operations that are working against time and weather in previous wilderness areas that have burned through the western states last year". "If you have been watching the news, you know that last year was one of the worst forest fire years on record" "Yes, we know"

John asks Hank about what seems to be a road going up along Goodyear Creek, where several years ago it was only open to A,T.V.s and Dirt Bikes, Hank tells them how the logging company is building a road up the old stage route from the 1800's, "Within a week we will be to the top of the ridge, then we will turn right along the ridge top into the burn and take logs down from there.

When we finish that area, we'll start on the west side of the road and follow the old stage route all the way to Marysville. The company has a road building crew already on the Marysville side building the road from there. As soon as our crew finishes the road going to the right, they will start to build the road going to Marysville, and the two crews will meet in the middle somewhere. The road going to the Marysville Saw Mill will be wide enough and straight enough, so the trucks will be able to carry the normal forty foot logs.

The reason we are only taking twenties to the Grass Valley Mill is because of the narrow and twisting road that highway 49 is from here to there.

"Anyway, you folks seem to have an uncommon interest in this operation, may .1 ask why?", "Sure! a few years ago we discovered an old placer mine in the area of the wilderness before it became a wilderness". "We were able to mine a sizable amount of nuggets from there before the weather forced us out, the following spring when we wanted to go back, the administration and their Enviro buddys had locked it up into a wilderness".

"When we heard the other day that the area was taken out of wilderness status, we jumped on the chance to put a placer claim on the area we worked". "We were coming back from Downieville after filing the claim, when We saw your operation"

"Whereabouts is this claim if you don't mind my asking?" "Well now that we have a valid claim on it, I can tell you where it is", says John. "Going northeast or turning right at the top of the ridge, you go about a mile and a half till you come to a large flat, then almost straight down the mountain towards a stream in the bottom of the canyon you will find a small ravine with the dried up remnants of an old stream channel". "The gravel has enough gold in it to warrant a small pick and shovel operation". "In three days Sue and I picked and shoveled at the gravel". "We uncovered enough bedrock to use our metal detectors on, and recovered a little over five ounces of gold nuggets". Then we took a couple of buckets of the bedrock gravel down to the stream and panned them out, and recovered almost another three quarters of and ounce of fine gold and small nuggets from the gravel". "This told us we had a spot we could mine with a small mining machine that we could shovel into by hand"

Hank asks if we could show him the spot on a Topo map, stating that he thinks he knows whereabout we are talking about, "I guess there would be no harm in that" answers John

Hank gets out his map, and pointing to almost the exact spot asks is that where it is? "Yeah, says John, but how did you know?" "When getting ready to do this job, we spent a week in a chopper taking aerial photos of the burn". "As we were flying over the area of your claim I noticed a couple of things that were out of the ordinary". "From the flat we could see where someone had cut a trail through the buck brush, even though the fire had burned most of the brush away, it was still visible from the air". The trail followed the ridge line for a couple of miles, then it turned back on itself, and transversed down the mountain toward the bottom of the canyon".

"We could see where it stopped at a small ravine, where the gravel is much lighter in color than the surrounding ground", "Now having logged around several old hydraulic mines, where the gravel is about the same color, I surmised that it could possibly be a placer deposit". And that at sometime, someone was trying to work it". "There were really old tailings just down the hill from the ravine". "But what struck me funny was the fact that the trail was new, having been cut through in the last five years or so"

"You're right Hank, Sue and I spent two weeks with a chain saw and pruning loppers cutting that trail". "Then three days checking the gravel out, before the weather forced us to quit". "Then as we said, the next spring it became a wilderness, so we couldn't get back into it with out hiking twenty miles one way". "With Sue's arthritic hip and our age factor, we figured it was too much of a challenge for us, so we gave up on the idea of coming back". "Besides it is illegal to mine or use a detector in a wilderness".

"But now, with the wilderness designation gone we can again get to within about four miles of the spot, and maybe set up a small mining operation".

"Well, I've got some good news for you said Hank, we plan on punching a skid trail down the ridge, then down the trail line to the next ravine just beyond your claim". "You will be able to take a Jeep right to the mine, when we get done". "Plus onto the next ravine where there is another gravel deposit".

"Did I hear you right?" "You said there is another ravine full of stream gravel just beyond the one we were at", "Yes, It's just a couple of hundred feet away, here let me show you the aerial photo". With that Hank looks through his file and brings out a photo that shows the two ravines, the old tailings below the first one and nothing but old gravel in the second ravine. John and Sue also note that the fire had stopped just a few feet below the two ravines outlets, and that the timber down to the stream and up the other mountain side was left unburned. John asked Hank if he knew what stopped the fire along that line? "I was told that the fire was going down hill at that time, and between fire retardant drops from the fire bombers and choppers, the fire was stopped there"

"Wow! how lucky can we get, the fire didn't hurt the stream, and we have another gravel bed that might have some gold in it". "And with the fact that we included that area in the claim we just filed we just might be in the mining business again"

"Hank, if that other gravel deposit has gold in it, how would you like a fifth interest in a gold mine". "If you hadn't told us of the other ravine, we might not have bothered with looking for it, and therefore have missed it". "So what do you say Sue, we give Hank twenty percent of the gold that comes out of that ravine?" "You bet John, with the skid trail right down to the ravines, even I will be able to have a little fun mining there again even with this damn hip implant that acts up pain wise every so often, and the knowledge we have gained here is worth every bit of the percentage we will give Hank".

"So Hank, when can we get in there without interfering with your logging operation?" "How about two weeks",

"We plan to have the road over to the flat, where we are going to set up a yarder, then the skid trail down to the ravines" "You can call me on Friday evening in two weeks, and if we are set up as planned, you can come up and drive your Suzuki into the mine, and start looking the situation over".

"You'll only have the weekend to work there as we will be logging during the week, which means heavy equipment, and logging trucks all over the place". "We know just what you're talking about, Sue's son Dan is a hot saw operator down in the El Dorado forest, and a couple of years ago we were allowed to watch his operation during a working day, what a wild dance of men and machinery that was", "Trees being sawed down, skidders running back and forth to the landing, where some of the logs were being loaded onto trucks to be hauled to the saw mill, while other trees were being chipped into bio-mass for the co-gen plants". "As I said, what a wild dance".

"Hank, give us your phone number, and your last name, when we come up we will have a piece of paper making you a fifth owner of the mine, so that you will have legal recourse in case we are in an accident". So Hank tells them his last name is Schofield, and the phone is 555-1213, and that he is looking forward to being a part time miner, "Well Hank it has been a pleasure, but we should be getting home, so let me leave you with this thought, Gold is good, and if the gold god is looking out for us, we will recover some of his bounty, and enjoy the soft yellow hue that it gives off to all who gaze upon it".

"On the way home, Sue tells John, now that was a nice sentiment you left Hank, but what I want to know is where you get all these stories you make up?" "I've been watching you for years, giving Grouchy stories of how we can afford certain things, and now you come up with a plausible story of how we found the mine". "How do you do it?. "I don't know, they just come to me". "But seriously Sue, do you realize that possibly in two weeks we will be able to recover the rest of Theo's stash, and maybe set up another operation on his mine, what a rush as the young folks say". So it's home to dream and plan their next adventure.

CHAPTER FORTY FOUR

The next day being Saturday, Sue's sons came over to see what was going on. They hadn't seen so much excitement in John and Sue over mining for several years now.

"What's up mom?", asks Dan. "Dan, Rich, come on in and we are going to tell you all about our new adventure". Dan is Sue's youngest boy, and works in the logging industry as a hot saw operator. Rich is her oldest boy, and he works in construction as a cabinet maker and installer.

"So what is going on?" asks Rich. "How come you wanted us to be listed on a new mining claim?"

"Sit down and listen boys, because we have a story for you" "Do you remember several years ago when John and I recovered a sizable amount of gold off of and old mining claim?"

"And we told you that before we could finish mining the spot, the past liberal administration put the area in a wilderness". "And that later on the wilderness was involved in a terrible forest fire". "Well the new administration has rescinded the wilderness designation there, and all over the western states, especially those areas that were involved in forest fires". "As you know last year was the worst fire season in recent years". "Anyway the new administration found the wilderness areas to have been brought about illegally, and with the fires, the loss of timber for lumber use, to be detrimental to the overall economy of the country, so they opened all the burned areas for immediate salvage logging".

"And now with the energy crisis, here in California, the Forest Service has been ordered to log all the burned areas, and turn the wood into biomass and saw logs where possible, immediately". "The state of California wants all the biomass chips they can get to keep all the co-gen electric plants on line seven days a week to help eliminate the possibility of power outages".

"Which brings us to the mining claim". "With the wilderness designation gone, we were able to put a claim on the area we wanted to mine". "So yesterday we went up to Downieville and filed an eighty acre association placer claim". "That's why we needed your names on the papers".

"On the way back from Downieville we stopped at the Goodyears Bar campground and talked to the forman of a logging operation, you tell them John". "Well boys, we met with the boss of the loggers, and he showed us where they are going to log". "As it happens they are going to put in roads and skid trails right down to our claim". "And furthermore, the Side rod showed us an aerial photo of the ravine we want to work, and we saw another one about a couple of hundred feet away that has the possibility of being as rich as the first one".

"The forman was so helpful, plus showing us the other ravine we are going to give him a fifth of the gold that comes out of that spot". "Dan you might know this guy, his name is Hank Schofield".

"Hank 'mission impossible' Schofield". "Yeah, I know of him, I met him at the logging show in Medford last year". "He's a legend among the logging community". "The story I have heard is he was a chopper pilot during the last year of Viet-Nam, flying Chinooks and Siskorsky flying cranes", "When he got back home, he went back to work in the logging industry, and when a particularly ground sensitive logging operation was proposed, he suggested using choppers to haul out the trees, thereby eliminating the surface damage caused by Cats and Skidders". "The idea worked so well that they do it all the time now". "So that's how he got his nickname, 'mission impossible'. "He has the reputation of being the best Side rod in the business". "His crew will tackle jobs that other outfits will walk away from as being too difficult to do and make a profit from".

"Well that's great to hear, I knew when we were talking to him, that there was something special about the man". "Anyway he is going to push in a road to the ravines, and we are to call him in two weeks and see if we can get into the spot with our Suzuki". "Knowing his rep, he will have a superhighway waiting for you" remarks Dan.

So for the next two weeks, John and Sue plan to go to Theo's mine to recover the rest of the gold hidden in the hot tub furnace. John has checked over the Rubicon Suzuki, and mounted one of the metal boxes they used on the camp trailer before, in the back of the Suzuki as a lockable safe to put the rest of Theo's gold in to bring home. He is also getting the camp trailer they used before ready, filling the water tank, servicing the port-o-potty, filling the propane for the cook stove. He also goes and gets a new supply of backpacking freeze dried food. As they plan to stay over the weekend, he is getting everything ready so they can be as comfortable as possible.

John is also developing a plan to mine the two ravines. Knowing that the old spring might still be there and running, he feels that we could get a machine called a Gold Screw, and use it to recover the gold in the gravel. The machine comes with an optional water tub so it can be operated in dry areas such as the desert. With the spring there, they can get enough water to fill the tub, then operate with the water recycling itself in the tub. Checking with his mining shop owner friend Sully, he finds the machines are still available, and if we look around we might find a used one for a pretty reasonable price.

We are getting ready and excited. We never expected to be able to get back into Theo's mine again, it's funny how life has its twists and turns, and how outside influences affect everybodys lives. We are ready and waiting for Friday evening, so we can call Hank

CHAPTER FORTY FIVE

Finally :Friday evening, time to call Hank. A couple of rings, and Hank answers the phone, Hank Schofield here. "Hank, this is John, the miner", "I figured it was you" said Hank "I've got lots of good news for you John". "Let me start with the fact that the road and skid trail is completed down to the second ravine". "Plus, I had the cat skinner push some of the gravel in each ravine up on itself, thereby exposing about ten feet of bedrock at the beginning of the ravines", "That's great exclaims John, we never expected you to do something like that, it will sure make it easier to test the ground in both ravines". "Also I don't know if you realize it, but this weekend is Memorial Day, which means we won't be back to work until next Tuesday, that will give you three days to do your testing".

"Hank, I don't know how to thank you". "Bring me some gold Monday evening, so I have something to brag about later on". "Will do, we will be there bright and early tomorrow, and start testing, and if there is any gold in that ravine, we will see you Monday evening on our way home, and give you something to tell your grandchildren about".

"Ok, just to let you know what we are doing, the plan is to start the fallers dropping trees Tuesday at sunup, then the choke setters will be hooking them up to the high line on Wednesday, and the yarder will be hauling them up to the landing". "There the trees will be sorted into saw logs, or food for the chipper to be turned into bio-rnass for the co-gen plants".

"We figure we can have the area around the ravines done in a couple of weeks". "That's when you can get in there and start some serious mining if the ground warrants it". "Hank, again, that's great, I can assure you that from our previous experience in the first ravine, that the gound is rich enough to mine", "I think you're going to be surprised at the recovery we will be making there". "So we will see you Monday evening, till then have a nice holiday".

Not much sleep that night, too excited over the new adventure, up before daylight, on the road at sunup. Sue points out what a beautiful sunrise we have this morning. By seven we are starting up the Goodyears Creek logging road, we arrive at the first ravine by eight. The logging road and skid trail are like super highways compared to what we had to contend with three years before.

There's a wide spot at the foot of Theo's ravine where we put the camp trailer, and set up camp. Then it's grab the backpacks and tools to go down to the hot tub furnace to retrieve what's left of Theo's stash, Again, like three years before we are prepared to put the old leather pouches in strong freezer bags to transport them home. Getting down to the furnace we are amazed at the fact that nobody has been there since we were. Sue went over to the cabin and found that it had not been disturbed, and that everything was just as we left it.

Taking the pry bars and removing the slate rock at the base of the furnace, I again opened the metal safe box, and there just as pretty as before, were Theo's pouches full of gold.

With Sue's help, I started to remove the pouches, and one by one put them in the freezer bags. Loading Sue's backpack with fifteen of the bags, and mine with thirty five, we hiked up the hill to the Suzuki. Opening the back of the rig, I unlocked the metal box and put the gold in it, then down to the furnace for another load. It took three loads to get all the gold up to the Suzuki, we counted a hundred and twenty seven pouches. That means we had just brought 127 Troy pounds of gold up the hill to the Suzuki. By this time it was noon and time to take a lunch break. So while Sue broke out a couple of backpack lunches and heated them up, I went back down to the furnace, and closed it up, and made it look like it hadn't been disturbed, figuring that we may need it in the future when we are mining.

After lunch, we drove the Suzuki down to the second ravine where the cat skinner had put in a turn around, and had pushed gravel off the bedrock like Hank said.

Unloading several buckets, a plastic pan that Sue preferred to use, her detector, a Molly that I had made after Cuss's original tool, rock pick, three foot long bar, and Sue's plastic scoop she used with her detector, we were set up to start digging. Sue gabbed her detector and turned it on, ground balanced it and went to work. She hadn't moved more then a foot into the scraped bedrock when she started getting signals. One in particular was quite strong, so she dug it up and came up with a nugget as large as my thumb. "John, look at the size of this nugget, I bet it weighs over a couple of ounces. With that she put it in her keeper pouch that she had on her hip.

"Ok, Sue, you keep working here, I'm going back to the first ravine and find the spring and set up the wash tub so we can pan some of this gravel and give it a good testing.

So Sue keeps on detecting, digging up the better signals, and soon has her keeper pouch full of good sized nuggets. Then it's time to do some serious digging, with the Molly and the rock hammer she starts cleaning the bedrock. Using the plastic scoop she runs each scoop full over the detector. Each one that gives a signal, she sorts the gravel until only the signal ends up in one of the plastic buckets, thus classifying the gravel as to gold and no gold.

Meanwhile John has found the spring, and is setting up a small horse trough he had brought along for the purpose of panning the gravel that they are testing. Using sections of plastic pvc pipe, he rigs a pipe line from the spring down to the tub, which is sitting in almost the same spot as Theo's old water tub. The spring is running about a half gal a minute, so it won't take too long to have enough water to pan with.

Back at the second ravine, Sue is filling the plastic buckets. When John has the tub set up, he drives the Suzuki back to Sue and loads up the buckets to take them to the panning tub, Sue takes a break from the digging and goes back to the panning tub to help John pan out the gravel. John had set up the horse trough so that they could pan without bending over, thus saving them from a back ache. The trough was long enough that they could pan side by side.

Sue likes to use a twelve inch plastic pan, while John used an eighteen inch metal pan with a drop center. The tub was full enough to start panning. By the time the first two pans were done, the water was so muddy they couldn't see, so they had to pan more by feel than by seeing. As they were panning into a tub they didn't have to worry about losing any gold as it couldn't go anywhere but into the tub.

Each pan had a sizable amount of gold in it. John had a small eight inch metal pan that they were putting the gold in, so they could later dry it over the camp stove, and then weigh it. So a routine was established, after panning the first batch of gravel, Sue and John took the buckets back to the second ravine and scraped and cleaned bedrock, filling the buckets, then back to the panning tub, pan out the buckets, then back to the ravine. By late that afternoon, they had almost cleaned up the bedrock that the cat skinner had exposed. Looking at his watch, John said to Sue, "Why don't you knock off for today, I'll finish up here, while you can get cleaned up and make supper". "After supper I'll finish panning out, then dry the gold an weigh it". "Then a well deserved rest before bedtime". Sue tells him, that idea works for her. So off to the camp site she goes.

After supper, and the final panning out, they dry the gold and weigh it. Now John knowing that his scale would only weigh four ounces at a time, sat down one day and made a portable scale with bigger pans so he could weigh more gold at a time. He got this scale out of the Suzuki, and set it up. For weights, he had real copper pennies, that he knew weighed 2 dwt's each, thereby ten weighed an ounce, a roll weighed five ounces, having three rolls, he could weigh fifteen ounces at a time. Using the pennies and the weights from his other scale he could weigh nineteen ounces total, or any number in between,

So the weighing begins. Putting the full nineteen ounces of weights on the scale, he carefully poured the gold on the other scale pan until the scale beam was balanced. Nineteen ounces, which they poured into a freezer bag and labled, nineteen ounces, Hanks ravine. Then repeating the process over until the gold was all weighed. "John, we have a total of ninety five and a half ounces, plus what I have in the keeper pouch, that we haven't cleaned and weighed yet"

So Sue takes off her keeper pouch, and dumps the gold into her plastic pan. She takes the pan over to the tub and washes the dirt off the nuggets, then puts the gold in the small metal pan so it can be dried. After weighing Sue's gold, we find that she had dug up over twenty five ounces using her detector. Her biggest piece was just over five ounces, the first piece she had found weighed two and a half ounces. Quite a haul for the first day of testing. " Sue, I think we have a real gold mine here, I can't wait till tomorrow, to see what we will finish up with in Hanks ravine, then on to Theo's spot". "Won't Hank be surprised and pleased with what we have found here remarks Sue", "Boy won't he ever" says John. As it is getting late, they button up for the day, John gets the camper bed ready. Sue puts the gold away in the Suzuki. John lights the lantern, so they can read awhile in bed. Then both yawning, it's lights out and off to dreamland.

CHAPTER FORTY SIX

Next morning, the sunrise wakes us. Coffee for Sue, Hot chocolate for me, Sue then cooks two of the backpack breakfasts, we eat, then cleanup and off to Hanks ravine to finish the testing. By noon we have the bedrock scoured, and are panning out the last of the buckets.

While Sue cooks us lunch, I dry the gold, then start weighing it "Sue we got another 34 ounces, from that last stretch of bedrock". "I think Hanks ravine, as we are calling it now is going to be as rich as Theo's diggings". "After lunch, I'll divide the gold into five parts, and then put it away". "Won't Hank be surprised when he gets his share, roughly speaking he has close to thirty ounces coming". "Remember when we thought that thirty ounces a year was great, and by making it into jewelry we could live quite comfortably on the sales of the jewelry made from the gold nuggets". "I sure do" remarks Sue.

Putting the gold into the metal lock box, we start working on Theo's ravine. Same routine as before, detect for the larger nuggets, then scrape the crevices clean, break them down further with the rock hammer and short bar, fill the buckets, pan them out. At last its time to quit for the day and have supper. After supper, dry and weigh the gold, again several large nuggets detecting, plus another small pan full of smaller gold. With only half of the Cat scraped bedrock cleaned, we have a total of 79 ounces and three dwts. of gold. Again a phenomenal amount of gold for the area we worked. It just goes to show that the stories from the gold rush of finds like this are true.

Next morning, same routine. We continue with the cleaning of the bedrock, finishing the area by one that afternoon. Lunch, dry and weigh the gold, another great recovery, 54 ounces and 11 dwt. Then pack up to leave. We stack the plastic buckets next to the water tub, so they will be there for next time. Pack up our hand tools, close up the camp trailer and hook it to the Suzuki and get ready to leave. Slow climb up to the big flat where the Yarder is set up, then down logging road to Goodyears Bar camp ground. We get to Hanks trailer around four thirty in the afternoon.

Hank is on his veranda, and sees us coming. "Hey, guys that's not the same Suzuki I saw before, same color but it looks meaner, big tires, lifted, winch, etc." "Yeah, Hank, this is my Rubicon Rig, its geared lower, thus can carry the bigger tires, and go more places then Sue's Suzuki". "Well how did you do?" "Hank, let's go inside away from prying eyes and ears, and I'll show you enough gold to make your eyes bug out" "Sue, bring the gold and let's give him a real case of gold fever". In Hank's trailer, they sit down at his table. "Hank, get a dinner plate out and we will put the gold on it so you can play with it", "A dinner plate, you're kidding, there isn't that much gold left in these old mountains". With that Sue produces five leather pouches of gold. "Hank, we separated the gold into five equal shares, pick one of the pouches, and that will be your share from the second ravine, which by the way we named after you, from now on it is Hank's ravine".

Hank picks a pouch, then slowly pours the gold onto the dinner plate. "My god, look at it, it's beautiful, and so much, are my eyes bugging out enough?" "Yes, they are" Sue tells him "Hank, we recovered 154 ounces from that ravine, which definitely makes it worth mining", John tells him. "I should say so" Hank exclaims "There is one thing, though, you're going to have to keep it under your hat, otherwise we will have a gold rush up there, which will interfere with your logging operation, and our mining" "I can do that" says Hank

"Good, here's the paper that gives you one fifth of the second ravine, and of course your first dividend in the mining operation". "For bragging purpose's, put about an ounce of gold in an aspirin bottle, and tell your crew, that we gave you half of the gold from the second ravine, since you opened up the bedrock with the Cat, that way it won't look so rich that it will give anybody the wrong idea". "Ok", says Hank, "I'll downplay the richness of the claim"

"Next step, when can we get in there to do some serious work?" "Like I said before, probably two weeks, we should have most of the timber out of that area". "Best you call me like before, then we can coordinate your getting equipment in there". "Have you figured out how you're going to mine those two ravines?" "Yes, pretty much so, I plan on using a small placer machine with a self contained water supply". "The spring up there is running enough to fill the tub under the machine, plus keep make up water flowing into the tub". "The unit I'm thinking of can process a couple of yards an hour, that's more than two guys can shovel on a continual basis all day". "The nice thing is the portability of the machine". "I can bring it in behind my Suzuki without any problem".

"That sounds great", "Well, it's settled then, call me in two weeks, and we will get you in there on the weekend when the crews are off". "Ok Hank, I'll call you on Friday evening two weeks from now, have fun with your gold". So it's head for home, stopping in grass valley for a restaurant meal, then on to the house,

Arriving home, John drives the Suzuki into the shop with the camp trailer, then locks up. Meanwhile Sue is taking a shower to get rid of the weekends dirt, then off to bed to watch TV. John is right behind her. They relax and are soon dozing. John rolls over, and wakes up enough to turn off the TV with the remote, then off to dreamland again.

Next morning they take their time in getting up, Sue with her coffee, and her pocket poker game she likes to play while drinking her coffee and waking up. John normally jumps out of bed raring to get the day started, but this morning he takes his time getting up. It's almost nine before John gets out of bed, then S--, Shower, and shave, a three day growth of beard which John hasn't had in thirty years, ever since he tried to grow a beard and found out he had too many blank spots, no sideburns, two blank spots under his chin, and now with his age, the beard was silver white.

So off it came.

After breakfast, John put in a call to Sully at the mining shop, and asked how long it would take to get a Gold Screw with a water tub. Sully told him a week, so John ordered one, and told Sully he would be in later with a deposit. That done it was time to get the gold out of the lock box and sort it out for size as they had done with the original gold from Theo's mine. By noon he and Sue had half of the gold sorted. John told Sue "let's take a break and run up to Sully's and give him the deposit for the machine, then have lunch at the steak house that you like so much".

At Sully's they gave him the deposit. Sully starts to quiz John about him buying a brand new machine, as in the past he was always trying to find a deal on a used whatever.

John told him that an uncle left him some money, so he figured he could finally afford a new machine to play with. "I've always wanted to check out some of the hydraulic diggings for fine gold". "I've been told that there is more fine gold in these diggings then you can find in nuggets, so I thought I would try it". "By the way Sully, can you get me two extra gold wheels that go on the machine, I've got an idea on a modification for the machine that will get all the fine gold that is recoverable". "Sure, I'll call the guy back and get two more wheels for you" "Ok, call me when it comes in, and I'll drive the old Power Wagon up and pick it up" "Do you still have that old truck?" Asks Sully?" "Yep, can't find anything to replace it for getting down and dirty work done.

"The old truck is thirty one years old this year, and I figure it costs me between two and three hundred dollars a year for maintenance and gas, plus the license, and my insurance company, only insures it when I need to drive it". "All I do is call them the day before, and they cover it for liability, etc, then when I'm through, I call them back and they take off the coverage, except fire and theft". "Saves me a couple of hundred a year that way"

So off to the steak house, a great lunch, then back home to finish the gold sorting. They get about half way through by supper time. So they quit for the day, and have supper, then relax watching TV, then off to bed.

Next morning, up at eight, in the shop by nine to finish the sorting job. By that evening it's done, the fines amount to just over thirty nine troy pounds, which they will send off to the refiner to have it made into fourteen karat casting shot to make jewelry with. The rest is put into the floor safe, which is getting pretty full.

The next day old Grouchy is lurking around, curious as ever, "Hey, John, How did you and Sue do this weekend?"

"Oh, the usual, went up to one of the hydraulic digs, and detected, as usual Sue got more than I did". "I had to kill a rattler that was being too aggressive. I accidently hit him with the detector coil, and instead of crawling away he kept striking at the coil, so I picked up a long stick, and beat him to death, poor creature". "Poor creature, why they don't have any good use on this earth," Grouchy growl's" "Sure they do, I said in defense of the snake, they eat mice and rats. "Just think how overrun the world would be with rodents if there weren't snakes to eat them". "Just the same the only good rattler is a dead rattler I always say", grouses Grouchy.

Four days later, John gets a call from Sully, the machine, water tub, and extra wheels are in. John tells Sully, he'll be right there to pick them up. "Sue, do you want to go with me to pick up the gold machine?" "Sure, John, maybe we can pick up some Chinese food for lunch on the way back" "You bet" he tells her

To the mining shop, pick up the machine and accessories, stop at the Chinese take out, then home. Have lunch, and then unload the mining machine. "Here comes Grouchy", Sue whispers to John. "What in the world have you got now" he asks? "Oh, just a new toy to play with", exclaims John "It's a gold saving machine, see you put the machine in that tub, then fill the tub with water, then start the engine and pump, then you break your back all day shoveling gravel into the machine, at the end of the day you look in the little bucket that hangs under the wheel down there to see how much gold you have recovered from the tons of gravel you have shoveled". "Sounds like a lot of work to me". "Sure, but you know how gold fever is, every little piece counts". "Someone said once, he who has the most gold when he dies wins". "Wins what?", asks Grouchy. "I don't know, he just wins".

With the machine in the shop, John is figuring out how to add the extra gold wheels to the machine. "The idea Sue is to have all the processing done while we are feeding the machine". "The way it works now you end up with either a bucket full of black sand with gold in it, or a bucket of just gold, throwing the black sand away". "As tests have shown, there is micron gold in the black sand that can only be recovered by grinding the black sand, then treating it with mercury or leaching chemicals to recover the micron size gold". "So I have an idea that we can save the fines by using a series of gold wheels, with mercury in the last wheel to glue the fine particles of gold together into an amalgam ball, much like a Berdan bowl that used to be used in some of the hard rock mills". "you'll see after I get it set up",

So John spends the rest of the week modifying the gold machine, when it's done he gets Sue to come and watch how the process works. Using some of the black sand they have accumulated over the years, John turns on the machine, then puts a small amount of mercury in the last wheel, which Sue notices is turning backward. John then pours black sand into the hopper of the machine, and watches as it goes through the machine. When the black sand hits the last wheel it is being ground into finer pieces, and the mercury is picking up the fine gold and making an amalgam ball.

When all the black sand has run through the machine, John lets it run another five minutes, then shuts it off. He then changes the drive belt on the last wheel so it will run normally, placing a small plastic bucket under the outlet of the wheel, he turns on the machine again. They watch as the mercury climbs the screw riffles in the bowl and out into the plastic bucket. When there isn't any more mercury showing in the riffles, John shuts the machine off. Taking the little bucket off the wheel, he takes it over to the sink in the shop. There he has a plastic dish washing tub.

Putting on some latex gloves, he pours the mercury into a wet chamois. Then he twists the chamois into a ball, and squeezes the excess mercury out. When he is done, he opens the chamois, and there is a small amalgam ball. He takes the amalgam ball and places it into a glass jar, Then he takes a small plastic jar of nitric acid off a shelf. Taking the jars outside, he pours the nitric acid into the amalgam jar, where it removes the mercury from the fine gold it has collected.

Since the fumes that are given off by the acid working on the mercury are harmful, it has to be done outside so the fumes will not harm anybody. When the acid is done working, it is poured back into the plastic bottle and saved for the next time it is needed. Carefully rinsing the gold with clean water. John removes all trace of the acid. There in the jar is a small quantity of clean shiny fine gold. "That's pretty slick" exclaims Sue. "Yeah, it should make the ravines pay even more than what we have seen so far there".

The rest of the week is spent restocking the camp trailer, getting the machine loaded into the Power Wagon, what tools to take, gas and oil for the machine, food, drinking water, should we take the ATV, in case the Power Wagon has a problem, and all the other myriad little things we think we will need.

At last Friday evening, time to call Hank. "Hank, John here, how's the weather? "Just great, we have the ravine section done, you can come up for the week end". "It's going to take two and a half to three weeks to finish the logging to the switchback, then it's all yours".

"You will be able to mine without any fear of being in. our way and vice versa". "That is just great, we're looking forward to setting up the machine and give the gravel a good run". "Good" says Hank, "I'll be looking forward to seeing you". "If I have time, I'll drive my Jeep up and help you if I can". "Tomorrow I have to check on the progress of the road crew that's building the road to Marysville". "But I should be free Sunday to come up, and see how this operation is going to work". "We will be looking forward to seeing you, and I'll bet Sue will have a fresh strawberry pie for you to have with coffee in the afternoon, for a break from the hard work of mining". "In that case I'll put a shovel in both hands to double the production, I love fresh homemade strawberry pie ". "Ok, Hank, see you then".

CHAPTER FORTY SEVEN

The next morning, up before light, Sue complaining, that she thought we were semi-retired and didn't have to do mornings anymore. "Yes, I know what you mean, I never did like to get up this early except to take a picture of a spectacular sunrise, like we have seen in Arizona or Nevada.

So We are off and running. Goodyears creek by seven, Theo's ravine by eight. Take a small break, then start to set up camp and the gold machine. With the skid trail going right to the ravine, it is an easy job to get the machine set up. I back the Power Wagon into the ravine close to the face of the gravel, then off load the machine there. Next all the tools we will need to dig with. Level up the machine and water tub, and then bring the spring water to the tub. Time for a lunch break, Sue has brought fried chicken, and fresh white corn on the cob, lunch fit for a king and queen.

Now to start digging, pick the gravel down onto a couple of refrigerator door panels we brought along for slick sheets, then sort the bigger cobble stones out. Load the wheel barrow and put it next to the gold machine. Start the engine and pump, and start shoveling. Within thirty seconds the machine starts to tell us whether we have gold in the gravel, as the gold can be seen traveling down the black plastic chute into the wheels. We watch and see not only fine gold but small nuggets, so the machine tells us we will have to process all the gravel. Usually the gold is concentrated on or just above the bedrock, but in this case the gravel is rich enough to run it all,

So for the next couple of hours we set up a routine, Pick and shovel the gravel into the wheel barrow, Sue feeds the machine. Then it's time for a break. Getting out a couple of cold drinks from the cooler, we sit in the shade of the Power Wagon and catch our breath. "Damn, Sue if we didn't have gold fever so bad this would be really hard work". "I know just what you're saying John, the sun is hot, we need some shade". "Next week we'll bring some tarps and poles to get the machine into the shade, same for the face of the gravel".

"Meantime we will just have to grin and bear it" "Let's go look in the little bucket under the second wheel and see how much gold we have". "Sue, bring your plastic pan and we will empty the bucket into it". John takes the bucket off its hanger and remarks to Sue it's pretty heavy, then dumping the bucket into the pan, Sue looks at the amount of gold, and exclaims, "Wow, did we do that?" "There must be twenty ounces there" "That gravel is richer then we thought it was going to be". "What is the bedrock going to be like she asks?" "Just like it was two weeks ago, I would imagine John tells her:.

"Sue get your detector and earphones, I want to check out the tailings for larger nuggets that might have gone through the machine and were too big to go through the screen". As John rakes down the tailings, Sue detects them, getting an occasional signal; they locate the nugget and put it in Sue's keeper pouch. "Just as I thought John remarks, with the history of this mine for big nuggets, I figured we would find some nuggets too big to go through the screen in the machine". "well it's almost three thirty, what say we knock off the digging and machine running and scrape some bedrock to see what we can find, then quit for the day?" "Ok, by me John, let me detect the bedrock first, then let's got our knee pads and scrape the crevices".

Sue detects the bedrock and finds several large nuggets along with lots of smaller ones. John meantime gets the knee pads, Molly tools, rock hammers, and three foot bar, so they can go to work on the bedrock. By five they are exhausted from the long work day and call it quits. Sue washes up, then goes to get supper going, while John pans out the buckets of gravel from the bedrock. After supper and a rest, they clean up the gold, dry it, then weigh it. Forty three plus ounces John tells Sue, not bad for today. "Plus we don't know what we have in our mercury trap wheel, that's going to be interesting, but let's leave it for tomorrow", "It will be fun to show Hank how the mercury wheel works".

Cleaning up the supper dishes and taking a shower from the shower set up on the camper trailer, they open the bed and crawl in. Read until it is too dark to see, then off to sleep.

CHAPTER FORTY EIGHT

Next morning up at sunrise again, coffee, breakfast, get dressed, ready to go to work. Hank arrives just before nine, and asks what he can do to help. John shows him the machine, and the gravel face, and how we pick and shovel onto the slick sheet, sort out the bigger rocks and boulders, stockpile the gravel next to the machine, and push the rocks and boulders over the hill side out of the way.

John and Hank start mining the gravel, while Sue starts the machine and begins feeding it. Couple of hours later, break time. Sue shuts down the machine, and goes to the camper trailer and pulls out the strawberry pie and whip cream to put on it, from the cooler. Hank is wide eyed at the decadent looking pie. Sue asks Hank if he wants's coffee, milk, or a cold drink with his pie? Hank tells her coffee if it is not too much trouble. Sue gets a thermos bottle out with coffee left over from this morning and pours Hank a cup. "Cream and or sugar" she asks? Hank tells her black. "The pie is delicious" states Hank as he devours it, "Is there enough for seconds?" "Of course, here let me get you another piece". So they have a break, and chit chat about the mining process. Then back to work. Soon its lunch time, again Sue shuts down the machine, and starts to fix lunch. John shows Hank how the wheels recover the gold, then taking the bucket from the second wheel, be pans it out. Hank is again wide eyed at the amount of gold in the pan. "Is it always this good?" asks Hank. "Only here at this and the other ravine" John tells him "We have never seen a richer spot in all our years of mining".

Lunch, then back to work, afternoon break, then John asks Sue to bring the detector up and let's check the bedrock. Sue is detecting and finding nuggets, when all of a sudden, she cries OW!, and rips off the head phones. "What's the matter?" asks John "Here listen to this she tells him", with that she unplugs the head phones so they can hear the regular speaker on the machine. As she swings the detector over a certain spot the signal' screams louder then John has ever heard it. "My god, what do you have there" "Bare, bedrock as far as I can see she says" "Ok pinpoint the spot, and I'll get the tools and start digging". Sue tells him it goes from there to here, about three feet long

John takes a stiff brush and sweeps the gravel off the bedrock, and exposes a crevice three feet long, about an inch wide full of small pebbles. Taking the rock hammer and the three foot bar, he starts breaking the crevice open. Removing the pebbles from the crevice he sees gold.

As he cleans the full length of the crevice they see a solid line of gold nuggets. Getting the Molly tool and a big pan, John starts to pull nuggets out and puts them in the pan. "Hank, get the other Molly and a pan and you can start from the other end". "Sue, why don't you finish checking out the rest of the bedrock, with the detector, while Hank and I finish cleaning out this crevice"

Half an hour later, Sue has filled her keeper pouch full of nuggets. John and Hank are just finishing the crevice. "Will you look at all those nuggets" exclaims Hank. "Now

I understand how people get gold fever". "Is there anything ,on earth more beautiful?" "Yes there is" says John, "my lovely wife Sue" "Why thank you John, what a nice thing to say)" .

"Hank, bring your pan down to the panning tub, and I'll show you how we get rid of the dirt" John pans down both pans, then putting all the gold in one metal pan he takes it over to the camp stove to heat it up and dry the water out of the pan.

Getting the gold scales out, he weighs the gold from the crevice. Just over twenty troy pounds he tells Hank and Sue. "Twenty pounds!" exclaims Hank, "what is that in ounces?"

Just over two hundred and forty ounces John tells him. "Gold's around three hundred an ounce right" "That's right" Sue tells Hank "So at three hundred an ounce, an we have two hundred and forty ounces, that comes out to seventy two thousand dollars". "Is that right?" "Yep" says John, "Not bad for one days crevice is it?"

"I've got to sit down, that's incredible, one crevice full of gold nuggets worth seventy two thousand dollars". "Now you know why we wanted to get back up here to mine this spot", John tells him. "We were pretty upset three years ago when the Administration and the Enviros locked this area up into a wilderness". "We would have had to hike in twenty miles one way, and then it was illegal to mine". "So that's why we jumped on the spot with a mining claim as soon as we found out they had rescinded the wilderness". "And because we knew the history of the place, we could make you a twenty percent partner without it costing us".

"You say you know the history of the place?" asks Hank, "What do you mean by that?" "Hank, have you been to Downieville?" "Yes" "Did you by any chance pick up their souvenir newspaper, telling about the hanging of the Mexican woman, and the shooting of a miner named Theo Calhoun by three owlhoots who were trying to rob him". "Yeah, if I remember right, this Theo killed the robbers, but got gut shot doing it, then managed to ride to Downieville before he died", "The article said he had an enormous amount of gold on his pack mule, and that the Deputy, named Charlie took his body back to his wife in Auburn, along with the loaded mule".

"Well, Hank you're standing in Theo's ravine, one of the richest gold placers in California". "But how did you find it?" "The article went on to say, that people have been trying to find this mine for over a hundred years". "To keep a long story short, we inherited it from the last descendent of Theo, that's why we spent two grueling weeks cutting through the Buck brush, to get here three years ago". "We recovered enough gold then, before we got weathered out to know we could get a rather comfortable income if we could mine here".

"So now you know the story, but as we said before, you have to keep it a secret until we are through mining, otherwise we will be invaded by every miner and scumbag that roams these hills looking for easy pickings".

"Hank, I'm going to show you one more facet of this machine we are using". "I modified the wheel set up so we could recover more of the fine gold". "The machine usually comes with one wheel, you'll notice that we have three". "The last wheel runs backwards so it will grind the black sand, thus cleaning it and releasing the fine gold locked up in it". "By using a chemically enhanced Mercury compound we recover all the fine gold that is recoverable in the black sand". "Let me change the belt drive, and we will run the wheel forward and watch as the mercury amalgam climbs out of the wheel into the small bucket under the outlet".

Starting the machine John and Hank watch the Mercury. When there isn't any more Mercury climbing the riffles, John shuts down the machine. Taking the bucket of Mercury amalgam off the wheel, he pours it into a Mercury press, and presses out the excess. Then he opens the press and dumps the amalgam ball into a plastic pan. From out of the tool box on the Power Wagon he gets a plastic bottle filled with Nitric acid. "Hank, stand back enough so you don't breath the fumes that will be given off". Holding his breath John pours the Nitric acid into the plastic gold pan, then watch's it work from a safe distance. When the fuming stops, he pours the acid back into the plastic bottle, then takes the gold pan over to the panning tub, and rinses the fine gold in the pan with fresh water and a drop of shampoo soap, which causes the fine gold to drop to the bottom of the pan, "Will you look at that", exclaims Hank. "Why that gold is almost as fine as face powder, but just as shiny as the nuggets". "Yes, and most miners throw it away, because they don't know how to recover it". "I'll bet we have another ten ounces in just fine gold". "That means we have paid for the wheels four times over already"

"It's getting late, let's pack up and get out of here. So they gather up all the tools, and put them with the machine, close up the camper trailer in case of rain, chain the ATV up to a tree, put the extra gas cans in a safe spot, put the gold in a plastic box they brought for that purpose, and head up the hill. At Hank's trailer, they take a break, and Hank tells them that he will have the crew watch over the mine to keep anybody out that shouldn't be there. "Great", says Sue. "Hank, should we call you first next weekend before coming up?", asks John

"Yeah, just in case something comes up we don't expect, and Sue can you spoil me with another one of your pies?" "You betcha" With that they leave. Supper in Grass valley, then onto home. Grouchy is waiting, all eyes and ears to see how they did. "Where's all of your stuff, he asks?" "Oh we left it up at our new mining claim". "New mining claim!, you didn't tell me you have a new claim". "Gee, I didn't, did I" says John. "Well we have a new mine up the hill a ways, it even has some gold in it" Although, a little less, now that we recovered a little over and ounce this weekend". "Next weekend we hope to get some more".

So Grouchy goes home, we put the Power Wagon in the shop, then off to the shower, and bed, read awhile, then watch the news, then lights out, and off to la la land.

CHAPTER FORTY NINE

Then next morning, we sleep in till nine, then up and slowly get the day started. "Sue with her morning coffee, me with a bowl of cereal", Finally out in the shop, we sort out the gold, the amalgam fines, we are keeping separate, so that when we send it in to the refiner,we can tell them that it was recovered with mercury, and then they can treat it accordingly. Next the small screen fines are sorted out, then on up to the largest nugget. After the sorting, they weigh the gold, it totals out at two hundred and ninety four ounces, "What a week end, Sue exclaims". "Even giving Hank twenty percent, we did one hell'va recovery job at Theo's digs for us".

Sorting out what we call a river run average, we pack up a package of gold for Hank, almost sixty ounces. "Sue laughs, as she remarks; I wonder what will make him happier, the gold or my strawberry pie". "Pie, honey, gold can be had anywhere, but your pies are one of a kind".

Taking the afternoon easy, they kind of putter around, not doing anything special. Sue's hip implant is stiff and sore from all the shoveling, so she takes a soak in the hot tub, then reads awhile until time for supper. That evening after supper, Rich and Dan show up. How did it go they ask? "Great, we picked and shoveled so hard we have blisters on our blisters, the machine overworked us trying to keep up with it, Your mom has a ringing in her ear because her detector screamed at her when she swung it over a large nugget, plus her hip is killing her",

"Other then that we had a great weekend". "Well show us the gold", Dan insists. "Ok, but you have to promise not to faint, because I can't pick up that much lead weight at one time". "Listen old man" "Yesss"...

"Come out to the shop and keep your voice down, we don't want Grouchy to hear how much we got". John takes the plastic box down off a shelf and opens it up, taking out freezer bags full of nuggets, he lays them on the workbench. The boys are speechless. Dan gets his voice back first, and in a low whisper, "he says you got to be kidding, those are just painted rocks, right?" "You're playing a joke on us, right?" "Come-on boys, you've seen enough gold to know the real thing when you see it". "Pick up one of the bags and feel the weight".

"My god, Rich, it's real, we've never seen this much gold except in a gold show". "When do we get to go to work up there?" asks Rich. "Whenever you're available" John tells him, "I'll get another gold machine and you can set it up and pick and shovel to your hearts content".

"How about three weeks?, we should have the job we are on finished, and the boss and I are at each others throats again, so I was getting ready to quit anyway". "Ok, that should work out just right, as Hank said they should be done logging in our area, and that we can have the mine all to ourselves then".

"What about me" asks Dan, "when do I get to play?" "Whenever you're ready, like I told your brother". "Well, I heard just today that the Forest Service might be shutting down all hot saw jobs because of how dry it is". "It's real easy to start a fire with my machine". "Let me find out for sure, and maybe I can work with Rich". "That would be great, Hanks ravine looks like it is going to be just as rich as Theo's". "Hanks ravine?" "Yeah, we decided to name it after Hank, as he is the one who discovered it when he did his chopper fly over and aerial photo shoot of the burn area he was given the job to log".

John puts the gold away, and they go in the house and make plans to go up and work. Sue makes a peach pie, while the boys are voicing their fantasy's over working at the mine,

"Dan, Rich, It's not going to be a picnic up there, the work is physically hard and will become very boring after a while, but the rewards should be fantastic", John tells them.

"How about camping gear?, are we going to need a tent or trailer to sleep in?" asks Dan "Sue, what do you think?, can the old cabin be cleaned up enough, so these boys can stay in it". "I don't see why not, a gallon of bleach will disinfect the place, and Rich can build a bunk over the existing bed to sleep on". "I would think it would be rather comfortable there, certainly better than a tent".

"Rich, can you come up this weekend or next?" "If you can, you can get a feel for the place, and what needs to be done". "Sure, when do we leave for the mine?" "Be here at six Saturday morning, and we can all go up in the Power Wagon". "In the meantime, Dan, you find out for sure about your possible shut down, and I'll order another Gold Machine and extra wheels to set up for Hanks ravine",

So the plan is set in motion. Saturday morning they head up to the mine. stopping at Hank's to let him meet Rich. Hank tells them he will be up tomorrow, to help out. "Sue tells Hank, she has another pie for him to sample, " Maybe I'll just come up tonight, nothing like pie for desert".

"John, don't ever take your eyes off her, I just might kidnap her and make her bake pies for me forever", which they all have a laugh over his joking threat,

"Oh, Hank here's your percentage from last week" "But I thought I was only getting a percentage from the second ravine?" "Well, we figured since you have done so much in helping this operation get going that we would just give you a full twenty percent". "Well thank you, I don't know what to say".

Reaching the mine, they unload the food, cold drinks, and ice. Opening up the camp trailer they put the ice, drinks, pie and whip cream into the cooler. Unload the extra gas for the gold machine, and miscellaneous other items. Then John and Sue take Rich down to the cabin. He is amazed at the condition of it, looking at the construction features he sees real craftsmanship like none he has seen in modern buildings of today. Putting on respirator masks, they open the door, and go inside. The interior is just as they left it three years ago. Sue tells Rich, "See it won't take to much to clean it up, and like I said the other night, you can build a bunk over the old bed to sleep on". "You're right mom; I can come up next week end and get started". "I'll bring the necessary tools and materials, and have this place shipshape in no time",

"Rich, let me show you something else that you might find interesting". John takes Rich out to where the hot tub used to be. "Look at the way Theo set up a hot tub", "He brought water from the spring through those cedar pipes". "The tub was built of redwood in his shop in Auburn, then assembled here". "He also built the water tank, and the furnace to heat the water", "Pretty clever for the 1860's, don't you think?" "His journal, states that he and his wife spent many an hour soaking away the ache's and pain's of the daily mining routine".

"What do you think? want to resurrect the old tub?" "Sure, If you can make a new water tank, I'll make a tub, plumb it, and we can have a hot tub out here in the wilds, what a kick that would be",

"Ok, time to get mining". So up the hill they go. Sue gets the gold machine running, while John and Rich start the pick and shovel work. John has brought another wheelbarrow up so they could load rocks in it, while putting the gravel in the other one, making it easier to get rid of the rocks and small boulders over the hillside. He has also brought another slick sheet up for Sue to shovel off of making it easier for her. So the mining progresses. Lunch break, after which Sue detects the newly opened bedrock, lots of nuggets up to a half ounce in size. No screaming crevice, like last week, but still a sizable amount of gold. Clean up that evening produces a little over sixty seven ounces. Rich is flabbergasted He knows that it is hard to come up with that much gold in a year or two, let alone recover that much in a day. Needless to say he is hooked.

Hank, true to his word, shows up that evening, with his bedroll, and kiddingly insisting on having his pie. Sue gets the peach pie she made this week out, and they all have a piece. Again, Hank warns John to keep a tight leash on Sue. Sue leans over to John, and whispers in his ear, "little does Hank know that I have another strawberry pie in the cooler for tomorrow."

Next day the mining starts, with four people they uncover a sizable amount of bedrock in a hurry. Rich and Hank are picking and shoveling, John is pushing the wheelbarrows, getting rid of the tailings and stacking up gravel for Sue to run in the machine. Lunch break, Sue has brought a pot roast with fresh vegetables and mashed potatoes and gravy. After the meal, she breaks out the strawberry pie and gives

Hank a double serving. The poor man is so bloated after all that food, that he can hardly move.

After a rest, they get back to mining. Around four, John tells them it's time to start the clean up. Sue shuts down the machine, and gets her detector out. John and Hank grab the Molly's and start scraping out the crevices as Sue pinpoints the gold. Rich is filling the buckets, and setting them next to the machine to be run. Sue then has Rich help her rake down the tailings from the machine while she detects them for nuggets, between the bedrock and the tailings she again fills her keeper pouch.

Completing the cleanup, they weigh the gold. I come up with right at 99 ounces, with the 67 ounces we got yesterday; I would say we have had a good weekend. Rich and Hank are still amazed at the richness of this spot. Closing up the operation for this weekend, they head down the mountain to Hanks trailer. When they get there John and Hank go in and John weighs out Hanks share of gold, just a tad over 33 ounces. Again Hank is amazed at the quantity of gold they have recovered.

John then tells him of the plan of the boys to come up and mine the second ravine. That way we can double the production, plus they will be earning their share. "Sounds great to me". "What can I do to help?" "Oh, just keep coming up on Sundays, and get fat on Sue's pies" "I can sure do that". "Oh, while I'm thinking about it, we are still on schedule with the logging, so you ought to be able to set up your operation to work all week two weeks from now". "That's great, I was telling the boys that we could probably do that". "They are anxious to get started".

So they head for home. Supper in Grass Valley as usual. Home and unload. Rich says goodnight, and heads for his home. Has to be to work early. Sue and John take showers then a soak in the hot tub, then off to bed.

CHAPTER FIFTY

The next morning. John and Sue sort out the gold. Around ten o clock Sully calls and tells John the gold machine is in. "Ok, I'll be down to pick it up shortly". "Sue, want to go to Auburn to pick up the new machine?" "I'll treat you to lunch". "Sure, let me wash up and I'll be ready to go". So off to the mining shop in Auburn

Sully greets them at the door, and asks John what is happening? "That's the second machine you've gotten in a month", "Yeah, we found a spot that has a considerable amount of fine gold, and Sue's boys want to play along with us". "So I figure why not, you only live once, and we've already recovered enough fine gold to pay for this machine", "Besides, when we finish the spot, we can sell the machine and recoup some of our investment in it", "That makes sense", Sully agrees,

Load up the machine. Lunch at Sue's favorite Auburn restaurant, then onto home to begin the modifications on the gold machine. Friday evening, call Hank, the coast is clear for the weekend. Sue gets on phone, and asks Hank what kind of pie would he like this week? "How about a deep dish apple, he asks?" "Ok, one apple pie coming up,

Saturday evening or just for Sunday", "Lady, if I have pie Saturday and Sunday both, I'm going to get so fat you'll have to roll me home like a bowling ball". "Naw, we will work it off you in Hank's ravine". "Hank's ravine?" "Yes, John decided to call the second ravine Hank's ravine since you're the one who discovered it". "Here, John wants to talk to you". "Hank, I picked up another gold machine". "Rich is supposed to come up again this weekend, so by the time you get there Sunday, we'll have it set up and you can shovel till you lose all the fat from Sue's pies".

"Alright, I'm going to be there after work Saturday, see you then". Six the next morning, Rich is here, time to get going. Sue says, wait a minute, "I have to load up the pies and Sunday dinner". "Ok, but daylight is burning, so come on my sweet little turtle dove".

Getting to the mine by nine, John and Rich unload the machine at Hanks ravine, along with the necessary PVC pipe to bring water to it from the spring, and extra tools and wheel barrows. It takes all morning to set up the water supply, but at last it is ready to go. Meanwhile Sue has her machine going and has been shoveling all morning to catch up on the stock pile of gravel left over from last week end.

Lunch break. John tells Rich to pick and shovel in Hanks ravine for about and hour, then start the gold machine and feed it, till the pile of gravel is gone. Then more pick and shovel, again feeding the machine. "Quit around four, then your mom can come over an detect the bedrock you will have uncovered". "I'll finish up Theo's ravine for the day". "Tomorrow, with Hanks help, the two of you will be able to accomplish more". "The clean up should be interesting"

That evening, after supper and Hank gorging himself on one of Sue's pies, They clean up the gold from the two ravines, Hanks ravine had given up a respectable twenty nine plus ounces. Theo's ravine came out to seventeen and a half ounces. Down from last weekend, but still a goodly amount of gold.

Next morning, up with the sun, breakfast, then off to work. With four people working both ravines, the place is humming with activity. Lunch, Hank with another double portion of pie. Back to work. Quit at four as usual, then the cleanup. Sue detecting both ravines fills her keeper pouch twice. The total weight from Hanks ravine for today, comes to forty six ounces, including the fines in the wheel. Theo's ravine only came to twenty two ounces. "It seems to be falling off a little", Sue said. "Well maybe not, John remarks, I only uncovered a third of the bedrock this weekend, compared to last week". "So the gold recovered figures about right", "Besides, who do you know that is finding as much gold as we are except the big companys over in Nevada, with their big earth moving equipment, and ten million dollar processing mills".

So it's button up for this week. Hank tells John and Sue, they can probably plan on moving in and staying all week if they feel like it The logging should be done here, and they will be working on the west side of the ridge, of course there will still be logging and chip trucks going up and down Goodyears Creek road. "But you will be able to get out after four during the week without any danger of running into any of the trucks until four the next morning".

"Sounds good to me, Sue are you ready to move up here with the Bears and dig for gold all week?" "Sure, as long as you set up an oven to bake pies, so I can feed them Bears and keep them fat and happy". With that everybody laughs until it hurts.

CHAPTER FIFTY ONE

This next week has been busy for us. We spent a day in Sacramento at the large Army, Navy Surplus store where we picked up several olive drab colored tarps to put over the gold machines and the diggings to get them in the shade out of the hot sun. A large screen tent that we can put the camper trailer in and sit an read with out being bothered by pesky mosquitos.

We also found a heavy cast iron two burner stove unit, with the idea of setting up an outdoor kitchen to cook in, And the prize of the day, an old Servel! gas powered refrigerator that still works. Now we can have cold drinks, ice, real food, etc., without having to run into town to get ice and fresh food the same day we want to eat it. We also found a five gal gas fired water heater tank from an old RV, that we can use for the hot tub. Sue said to me, "we're going to be styling first class, with all these modern convenience's".

That evening, got ahold of Rich, and told him what we had gotten, and asked him if he can come up with a lean-to covered kitchen for the mine. "Sure, I just need to get the measurements of the fridge and stove", "Then figure some counter space", "How about a sink to do dishes in?" "Good idea", remarks Sue

So Rich comes over to the house and gets the measurements he needs. He tells John, "you know, we can use shipping pallets for the floor, I have some out back of the shop that have tightly spaced boards on the top deck that would work just great, and best of all they are free". "Alright Rich, I always like free or cheap stuff'.

So he goes home to plan out the kitchen, and figure what materials we will need. "In the meantime I picked up three new five gal propane tanks and had them filled to run the stove, refrigerator, and hot tub".

The next evening Rich shows up with some pallets, a couple of sheets of plywood and a used kitchen sink, and a plan on how to put it together into a usable kitchen. Dan calls and tells us he will be laid off because of the fire danger. So we are going to have a crew to mine with.

The rest of the week is filled with getting backpack food packs, water jugs, extra gas cans and all the other sundry items to make life comfortable while we are working at the mine.

Friday evening, call Hank, everything's a go. Saturday morning the expedition takes off, the boys are in the Power Wagon, while John and Sue are driving up in the Rubincon Suzuki.

Lots of picture taking, for the family album. Spend all day Saturday putting up tarps, screen tent, and building the kitchen. Leveling the Servel!, so it will work properly. Then Dan and Rich tackle the old cabin with a lot of bleach and soap to make it safe to live in. After supper, Rich starts building the bunk bed, with John and Dan's help he finishes it in time to use it for the night

Sue tells John, "the Servel! Refrigerator isn't getting cold". "It's probably because the ammonia gas in it got all shook up coming up here, what we need to do is turn it upside down and let it burp itself over night, then in the morning we turn it right side up, let it rest for a few hours, then light it and see if will work". "It's a trick I learned from an old gas man, who worked on these machines back when they were popular".

The next morning Rich and Dan start to put the hot tub system together. While Dan is bringing the spring water down to the hot tub site, Rich is building the new hot tub out of Redwood two by six decking material. Rich had brought his small electric generator to run his skill saw and electric hand planer. The planer made quick work of getting the right bevel needed to assemble the barrel staves together so that they needed very little caulking between them.

Meanwhile John, Sue and Hank were picking and shoveling on Theo's ravine. By lunch there were several feet of bedrock exposed. After lunch, and Hanks usual overdose of pie, Sue detected the bedrock, with the usual gathering of nuggets for her keeper pouch.

Late afternoon, the boys have the hot tub ready for its first filling and hot water test.

Turning on the valve on the PVC pipe Dan had brought down from the spring, they start to fill the tub. While the tub is filling, they go up to the diggings and help with the cleanup. Since this is Dan's first cleanup at the mine, he is all excited, and unbelieving at the amount of gold recovered. The gold nuggets recovered from the machine weighed out at just over seventeen ounces, the fines from the mercury trap, eight and a quarter ounces, the nuggets in Sue's keeper pouch from the bedrock and tailings pile came to over twenty one ounces. A grand total of forty six and a third ounces of gold. Another good day at the mine.

Meantime the hot tub has filled, and Rich has started the propane water heater going, it takes till after supper to get the tub hot enough for the first test. The tub has some seepage from the seams, but Rich said that would stop as soon as the wood swells and he can do the final tightening of the bands that hold the tub together. Dan and Rich get to do the first soak, and state its great, what a way to end a day of mining.

So the routine starts at the mine. Up at daylight, breakfast, dig until lunch time, detect the bedrock and tailings piles, start cleanup at around four in the afternoon, supper, then shower, and a soak in the hot tub. Once a week, take a trip to Grass Valley and stock up on groceries at the supermarket there. Once a month, John and Sue go home, to put the gold in the safe there.

They have been keeping the gold in the hot tub furnace safe at the mine. Hank comes up on Sunday to help out. Missed a couple of weeks of pies until Sue and John went home, where she could make a few to bring up to the mine Poor Hank had to fight the boys for his share, since they are dessert hounds too. John brought back one of the metal boxes they had used before to keep food in, as an experiment to make an oven to make pies at the mine. He put a couple of used refrigerator racks in the box, plus installed a candy thermometer in the door, and. had a make shift oven.

By mounting it over the two burner stove, and watching the thermometer Sue could bake fresh pies and rolls, and even make pizza for the boys. This is camping out at the mine? What a life, the great outdoors, lots of gold, and homemade pies and pizza, plus a hot tub.

At the end of July, the boys and Hank run into a monster boulder, the size of a full size pickup truck, in Hanks ravine. With the fire danger, and the red tape involved in getting dynamite, and the hiring of a certified blaster, John tells them, he will check into getting some of the expanding cement, that some of the demolition companies use in areas where they want to break up concrete or rock without the noise, fumes, and danger of flying rock that using dynamite would do.

The next morning John and Sue go into Sacramento to a big industrial construction supply house. There they explain their situation to the manager of the store, about how they have to break up the boulder to mine the bedrock underneath. "I have just the stuff you need. I need the dimensions of the boulder, so I can sell you the appropriate amount you will need". "Also do you have tools to drill holes with?" "No", said John, "What do we need?" "A couple of Star drills of varying lengths, and a single jack to pound with". "Ok, let me have two of every tool, that way both the boys can be drilling at the same time, plus if we break something, we will have a spare". Then it's an overnight stop at the house. Rattle Grouchy's cage a little, while thanking him for keeping an eye on the place. Putting more gold into the safe, supper, shower, and bed.

Up the next morning, back at the mine by eight o'clock. "Here boys, we are going to drill holes into the boulder, and then pack them full of this cement, then wait for it to break into smaller pieces that we can move. It takes all day to get the proper amount of holes drilled, then mix the cement, and pack the holes. The instructions say it will take up to twenty four hours for the cement to cure and expand and therefore break the boulder, So it's clean up the machine Sue had fed gravel all day. Then supper, a rousing game of poker, then off to bed.

During the night John is awakened by a strange sound, listening for it again, he hears it coming from Hanks ravine. He gets up, puts on his pants, shirt, and boots, then grabs the powerful flashlight he has and walks down to the ravine. On the way he hears the strange sound again. It dawns on him, the noise is the boulder cracking. Sure enough, when he gets to the boulder, it is literally breaking apart in front of his eyes.

Alright!, he exclaims to himself. The boys should be able to muck it out starting in the morning. Back to bed, Sue asks where he had gone? "Been looking at the boulder, and watching it break apart". "By morning it will be small boulders that the boys can move".

Next morning, after breakfast, John shows the boys what he saw in the middle of the night. The boulder is in small enough pieces, that the boys can move them, and stack them out of the way. Well boys you have your work cut out for you today, and. possibly tomorrow. I figured that hunk weighed around 18,000 pounds. That's a lot of rock to move, no matter how you look at it.

Leaving them to their job for the day, and tomorrow, John goes back to Theo's ravine and continues the mining process.

Just before supper the next day the boys announce that they had finished mucking out the boulder pieces. "And look here folks, Dan exclaims, we have already found several large nuggets", "Rich thinks it is loaded under where the boulder was.

"Sue, get your detector, and let's go see this bonanza these youngsters think they have found". At the place of the former boulder, Sue turns on her detector, ground balances it, then starts to swing over the area. She screams, and quickly pulls off her head phones. The

The Detector signal is so loud that we can hear it through the ear phones. "John, there is a solid patch of gold nuggets there. We get the buckets, and Molly tools,_rock hammer, bar, and stiff brushes, and_start cleaning up the bedrock. There are three-distinct crevices, full of nuggets

We are grabbing hands f ull of them and putting them in the buckets. "John, boys, how about supper?" Sue asks.

Theo's Gold

"Who can eat at a time like this," said John. "Yeah, mom, look at all the gold here," Dan exclaims". Rich just shakes his head yes, and continues to dig:

"Ok, just thought I would ask," as she gets down on her knee pad and digs along with the men., Just before dark, they decide to quit for the day, and go get something to eat. At the kitchen, the boys grab some lunch meat, bread, and cold drinks from the Servel, and start to wolf it down. "Dan, we could set up a couple of lanterns, and continue to clean up the crevices tonight". "Not a bad idea Rich", Dan agrees. "Boys, give it a break, you've been busting butt for two days now, the gold isn't going anywhere, it'll be there in the morning after a good nights sleep". "Mom, who can sleep at a time like this, this is probably the most exciting gold mining experience a person can have in an entire life time". "What do you say Dan, should we continue to work now in the cool of the evening?" "Sure, why not".

So taking a couple of lanterns, the boys go back to work, while John and Sue take a shower, and a soak in the hot tub. "Were we like that when we were their age asks Sue?" "Probably" remarks John.

The next morning the boys sleep in, and when they finally get up, they announce that they think the crevices are done, "Did you break them down like we taught you?" "Yes", says Rich,

"We also brought the buckets over here by the scales so we can weigh the gold".

Taking the buckets over to the panning tub, John and the boys do a final cleaning of the gold. Meantime Sue has the two burner stove lit and is making coffee. Bringing over a metal pan of gold nuggets, John puts it on one burner, and dries the gold. Then two more pans fall.

After the gold has cooled. John announces, "Now comes the moment of truth". He takes all the weights he has and

359

tries to weigh the two biggest nuggets. They are more then the total nineteen ounces of weights he has, So he sets them aside, and weighs up nineteen ounces of small nuggets. Then he puts the largest nugget on the opposite side of the scale, and adds weights till he has the equal of the nugget. "Boys, Sue, that nugget weighs twenty nine ounces two dwt. and four grains". "Because it is such a beautiful specimen piece, I bet we could get a thousand an ounce for it, even at todays low price". Taking the nugget off the scale, he puts the other one on, and removing weights, comes up with a total of twenty one ounces even. "Another great specimen piece, he declares".

After and hour they have a total of the gold from under the boulder. "Eight hundred and seventy ounces, plus a few grains, John states", "Not too shabby, for this little diggings, I would say". "Old Theo sure knew how to find a real gold mine, didn't he?"

The following Sunday, John shows Hank what the boys found under the large boulder they had unearthed, then he and Sue head down to Newcastle to put the gold away for safe keeping.

As usual Grouchy is waiting for them. "how did you do?" "Oh, we got a few ounces John tells him", and whips out a leather pouch, and opens it up to show Grouchy around five ounces of nice nuggets. "Wow", declares Grouchy, "ain't they beautiful". "Yep", Sue agrees, "Well old friend, we have to put this away, and get back up to the mine, the boys are hungry for more of their moms pies, so we have to get the fixings and make some more to take back with us". "See you later".

CHAPTER FIFTY TWO

The next morning, they head back up to the mine, with half a dozen fresh pies. When they get there, naturally the boys have to take a pie and coffee break. Since it's midafternoon, John and Sue decide not to work in the diggings today. Instead, John suggests they go fishing. They haven't fished since they have been here, plus it would give everybody a break from the normal food menu, if they could catch a few trout.

The rest of the afternoon is spent on the stream catching fish, When they have six good pan size trout, they head for the camp to clean them and get them ready for the frying pan. Salt and pepper, rolled in cornmeal, they have a fresh fish dinner. While John cooked the fish, Sue made hush puppies, and a fresh spinach salad. "I wonder what the rich folks are doing now?" John asks. "Life doesn't get much better than this"

And so the summer goes. Mining, getting lots of gold, enjoying the outdoors, the companionship of good friends and family. All too soon it is the start of fall weather, time to start thinking about closing up the mine for the winter. Since they still have enough gravel left for one more season, John and Rich come up with an idea to protect the equipment from the ravages of the rain and snow. They are going to build three A frame sheds to cover the gold machines and the new hot tub.

Rich takes the Power Wagon down to the valley, and picks up a load of pallets, and several rolls of roll roofing material. Meanwhile Hank and John gather up enough small trees to make poles with from the logging operation. When Rich gets back, they put up the three sheds, covering them with the roll roofing. Putting a door in the end of each one they can store all their tools, tarps, screen tent, etc. Since the kitchen is already a lean-to, all they have to do is close up the front and sides. The Servel is defrosted, and the bottom is boarded in, to try and keep out mice and bugs, that like to get into the works in the back of the fridge.

It's time to leave for the winter. The rains are threatening. Hank and his crew, are packing up to go up to the Klamath River areas where they can work during the winter as the elevation is lower, therefore very little problem with snow. Hank informed us that he has one more season of work here, so he will be with us next year. "That's great Hank, I'm sure I can keep you in enough pies to keep your girlish figure intact", Sue kids him.

So they leave the mountains, to await next spring, when it is time to open the mine up again. The mining has produced a phenomenal amount of gold, after cleaning and weighing it all, they had recovered thirty eight hundred ounces, With the spot price of gold around 300.00 an ounce, they have approximately, one million one hundred and forty thousand dollars worth of gold.

With John and Sue making jewelry out of their share, they of course make much more than three hundred an ounce. The boys are willing to sell their share, so they can invest in something that will give them interest on their dollars. Rich has decided that he will set up a cabinet shop in the Lincoln area, where they are having a building boom. Dan's going to bank his for now, until he finds the right project for his money to go to work in to make more. Hank told us he had his eye on a piece of property up near Yreka, where he could become a cowboy, and raise horses. So he's going to put a down payment on the place.

We connect them with some of the gold buyers we know, and help them get the best price, so each of them has a sizable bank account now.

As this is October, John gets busy making gold nugget jewelry to take down to Quartzsite, And this year, we decide to do the show in Tucson, to see if we can get some of the big money buyers interested in our line of jewelry.

We spend a month in Arizona, Sell out, and get enough orders for more, so that when we get home, John has to look for a couple of independent bench jewelers who can help us make our line of goods. "John is busy every day casting rings and pendants, for the other bench men to finish". "He even has me designing new pieces to make". We fill all our orders first, then make up a stock to carry us through the summer, so we don't have to stop mining to sit down and make jewelry

We are so busy, we don't realize that spring is almost here. Hank calls to inform us that he and his crew are back, and are starting to go to work. The snow pack is melting, and they have been opening up the Goodyears Creek road so they can start hauling soon. Plus the old stage route to Marysville is going to be used almost exclusively this season so they can haul forty footers to the Mill. They not only had finished cutting the road through to Marysville, but it is graveled in such a way as to make it a smooth highway for the logging trucks, with passing zones so they can have two way traffic.

So its time to get our mind in gear to go mining. Dan is back to work, running his hot saw, and won't be able to mine unless the Forest Service shuts them down because of fire danger again. Rich's shop is doing so good, that he has several employee's working for him. So he will only be able to get up there on the week ends. Hank will be there with bell's on for Sunday pie and work in Hank's ravine. We figure we will be able to finish Theo's ravine by the middle of summer by ourselves, then go to work on Hank's ravine during the week, and rest up on the weekends while Rich and Hank work there.

That's the plan, and if Dan can come up we know that we will finish the project this summer. So, now it's wait for the snow to melt, so we can go back to work.

CHAPTER FIFTY THREE

Finally we hear from Hank that the snow is gone and we can get into the mine. So we plan for the weekend coming up which happens to be the Memorial Day holiday. Both Dan and Rich can be there. That will give us many hands to get the mine open for work.

Hank asked us to stop at his trailer on the way up to say hello, and to meet someone he thought we would like, "Sue, he's being very mysterious about this person he wants us to meet, do you suppose he has a lady friend?" "Quite possible John".

Rich and Dan show up first thing Saturday morning, to drive the Power Wagon full of supplies up to the mine. John and Sue are in the Rubicon Rig towing the camper trailer.

At Hanks we get to meet the mysterious person who we believed would be a lady friend, and sure enough it is. "John, Sue, Dan, and Rich, this is Carol, my neighbor who lives in that small motor home next to my trailer". "Carol, this is the mining crew I have been telling you about". Hank goes on to tell John and Sue how Carol had moved into the campground the same day he had put his trailer back in his old spot. "Carol had only planned to stay a week as she is

365

on a tour of the country". "But we hit it off so good, and she was so fascinated with the logging and mining stories I told her, that she had to stay and meet you all and see if it would be ok to visit the mine with me",

"I don't see why not, what do you think John?" "Hank, you just bring Carol up and we'll put her in charge of sight seeing", "Good, I thought it would be alright, but I had to check with you first". "Anyway we got the Jeep packed, and ready to go, so we'll follow you up". "By the way, the skid trail was a little muddy the other day when I checked it, but I made it through with out having to chain up", "The mine looks like it did when we left it last fall".

The boys lead the way with the Power Wagon. John and Sue next, then Hank and his new friend and the Jeep. The skid trail was a little muddy, but not as bad as the other day according to Hank. Arriving at the mine, we unload the Power Wagon, and start to get the kitchen area opened up. Removing the temporary front and end walls, the women wash down the counter and freshen up the inside of the Servel!. John hooks up the propane to the stove and the refrigerator, then lights the Servel burner to get it going. Carol remarks, that she remembers these refrigerators being used by a lot by the folks who lived in the Runs and Holler's of Kentucky.

"It's only been recently that electric power has been available to everyone in the state"

"Is Kentucky your home" asks Sue? "Why yes, my late husband and I had a small horse farm there", "We raised a breed of horse called Morgan's, for the horse and buggy trade". "Horse and buggy trade, asks Sue?" "Yes, we have a lot of Amish and Mennonite farmers in the area, who still use horse and buggy for transportation". "We sold horses from our farm all the way up into Pennsylvania". "And most of the older big towns have a lively tourist trade who like to take old fashioned buggy rides to see the sights". "So we had quite a nice business going until my husband was killed in an auto accident while coming home from an Elks club meeting one night".

"Oh, I'm sorry to hear that". "It's alright Sue, it happened over three years ago; I'm quite over the loss now". "After I got over the mourning period, I sold the farm, and bought the motor home, with the idea to see the country". "I've been on the road for over two years, until I met Hank a few weeks ago". "Oh?" "Yes, there is something about that man that makes me want to nest again". "Does Hank know this" asks Sue? "Not that we have voiced out loud, but I think he feels the same way, the signs are there".

"Yeah, I felt the difference in Hank right away, when he introduced us". "Anyway, Hank wants me to go up to Yreka where he is buying his property over the forth of July, when he has another holiday". "So I said yes, besides it'll give us more time to get to know each other better, as that's a month away". "We seem to have compatible likes and dislikes, so I want to learn more about this man who I seem to have a large attraction for", "Good thinking" says Sue.

"Well Carol, we better get to work, or the men will try to get all over our case for wasting daylight, as they like to say". So they walk over to Theo's ravine where the guys have dismantled the A frame shed over the gold machine, and are starting to put up the tarps to give them shade. Sue explains to Carol how the gold machine works. Then takes her up the ravine to where the actual diggings are, and explains the process by which they pick and shovel the gravel onto the slick sheets, then using the wheelbarrows transfer the gravel down to the gold machine to be worked.

The guys are finished here, so they are going down to Hanks ravine to repeat the process. John asks Sue and Carol, if they could put up the screen tent? "Sure honey, we can give it a try", Sue tells John. So they go back to the kitchen and camp area and drag the screen tent over to where it was set up last year, and start to put it up. Luckily the poles are numbered so they can figure out the way it goes up. Soon they have the tent up and are pretty proud of themselves.

"Come on Carol, and I'll show you the cabin the original miner built back in the eighteen sixtys". As Sue opens the door of the cabin, a mouse runs out between their legs, causing both of them to scream and jump. "Oh!, oh!, says Sue, we better not go in there until we get the respirator masks on, these little deer mice can carry the Hanta Virus". "Anyway you can see some of the layout from out here", "Yeah, it looks pretty cozy, Carol remarks". "Now over here, under that A frame shed is the hot tub". "Hot tub, you got to be kidding?" "No Im not, we have a bonafide redwood hot tub, that we soak our tired sore bodies in after working all day in the mine". "Pun intended".

"Well I'll be, when can I come work in the mine, so I can have the excuse to use the hot tub?" "Well we kinda sorta have to leave the guys make that decision", Sue says. "It helps with their egos to know they made such a big decision". "Yes, I know what you mean".

By this time it's time for a late lunch, so the ladies cook up a hamburger macroni goulash, tasty and easy to make, and of course the pies for the dessert hounds. Carol asks if we always eat this well up here? "Sure we do, why shouldn't we, when we are working at the mining process, we're expending a lot of energy and calories, so I spoil the guys with pies".

"Hey guys, when can I start working here?", asks Carol. "The way I see it, the benefits in food alone makes it a pretty good job". John looks at the boys and Hank, Hank is shaking his head yes, the boys agree, so Carol has now become part of the family of miners at the Deja-vu mine.

After the weekend, the boys head back home. John has given Rich a list of things to bring up next weekend, including the ATV, they have decided that Carol can use it to commute from the Goodyears Bar campground up to the mine each day. While in the evenings she and Hank can get to know each other better, So a new routine, two ladies working together, feeding the gold machine, while John attacks the gravel face.

The gold keeps coming as before, a couple of ear busting detector crevices, many sizable nuggets, and lots of fines in the mercury trap. All too soon it's time for Hank and Carol to go up to Hanks new property near Yreka. Dan gets the holiday off, so he shows up with Rich. So the four of them are digging. Theo's ravine is nearing the end of the gravel, maybe another month, and it will be done. Hanks ravine is also getting close to the end. John guess's it should be done by October. Then it will be time to close up the mine, remove the equipment, spread top soil over the bedrock, and plant tree seedlings.

Hank and Carol return from Yreka, all aglow. She can't say enough good over the place Hank is buying. It has an old two story farm house still in good shape, but in need of paint and some TLC. A good well and small year round stream with which to irrigate the pastures, fences in reasonable condition. And with over two hundred acres, there is enough room to raise a small herd of good horses, Best of all Hank and Carol have decided to partner up on the small ranch as they call it. "Partner up?" John asks. "Yeah, I've asked Carol if she would like to be my steady cowgirl lady, ring and all, Hank declares with a big blushing smile on his face. "Well I'll be damned", exclaims John, "and what did the cowgirl say when you proposed this arrangement?" "Why, yes of course, where else can I find a rich logger, miner, and horse lover my age, and good looking to boot, to spend time with". "Ah gee, girl you're making me turn all red in the face again".

So Hank and Carol are making their plans to marry and start the ranch. Both of them happen to have lap top computers, and in the evening they are researching the internet for information concerning horses, and what breed they could raise to have something different, yet very desirable for other people to want to own, Carol being familiar with the Morgan breed, was doing some market research on the various needs of the horse crowd, and the potential for selling Morgan's here in the west. She found that the breed had potential, if it were taller then the normal Morgan's. Remembering once hearing about a Morgan and Thoroughbred cross, which combined the strong endurance of the Morgan's and the taller stature of the Thoroughbred, she started searching for a breeding farm that handled the breed. Low and behold the original breeders from the 1860's were still in business. The family had handed down the farm from generation to generation, and were still raising the rare breed developed so many years ago.

"Hank, I think I have found the breed we can raise here and make the ranch a payable business". "What breed is that Hank asks?" "They are called a Chastain Morgan Cross". "Never heard of them". "I know, they are very rare". Carol goes on to explain the origin of the breed, "It's all here on their website, *see*"

The story tells how during the last part of the 1850's, the Chastain farm, cross bred Morgan's with Thoroughbreds and came up with the best characteristics of the two breeds, the strength and stamina of the shorter Morgan, and the height of the Thoroughbred. They make a great buggy horse, easy gait for riding, and a winning stride for sulky racing. The story goes on to say how the breed survived the Civil War.

The original breeders, a gentleman named Chastain Castle and his wife Sara were able to hide several of their top breeding stock from the ravages of the war. And after the war he was able to keep the farm out of the hands of the crooked reconstructionists, and therefore keep the breed alive. The original farm is still in business near the town of Dahlonega, Georgia. "Well I'll be, exclaims Hank". "Have John or Sue told you about the original miner who discovered the mine?" "No, I only know what I read in the old Downieville paper, about how he was shot and killed, while killing the owlhoots who were trying to rob him".

"Well Theo came from Dahlonega, where he worked for a miner named Cuss". "His real name was Chastain Castle, and he married a women whose name was Sara". "After the mine he owned was worked out, he and his wife bought a farm where they raised Morgan horses". "Obviously the same farm you have found on the internet. "Wait till I tell John and Sue about this". "Won't they be surprised".

The next morning, being Sunday, Hank and Carol drive up to the mine in his Jeep.

When they get there they tell John and Sue what they had found on the internet about the history of the Chastain Morgan's. "John, you once told me that Theo worked for a Cuss, whose real name was Chastain Castle". "Yeah, it was in his first journal, how he and Cuss worked the mine together for almost five years". "It was where Theo learned to mine and how to recognize a good prospect like he did here". "The journal also tells of the horse farm that Cuss and Sara were going to set up, and they had planned to raise Morgan's, as Sara was already familiar with the breed".

"Well the Chastain farm is still in existence, and they have the horse breed we are thinking of raising". "That's great", remarks Sue, "and what a coincidence that a hundred and forty years later, you would be working Theo's mine, and now you want to buy horses from his original mentors farm". "Small world isn't it".

CHAPTER FIFTY FOUR

And so the mining progresses. Labor Day week end and the whole crew is there. John decides to take advantage of everybody being there and wants to attack Theo 's ravine and finish it off this weekend. So they do, by Monday it is done. The ravine gave up gold right up to the last. And what a rich history it has had, with many thousands of ounces of gold recovered.

On to Hanks ravine, they move the gold machine from Theo's to Hanks, so that they have two machines for the ladies to shovel into. During the week John tries to keep up with the ladies feeding the machines, picking and shoveling. On the weekends, Hank, Rich, and John are working the last section of the gravel, getting a stockpile put up so as to keep the gold machines busy.

Finally as the first of October comes around, the miners finish the last of Hanks ravine. Another rich history, as many Troy pounds of gold have been recovered. It's time to close down the successful operation. They pack up the two gold machines, and all the hand tools and take them down to Newcastle to the house. Spreading as much top soil as they can in the ravines, they plant tree seedlings that they had gotten from the tree planters who were working in the burned out areas,

The weather is changing fast, and they finish closing down the mine as the first rain threatens. John and Sue are the last to leave, and as a last gesture of thanks for all their good luck, they take a special leather pouch that Sue had made, and putting a pound of Theo's ravine gold in it, John takes it down to the hot tub furnace and puts it into the safe in the bottom. Spending a few minutes in thoughts of Theo, and the rest of his family, he finally says goodbye.

By the time John and Sue get up to the flat, it starts to drizzle, as they get to the campground at Goodyears Bar, it is raining pretty good. Stopping to say goodbye to Hank and Carol, and getting their invite to the upcoming wedding, they are finally on the road to home. "What a sad and yet happy day", remarks Sue. "Sad that we are closing the mine, but happy for Hank and Carol". "Yes", John agrees.

The next day John and Sue sort out the gold, weigh it and then separate it into five equal shares. They call Hank that evening and ask if he is going to be at his trailer tomorrow evening? "Yes, I am", "Good" says John, "we'll be up to see you and bring you your share of the recovery".

The next evening, John and Sue arrive just in time for supper with Hank and Carol. After supper John opens the box he has put the gold in, and brings out freezer bags full of gold nuggets. "Will you look at that Carol, have you ever seen anything so pretty, that comes out of the ground all covered with dirt and clay?" "No! I haven't", Sue tells Hank, John tells Hank "The total comes to 540 ounces this year, down a little from last year, but we kinda expected that".

"What does that come to in money?" asks Hank "We can probably get you three hundred an ounce from one of the big buyers, so that would come to around 162 thousand". "Carol, that would pay off the ranch, and with my regular savings we should have enough to get a couple of the Chastain Morgan's you have your heart set on", "Hank, you forget I have some money to put into this venture too", she exclaims. "Ok, I almost forgot we are partners in the money department too", "Well Mr... you better remember it's takes two to Tango, or I'm going to have to take one of your logging boots to your body", with that she laughs, and gives him a big hug and kiss. Whereupon he turns beet red.

Just before John and Sue leave to go home, Hank and Carol are trying to talk them into getting a computer. "Why? John asks, "Do I need a computer, can a computer sit down at my jewelers bench and make jewelry, or carve a wax model for a new design?" "No, but it can help you sell your jewelry all over the world, instead of the limited customer base you have now", Hank tells him "And look at how easy it would be to keep in touch through E-mail" says Carol. "Sue, tell the stubborn old coot it's about time he comes into the 21st century" said Hank "Old coot, am I. "Hank if you weren't such a good friend, I would have to take you out behind the wood shed and give you an attitude adjustment". "See what I mean, nobody has a wood shed any more, so where are you to go for this adjustment". "Ok, I know when I'm beaten" declares John, "Sue, tomorrow we get a new computer, and hope Bryce will help us learn how to turn the new fangled thing on",

"I can't believe it, exclaims Sue, I've been trying to talk him into a computer for two years now, and you folks do it in ten minutes". "Talked into hell, I was coerced, the whole bunch of you have ganged up on me". This sets everybody to laughing. "Come on Sue, If I'm going to learn how to be a computer nerd, I'm going to need my beauty sleep".

The next day they go looking at computers, the offerings are pretty confusing to both of them. John tells Sue, "let's talk to Bryce tonight and see what he recommends, and if he will be willing to help us learn how to get around in cyberspace". That evening they go over to Bryce's house and explain to him their problem, and ask if he would be willing to help? "You bet", he tells them, "there's nothing I like more then to show people the interesting world of computers". "Why don't we get together Saturday, and go find you a new computer, then help you set it up, and Monday you can get a server, so you can be online, and be able to talk to the world". "Eh, what's a server, and being online mean?" asks John. "You'll see John, we'll take you through the process one step at a time". "Six months from now you'll laugh at your ignorance that you have now". "Oh, now I'm ignorant, yesterday I was an old coot" "All I can say is these machines better be what they are all hyped up to be". "It will be old coot" says Sue, "just you wait and see".

Six months later John is telling Sue how the computer has changed their lives, we don't have to spend days getting the motor home ready to go to a show two states away. A show that might be profitable or might not like our last trip to Arizona, "All I have to do is make an especially nice piece, take a picture of it, then put it on the big auction web site and wait for it to sell". "I don't even have to leave my house to make a living any more, course I miss the friends we have made over the years". "But even most of them are on line so we can talk to them whenever we want". "I guess we should have bought this new fangled machine years sooner eh, Sue". "That's what I tried to tell you, you stubborn old coot", she says, and laughs.

A few months earlier, at thanksgiving time John and Sue and the boys, went up to Yreka, to be a part of the wedding. John is to be best man for Hank, and Sue maid of honor for Carol. Carol wore a white buckskin outfit, complete with fringe and fancy bead work, and a white Stetson hat. Hank had on an old fashioned gamblers outfit, black twill pants with pin stripes, a black frock coat, white shirt with fancy ruffles, and a black flat top Stetson hat. A mighty handsome couple in their finery. The reception was a fine western barbeque, with the usual champagne toast, and plenty of beer to go with the food. The crowd was small, just about twenty of their best friends. Everybody had a great time. Just before it was time to leave, Rich and Dan get the groom and bride off to the side. They want to give them a special wedding gift. "What's this?" asks Hank, as the boys hand them two small very heavy boxes. "You'll see", says Dan, "Just promise you won't open them until after we are gone". "Ok, I guess we can do that".

Later, after everybody has left for home or a motel to stay in overnight, Hank and Carol open the two boxes from the boys. In the boxes is a card telling them that since Carol spent her whole summer breaking her back, and getting blisters on top of blisters, shoveling, that she deserved a share of the gold she could call her own. In each box there is a hundred ounces of nuggets, also a note that says, thank you for being such a good friend to our folks, and hopefully this will help you get the Morgan's you want.

"Wow, what great young men", Carol exclaims, "This will help us get a couple of very fine breeders". Two days later, John and Sue get an E-mail from the newly weds, thanking them for being best man and maid of honor, and telling them of the gift the boys had given them, what a surprise, for all of them.

CHAPTER FIFTY FIVE

Two years have now passed since the crew have closed down the mine. John and Sue have been traveling a lot more, checking out old ghost towns in Nevada, Arizona, and New Mexico. Metal detecting for gold nuggets and taking lots of pictures. Sue took a water color painting class the winter after closing the mine, so she has been painting some of the ghost town scenes she has found interesting. John's jewelry sales on the internet is just enough to keep him somewhat busy, without interfering with their traveling. They go up to Yreka to visit Hank and Carol quite often. The horse ranch is coming along. Hank has just retired from the logging company, so he can devote full time to the ranch. They have had their first foals, a colt and a filly. Both animals have the makings of superb examples of the breed that Hank and Carol want.

Rich's cabinet shop is doing well, and he has met a very nice young lady that he seems to be serious about. Dan has been made Side rod for the logging company he works for, better pay and benefits. He also has met a young lady, that he is interested in, she's a divorcee with two boys. He's having problems with the idea of a ready made family. We hope he works it out.

One summer evening John tells Sue that he has this urge to go visit the Deja-vu, and see what if anything has happened there. So the next day Sue packs a picnic lunch and cold drinks, and they get in the Rubicon Rig and head for the old mine. The logging road up Goodyears Creek is still in good shape, all the way to the flat. The skid trail is strictly four wheel drive now, they have to dodge seedling trees that have taken root, and traverse a few deep ruts caused by rain and snow melt. Reaching Theo's ravine, they see that the seedlings they planted are doing quite well. Walking down to Hanks ravine, they see the seedlings are doing well there too.

Walking back to the Suzuki, they grab the picnic and a couple of cold drinks, and a blanket to sit on and go down the hill to the old cabin. Nothing has changed at the cabin site, except for a little more growth from the vines and trees around the cabin.

Spreading the blanket, they sit down and start eating, and talk of memories of their time mining here, and the discovery of the old mine and the gold stashed in the base of the furnace. Finished eating, John gets up and walks over to the hot tub and furnace. Sue is packing up the picnic basket and blanket, when John asks her to come over to the furnace. "Sue, look at this, the access stone to the safe is ajar". "I remember distinctly putting it back the way it belongs when we left here two years ago". "You're right John, I remember too".

John gets down on his knees and starts to pry the stone out, Sue is kneeling next to him and trying to help. They remove the stone, and then open the metal door, and inside the safe they find that the leather pouch they had left there is gone, and in its place is a piece of paper rolled up with a faded yellow ribbon around it. John removes the paper, and hands it to Sue, whereupon she slides the ribbon off and unrolls the paper and starts to read it. The note reads

John and Sue, thank you for taking such good care of Melissa during her last days in the mortal world. And thank you for completing the mining project that Amy and I started. Enjoy your lives, and when you get to this side of the big river, we will have a special place waiting for you.

Sincerely,
Theolonius. Raphial Calhoun.

Sue looks at John and then faints. John catches her and lays her down in his lap, then he reads the note. "Well I'll be", he exclaims, and then sits there staring dumbfounded off into space. A minute or so later Sue starts coming around. John snaps out of his reverie, and helps Sue to get up. "Are you alright Sue?" "Yes, it was quite a shock seeing that note". "Yes it was" he says. "Why don't you go get the picnic basket, and I'll close up the safe, then we can head for home". On the way up the hill, they both turn back to look at the cabin site for the last time, and there standing next to the cabin they see a young couple, he is tall and very well built, wearing buckskins and a floppy miners hat. On his belt he has the special leather pouch that Sue made. Next to him is a comely young woman wearing jeans, flannel shirt, a levy vest, and straw hat. They are smiling and waving goodbye to John and Sue.

As they watch, the apparition slowly fades away. John takes Sue by the hand and helps her up to the Suzuki, Putting the picnic basket in the back, they get in the car, buckle up and drive up the hill. Up at the flat, John takes the rig out of four wheel drive, and they head for home. They are very quiet on the way back to the house, both lost in their own thoughts of what has happened today. At home, John drives the Rubicon Rig into the shop and closes the door. Sue goes into the house, and even though it is early, she takes a shower and gets into her P.J.s and goes to bed. John meantime, takes the note over to his desk, and notices that the paper is a page torn out of a book. On a hunch he opens his glass front bookcase, and takes down Theo's last journal. Opening the book to the last page, he sees that the second to the last page is missing. "That page was blank when we read the journal" he says to himself. He takes the note, from Theo, and unrolling it, he places it in the journal. Sure enough it is the missing page. Sitting there for a couple of minutes to adsorb what he has just discovered, John carefully puts the page in the book along with the yellow ribbon, closes it up and puts it on the shelf where it belongs.

Going into the house, he remembers he is hungry, taking a piece of chocolate cake out of the refrigerator, and a glass of milk, he eats the cake and drinks the milk, then rinses the dishes off. Taking a shower, he also gets ready for bed. In bed, Sue is just kind of staring at the TV, not really paying attention to it. John asks what she is watching? "I don't know, I can't get today Out of my mind". "Me neither" John tells her.

"Sue, I've been thinking, we have had one hell've an adventure since we opened that trunk full of junk that Melissa gave us". "Amen" Sue says as she starts to drift off to sleep. "And I think to myself, that I want to thank Theo and his spirit friends for allowing us this chance to share in the discovery of Theo's gold".

END.

Author with gold nugget worth 150.00 he just recovered while dredging for gold on his mining claim in Northern California

ABOUT THE AUTHOR

Gordon Knight has 40 plus years experience making a modest income as a small scale gold miner. Coupled with the study of Gold mining history, he used that knowledge and imagination to create this book. It is his hope that the reader will enjoy the book as much as he did in writing it.

.